The Great
of the

A young tough named Artemis Entreri plays a treacherous game of death with a master assassin in Calimport's squalid back streets. . . .

In the days before the destruction of Zhentil Keep, Manshoon schemes to seize control of that black-walled city for the newly formed alliance of evil mages known as the Zhentarim. . . .

Renegade elflord Elaith Craulnober reaches for the magical moonblade that is his heritage, but finds himself denied by shackles from which neither time nor distance can provide an escape. . . .

Stalked by a relentless nemesis of the undead, the elven vampire Jander Sunstar is drawn into a battle with a foe more soulless even than he. . . .

Two members of the Society of Stalwart Adventurers set off to map the Realm of the Dead's uncharted boundaries, but discover instead that the dark kingdom's lord —Cyric, lunatic Prince of Lies—has residences in the mortal world, as well.

Thieves and assassins, misers seeking immortal life and creatures bent on destroying humankind—these and many more of the villains from the best-selling FORGOTTEN REALMS® novels come together in this collection of sixteen chilling tales.

Other Fantasy Anthologies from TSR

Realms of Valor
Edited by James Lowder

BOOKS

Tales of Ravenloft
Edited by Brian Thomsen

SAGA

Tales Vol. 1
The Magic of Krynn
Edited by Margaret Weis and Tracy Hickman

Tales Vol. 2
Kender, Gully Dwarves, and Gnomes
Edited by Margaret Weis and Tracy Hickman

Tales Vol. 3
Love and War
Edited by Margaret Weis and Tracy Hickman

Tales II Vol. 1
The Reign of Istar
Edited by Margaret Weis and Tracy Hickman

Tales II Vol. 2
The Cataclysm
Edited by Margaret Weis and Tracy Hickman

Tales II Vol. 3
The War of the Lance
Edited by Margaret Weis and Tracy Hickman

The Dragons of Krynn
Edited by Margaret Weis and Tracy Hickman

FANTASY ADVENTURE

Realms of Infamy

Edited by James Lowder

REALMS OF INFAMY

Cover art by Blas Gallego.

Interior Art by Ned Dameron.

First Printing: December 1994
Printed in the United States of America
Library of Congress Catalog Card Number: 94-60109

9 8 7 6 5 4 3 2 1

ISBN: 1-56076-911-4

TSR, Inc.
P.O. Box 756
Lake Geneva, WI 53147
United States of America

TSR Ltd.
120 Church End, Cherry Hinton
Cambridge CB1 3LB
United Kingdom

My conscience hath a thousand several tongues,
And every tongue brings in a several tale,
And every tale condemns me for a villain.

Richard III Act V.iii

CONTENTS

SO HIGH A PRICE 3
  Ed Greenwood

THE MORE THINGS CHANGE 27
  Elaine Cunningham

THE MEANING OF LORE 43
  Barb Hendee

RAVEN'S EGG 61
  Elaine Bergstrom

THE THIRD LEVEL 79
  R. A. Salvatore

BLOOD SPORT 101
  Christie Golden

GALLOWS DAY 121
  David Cook

A MATTER OF THORNS 145
  James M. Ward

STOLEN SPELLS 163
  Denise Vitola

THE GREATEST HERO WHO EVER DIED 183
  J. Robert King

TWILIGHT 201
  Troy Denning

THE WALLS OF MIDNIGHT 225
  Mark Anthony

AND WRINGING OF HANDS 247
  Jane Cooper Hong

THIEVES' HONOR 273
  Mary H. Herbert

LAUGHTER IN THE FLAMES 293
  James Lowder

VISION 317
  Roger E. Moore

CONTRIBUTORS' NOTES 343

SO HIGH A PRICE

Ed Greenwood

So high a price
So willingly paid
Hot blood flows
And a ruler is made.
Mintiper Moonsilver
Ballad of a Tyrant
Year of the Turret

Sunlight flashed from the highest towers of Zhentil Keep and flung dazzling reflections through nearby windows. It was a hot Mirtul day in the Year of the Blazing Brand.

A ledgebird darted past one window, wheeled on nimble wings, and called like a carefree trumpet. But then, it did not know how little time it had left to live.

Manshoon smiled slightly and crooked a finger. The bird exploded in a puff of green flame. Humming the latest minstrel tune, the wizard watched scorched feathers drift away. Trust a bird of Zhentil Keep to fly unwittingly to its doom, singing off-key. Well, things might not be that way much longer. . . .

The first lord of Zhentil Keep smiled as he caught sight of himself in an oval mirror floating upright in a corner. The image, jet-black hair gleaming, returned the expression. Its robes were of the finest purple silk, worked with rearing behirs in gold. The sleeves were the latest flaring fashion, and the upswept collar was cut in the style of city lords.

With the faintest of rustlings, Taersel drew a hanging tapestry aside and murmured, "The one you expected is here, Lord."

Manshoon signaled for his servant to bring the guest and withdraw, but then to wait unseen behind a tapestry. To show he understood, Taersel touched the hilt of the throwing knife hidden in his ornate belt buckle.

"Arglath," Taersel announced, then bowed out. The cloaked guest moved forward with a strange gliding motion, as if his feet didn't quite touch the floor.

"Yes?" Manshoon asked coldly.

His guest shrugged off his cloak and replied in tones just as glacial, "I presume you're finally ready to move?"

"I believe so," Manshoon said flatly.

His guest had soft, unfinished features. On second glance, most folk would have guessed him a mongrelman—something not quite human—and have drawn back, muttering and reaching for weapons. They'd have acted rightly.

Hair melted and fell away as the man's features swam, glistened, and split to reveal a single green, liquid eye. That unblinking orb grew until Manshoon looked into a giant eye that swayed at the end of a long, snakelike neck. The body beneath hung shrunken and empty, like discarded clothes drooping from a wall peg.

"Speak, then," the strange visitor's cold voice came again. "I've little patience for humans who enjoy being mysterious."

Manshoon gave his guest a wintry smile. "There will be open slaughter at the next council meeting. Those who oppose me will die there. When Zhentil Keep is mine, your kind will have what they desire: a powerful city full of hands to do your bidding, fresh meat to feed you, and men who fear and kneel before you."

"Do not presume to understand my kind so well," the creature responded, drifting slightly nearer. "More than that, Manshoon, do not presume to understand—or imagine that you can command—*me*." Writhing worms of flesh sprouted from its spherical body.

A gasp of horror came from behind a nearby tapestry. Then a crossbow bolt burst out of that same curtain, whipped across the chamber, and was driven sharply aside by an unseen magical force just in front of the floating eye. The bolt ended its flight in a splintering crash against a wall.

Eyes opened in the ends of the monster's still lengthening stalks. One blinked.

The tapestry drew aside by itself to reveal the mouth of a passage—and Taersel, who was now sprawled on his face, crossbow still in his hands. Thin wisps of smoke rose from his body.

"It is not wise," the eye tyrant said silkily, "to threaten 'my kind.' "

Manshoon stared into the beholder's many eyes and replied steadily, "I am too useful for you to slay—and too wise to attempt an attack upon you." He nodded at his sprawled servant. "This man acted of his own accord to protect me. Foolhardy, yet he is as useful to me as I am to you. I trust he has not been harmed."

"Not overmuch." The beholder drew nearer, its many eyes yellow with displeasure. "When next you speak in council, we shall be there. Yet know this, Lordling: unless you and your minions take greater care, a day of harm may soon come to you all."

* * * * *

"Unless we take great care," Lord Chess said in an inner room of another tower not far from Manshoon's home, "a day of harm may soon come to us all."

The other nobles at his table shifted in their seats. Most of the city's young noblemen were present. Some hid nervousness by taking flamboyant sips of the Mulhorandan lion-wine in their goblets. Others assumed superior smiles and settled into even more indolent poses in their great, finely carved chairs.

"We do not fear upstart mages," one said with a practiced sneer. "Our sires and our grandsires smashed such foes. Why should we quail? The least of our guards can destroy these Zhentarim."

"Aye," another rumbled amid murmurs of agreement. "Let the graybeards in council yap and snap all the day long! I see naught to threaten Zhentil Keep or to prevent our coins piling up. The council responds whenever those dolts in Mulmaster dare another challenge, or a Thayan wizard deludes himself into thinking he's mighty enough to rule us. On most days, the council simply keeps our fathers and the rest of the dotards busy—and keeps their noses out of our affairs!"

"And just how many affairs *have* you had, Thaerun?" one noble asked slyly.

"Aye, this tenday?" someone added through the general mirth.

Chess frowned. "Have you no care for the snakes in our midst? Agents of Thay, of the Dragon Cult—even of Sembia and Calimshan—are unmasked every month! Their dagger points are always closer than you credit."

"Ah," Thaerun said, leaning forward to tap the table in triumphant emphasis. "That's the point, Chess. They *are* unmasked—by the watchful wizards Manshoon commands, and by Fzoul's tame priests. That's why we tolerate these haughty longrobes in the first place! They watch our backs so we can get on with the business of getting rich!"

"And wenching," someone murmured.

"Drinking," another added. "What *is* this chamberpot-spill, anyway, Chess?"

"The finest Mulhorandan vintage," Chess said dryly. "Not that you'd recognize it, Naerh."

Naerh spat on the table. "That for your pretensions! My family's as old as yours!"

"And as debauched," Thaerun murmured.

Chess smiled thinly. "You do well to enjoy your ease while you can, Lords. 'Tis a precious luxury, lost if just one of our foes decides to make war on us."

Thaerun leaned forward again, his eyes cold. "I do enjoy it . . . and I shall. Every luxury has its price—but our ease costs us only the blood of a few fool altar-kneelers and hireswords from time to time. That's a fee I'll pay willingly. Save your veiled threats. The Blackryn name is a proud one—and one I'm always ready to defend." Twinkling points of light burst forth around his hand. They coalesced into an ornate scepter whose tip pulsed and glowed.

A noble sighed. "Oh, put it away, Thaerun! You're always trying to prove how battle-bold you are, and showing instead your utter lack of subtlety. We've all got one or more of those! You think yourself the only one in Zhentil Keep with wits enough to carry magic, when we must all hang our blades by the door at feasts?"

Another noble scratched the untidy beginnings of a beard and added, "Aye, and if you ever use it, Blackryn, 'tis the blood of one of *us* that'll spill. Then the bloodfeuds'll begin again. That *is* too high a price for the liking of the council. They'd probably put you in beast-shape to spend your days as a patrol-hound north of Glister . . . for the few days before you met death."

He leaned forward, uncrossing glossy-booted legs, and added, "Enough hard words. More wine, Chess, and tell me of the maid with green hair you were with last eve! I'd not laid eyes on her before. Where've you been hiding her?"

Chess smiled as a silver tray bristling with bottles and decanters rose from the polished wood in front of him and floated slowly down the table. "Yes, her hair was green last night. The Shadowsil, she's called. One of Manshoon's mages—so don't even *think* of wenching her, Eldarr. She could slay us all with one wave of her hand."

"And *that*, Thaerun," Naerh said dryly, "would also be too high a price for your liking!"

A well-fed man in robes of the latest slashed, counter-folded Calishite finery spoke for the first time that night. "I have been long away," he said, "but word has spread far of the Zhentarim: dark wizards, ruthless mage-slayers who gather ever more mighty magic. I would know more. Tell me plainly: what befalls in our city? What lies ahead that you fear?"

Lord Chess sipped at his wine. "Manshoon, leader of these Zhentarim, has become first lord of the council. He plans to do much more than chair the debates of squabbling merchants. He speaks of Zhentil Keep as 'his,' as if he were king over it!"

More than one noble laughed in derisive dismissal, but Chess held up a quelling hand. "Manshoon is a mage of power. He's gathered wizards great and small who think as he does. He's slain or driven out many of the mages who might oppose him. These Zhentarim work together. Think on *that*, my lords, and consider how you'd fare if twenty came to your feast, drank less than they pretended, then attacked you with spells!"

There were dark murmurs. Chess looked around grimly. "Worms you may think them, but they can slay us all. Have you not noticed how many of our great lords—even our last battlelord—are ill and keep to their beds? Old age, aye. . . . But what if they're being helped to their graves? Before you scoff, consider: spells may not slip past all the expensive wards and amulets we wear, but there are other ways. I know Manshoon well. We grew up together. He is a master of slow, wasting poisons that deal gradual death and raise no alarm. He killed his parents thus, to gain their gold."

Chess set down his goblet, and his voice grew more urgent. "Each day the Zhentarim grow more haughty. I fear they'll seize power soon, using spells to sway the council. Manshoon must act before the council approves the opening of the wizard-school that the Beldenstones are sponsoring, which will draw independent mages by the score to our city. And final approval for that is to come when the council next meets."

"Aghh! Enough of this fear-talk!" Thaerun snarled. "We've heard you spout this before, Chess! How can any wizard—even a band acting together—break the spell-shields and the priests' scrutiny? *Those* blackrobes grow rich by keeping all of us striving against each other. Priests don't like rivals! They'll slap these Zhentarim into the dust as soon as the mages dare to act openly!"

"Think you so?" Lord Chess leaned forward. "What if I told you Manshoon meets often with the most powerful of the priests? Aye: Fzoul, the master of the Black Altar, himself."

Shocked silence fell, and Chess added with more calmness than he felt, "It is the 'impartial' priests' vigilance that keeps council meetings free of spell-deceit. Mayhap that is only a fancy-tale." He reached for his goblet again, bejeweled fingers trembling.

"There's more, isn't there?" Naerh asked, eyes on his host's face.

Lord Chess nodded. "Taersel tells me Manshoon meets with someone more powerful in magic than he—someone he keeps secret from High Priest Fzoul. You've heard rumors of beholders prowling the city by night. . . ."

He looked around at the silent, pale faces. "*Now* are you afraid, my lords?" He drained his goblet and added, "As the next council meeting is on the morrow, it may be too late to do anything *but* be afraid."

* * * * *

The beholder bit down. Blood spattered, and a suddenly headless body twisted and flopped like a landed fish.

Lord Rorst Amandon, battlelord of Zhentil Keep, passed a hand over his scrying crystal. The bloody scene faded.

"So passes Lord Hael's hope," he murmured. "Hardly a surprise—and probably not the only uninvited visitors to Manshoon's Tower who'll meet their gods this night. Such feeble attacks won't stop the Zhentarim now. Still . . . Hael's thieves got farther than I'd expected."

The old lord's hand trembled as he reached for a decanter beside the bed. As always, Etreth was there to put a drink into the palsied grip.

Possession of a scrying crystal that could pierce spell-shields meant death if either the city's priests or wizards learned of it—but Lord Amandon was past caring. He lay on his deathbed, and knew it. By the time Manshoon's poison had been detected, its ravages had gone too far in his aged body for magic to mend. The most expensive sages knew no antidote, once the poison took hold. The first lord had been thorough. Enough, at least, to slay Lord Amandon.

The old warrior looked wearily around his bedchamber, gazing at his favorite broadsword and the portrait of his wife, dead and gone these seven years. He might join her before morning, whatever befell the mad wizard's schemes.

"I . . . can wait no longer, Etreth," he muttered. "My body fails. I can barely drink without your aid, now."

Looking up, he saw bright, unshed tears in his loyal servant's eyes. Rorst turned his head away, moved. Years they'd been together, as he'd led the armies of Zhentil Keep to rule Thar and the northern coast of the Moonsea with brutal efficiency—something he was less and less proud of, as the years passed. He'd never noticed the gray creeping through Etreth's hair, and the man's moustache was white!

The battlelord sat up, cushions tumbling. "The time is come," he growled. "I have one last command, good Etreth: go and summon the one I told you of."

"Now, Lord? And . . . leave you? What if—?"

"I'll do without," the lord said firmly, "until the one I must deal with is here. Go, Etreth, for the honor of the Amandons."

He set down his goblet. It clattered in his trembling hand. Rorst frowned down at it, then raised fierce eyes. "Go," he said roughly, "if you care for me at all."

The old servant stood looking at him a moment, turned with what sounded like a sob, and hurried out.

Rorst Amandon glanced at the darkened scrying crystal and wondered if he'd last long enough to see this final battle through. His eyes wandered to Desil's portrait, drank in her familiar painted beauty, and turned again to the scrying crystal. I am a man of the sword, he reflected with a wan smile, itching to be part of the fight until the very last.

* * * * *

The well-oiled door to the chamber's secret exit closed behind the last guest, and Lord Chess sat alone. A full goblet rested forgotten before him as he idly turned a plain ring around and around on his finger.

Nothing short of an angry god could stop Manshoon now. The first lord was as powerful in sorcery as he was a master of strategy. He'd be ruler of Zhentil Keep before the snows came. That would have been unthinkable only a year ago, with all the wily, battle-hardened nobles of the Keep between the arrogant mage and mastery of the city.

Then old Iorltar had named Manshoon his successor as first lord—under magical compulsion, many thought. Within a tenday, many of the proudest nobles—those who had no love for the upstart first lord or commanded strong magic—fell ill. No cause could be found, but the tavern-rumors carried the truth. Now those same taverns housed talk of the Zhentarim slaying rivals openly. And when the uproar began, Manshoon was supposed to have some secret weapon to wield, one beyond the spells of his ever-growing band of gutter wizards.

The monied among the work-a-day Zhents fiercely opposed every plan and deed of the swift-rising Zhentarim, but that mattered little. The merchants learned early there was no safety to be bought after one opposes a magic-wielder. As for the rest of the populace—well, the rabble never played much of a role in politics, apart from being swayed to one cause or another by well-staged public spectacle. Not much different from the other folk of the Heartlands, really.

The ring Chess had been turning gleamed and caught his eye. He regarded it thoughtfully. The plain band had cost him his best hireswords; he'd paid very expensive assassins to kill them after they'd refused to part with it. But it was worth the bloodfees and the loss of their service. He wore it constantly these days.

Manshoon wasn't the only one in the Keep with secret weapons. Chess could call forth a loyal dragon from the ring whenever the need might come. That might be as soon as tomorrow, he thought grimly as he reached for his goblet once more.

* * * * *

"We've been foes more years than I can remember," Lord Amandon said, rising. His guest had arrived swiftly, indeed.

Sweat from the effort of standing sprang out on the old lord's brow. A moment later, he felt himself borne on unseen hands back to bed, to settle once more among the cushions. The pain and trembling eased—but all his will could not entirely stifle a whimper.

"Be at ease, Lord Amandon," said his guest, standing cloaked in shadow. "Greeting me should not bring ye death."

The old lord raised an eyebrow. "Myrkul stands ready at my door . . . 'tis why I sent for you. I need Manshoon stopped, but not slain."

"When, and how?"

"As soon as next highsun, I fear . . . at the meeting of the ruling council."

"A meeting so guarded by spells that my approach would call forth all the mages, priests, and armsmen Zhentil Keep can muster."

"There is a way in," Lord Amandon replied. "Take the shape of a being who is expected, and you'll be free to enter."

"I smell a trap."

"Aye," Amandon said. "There is. . . . But not for your skin. Certain secret names I've learned, coupled with your power, can entrap a being, to its death. I give you my word—as battlelord of Zhentil Keep and as an Amandon: I mean no attack against you."

"I believe ye," came the voice from the shadows.

Lord Amandon sighed. "You show more trust than most in this city, these days."

"Lack of trust is a more widespread problem than ye may think, Lord," was the dry reply. "Now, these secret names. . . ."

* * * * *

At the heart of the High Hall of Zhentil Keep was a vast, echoing room. Usually it stood empty. Today every seat was taken, and those who could not find seats in the council chamber, but had importance enough to force admittance, stood on the stairs, anxious at what might occur—and even more anxious not to appear so. Rumors about the rise of the Zhentarim and the growing anger of the nobles enfolded the city like a cloak on a chill night. Would the cold-faced priests of Bane stop the wizards' grab for power with spells of their own? That might plunge the city into spell-battle and ruin. Or would they remain as impartial as they'd always claimed to be?

Through the murmur of excited talk, bright morning light fell past the shoulders of standing citizens into the oval well of concentric benches to splash the central debating floor with sun-fire. Lord Chess looked grimly down from his seat into that pool of light and stroked one of his rings.

One man stood alone in the brightness—a man in rich robes, who surveyed the chamber as if he owned it and every person there; a man hated more than most, in a city of many hatreds: Manshoon of the Zhentarim, first lord of Zhentil Keep.

He gave the crowded benches that soft half-smile many had learned to fear, then said, "There is just one matter more."

Manshoon took a thick sheaf of parchment from a front bench and waved it. One scrip escaped his grasp and fluttered away. Someone snickered, but Manshoon crooked an eyebrow and let his hand fall open. The papers began circling his head in a slow, stately ring.

"These reports cite increased aggressions by our foes," he said, his voice carrying to the uppermost reaches of the chamber. "See how many there are?"

He indicated one paper. "Here we read of citizens slain by villainous, deluded followers of the discredited high imperceptor."

He pointed at a group of parchments. "There we read of unfair fees and taxes heaped upon our merchants by no less than seven cities of the Dragon Reach."

Manshoon's finger moved again. "Or perhaps you'd prefer to report of open assaults on our caravans by the brigands who style themselves the Cult of the Dragon!"

The first lord spread his hands. "Is this not monstrous? Should we not sharpen our swords and ready our spells?"

"No," someone replied flatly from the middle benches. There was a murmur of laughter.

Manshoon let it run its course and die. "Yet there's more. Much more. The survival of our very city is at stake!"

"It always has been," someone called.

"Aye, show us something new to back up those old words!"

Manshoon replied, "Very well. Look, all! *Look well!*"

He waved a hand and stepped back. The debating floor darkened. Motes of light winked and sparkled in that magical gloom, swirling suddenly into the ghost-form of a robed man. The stranger sneered, then raised one hand to shape an intricate gesture. A soundless bolt of lightning lashed out from that hand into the upper benches. Councilors cringed back—and then gaped as images of three Zhentarim wizards well-known in the city suddenly appeared among the benches. These ghost mages hurled back magics of their own.

The harmless shadows of sparking, slaying spells flashed and leapt. Manshoon stood calmly in the midst of their silent fury and said, "I call on the high priest of the Black Altar!"

Fzoul rose and bowed gravely. His flowing red hair and moustache stood out like frozen flames against the dark splendor of his robes.

Manshoon asked in loud, solemn tones, "Are these images false?"

Fzoul held up a gem that filled his fist and glowed with magical radiance. He peered through it at the spell-phantoms, then shook his head. "No. These images record what truly befell." He bowed again and sat down.

"Behold," Manshoon said triumphantly, pointing at the image of the stranger-phantom. "A Red Wizard of Thay!" He surveyed the dumbfounded councilors and added, "Confronted as you see, in *this very chamber*, two nights ago!"

Silent spells splashed and grappled. Sudden green flames raced up the Red Wizard's limbs. The struggling man's flesh dissolved in the inferno until only black, writhing bones remained. The watching councilors saw those bones collapse into ash.

In the hushed silence that followed, Manshoon's voice carried clearly. "Saw you the scroll at his belt?" The smoking image faded as he waved at it, but many councilors nodded.

"I recognized it," the first lord said grimly, "and checked our records chamber. The naval treaty we recently signed with Thay is missing! We are defenseless against Thayan piracy—but the concessions we surrendered to get that agreement are still lost to us."

Manshoon raised his arms and voice together as he looked around at the benches. "And this is but a piece of paper! What if this wizard had come with killing spells, seeking your money? Or your throat? Or your children, to sell into slavery?"

There was an excited, angry buzz, as councilor looked to councilor. Manshoon let it grow into a roar, then waved for silence.

"Zhentil Keep needs strong guardians against such perils. You saw the bravery and skill of three Zhentarim with your own eyes, preventing the destruction of this hall—or worse. I can keep this city safe with more stalwart, loyal mages such as these. . . . But I need your permission to do so." He stepped forward grandly, so sunlight outlined him. "I must have the right and the power to defend you!"

Then Manshoon continued more quietly, "I must be free to train and equip forces to properly defend our city. I must have the authority to whelm and direct them in emergencies. I move that the formal powers of the first lord of Zhentil Keep—*my* powers—be so increased."

The chamber erupted. Red-faced old nobles pounded fists on their benches and bellowed, "Never!" There were shouts of "Tyranny!" and others of "Well said!" There were also cries of "Let the lord speak!" and "Wisdom at last!"

From out of the tumult, somewhere in the upper benches, came the wink and flash of a dagger spinning end-over-end through the air. Manshoon calmly watched it come. At the last instant, after most councilors had seen the whirling blade, the first lord waved his hand and muttered a word. The blade blossomed into a small shower of sparks and was gone.

Fzoul Chembryl rose, dark robes swirling. His voice was loud and level. "From chaos and strife can come only harm. Whatever is decided here, we *must* have order in this city, and the rule of law." He surveyed the hall slowly and sternly before he added, "We have heard a proposal of some controversy—and seen the clear urgency behind that proposal. Let us put this matter to a vote. Let this council decide—*now!*"

One old nobleman protested, "Matters of import shouldn't be decided in haste! This is *not* well done! This council never speaks or acts hastily!"

High Priest Fzoul answered coolly, "Daggers are never thrown in this council chamber, either." He folded his robes around himself with dignity and sat down.

A young lord rose and shouted over the angry talk that followed. "Let us have a vote. Something must be done, or we all waste our time here!"

There were supportive cries of "A vote! A vote!" Most seemed to come from the benches where wizards sat.

Manshoon nodded. "A vote has been called. Will any other councilor speak for it?"

"*I* speak for it!" cried an excited young noble in the upper benches, to be answered by a slithering of hisses.

Manshoon's voice silenced them all. "A vote has been twice called, and the duty of this council is clear. Let us vote."

Fzoul stood again. "By rule, any vote for or against a first lord is called by the senior priest present—yet I think it not right for the servants of holy Bane to act so boldly in this purely secular business of Zhentil Keep. If Councilor Urathyl will honor us?"

The young noble who'd seconded the call rose, flushed with pride. "The first lord asks this council to increase his powers and those of the Zhentarim he commands. Who stands in support of this request?"

Here and there around the chamber councilors came silently to their feet. There were not many. Urathyl counted them twice, including himself, and called the count— nineteen—to Fzoul, who confirmed it.

Less happily, the young noble drew breath and said, "Let all against the request stand to be counted."

Benches scraped and echoed all over the chamber. Urathyl counted and called forty-six councilors.

Fzoul bowed. "The count is correct, and has Bane's blessing. The request is den—"

"Wait!" The strong, sour voice of Lord Phandymm cut across the high priest's words. Fzoul bowed, surrendered the floor with a gesture, and sat down.

The senior noble, known as a loud opponent of the Zhentarim, struggled to his feet. He was trembling, and his solemn face slipped into fleeting contortions several times. His hands clutched at his bench for support. "I—I think we are too hasty, and have voted with our hearts, with too little regard for the safety of fair Zhentil Keep. It irks many of us—myself included—"

Phandymm's eyes grew wild, and he gabbled for a moment before his voice cleared. "Irks us, I say, to see one so young making what some see as an arrogant, dangerous grab for the scepter of absolute rule over our city. And yet . . . if we set aside our anger, what he proposes is only sensible! Have we not seen the perils lurking in the shadows of this very hall? Have w-w-weee—?"

The noble's face twisted and spasmed again. His body jerked about as if buffeted by unseen hands. He passed trembling fingers over his face, and sat down. "I—I cannot say more," he mumbled.

"Magic," a councilor shouted suddenly. "Someone's using magic on Phandymm!"

"Magic! Through the spell-shields?"

"Aye, *Zhentarim* magic!"

A Zhentarim wizard rose angrily. "I resent that charge! Will the high priest examine Lord Phandymm? I am confident no spell will be found upon him!"

Fzoul rose and bowed again. "As this meeting unfolds," he said dryly, "it occurs to me that perhaps I should simply remain standing." There were chuckles amid the growing tension. Again Fzoul peered through the glowing gem to seek out any trace of sorcery—and frowned.

"I find no magic," the high priest said firmly. "But there is *some*thing. . . ."

He crooked a finger, and a small flask rose from the breast of the hunched lord's robe, sparkling as it drifted smoothly into the air. All could see the potent wine within.

"Ah," Fzoul said, amid a spreading ripple of laughter. When the mirth had diminished, he let the flask sink back and said delicately, "Lord Phandymm seems in some . . . *emotional* distress, but his deep feelings for the safety of our city are clear. And from the wisdom of more years than most of us boast, he has called for a revote."

The Zhentarim wizard who'd denied the presence of magic sprang to his feet, voice triumphant. "I move a revote proceed!"

Councilor Urathyl almost fell over his feet as he rose to shout, "I speak in support!"

Fzoul bowed again. "A revote must now occur."

Manshoon sat silently at his front bench, smiling a little. His gaze never left the face of the sweating Lord Phandymm.

From his high vantage, Lord Chess saw a little glow in the first lord's eyes, and was sure: magic. He leapt to his feet. "Enough, Manshoon—and all of you Zhentarim! Let *all* foul magic be left outside this hall. The councilors of Zhentil Keep must deliberate with clear wits!"

Manshoon turned his burning gaze from Phandymm—who fell back senseless in his seat, head lolling—to Chess.

The nobleman felt a sudden heaviness tearing at his mind. He gasped, then roared in fury as he felt his tongue thicken and words come unbidden into his mouth.

The first lord smiled at him as cruelly as any cat cornering his prey.

Chess glared into that mocking smile as he struggled against his own muscles. The lesser rings of protection on his fingers smoked, flared into tiny blue flames, and burned away. The searing pain cleared his senses. Desperately, Chess drove his arm up—it moved slowly, as if coming from a great distance—to stare at the one ring still on his hand. It flashed.

Sudden golden radiance swirled in the air over the central well of the High Hall. It spun ever-brighter until the stunned councilors saw it become a large black dragon, vast and scaled, its head like a gigantic horned snake. Mighty wings clapped, once.

The wind of that wingbeat smashed many men flat against their benches. The dragon hissed, loud and angry. Acid foamed and bubbled at the edges of its jaws, and the chamber was suddenly full of the eye-watering stink of its breath.

Men screamed. The dragon turned its snakelike head, terrible hunger and mirth in its eyes. With its tail, the wyrm casually smashed a councilor and his bench into a bloody heap of pulp and splinters.

That crash was answered with a ringing like angry bells as the tall windows of the chamber shattered—and true nightmare descended on the council.

The dragon whirled, gleaming scales shifting.

Three orbs, black against the bright sunlight, drifted into the chamber through the broken windows. Eyestalks writhed as each dark sphere looked down with a single unwinking, central eye. A large, many-toothed mouth split one sphere in cruel laughter.

"Beholders!" a councilor shrieked.

"The rumors were true!" another shouted. "The Zhentarim are in league with beholders!"

All across the chamber, councilors and citizens shrieked

and scrambled over benches in a frantic rush to flee. The dragon roared and spat a smoking plume of acid at the foremost beholder, but the air suddenly filled with glowing rays, which lanced out from the beholders' many eyes. At their touch, the acid hissed into smoke.

Lord Chess felt Manshoon's mind-attack falter and fade. The noble flung himself under his bench and tried to reach the dragon's mind, to turn its fury on the first lord before Manshoon could work worse magic.

The dragon's will was clear and hard, far mightier than the nobleman's. Bent on destroying its many-eyed foes, the dragon ignored his silent commands. Chess growled in exasperation.

Across the hall, Zhentarim mages came to their feet. They boldly ignored the dragon's lashing tail and used the panic to follow their own dark plot. Triumphant sneers twisted their faces as they hurled balls of fire and bolts of lightning at the keep's proudest and most powerful nobles. Many lords snatched out magical rods and wands of their own, striking back with fury.

Overhead the dragon roared in pain, writhing, as many rays stabbed at—and through—it. Smoking wounds appeared all over its body, raining hot blood down on the men fighting below. Swords and knives flashed as men slashed and grappled along the benches. Chess tried again to reach the dragon's mind, but felt from it pain that made him shout aloud and recoil so violently he cracked his head on the underside of the bench. When he'd recovered his senses, he settled on drawing his slim ceremonial sword.

A Zhentarim mage hurried past. Chess rose as another wizard rushed by. Coolly, he ran the man through.

The wizard coughed, convulsed, and hung heavily on the noble's blade. As Chess wrested his steel free, ripples of radiant magic rolled out from the beholders to strike the dragon.

The mighty wyrm flickered and grew pale as wave after wave of bright magic broke over it . . . until Chess thought he could see benches and struggling men *through* it.

A breath later, the still-roaring dragon simply faded away.

The noble looked around, blade raised. Zhentarim wizards were blocking every exit, using magic to hurl back fearful councilors, preventing all from leaving. Spells snatched blades from hands all over the chamber, or made drawn steel burn as if aflame. Even as his own blade seemed to catch fire, Chess saw a man curse as his sword clanged to the floor. Then Chess was forced to let his own weapon fall.

Manshoon stood at the center of the hall, gloating openly. The wizard's grin was wide as his gaze took in the moaning and the fallen. Then the first lord glanced up at the three beholders.

His triumphant smile slid suddenly into open-mouthed astonishment. The beholder Manshoon knew as Arglath had turned—and rays lashed from its eyes to rend its two fellows.

One eye tyrant burst, spattering stunned priests and mages below with its gore. The other spun through the air, torn apart and blazing, to crash down in ruin on a cluster of vainly shouting Zhentarim wizards. The treacherous beholder floated slowly across the chamber. Lord Chess cowered as its dark, awesome bulk halted above him, eyestalks curling like a nest of angry snakes.

"Enough killing," the eye tyrant hissed in a deep and terrible voice that brought the hall to sudden silence. "Let order be restored and all magic cease. Let all able councilors return to their seats—and I do mean *all*, Manshoon."

The first lord of Zhentil Keep froze in the midst of frantic spellweaving. Failing magic flashed and faded around him as he glared up at the beholder. Chess saw fear and hatred war with each other in Manshoon's eyes.

Fear won. For now.

* * * * *

The second vote, taken with the beholder hanging dark over the terrified councilors, was not even close. The special powers requested by the first lord were denied.

At the beholder's bidding, Lord Chess was named "Watchlord of the Council." His vote was stripped from him, along with any authority over the armsmen of Zhentil Keep. But he was made supreme in directing council affairs. None could now lawfully set aside the council to seize rule over the city . . . not even ambitious archmages.

More than a few eyes saw Fzoul, the supposedly impartial high priest of Bane, turn white with fury. There was a general hiss of anger at his revealed connivance when Manshoon strode around the ring of benches to lean over the priest and murmur a few words. The price of the uncloaking was high, but the words needed to be said.

"Make no defiance," Manshoon breathed. His face was a calm mask; only his burning eyes betrayed the fear and rage that were almost choking him. "I was close with Chess once, and can be again . . . close enough, at least, to make him move at our bidding."

Whatever reply Fzoul might have made, his own eyes still dark and ugly with rage, was drowned out by the beholder's cold, hissing voice. It had silently descended to hang close above the two men.

"It is hoped among my kind," the eye tyrant said with deep sarcasm, "that the events of today have taught you both the folly of such clumsy, drawn-swords villainy. Those who deal in rashness are changed by their dealing—and not for the better. The *waste* caused by the violence you began should make your lesson as clear and as painful to you as it has been to the rest of this council."

The beholder rose swiftly, eyestalks still trained in a deadly array on the two. Then it added almost bitterly, "But the curse of humans seems to be the nimbleness with which they forget."

Manshoon straightened, opening his mouth. His expression foretold words of proud defiance, but the beholder was already disappearing through a shattered window. Its parting words echoed around the hall. "Behave with rather more subtlety in the future, Manshoon, if you wish to enjoy our continued support!"

Silence fell. The councilors sat frozen in fear of what the first lord might do in his rage.

Manshoon stared up at the window for a very long time. Then he smiled thinly, raised one hand in what might have been a salute—or a wave of dismissal—and quietly walked out of the hall. Wordlessly the surviving Zhentarim rose and followed, their dark cloaks sweeping out like the wings of so many determined birds of prey.

Lord Chess watched them go and let out a breath he'd been holding a long time. As he made his own way out, he was careful not to glance at Fzoul Chembryl. He could feel the cold weight of the priest's gaze. The master of the Black Altar had been known to lash out in fury himself.

Cold sweat was trickling down the newly appointed watchlord's back by the time he strode out of the chamber and turned hastily aside to where hurled spells could not reach. He sighed then. There were still some chasms, it seemed, even the Zhentarim and the priests of Bane did not quite dare to hurl their spells across. Yet.

Chess sighed again and hurried away, keeping a wary watch behind as he went.

* * * * *

Awe and terror filled the streets of Zhentil Keep when a beholder of gigantic size drifted, dark and silent, over the city in the brightness of highsun. Ignoring the startled folk below, it floated between spires and high turrets with menacing purpose. Coming at last to the clustered towers of a high, grand stone castle, it paused by a certain window.

There it erupted in a puff of smoke that seemed to draw the window open. None below could see a robed, bearded man in the heart of the smoke. He stepped over the sill into the tower beyond. The beholder drifted away, its body beginning to dwindle, until it was only wisps of darkness that soon faded to nothing.

* * * * *

It had been a long wait. Lord Amandon was breathing raggedly as the high window of his bedchamber squealed open and the chill north breeze slipped in. The surface of his scrying crystal misted over.

Etreth started forward, sword drawn, when he met the challenging gaze of a white-bearded old man who stepped through the window and strode down empty air.

"Well met, Rorst Amandon," the newcomer said in a voice both dry and deep.

"Welcome, Elminster," the old lord managed to gasp. Etreth came to a halt, open-mouthed. Only then did he remember he held a sword.

Elminster looked at him and, in tones that were not unkind, said, "Put that toy away."

Lord Amandon struggled to speak. "I've . . . no time left to waste words. That was well done, Lord Mage. You kept your word. My price is met. I'm glad I lived to see the bargain sealed."

Elminster bowed. "I shall keep my word in times to come. This I swear: neither Fzoul nor Manshoon shall die by *my* hand or spells . . . however much ill they work." He bowed. "My payment, as agreed, for the names you gave."

Etreth stared from one old man to the other. Lord Amandon nodded. "I do not want Manshoon dead, whatever he may have done to me," he said. "Zhentil Keep needs a strong leader against growing foes. . . . But I did want him held back from becoming a tyrant, ruling over a city twisted into little more than a fortress." His breath faltered. For a long moment the nobleman struggled to gather strength—and then spent it in a shrug. "So . . . even evil old men can be of use to you, eh?"

"Aye," Elminster said, watching the battlelord with something rather like sadness in his eyes. "I salute ye, Lord. It has been an honor to do battle against ye, all these years."

Lord Amandon lay back against his pillows and said faintly, "And now I fear it is ended, Elminster." He turned his head to look into the eyes of his servant one last time. "Farewell, Etreth. Have my thanks—and all my wealth." Then his gaze swept across his broadsword to the portrait of Lady Amandon. Elminster's eyes followed.

Tears welled up in Etreth's eyes, so he never saw the mage lift a hand and murmur something, face very gentle.

A moment later, the slim, demure lady in the painting seemed to turn, recognize her lord, and smile. The painting glowed as she stepped out of it, a figure outlined in faint white fire, face radiant with welcome as she extended loving arms to her lord.

"Desil," Lord Amandon quavered, tears in his voice. "Oh, Desil!" He raised his wasted arms with surprising speed, reaching for her.

As she came to him, the old nobleman struggled up from the bed to meet her—and fell headlong, crumpling to the carpets without a sound.

The radiant figure hung above him for a moment, looking down with a smile before fading away. Etreth made a convulsive moment toward his lord, then looked at Elminster. They both knew Amandon was dead.

"Lady Amandon," Etreth said, weeping. "Oh, the gods are merciful! She—" The faithful servant froze and brushed away his tears. " 'Twas *thou* conjured her up," he said slowly. "Why? Why help one who stood against you down the years?"

Elminster raised an eyebrow, but his voice was empty of sarcasm as he replied, "As your master said, even evil old men can be useful. Thy lord was useful to me as well as to his city. . . . And as we old men know, if long years are to be ours, debts must be paid."

As the Old Mage turned toward the window, Etreth saw that his hands shook with weariness.

One of those hands rose in a salute as Elminster gained the windowsill, turned, and added softly, "No matter how high the price."

THE MORE THINGS CHANGE

Elaine Cunningham

Whenever Elaith Craulnober wished to find his future wife, he knew precisely where to look. He knew also what she would be doing. Although he didn't entirely approve, he'd long ago abandoned any notion of taming the fierce elven lass.

The young elflord hurried through the palace gardens and down a path that took him deep into Evermeet's royal forest. He made his way to a grassy clearing shaded by a canopy of ancient trees. As sure as sunrise, Princess Amnestria was there, sword in hand and skirts kilted up around her knees. Her blue eyes blazed with concentration as she faced off against the finest swordmaster in the kingdom, and her pale face shone like a damp pearl. With both hands she clung to her practice sword—a long, broad blade that looked far too heavy for her slender strength. Her knuckles were white and her arms shook from the strain of balancing the oversized weapon.

Elaith's jaw firmed. He strode forward into the glen, determined to have a few words with the princess's instructor.

When Amnestria caught sight of the handsome, silver-haired elf, she dropped her sword and flew into his arms like a delighted child. Elaith caught the elfmaiden and swung her off her feet in an exuberant spin, delighting in the playful mood she always invoked in him. Theirs was an arranged marriage, but in this as in all things, Elaith considered himself the most fortunate of elves. He was extremely fond of the princess, and justly proud of the brilliant match.

Even without her royal lineage, Amnestria was remarkable. She possessed rare spirit and inner fire, a pragmatic intelligence and unusual perceptivity. Her beauty was not yet in full flower, but already minstrels had begun comparing her to Hanali Celanil, the elven goddess of love. She had blue eyes flecked with gold, and the rarest hair color among moon elves: a deep, vibrant blue that the poets likened to spun sapphires. Her features were delicately molded, her form exquisite. Amnestria was the very embodiment of moon elven beauty.

Yet something about her often struck Elaith as too . . . *human*. That was the only word for it. Despite her merry nature, the princess displayed the intensity of purpose and singular focus usually associated with that vigorous, short-lived race. Battlecraft was her passion, and she divided her spare time between her swordmaster and the war wizard who tutored her in battle magic.

Remembering the source of his ire, Elaith set Amnestria down and prepared to castigate her swordmaster. The older elf, however, had discreetly slipped out of the clearing and was heading down the forest path, sympathy and nostalgia etched on his angular face.

Amnestria noted his departure and wrinkled her nose. "My teacher is deserting me before I'm ready to stop," she said. "Let's have a match!"

"A princess does not fence with the captain of the king's guard," Elaith said in the patient, gentle tone he used rather frequently with the girl.

She dimpled, and her eyes mocked him. "You're just afraid that I'll best you, and then Father will turn your job over to me!"

"The guard exists to protect you, my dear princess, not

employ you. No member of the royal house has ever served in the ranks, and you're not likely to change things," he reminded her. "The king has too much regard for tradition."

Amnestria responded with an inelegant snort. "Tell me something I don't know!"

"You misread me, *damia*," Elaith said earnestly, using an elven endearment directed to sweethearts or children. "I meant no disrespect to the king."

"Of course not." Amnestria sighed heavily, but her dancing eyes still teased him. "That would be hoping for too much."

"What do you mean?" His tone was sharper now.

"You're a dear, Elaith, but sometimes I worry for you." She paused, reflecting. "It's the hardest thing to explain," she mused.

"Make an attempt," he requested coolly.

"You're always so proper, and you follow the rules as if they were graven in alabaster. You're—" Amnestria broke off, clearly at loss for an explanation. Her slender hands milled in small circles as if she could create an air current strong enough to draw out the right words. "You're . . . you're such an *elf*."

"Of course, *damia*," he agreed, a little amusement creeping back into his voice. "What else would I be?"

"But don't you ever think about all this?" she persisted with the earnestness of the very young. Her slender hand traced an arc in the direction of the nearby palace, the wondrous moonstone castle that was the very heart of Evermeet. "I've never heard you wonder why, or question, or challenge *anything*. You just do whatever's expected, and you do it better than anyone else. You're the consummate elf," she repeated. Her natural effervescence asserted itself, and the golden lights in her eyes danced like giddy fireflies. "An elf's elf. The very epitome of elfdom," she elaborated, then bubbled over into giggles.

With another lightening change of mood, the girl snatched up her sword and whirled on her betrothed. "Fight with me!" The words were half request, half demand.

Elaith made her a formal bow. "But Your Highness, is that not what we are doing?" The glint of humor in his amber eyes belied his words, and Amnestria let out another peal of laughter.

"I suppose we are." She struck a pose straight out of an ancient, illustrated tome: sword tip resting on the ground before her, one elegant hand extended. "My lord, let us make peace. You are my silver knight, and I your only love," she said, mimicking the courtly language of an elven legend.

Responding in kind, Elaith bent low over her hand and pressed it to his lips. With a sudden flash of insight, he realized that despite her lighthearted game Amnestria spoke simple truth. He loved this child-woman with all his heart. He averted his eyes from her frank gaze, lest he reveal emotions she was not yet ready to comprehend. For Amnestria's sake, he tucked away the pang and the joy of this revelation, hoarding it like a red dragon guards its dearest treasure.

"Why are you practicing an ancient fighting technique?" he asked, turning the conversation to the subject dearest to her heart. "Are you performing in an historical masque for the midsummer entertainments?"

"No! This is swordcraft, not play," she told him in a stern voice.

"Then why?"

Her dimples flashed again. "You've met my great-aunt Thasitalia?"

"Yes," he said flatly. The elfwoman was a free-sword who'd traveled widely, debasing her ancient moonblade by lending her skills to anyone who could offer gold and adventure. The mercenary's tales enthralled Amnestria, and Elaith considered Thasitalia a bad influence on the restless princess. Still, he had to give the elfwoman credit. Moonblades were rare and so powerful that few could wield them. As the last in his family line, Elaith stood to inherit such a blade from his grandsire. He considered this his greatest honor, a mark of his heritage no less cherished than the elven princess he loved.

"Thasitalia made me her blade-heir!" Amnestria announced, holding out both hands to him. "Now we will each have a moonblade. Isn't that marvelous!"

"It is indeed," he said with genuine warmth, taking her hands and giving them a little squeeze.

"We'll need to have scads of children, so we can choose the strongest among them as blade-heirs," she said in a matter-of-fact tone that brought heat to Elaith's cheeks. Seeing this, the maiden rolled her eyes and dropped his hands. She arranged her face in a lugubrious pose and intoned, "It is not seemly to speak of such matters, Your Highness," in a wicked imitation of Elaith's precise, mellifluous tones.

"But anyway," she continued in her own voice, "Thasitalia told me to start practicing with a two-handed grip and a heavy sword. Her moonblade's magic adds unusual speed and power to the strike, and she says that I must develop strength and quick reflexes, or I won't be able to control the sword."

"So you're in training, preparing to inherit a moonblade?"

"Of course. Aren't you?"

Smiling, Elaith touched the shoulder of the white uniform of King Zaor's elite guard. The insignia there proclaimed his rank, and finely wrought pins attested to his expertise in a number of arts and weapons. "All my life I have prepared."

* * * * *

Directly across the street from Waterdeep's southernmost docks stood a ramshackle barn of a tavern, optimistically named the Tumbled Wench. The tavern was frequented by sailors and dockhands, free-swords in search of adventure, merchant captains, bored local dandies, and bemused travelers from a hundred ports and a dozen races. Local wisdom had it that the Tumbled Wench wove as good a picture of Waterdeep as a visitor was likely to get: a chaotic tapestry of splendor and squalor.

Exotic smoke filled the air with fragrant haze, and business deals mingled with bawdy laughter in cheerful cacophony. Wealthy merchants and noblefolk with a taste for gritty adventure bumped elbows with low-rent escorts and tattered street people. The prospect served the needs and tastes of all: for a few coppers, patrons could eat their fill or drown their miseries. Efficient barmaids bustled about with trenchers of seafood stew and tankards of foaming ale. More expensive libations were available, and the kitchen would roast herb-stuffed fowl to order, but patrons seldom lingered.

Oblivious to the bustle around him, a dazed young elflord sat at the long wooden bar, nursing a single glass of Evereska sparkling water. His choice of beverage, so unusual in the rough taverns of the Dock Ward, caused more than one patron to smirk and nudge his neighbor. The snide witticisms were spoken softly, though, for few seasoned fighters offered open challenge to a well-armed elf.

Elaith sipped at his water, and the vague sickness that had haunted him throughout his long and unaccustomed sea voyage slipped away. As his discomfort ebbed, he was all the more aware of the aching void that both filled and consumed him. Evermeet had been his life, Amnestria his love, and he had chosen to leave them both. His meeting with the princess in the forest glade had been their last; that very night his grandsire's spirit had passed on to Arvanaith, and the Craulnober moonblade had become Elaith's to claim.

Never would Elaith forget the horror of watching the pale light of the moonstone, the magic-bearing gem in the hilt of his inherited sword, fade to the dead, milky whiteness of a blinded eye. The moonblade had rejected him, choosing dormancy over an unworthy heir.

This possibility had never occurred to Elaith. He had felt neither doubt nor fear as he'd unsheathed the sword, although he well knew that many had failed an attempt to claim a moonblade. Most of these unfortunates had been struck dead by the swords, but if an elf were the last in a family line, the hereditary blade would merely fall dormant. To safeguard the potent artifacts from misuse, the original crafters had endowed the swords with the ability to discern character and motivation. The moonblade apparently sensed something about me, Elaith noted with deep bitterness, some flaw that I have yet to discover for myself.

"Your mother uses gray squirrels for currency!"

The cryptic remark, spoken in loud and badly accented Elvish, shattered Elaith's reverie. He spun about on the barstool to face the man who had spoken.

"Are you addressing me?" Elaith asked politely, speaking the widely used trade language referred to as Common.

A nasty grin split the man's bearded face. "I knowed it! The elf ain't deaf, just too good to speak when spoke to."

Belatedly, it occurred to Elaith what the human had been trying to say. The man had delivered a mangled version of an insult, of the sort elven children tossed at each other in fits of pique. More amused than insulted, Elaith studied the human with open curiosity.

The man stood a hand's span over six feet, and he appeared fit and heavily muscled. He wore a uniform of sorts—black leather armor that sported an elaborately tooled crest on the shoulder. Curly brown hair rioted over his shoulders and spilled into an abundant beard, and his face was twisted into a leer of challenge. One meaty hand rested on the grip of a dagger, and his booted feet were planted wide. Yet his bravado was marred by a pair of red-rimmed eyes. The scent of cheap whiskey rolled off him in pungent waves.

Elaith was not tempted by the challenge. Even if the drunken soldier had possessed the full measure of his wits, there were strict rules against dueling someone of lesser rank. "I will not fight you," Elaith said in a calm voice. "It would not be—" He broke off abruptly, for the word *honorable* no longer seemed to apply to him.

The man sneered, mistaking Elaith's hesitation for cowardice. "You'll fight if I say you will." He kicked the barstool out from under the elf.

Elaith saw the move coming and leapt lightly to his feet. The stool upended with a clatter that echoed through the suddenly silent taproom, and patrons seated by the bar quickly remembered urgent business at the far side of the tavern. The elf was not pleased to be the focus of attention.

He resolved to end the matter swiftly.

With a theatrical flourish, the huge drunk pulled his dagger and lunged. Elaith stepped to the left and seized the man's thick wrist with both hands. A slight twist brought the man to his knees. The elf slammed the back of the beefy hand onto the barstool, locking his opponent's arm in an extended position. Then Elaith lifted one booted foot and stomped on the elbow. Bone gave way with a cruel splinter. The man fainted away without uttering a single cry.

Silence reigned in the tavern for only a moment. Another, even larger man stepped forward, clad in the same black leather armor. He nodded at his fallen fellow. "That's my brother," he growled.

Elaith folded his arms. "My condolences," he said wryly. "Since none of us can choose our kin, I shall not hold this misfortune against you."

"We can choose our friends, though, and you ain't one of mine." The mercenary reached over his shoulder and drew a broadsword from the sheath on his back. Chairs scraped across the floor as the patrons cleared an impromptu arena in the middle of the taproom with an alacrity that suggested such fights were far from uncommon. The barkeep glanced up, then went back to polishing the pewter mugs.

"Borodin," the man said firmly. "Remember it. That's the name of the man who's gonna kill you." He raised his weapon in challenge.

Elaith reached for his sword, but hesitated when his fingers touched the lifeless moonstone. Borodin marked this hesitation with a derisive snort.

Something snapped within the elf's heart.

Stooping, Elaith pulled the sword from the fallen man's belt. The weapon needed a good oiling and sharpening, for the sword was blunt and the edge visibly pitted. Elaith studied it for a moment, then pointedly raised an eyebrow and met his opponent's glare.

"This should do," he said. His tone conveyed utter contempt for both the weapon and his challenger.

Borodin swung his sword high for a sweeping cut. The

blade hissed downward as he lunged. Instead of the satisfying clash of steel on steel, though, the fighter heard a dull thud as his sword cut a leg from an úpended bar stool. An instant later he plowed heavily into the bar. Mugs scattered with a mocking clatter.

The elf was simply not there. Elaith had danced aside with uncommon grace and speed. For good measure, he smacked Borodin's backside with the flat of his borrowed blade. Guffaws echoed throughout the tavern.

Borodin whirled and delivered a backhanded slash. Elaith parried the blow easily, but he was startled and jarred by the power of the attack. He could not match the man's size or strength, but the elf had the advantage of technique and speed.

With practiced grace, Elaith spun his blade outward in a lightning-fast circle, flinging Borodin's sword arm wide. In the same movement, he pulled a dagger from his belt and stepped in close. The point of the dagger bit into Borodin's throat, and cold amber eyes promised death. Then, with a deft, downward flick, Elaith slashed open the leather lacings on the man's jerkin. He leapt back, tucking the dagger into its sheath, and in a gesture of utter contempt, he lowered his sword arm to his side and beckoned for Borodin to attack.

"Ten coppers on the elf!" shouted a gravel-voiced sailor. Other patrons joined in, making wages and laying odds.

The man advanced, his bearded face crimson but set in determination. With his initial rage spent, he fell back into a more disciplined fighting style. At one time, Elaith noted as he parried the blows, the man had been well trained. By the elf's standards, however, Borodin possessed neither finesse nor imagination. Elaith easily anticipated and met every strike.

By honor and custom, he should have ended the matter at once, for his opponent was clearly outmatched. Yet Elaith continued, openly taunting the man with his superior skill. The elf was driven by a cold anger he'd never known he possessed, an icy temper than numbed the pain in his own heart. For the first time since he'd left Evermeet, Elaith could put aside his sense of disgrace and failure. With cruel humor and stunning swordcraft, he played the fight out for the amusement and delight of the rough patrons.

As the minutes ticked by, Borodin's mighty sword arm slowed and his breathing grew labored and raspy. Finally he could take no more. He fell to his knees, and then his forehead met the floor with a resounding thud. Several of his mates came forward and pulled him to his feet. They staggered out into the night with their burden, running a gauntlet of mockery.

A roar of approval and laughter engulfed the tavern, and Elaith found himself in the center of a back-slapping throng. A plump, red-bearded man, also wearing the tooled leather uniform, offered to buy the victorious elf a drink. "After all," he said as he dangled a small leather purse in front of Elaith's face, "you won the money for me! The name's Rix, by the by."

The friendly overture struck Elaith as odd behavior indeed, but he accepted the offer and followed the man to the far end of the bar. At Rix's signal, the barkeep handed them each a tall, narrow glass filled with a thin liquid as golden as honey.

"What is this?"

"Firewine." The soldier winked and slurped at his drink. "Bottoms up!"

Elaith took an experimental sip. The pale liqueur had none of the subtlety or complexity of elven spirits, but it was nearly as powerful. He drained the glass with dark pleasure; the firewine filled his mouth with a dry, bitter heat. His new companion gaped, then guffawed.

"Never trust a man—or an elf—until you've seen him fight and drink," Rix said cheerfully. "And on both counts, you're surely not to be trusted!"

He craned his neck and shouted at a knot of black-clad fighters near the tavern door. "Xander! Sign up this elf! Tonight, mind you, or the whole lot of us will quit!"

One of the men broke from the group and made his way

toward the bar. With a mixture of puzzlement and deep interest, Elaith watched his approach. Xander was a man of middle years, in the prime of his strength. He was slender and tall, with skin the color of polished teak, wavy black hair plaited into a single long braid, and mocking black eyes. He walked with sinuous grace, but Elaith noted a military bearing and air of command. The elf could recognize a leader in any guise, and he rose to his feet in an instinctive gesture of respect.

Xander studied the young elflord for a long moment. "A good recommendation, Rix. Tell Malcolm to give you twice the usual finder's fee, by my command. Now, off with you. I need to speak with our new recruit."

The red-bearded mercenary picked up his glass and strolled off, grinning broadly. Xander took the seat Rix had vacated and gestured for Elaith to resume the one beside it.

The bewildered elf sank onto the barstool. "You wish me to join your regiment?"

"Regiment? Oh, that's priceless!" Xander's white teeth flashed in a smile of genuine amusement. He took a gleaming black pipe from a bag at his belt and pressed a bit of tobacco into the bowl. The barkeep at once held out a lighted brand, his manner clearly deferential. Xander puffed for a moment, then leaned casually against the bar. "I'm the leader of a mercenary band. Treasure hunters."

Elaith nodded slowly. By all reports, the humans of Waterdeep were like so many dragons, hoarding useless wealth and measuring their success by the height and luster of the pile. That had always seemed strange to Elaith. A life of acquisition was entirely foreign to the values that had hitherto ordered his life. As he considered the matter now, however, the wonderful simplicity in this system appealed to him.

"You should have killed Borodin, you know," Xander observed.

Elaith stared. That was the last piece of advice he would have expected, even from this amazing man.

"Although your performance was amusing and your swordsmanship most impressive, you've made yourself an enemy. That was totally unnecessary. As a rule, you ought to eliminate enemies as they occur, not create them and let them linger to trouble you again later."

"I am unfamiliar with such . . . rules."

"They're easy enough to learn. Just do whatever needs doing to get rich and stay alive in the process. Above all, look out for your own interests." Xander took a long draw, then blew a wreath of clove-scented smoke at the elf. "You could do quite well for yourself if you cast your lot in with the Claw."

"You would have me? I disabled two of your men!"

"That you did." The mercenary captain considered Elaith for a time, sipping thoughtfully at his pipe. "With your skills, I can replace two men with one elf—and pocket another share of the treasure myself."

Elaith paused to ponder the unfamiliar logic. "Treasure," he repeated, more to buy time than to signify interest.

"Big treasure. Ever heard of Erlunn?"

"Of course." Erlunn had been one of the great centers of elven culture in the Northlands. The elves had long since retreated, and their civilization had been swallowed by the ancient wood known as the High Forest.

Xander pulled a metal tube from his belt and removed a small roll of parchment. He spread it out and tapped at a spot near the river known as the Unicorn Run.

"Rumor has it that, centuries back, the elves buried their dead and all their wealth among the roots of oak trees. Your good friend Borodin—" Xander paused and tossed his head toward the tavern door "—found a stand of ancient oaks surrounding a circle of stones. When he pulled the moss off the foot of the stones, he found these markings. We copied them here on the map, and later paid a priest of Lathander to translate them."

Xander traced the runes scrawled along the bottom of the parchment. "According to this, Borodin found a burial site."

Tomb robbing, the elf thought with a touch of horror. His dismay must had shown on his face, for Xander lifted one black eyebrow in inquiry.

Elaith's thoughts whirled. The life Xander offered him was as far from the peace and discipline of Evermeet as anything the elf could imagine. No traditions, no rules but expediency, no goals but power and wealth. The elf nodded slowly as the new mode of thinking began to take root in his mind.

"Borodin's an even bigger fool than I took him for. Your hired priest was not much better. These are runes of protection," Elaith said, tapping the curving symbols. "The standing stones and the oak trees are guardians. The actual grave sites would be much deeper in the forest."

"You could find the true site?" Xander asked.

"It might be that I can," the elf said tentatively. "But if I am to join your ranks, I must know more about the life you lead."

"What's to know? Just do what you're told and don't spend much time wondering why."

Elaith recoiled, for the mercenary's advice was an uncanny echo of words Amnestria had spoken at their final meeting. The life that Elaith had lived on Evermeet felt as distant as a forgotten dream, but it seemed that some things remained the same. As Amnestria had so perceptively noted, he could do whatever was expected of him, and do it better than anyone else.

Elaith leaned back in his chair and returned Xander's steady, cynical gaze. "If I am to replace two men, I expect to receive two full shares of the treasure."

An approving smile split the mercenary's dark face. He gestured to the barkeep, who produced two new glasses of firewine. Xander lifted his glass to the elf in a silent salute. Elaith raised his own glass and tapped it against his new employer's, in a manner he had seen among the fighters. A toast, they called it, a ritual used to seal a pact.

The elf drained the firewine in one long draught. As the golden liquid seared his throat, Elaith willed it to burn away his past, as well.

* * * * *

Many years passed, and Elaith seldom thought about Evermeet or pondered how vastly his life had changed since he'd left. He could not help but do so now as he faced the two women seated in his lavish study. One was his daughter; the other should have been.

Elaith studied Azariah, his blade-heir and only child. The proper elfmaiden sat with downcast eyes. Her golden hands were demurely folded in her lap. She had been raised on Evermeet as a ward of the royal court, and was everything Elaith once had been. This was her first visit to Waterdeep, and her confrontation with her father's dark reputation had visibly shaken her. Although Azariah tried to hide it, she was also daunted by Arilyn Moonblade, the half-elven woman beside her.

Arilyn waited calmly for Elaith to speak, all the while regarding him with Amnestria's gold-flecked blue eyes. He had known the half-elf for years, and had observed her with a mixture of admiration and longing. Arilyn was a fierce, stubborn woman who had made her mother's moonblade her own. She had inherited Amnestria's beauty and spirit, and a certain wisdom that the elven princess had once tried to share with Elaith. It was this that prompted Elaith to entrust his daughter's training to her.

He had endured much to restore the magic to the family's moonblade. Azariah's heritage, her success, was more important to Elaith than his next breath. Yet as he studied the beautiful elven maiden and reflected on all the qualities she embodied, he realized that there was not so much difference between his old life and his new. Granted, he had amassed tremendous wealth and a well-earned reputation for treachery and cruel humor. He was feared and envied for his success as a treasure-hunting mercenary, and for the unofficial power he wielded in Waterdeep. Yet the changes were more a matter of style than substance. He did what was expected of him, acted in ways defined by his chosen role. And as Amnestria had noted that afternoon on Evermeet, he did it better than anyone.

Elaith no longer wondered why his moonblade had

rejected him, those many years ago.

The elf handed Arilyn a tightly rolled scroll. "This is a history of the Craulnober moonblade—its wielders, its magic. This is what Azariah must know. Teach her the necessary skills, make sure she understands the rules."

Elaith paused, and his amber eyes held the sadness that comes in wisdom's shadow. "Make sure she learns the rules," he repeated softly, "and then, above all, teach her to question them."

THE MEANING OF LORE

Barb Hendee

The corridors of Twilight Hall dawned cold and quiet that morning. Dealing with freezing temperatures, even in early fall, was a common annoyance that every citizen of Berdusk adjusted to quickly. "Colder than a Berduskan attic in winter," was a phrase familiar throughout the Heartlands.

Chane Troiban drew his floor-length wool cloak a bit tighter around his neck, picked up a small canvas bag for his journey, and slipped out into the long stone hallway. He hoped to reach the courtyard before anyone noticed him.

"Master Chane! Master Chane, please wait," an irritating voice called from nowhere.

Master Chane. How hollow those words sounded to his ears. To be such a talented priest of Oghma among a score of inferior loremasters was to be less than nothing. To be a perfect rose obscured by a vast bundle of red carnations meant oblivion. Clutching his bag, fingers twisting in a hidden expression of frustration, he turned and smiled.

"Yes, Triska, you needn't shout. I am here."

Running toward him up the stone corridor, panting with lost breath, came Triska, the pudgy apprentice of Master Minstrelwish. Roles of flesh jiggled beneath the young man's burlap robe, making him appear even more ridiculous than usual. "Please—" he paused and gasped for breath "—the others have been waiting. You must help screen two new applicants for the guard. Have you forgotten?"

"Forgotten?" Chane's smile melted into a bland look of brotherly patience. He pulled his hood back, exposing a mass of burnished red-gold hair and a smooth, narrow face. He knew well that his handsome features made most of the apprentices feel inferior. "Of course not, but I have been called away to Rysheos for diplomatic reasons. I sent a message to Narshanna. Did she not receive it?"

"I . . . No one said anything about . . . Shall I inform the council that you have gone to Rysheos?"

"Yes, how kind of you, Triska. Please tell them I will be back to Twilight Hall in a few tendays. I've booked passage on a caravan. The river is too treacherous this time of year."

Pulling his hood back up, Chane left the rotund apprentice staring in confusion after him. Once the tall priest reached the courtyard and found his saddled horse waiting, he smiled again.

* * * * *

Rysheos was situated along the trade routes between Cormyr and Waterdeep, a day's ride north of Soubar. The newly established boomtown bustled with life and color. Though still somewhat primitive in its architecture and inhabitants, the small city exhilarated Chane, filled as it was with smoke-scented trading shops and citizens seeking a fresh start. Until recent years, warring nobles—along with roving bands of goblins and orcs—had given rise to chaos as each fought for control of Rysheos. But one powerful lord and his followers managed to crush all other factions and bring about a fear-induced peace. As the city flourished, opportunities surfaced for those with the courage to seize them. So far, no loremasters had established a temple here.

Seated in the dining hall of the victorious Lord Teelo of Rysheos, Chane felt a sense of urgency tickling the tiny hairs of his forearms. While the city as a whole appealed to him, this one room expressed all the qualities he found so desirable. Rich scents of mulled wine, spiced meats, warm whole-nut bread, stale sweat, leather, and exotic perfume drifted comfortably into his nostrils. Closing his eyes for a moment, he listened to the sounds of laughter, music, clanking steel from mock fights, and toasts to good health.

He raised his eyelids again and focused briefly on a silver bowl brimming with a bright array of fruit. So much wealth here, and so few who knew how to use it. His mouth watered, but he did not hunger for the taste of food. Warriors, wealthy merchants, and barbarians—at least to Chane's perspective —occupied every chair. A wide array of humans, elves, dwarves, and gnomes surrounded him. It was not the mix that differed from that of the Twilight Hall; it was the feel and mood and code of dress. There were no minstrels here. No loremasters. No bards. No teachers of any kind. And for once, all gazes drifted to him. Here he was no perfect rose hidden behind a dozen other nondescript flowers. These people of Rysheos were thorns in the truest sense. Here he was truly appreciated.

"How is your lovely highlady, Cylyria?" Lord Teelo asked politely.

By the gods, Chane thought. Look at him sitting there in chain mail armor with food in his beard, trying to make pleasant conversation. "She is well and sends her greeting."

Everyone who knew anything of Berdusk was well aware that Highlady Cylyria had little do with the governing of her city. She relied on the mages, thieves, bards, and loremasters of Twilight Hall to govern it for her.

"Then why have you requested an audience?" Teelo continued. "Does some other matter need my attention?"

This was the crux of the matter, the heart of Chane's lie. He had not been called to Rysheos for diplomatic reasons. He had written to Lord Teelo a few tendays past, requesting an audience. This hand must be played carefully. Teelo may have possessed the manners of a Shadowdale goat, but he was no fool.

"I am concerned, my lord," Chane began, "about the state

of education in your vast city."

"Education?"

"Yes, there are no churches here, no loremasters to teach the knowledge of Oghma. You don't appear to even possess a bard who might teach your people music, art, or ancient history. Does this not concern you as well?"

Chane noticed a pretty, dark-haired merchant's daughter hanging on his every word. Perhaps she was interested in the conversation. Perhaps she was simply overcome by his charm. He enjoyed the company of women, but only if they were completely enamored of him. Pursuing a romantic challenge held no interest whatsoever. He liked to be adored.

"What are you suggesting?" Lord Teelo asked.

"Suggesting? Why nothing. The recent past of Rysheos has been colored by bloodshed. Now that you have brought order and justice, should not the next logical step be education? What will become of your people without music and history?"

The lines of Teelo's wide forehead narrowed. He had once been a warrior. Now he was a strong leader, and the welfare of his city took precedence over all else. "Yes, I see truth in your words. Should I bring in loremasters and bards, teachers to set up churches and schools?"

Chane smiled his warmest smile, turning his face toward the candlelight to make his smooth skin glow softly. "A brilliant idea, my lord. If you would, let me look into this matter for you. Perhaps a few members of Twilight Hall would be willing to relocate for the chance to undertake so worthy a challenge?"

"Good," Teelo's gaze shifted to a dwarven mock fight that appeared to be growing less mock each moment. "Do that for me, Master Chane. I appreciate your counsel."

Chane sipped his mulled wine as though the exchange meant nothing to him, but his heart beat fast beneath the tan cloak he wore. The lord had expressed a mild interest at best, but a mild interest was all Chane needed. A servant laid half a roast pheasant on the loremaster's plate. Unlike those around him, he cut into it carefully, making certain the bird's juices did not soil his sleeves or spatter his neighbor.

* * * * *

A caravan on its way to Iriaebor arrived in Berdusk late into the night nine days later. The bards, mages, and thieves of Twilight Hall paid no heed to the passengers on the incoming wagons, only the supplies they carried. They had no idea that one of their own traveled in the heart of the clamor.

Chane kept quietly hidden between two wagons, having exchanged his tasteful cream robes for leather breeches and a heavy black tunic. He told no one of his arrival. He told no one on the caravan his true identity. As far as Berdusk was concerned, Loremaster Chane was visiting Rysheos on diplomatic business.

As the horses and wagons began to separate near the marketplace to park safely for the night, Chane turned his mount down a side street and headed for the city's west end.

The Seat of Lore, temple to Oghma.

The very thought of the temple filled him with anticipation. Long ago, scores of ancient books had been spirited inside those sacred walls. Centuries-old texts of legends and lore waited for him like glittering jewels in a consecrated mine. The temple's overseer was a gnome called Bransuldyn Mirrortor, a former rogue and wanderer who now guarded one of the largest collections of ancient and rare texts that Chane could ever desire. And what did Mirrortor do with all his wealth? He simply locked it up like some sad old man hoarding coins under a mattress.

A familiar litany tripped through Chane's thoughts: Knowledge is power. Power is wealth. Wealth is adulation and respect. That sorry gnome knows nothing of possibilities. He deserves to die.

A not-so-charming smile twitched at the corners of Chane's lips. How would Teelo reward a loremaster who knew more archaic history than any other priest on the continent? What would he pay to keep such a prized scholar within the walls of Rysheos? Yes, in Rysheos, such a loremaster could have anything he desired. He would rule the colleges and dole out positions to other prospective teachers, priests, or bards—just as long as they weren't too educated and remembered their place. Life would finally be as it should . . . grand and glorious.

It would take a few years of study, of course. After stealing the texts, he'd have to hole up somewhere to read and prepare. But then, just think of Teelo's gratitude, to command such a loremaster. So much preserved knowledge would be at Chane's fingertips. He would soon be worshiped as the right hand of Oghma. No other position could offer so perfect an existence. His mouth began to water again.

* * * * *

The huge oak doors of Oghma's temple loomed up before him. How to proceed? Cultured charm always worked best for Chane, but he could frighten and bully if the need arose.

Opening the unlocked doors without knocking, he stepped into a cavernous room. All around him simple wooden benches littered the vast floor. Sparsely filled shelves had been pushed up against three of the walls. There was no hall or entryway. To his surprise, he found himself looking at the far wall and a mahogany desk. Sitting at the desk, busily writing, was a slender elven girl with light gold hair.

Her eyes lifted when he entered.

"Welcome," she said softly.

Chane cursed under his breath; all the stories he'd heard portrayed Mirrortor living alone. He could not leave any witnesses alive to testify of his presence in the temple, so this unfortunate girl would have to die as well. Mirrortor was a great, selfish waste of flesh, hiding history from the eyes of the world. Whatever evil befell him, he deserved. But Chane had not planned to turn this theft into a night of multiple murders. There was nothing to be done about it now, however.

"Good evening," he said smoothly. "I know it is late, but I wish to speak with Mirrortor."

The girl had serious eyes, clear gray that seemed to look through him. "One moment," she said. "Let me see if he has retired to his room yet."

She slipped through a door behind the desk. Instinctively he knew that charm would be wasted on her. Force and threats were the only persuasion these people would understand. All he had to do was make Mirrortor show him where the oldest texts were hidden. The rest would be easy. Kill the gnome, pack the books into the bag of holding he had concealed inside his tunic, come back to the main room, kill the girl, and slip away. The dagger in his boot should be enough to silence them.

The door opened again and the girl stepped out, followed by a white-haired gnome apparently dressed for bed. Not sure what he had expected, Chane felt almost amused. Perhaps he had unconsciously anticipated the famous gnome would exude an imposing air, that he would wear the robes of a highly placed loremaster. Instead Mirrortor wore an emerald green nightshirt and purple silk dressing gown with a bright red nightcap whose pointed top hung down past his shoulder.

"Can I help you, son?" the gnome yawned, making the tiny crinkles in his forehead and cheeks more apparent. "It's rather late."

"I'm here on business for Twilight Hall." Chane fell into his authoritative voice. "I need to see your most ancient texts, the very oldest that you keep."

"Twilight Hall you say? Business? Cylyria told me nothing about . . . Aren't you a bit young for a loremaster?"

"That is not your concern." Chane pulled an amulet from beneath his robe—the holy symbol of Oghma. "Show me the books."

Mirrortor shook his head and turned back to the door. "There's no need to be snippy. The texts are always open for all to see. We have no secrets here. You need only ask."

You need only ask? What did *that* mean? If the books were readily available, why did no one ever come here? Perhaps the other loremasters read Mirrortor's books and simply never mentioned it.

Chane dismissed the notion as impossible. Anyone in his right mind would have attempted to remove the books and lay claim to them. Chane knew the contents of the Twilight Hall library by heart. There were no texts as priceless as the ones surely stored here. Perhaps Mirrortor's books were written in languages so old the loremasters could not translate them. Chane smiled slightly in the darkness. Dead languages were his specialty.

As he followed the gnome through the exit and into a narrow hallway, Chane found himself puzzling over the entire situation. Could it be this easy? If the texts were available to all, how were thieves held at bay? And what did Mirrortor hope to gain by sitting on such treasures like a fat little spider, only to allow any ignorant peasant to come in and see the books, as though Oghma's temple were some second-class library? None of this made any sense.

"I wish to see your oldest collection, the most archaic you have," Chane repeated. "Nothing originating after 902 DR, when the Rotting War decimated Chondath."

"Couldn't your quest wait for morning? We could have breakfast before we start. I'm not a bad cook, you know."

"No. I must see the books tonight."

At the hall's end stood another door. It opened with a creak when the gnome touched it, and they both began descending a curved rock staircase. Dim lamplight made for poor visibility, and the endless circles as they made their way lower caused Chane to lose track of time and distance.

"How far?" he asked.

"Not far now. Almost there."

But the descent continued. Farther down, the lamps were replaced by thick candles flickering in iron holders on the wall. For all Chane's frustration, at least the temple itself met his expectations—hidden corridors, rock staircases.

Perhaps this was how the foolish gnome kept his texts safe. Such a downward journey into the darkness would frighten an ordinary thief to death. But theatrics meant nothing to the ambitious priest. It would take more than a few cobwebs to make him lose his bearings. He was a bit disoriented, but certainly he could find his way out again.

"Here we are," Mirrortor said finally. He stepped off the bottom landing into a corridor. "Just a few more paces. Most of the well-read texts are upstairs, where the light is better. Almost no one asks for these anymore."

"Probably because they are written in dead languages only a skilled loremaster would comprehend," Chane answered, finding it difficult to keep contempt from his tone.

"And you find those 'dead texts' the most desirable?"

"Of course. They are like jewels and wine, the older the rarer. The rarer, the more precious. I would have thought you'd figured that out years ago."

"That depends on your perspective. I often find value to be somewhat subjective."

Then you are a fool, Chane thought. He followed the gnome down another stair, six steps curving to the left. They passed though a cobwebbed entryway and into a dusty room.

Upon stepping inside, euphoria filled Chane's breast, and he sighed aloud. "I knew it would be like this."

There weren't even shelves, simply stacks and stacks of leatherbound texts resting one atop the other. Scores, possibly hundreds filled his eyes, tales of heroic quests and dark deeds, the roots of Faerûn's history. Gazing at one stack directly in front of him, he noticed runes along the spines of several texts glowing soft blue. "Wards," he whispered. Those books were to be avoided. His ultimate goal had always been attaining a high position among the priests of Oghma through knowledge of lore alone. He knew little of magic.

Spellbooks aside, plenty of other treasures surrounded him. Bindings of forest green and charcoal gray shone out in the darkness with a brighter intensity than any glowing runes—texts of long-forgotten myths and truths. He would translate and memorize them all, then teach stories that no one had heard in a dragon's age. People would stare at him in wonder. He would be revered and adored.

"Are these the most ancient in your temple?" he asked, reaching down as if to scratch his leg. His fingers brushed the knife's handle.

No one answered.

"Mirrortor?" He turned, but found himself alone. Where had the gnome gone? Perhaps he assumed Chane wanted time alone to read. It did not matter. He could find his victims upstairs without much trouble and silence them later.

He touched the spine of a faded brown cover and chills ran up his arm. Worn symbols, rather than actual words, had been etched deeply into the leather by some craftsman of a bygone era.

"Perfection." He picked it up and turned to the first page. Inside, he discovered yellowed pages much better preserved than the cover. The symbols were a form of hieroglyphics once used in the old empires of the South, Mulhorand and Unther. He recognized the mark for "barbarians," and his excitement grew. Could this be an account of ancient wars? He envisioned himself standing before a crowd in Lord Teelo's dining hall—candlelight reflecting off his red-gold hair—recounting tales a thousand years past.

Pulling the enchanted bag from inside his tunic, he placed the book carefully inside and began paging through another. Anything he could read too easily was discarded as too accessible. He wanted only the elusive, only the ones no other loremaster might already posses. After exhausting the possibilities in this room, he planned to move on to the next. There was no telling how many treasures lay hidden in the temple. And his bag allowed him to take as much from Mirrortor as he pleased. Although he'd never studied magic in detail, Chane found some of its creations quite useful.

Thinking again about the elven girl upstairs, he was

struck by a pang of something akin to guilt. "Oghma may be annoyed at first," he whispered, "but he'll cave in when he sees what a perfect rose I really am."

After he'd pillaged the first pile of its priceless tomes, Chane tried to move to a new stack. The bag's weight jolted him to a stop. The books were heavy. Quite heavy. How could this be? After he had placed only fourteen in the bag, it was nearly full and difficult to carry. The enchantment should have allowed him to fill it forever. But peering inside, he saw that his magic bag was working as if it were nothing more than an ordinary sack.

Mirrortor might be more clever than anticipated, Chane mused. Perhaps he had placed wards against magic on the library. Even for a strong man like Chane, fourteen of the oversized books made a formidable burden. Would he have to settle for this paltry haul?

He stared down in frustration. Fourteen texts of the most ancient lore on the continent were still enough to fulfil his dreams. Or perhaps he could make a second trip after killing the gnome and the girl. The vault had not been hard to find. Yes, that was the answer, make a second trip, possibly a third. After all, he did have a horse waiting outside.

Rising, he turned to leave. Then he saw that all four walls of the room contained exits. Strange. He hadn't noticed them before. From which one had he entered? The many stacks of books made direction difficult to remember.

"Mirrortor, I am ready to leave now," he called.

Nothing.

Had he come into this room from the entrance to his left? Yes, that must be it—the door to his left. Gathering his bag over one shoulder, he walked out into a familiar hallway. Or was it familiar? Fat, flickering candles in rusted holders still cast their dim light against the walls. But this could be any hall in the temple. These dirty gray stone walls probably stretched out through the entire underground.

Chane's dilemma fled his mind as something painfully cold touched his arm. He jumped a pace down the corridor.

"Who's there?"

The hall lay empty. But then Chane felt invisible icy fingers again, trying to grip his shoulder. Burning cold drained his strength, and he scrambled backward, jerking the books along the ground. Chane had always thought himself above such base emotions as fear, but for the first time in his memory, he was afraid.

Dragging the books, he ran, harsh breaths coming quickly. At the hall's end he was forced to choose between two stairwells, one going up, one going down. Perhaps I've outrun the . . . *thing*, he thought. But when he glanced behind him, a horrified gasp escaped his lips.

Grayish white shapes were slowly forming, taking shape. To his despair, two separate faces and bodies materialized into the hazy outlines of human form. They had teeth. Their hollow eyes were hungry.

Wraiths.

"Mirrortor!" Chane called. "Come guide me out. I am ready to leave."

A high-pitched keening from one of the wraiths answered him. The other hissed in hatred and floated forward at an impossible speed.

Chane bolted up the right stairwell. He was usually a swift runner but the weight of the books slowed him. He had no silver. No spells. Nothing to fight the undead.

"Mirrortor, you little wretch," Chane hissed. "Simply cutting your throat will be too kind. . . ."

A cold jerk on Chane's collar made him lose his footing. The wraith was right behind him, fighting for a hold on his tunic. He knew if the creature got a solid grip on his flesh, its very touch could kill him. He swung out desperately with the books. Perhaps the thing was corporeal enough to be swatted away.

To his joy, the thing released him. To his sorrow, his fingers lost their grip on the bag, and it flew out of his hands. He steeled himself for another attack . . . which did not come. The other wraith now moved into view as well. Yet they both ignored him and positioned themselves over the bag, floating in the narrow stone corridor above his treasure, hissing and keening in agitation.

"Guardians?" he asked sardonically, knowing they couldn't answer. "If you think I'm going to let a pair of phantoms take those books away, you are sorely mistaken."

But the pain in Chane's shoulder had spread to his elbow. The fingers of his left hand wouldn't close. He was injured, and he needed something to fight with. No amount of wit and charm would affect his phantasmal opponents. One of them looked up at him and spit out meaningless sounds, its face twisting and contorting. The thing appeared almost disappointed that he had dropped the books.

"Oghma, help me," Chane whispered, grasping the cord of his holy symbol. He drew it into view, confident his god would assist him. But the second wraith only spat strange sounds like the first.

A wave of despair washed over the priest. Was this some sort of test? Was Oghma toying with him to see how well he might fare on his own? If so, he had to find another weapon.

With his good hand, he searched his pockets. There had to be something. His dagger was steel—useless. Then he found his coin purse. Coins? Ripping off his belt, he dumped the contents onto a step and smiled. Silver coins. Six of them.

He took a step toward the writhing, angry creatures. "Time for me to leave now. We must do this again sometime."

Gathering all six coins, he pitched them as hard as he could, catching one wraith with four, the other with two. Chane heard faint, liquid sounds of metal splashing through ectoplasm. At any other moment, he would have stopped to congratulate himself on not having wasted any of his tiny weapons. But this was not the time. Both creatures screamed in pain and confusion when the hated silver passed through them. Chane lunged forward, clutched the bag tightly, and retreated back up the stairs.

He expected to come out somewhere near the corridor that led to the curving stairway up. Instead, he found himself in a another small, square room filled with dusty stacked books. Four exits marked the walls. Am I back where I started? he thought. At the same instant, a hateful keening filled his ears.

A labyrinth!

That wretched gnome. Back—the way out has to be back the way I came. No, that was impossible; the wraiths were coming from behind. All loremasters were taught survival skills in regard to mazes and labyrinths. Chane let his mind seek out those half-forgotten lessons. Left. Always turn left. Never panic or you will be lost.

He leapt into action, running always upward and to the left. He concentrated on what Mirrortor's throat would feel like as his windpipe cracked. The keening grew closer.

Then it stopped. So did Chane.

Where are they? he groaned inwardly. Have they given up? No, that would be too easy. More likely they're trying to trick me into slowing down.

Chane broke into a jog. Each time he fell out of a flight of stairs into a room or a corridor, he turned left and scrambled up the next staircase. The maze had to empty out somewhere aboveground, sooner or later. Hope soothed his trembling heart when he realized how sensible he was. Nothing could stop him now. Then the rage-filled keening began again.

Only this time it came from ahead of him.

How could they have gotten in front of me? Fear and uncertainty crawled back into his spine. This could not be the end of so perfect a priest, to die like a rat in some mad gnome's maze! Standing dead center in a narrow corridor, Chane looked at the upward-bound stairwell about ten paces ahead. There were no doorways in the hall behind him except for the one to the stairway at the end. He was loathe to turn back; moving up and left seemed to be the only viable plan.

Wailing, the first wraith boiled out of the entryway and came straight toward him. In the dim torchlight glowing off the wall, he could make out its hideous expression of both insane hunger and fierce protection. He knew it could smell his warm blood and longed to drain him of life.

With no other choice, he threw the bag forward. It landed a few paces from the bottom step.

"Here, take it," he said in angry, bitter defeat. "Take your master's precious books, but you won't have me."

The creature stopped over the books and glared at the loremaster as though, for an instant, the sacrifice did not matter. But the undead did not leave its post; it continued hissing and spitting over Chane's discarded treasure.

The pain in his left arm had now spread into his shoulder. Going back down lower into the labyrinth would probably mean death. He panted to catch his breath.

"Get out of the way," he said.

Pulling his silver holy symbol over his head, Chane felt a stab of regret. Oghma would understand. The situation had grown desperate. Drawing his hand back as if to throw, he repeated, "Get out of my way."

The wraith raged and keened. But as Chane hurled the symbol, the thing dodged to avoid the blessed metal, leaving just enough room for Chane to slip past into the stone stairwell. He hoped the other one had called off the chase and disappeared. But the guardians were no longer his main concern. His left arm was paralyzed, and thirst made breathing painful. His lips were beginning to dry out from the lengthy chase.

What a fool. What an absolute fool he had been, thinking he could waltz into a temple of Oghma, murder its overseer, take its treasures, and then just stroll back out again. He'd brought no real weapons. No water. No food. King of loremasters indeed. If he didn't find an exit soon, he would be king of skeletons.

The stairs and corridors stretched on endlessly. Chane shivered and sweated at the same time. After a while it seemed he traveled in circles and the rooms began to look the same. Or perhaps they didn't. Perhaps he only imagined they did. How far had he traveled? It seemed like miles, but he couldn't be sure it wasn't merely a floor or two. Icy discomfort in his shoulder was turning into agony. His teeth chattered. His legs ached. Finally he staggered against a stone wall. Whimpering, he slipped to the floor, chin resting on his knees.

"I've lost," he whispered through parched lips. "It's over."

"Getting tired, son?" a cheery voiced asked.

Chane's head jerked up to see Mirrortor in the room with him, still in his ridiculous purple dressing gown. The elven girl at his side was rapidly writing on her parchment.

"Am I close to the surface then?" Chane rasped.

"Close?" the gnome answered. "Well, that would depend on your perspective."

Wretch, Chane thought, but instead he said, "If you've come to hear me beg for help, you may as well leave. I'd sooner die than ask you about tomorrow's weather."

"Hear you beg?" Mirrortor said. "Oh, by Oghma's pen, no. We came to guide you out. There must be something sensible in that over-inflated head of yours or you wouldn't be breathing. You are intelligent enough to value your life over the power you lust after. That must count for something."

Chane stared at him. "You're guiding me out?"

"Yes, of course. But I warn you, those creatures are here to guard over more than just books."

"I'm too tired to hurt anyone. Get me out of here."

"You've come all this way. I think you ought to have something for your trouble." Mirrortor held out a clothbound, dark green book.

Chane looked at it suspiciously. "What is it?"

"Something I put to pen myself a few years ago. It is the recent history of Rysheos before the coming of Lord Teelo, an account of the wars of the noble families. Distasteful era. Something they will wish to avoid again. Take this book, Loremaster Chane. Go to Rysheos and teach this."

Chane's mouth tightened in disgust. "That is nothing! Maybe a few rare details, but there is not a tale in that book any common street peasant wouldn't already know. What wonders can be found in such easily attained lore?"

The gnome smiled slightly. "The kind that matter. The

lore we live and breathe and remember. Stories that can teach us to avoid folly."

Mirrortor turned and motioned the girl forward. Chane gazed into her serious face as she knelt down and revealed to him the title of her work: *The Tale of Chane Troiban, the Twilight Hall Priest Who Got Lost in the Labyrinth of Bransuldyn Mirrortor.*

Chane looked up, the truth of it finally dawning. Lore was not only the ancient and unknown. It was created with each passing moment. He was now part of the web of legend, part of the web of lore, ever changing, always spinning.

Reaching out slowly, he took the green book from Mirrortor. "Yes, I will go to Rysheos. I will teach this lore."

The gnome smiled wryly. "Come then. Your arm will heal in a tenday or two. Now it is time to leave. I should have been asleep hours ago."

Chane stood and followed his companions, paying little attention to which hallway they chose. Soon he would be out in the fresh air, free from this labyrinth. His mind churned with Mirrortor's words. Perhaps he *could* do more for his students by teaching them recent history, teaching them ways to avoid bloodshed and chaos.

Picturing himself in an ivory robe, standing before a crowd of eager listeners, he anticipated the reverence that might be given to such an unselfish scholar—a humble loremaster, dedicated to his calling. He envisioned the awestruck faces of his followers as he taught the lore of recent tales. Naturally his handsome countenance would impress them, but his wisdom would impress them even more.

He was almost to the main entryway when a sudden realization came unbidden to his mind. Lord Teelo might be very grateful to a loremaster who knew more details of Rysheos's history than any other priest on the continent. Such a priest would be rewarded and valued.

Perhaps. . . .

RAVEN'S EGG

Elaine Bergstrom

Soon I, Lord Sharven of Espar, shall attempt a most daring end to all my woes. I will not speak too plainly of my plans here; the purpose of this account is to justify my act, not to forewarn others what it might be. I wish I could be more blunt but, though I am a young man, my inheritance is vast. Because of my wealth, I have many enemies and many paid spies throughout my house. I see how they whisper in private, plotting against me as they go about their work. If I had proof of their treachery, I would kill them all. As it is, I must abide them.

Even Atera, my beloved wife, has turned against me. I cannot bear to cause her pain, so I lied and told her that there have been threats against us and placed her under guard in her chambers. She has requested no visitors save me and her aged physician, the wizard Raven of Saerloon.

Saerloon! Ah, the sound of that name—exotic, dangerous, calling to me even now. Saerloon—the place where I made my fortune. Saerloon—the place where I found my most precious possession: my wife.

My older brother had been sent to that distant city in Sembia by my father and the nobles of our humble town to forge a trade alliance with the merchants there. I'd always had a wanderlust that set me apart from my stoic friends in Espar and so asked to go along. I had expected father to refuse; he agreed readily. I rejoiced, but during the long journey east, I began to understand his indulgence toward me all too well. Gwendh, my brother, was to inherit the family estate. I could manage one of our smaller holdings, but would always be dependent on his charity unless I made a fortune of my own. If I did not, I was expendable.

As we rode into the city, I saw its wealth and its poverty. Pickpockets stole almost openly from rich merchants in the crowded streets, ignoring the example of less skillful thieves, whose rotting bodies hung from the city walls to feed the crows. Nobles sported knives and swords with jeweled hilts, and even the grimiest street urchin carried a simple blade. Indeed, our first stop was to purchase daggers and swords. It galled me that Gwendh had to make the purchase for me.

I said as much as we sat in the back of a dark, smoky tavern, washing down spicy sausages with the golden local ale. "No matter. I'll make my fortune soon enough in a city such as this," I commented.

"Soon enough," Gwendh echoed and chuckled, a sound I knew too well.

"What is it?" I asked. "What have you been plotting?"

"Not me, Brother. Father has. He wants you to take a wife here in Saerloon."

"A wife!" I stared at the tavern wenches, as drunk and foul mouthed as the patrons. "Where will I find a wife in a place such as this?"

"Father's already found her," Gwendh said, then covered his ears in anticipation of my angry explosion.

Shock stole all thoughts, all words I might have said.

"Father says that her dowry is huge," Gwendh added.

"The greater the dowry, the uglier the bride," I reminded him, and we laughed together.

"You'll get to judge her soon enough," Gwendh said. "You're meeting her tonight."

"And if I despise her?"

"Her father hasn't announced the match, more for her sake than yours. She may despise you just as easily as you might her, you know."

I doubted that, but nonetheless I was thankful when Gwendh bought us each a bath. We changed into our best clothes and went to meet my arranged bride.

The house was three times the size of our family's home in Espar, and its grounds smelled as exotic as they looked. The iron fence around the house and gardens was delicately wrought with sharp points at the top, as much for beauty as to keep out intruders. The ironwork pattern repeated in the railings of the balconies and in the tall, thin spires of the house. A castle fit for faeries, I thought.

Its interior did nothing to dispel that whimsical idea. The high, arched doorway opened into a sun-drenched court-yard where pots of tall, lacy ferns shaded cages of songbirds and a bubbling fountain. A servant dressed in white and with a tall turban on his head separated Gwendh and me. Gwendh would go to speak to the father. I would remain in the courtyard.

"My mistress will be here soon," the servant said as he left me. I sat beside the fountain and watched the slow ripples move across the water's surface, hoping their languid motion would still the beating of my heart.

She came alone, walking toward me from the dark house, her flowing skirts beating against her legs. I rejoiced at her lithe form, her delicate hands. From her shy stance, with her eyes fixed on a spot somewhere near the center of my chest, I saw that she was more flustered than I by this arrangement. It occurred to me that I had also overlooked one important detail. "What is your name?" I asked.

"Atera," she replied. "You might have asked your brother." She glanced up at me for a moment. Her slanted eyes were an incredible shade of emerald green that harmonized beautifully with her honey-colored hair.

"I'm sorry." I took her hands. Her nails were painted a soft pink, the color of seashells. "Are all noble women in Saerloon so demure?"

She smiled and looked up again. "Just me," she said.
"What are the courting customs here?"
She shrugged. "They're not important."
"Sit beside me," I said.

She did as I asked. During the rest of our hour together, she relaxed a bit. I thought her far more beautiful than any of the round-cheeked girls in Espar, and I wondered how her father could give her up to a man he did not know.

But in the tendays before our wedding, I came to understand his decision. Atera had a sensitive temperament better suited to the tranquility of Espar than the constant danger of Saerloon. On our rare rides through the city, she became anxious in the crowded streets that appealed so much to me. She also gave all her coins to the crafty urchins who, dodging my discreet kicks, managed to attract her attention. Before we wed, I promised her that we would settle in my father's country. I did not say precisely when.

For though I loved her, I loved her city more.

Saerloon was a cesspit of avarice and greed, but there were fortunes to be made there. Soon I had established contacts among the thieves and assassins of the city. My family's caravans moved untouched, and my own enterprises prospered from the information and protection I bought. I increased my wife's dowry fivefold within a year.

The earnings had their price. I acquired a dueling scar on one cheek that gave my face a sinister look. My sword arm was slashed and broken in a brawl. It healed badly and I lost much of its strength. Finally, I was set upon by thugs who left me for dead. The men who found me unconscious behind a stable knew me well, but after the beating they could recognize me only by the half-moon ring on my finger. Before they returned me to my wife, they had the wisdom to demand a reward.

Because of this, days passed before I was brought home. By then the wounds on my face had begun to fester, and a fever had taken hold of me. I could see little but the tears on Atera's face as she held my hand. I also saw a gray-haired, dark-eyed man who laid compresses on the worst of my wounds and muttered some words in a strange tongue. The pain increased, bringing the relief of unconsciousness.

When I woke some days later, Atera sat at my side. As soon as she saw me looking up at her, she embraced me. "Raven tended you," she said when I asked about the man.

"Raven? The wizard?" I replied incredulously.

"He calls himself a necromancer, but is skilled in healing arts above all others. He's been my friend for as long as I can remember. Now he's proven himself my friend again." She held a mirror in front of my face. My wounds were nearly healed. I doubted they would scar.

I sent for Raven and thanked him sincerely.

"How could I not help you," he replied. "I am oathbound to do the bidding of Atera and her family. Even without an oath, I could do nothing to cause that child harm." He smeared a sweet-smelling ointment on my wounds and promised to return later to see how I was.

After that, we talked often. I found him to be powerful and willing to teach his skill. I'd always had a fascination for magic and the might it imparted, so I went to my father-in-law and asked to have Raven put in my employ.

"I intend to send him to Espar with you when you go," he responded. "He's been Atera's physician and friend for so long that I wouldn't want her to leave my house without him."

I smiled. Though I still held out the promise of Espar to him as to Atera, I had no intention of keeping it. Power, wealth, and now, vengeance, were foremost on my mind.

My spies soon learned the names of the men who had attacked me. My assassins were quick and deadly. As for the jealous merchants who had paid to have me assaulted, Raven devised a fitting poison, one that caused oozing sores that healed slowly, leaving deep and painful blood-red pock-marks. They died by their own hands soon after.

Ah, the intrigues of Saerloon! Such a magnificent city, so magnificently suited to my tastes.

But some months later, fate determined that I would have to go home. My father died. My brother soon followed.

With Raven and hired guards to protect my fortune, I reluctantly brought my bride to Espar.

I found the land much changed. True, the fields were as green as always, the forests as dark and thick. But beneath the plodding rhythm of Espar's sleepy life, I sensed evil, hiding just out of sight, an evil as deadly as any in Saerloon.

The local nobles were curious about my life in Sembia and anxious to meet Atera. In the first days after we came home, we were invited to a homecoming feast held by my neighbor, Lord Romul. Romul had been an old friend of my father's. I had grown up with his children and spent many happy hours roaming his lands. Nonetheless, I felt an instinctive wariness.

There were plotters everywhere, I reminded myself. With a beautiful wife and vast wealth, I was a prime target.

As I entered Romul's house, I heard the whispers of the other guests. I thought at first that they were commenting on the beauty of my bride. Later, I realized that they whispered about me. I had been scarred and my arm maimed, but I sensed that their muttering meant more than that. I stood aside from the others, saying little while I watched protectively over Atera; she moved among them like a kitten, full of trust and happiness.

In the month that followed, I kept up my guard at the local festivals and remained tight-lipped about my business. As I expected, once everyone realized they would learn nothing of value from me, Atera and I were silently ostracized. Only Lord Romul and his wife, Laudrel, invited us back to their estate.

At our second meeting, I bluntly asked Romul why he felt such concern for me.

"Concern!" Romul laughed. "I recall your childhood well, Sharven. You were always one of my favorites. I am pleased to count you as a friend."

"Good," I responded. "Atera has been so lonely here."

"May I speak bluntly?" Romul asked.

I nodded.

"You changed much in Saerloon. I am not speaking of

your wounds, either, for a man's face means nothing. Your bride is lovely and everyone speaks well of her. But if you wish to gain acceptance, you must be less suspicious of your neighbors. You've been gone some time. People are wondering what you are hiding to make you so nervous."

"I hide nothing!" I retorted.

"You gave me leave to speak," he reminded me gently. "This is a peaceful land, Sharven. These are simple people. Remember that."

He wanted me to think so. Indeed, for a time I tried to take his advice. I understood his motives soon enough.

We exchanged breeding cattle to strengthen our herds. His appeared healthy, but as soon as they mixed with mine, my herd fell ill with a strange disease. Mine died. His were less ill, and recovered. I sent an angry note to Lord Romul.

He came immediately and rode my fields with me. I kept up with difficulty, using my good arm to guide my horse. Eventually he pointed out clumps of speargrass on the edges of the fence lines.

"Have your fieldhands move your herds more often so they stay clear of that weed," he said. "It slowly poisons an animal if too much is eaten."

"Your cattle didn't die," I reminded him.

"Speargrass is a mild poison. My ranges are clear of it, so the poison wouldn't have built up in them. Still, I can't be certain the grass was the cause, so I'm willing to bear some of the loss. Come pick another dozen cows from my herd."

And have the fever kill the rest! I railed inwardly. To him I stiffly replied, "I'd rather settle in coin."

"You'd be wiser to rebuild your stock," he began, then, seeing the resolution in my expression, became resigned. "Perhaps you weren't meant for the country life," he said wearily and agreed to all my terms.

While Romul and I had been riding, Atera had visited with Lady Laudrel. When we joined them, I saw that Atera's face was flushed, her eyes bright. "I don't think I've ever laughed this hard," she said to me as we went in to dine.

Throughout the meal, Romul entertained Atera with tales

of the hills and forests around Espar. I'd never seen her listen so intently to my stories, or laugh as pleasantly at my jests. It seemed that Romul did his best to charm her.

I mentioned this to Raven the following night. "Old men long for youth," he said. "However, I have never heard Atera speak of Lord Romul as anything more than friend—or of you as anything less than well-loved husband."

"What Romul feels may be equally important."

Raven did not reply. He was right to be silent. This was a matter between me and my wife.

I confronted her in the morning. She appeared genuinely distressed by my suspicions. "Lord Romul and his wife are the only people we ever see," she retorted. "They've been kind to me. I think highly of him, but nothing more."

"Are you certain that's the only way you think of him?"

Atera did something quite unexpected. She slapped me and stormed from the room. I heard her call for a servant. Some time later, I saw her ride off alone, galloping north through the fields on the bay mare she had brought from Saerloon. North—the direction to Lord Romul's lands.

The money from Lord Romul arrived just after highsun, along with a note inviting Atera and me for yet another visit. Seething at the gall of a man who would seduce my wife under my very nose, I returned to my library and laid the note on the table.

Atera did not return until evening. She did not explain or apologize for her absence. That night, when I went to her chamber door, I found it locked.

"If that's the way you wish it, stay in there!" I bellowed through the door. I ordered the servants to bar it so she could not leave. After overseeing the work, I went to my library. There I fell asleep trying to make sense out of some old and incomplete instructions for turning copper into gold.

A strange rustling woke me, as if the pages of the books on the shelves around me had somehow come alive. Even the closed book on which my head rested vibrated at my touch. Fearful of what I might find, I opened it.

Bookworms! A dozen of them feasted on the pages of the text, their tiny bodies the same parchment shade as their meal. I shook them to the floor. Their color hastily changed to that of the flagstones, and they scattered as I stomped on them. When I'd killed as many as I could find, I moved to the shelves where hundreds were devouring my other texts. I shook them free of each text, stomping them as soon as they hit the floor. Soon the flags were slimy with crushed bodies. Yet the hungry horde continued its destruction.

Words gone. Knowledge gone. The power of that knowledge gone! Mere wealth could not repair my loss.

"Raven!" I screamed. "Raven come here!"

As I turned back to the shelf nearest the wall, I glanced out the window and saw smoke rising from the stables, servants rushing to beat out the blaze. They were too late. When the doors opened, the fire flared. I heard the whinnies of the horses, the pounding of their hooves against their paddock doors, the cries of the stablehands. If I hadn't problems enough in the library, I would have gone to help.

As Raven and I labored to save the books, I saw Lord Romul's note lying on the floor. When I picked it up, it crumbled in my hand.

"Could he have sent bookworm eggs?" I asked Raven.

The wizard nodded. Hours later, after we had salvaged what we could, I went outside to see the ruins of my stables. Only three mounts had managed to escape the fire. Atera's bay mare was one of them.

"Quite a coincidence, don't you think?" I asked Raven as we examined the burns on the horse's left flank. I spoke coldly, finally convinced that all my suspicions were true.

"The mare was lucky," Raven responded. "I'm glad for Atera's sake."

"But suppose it wasn't luck. Suppose Atera is a part of the plot and would not let her mount be harmed," I insisted.

He paused before speaking, weighing his words carefully, "Atera loves you. Yet, there are ways in which she could be made unfaithful against her will," he said.

"Ensorceled! Yes, that must be it. She certainly hasn't

been herself since we returned to Espar." I felt suddenly glad I had guards at her door. "Raven, what can I do to end these plots?" I thought of the pockmarked merchants and felt a thrill of excitement I hadn't experienced since Saerloon.

His words disappointed me. "I am not certain. Let me consider it," he said. "In the meantime, write Lord Romul and tell him you accept his invitation."

"Of course! I must go see firsthand if he is gloating over my loss."

I penned a cordial reply, then took it to Atera. As she read my words, I told her that jealousy had turned me into an idiot. "I could never really doubt you," I said. "Forgive me."

Tears came to her beautiful eyes. She embraced me. Our reconciliation was long and satisfying.

* * * * *

The visit to Lord Romul accomplished everything I'd hoped for. He and his wife had arranged a magnificent meal, even hired some local musicians to play through the dinner. I tried to appear relaxed as I waited for some clue as to why the nobleman had become my enemy.

I discovered the cause after the meal, when he took me aside to speak to me privately. "Before your brother died, we had discussed the sale of your north fields that border my own grazing area. Since your livestock is so decimated and you have no interest in rebuilding the herd, I thought you might want to sell it to me," he explained.

Decimated livestock! Yes, he'd seen to that! "My father always said land is more precious than gold," I noted evenly.

He looked at me oddly. "So it is. But land is a tool like any other. It has to be used to be of any real value."

"I'll keep it," I responded, my tone convincing him I would not reconsider. "Now, if you don't mind, I think Atera and I should leave."

"I meant no offense, Sharven. I'm sorry if you misunderstood me."

"No offense was taken. It's just such a long ride back," I responded as pleasantly as I was able.

I hid my anger from Atera as well as I had from Lord Romul, venting it only when I was safely in Raven's chambers. "It's my land Romul wants," I told him.

Raven's long black robe brushed the floor as he paced. I'd never seen him so animated. "That's hardly a surprise. Now, we must determine what to do about his schemes."

We read well into the night. Eventually I suggested a plan so audacious that no one in Espar would ever suspect my hand in it. I went to Atera and instructed her to send word to all our neighbors that we were holding a feast and wanted everyone to attend.

"Sharven, thank you!" she exclaimed and kissed me.

Atera penned invitations all evening and sent the servants out with them in the morning. Most of the estates sent immediate acceptances.

While Atera worked with the seamstresses, the cooks, and the house servants, Raven and I read through our remaining books, preparing everything I needed for my revenge. Now we are prepared, and the party is at hand.

I have written what I can. Later, after I have dealt with my foes and my woes are over, I will finish this account.

* * * * *

It is difficult now to write, though the memories of my carefully orchestrated vengeance still burn clearly in my mind. And though it will take some time for me to capture all the events on paper, I will do so. . . .

The pigs and fowl for our feast were turning slowly on their spits when I knocked on Raven's door. Inside his room, with its scrolls and ancient tomes, its vials of herbs and exotic incense, I claimed the magic he had prepared.

I pocketed the love potion for Atera, then held out my hand for the other, darker magic we had discussed. He gave me a tiny blood-red egg, so light it seemed hollow. I looked doubtfully at it. "Are you certain?"

"Swallow it whole, as I instructed," he said. "The shell will dissolve inside of you, and the creature will merge with your body."

Now that I was actually going to eat the thing, I found myself more concerned about its nature. "What precisely is it?" I asked.

"A dark spirit summoned here from the nether-realms to do exactly what you requested: destroy your worst enemy."

"A dark spirit." What little I knew about supernatural creatures made me less certain I should go through with this.

"Your victim will feel his life slowly drained by a force he cannot see."

Exactly the sort of end for Romul that I'd demanded! I swallowed the egg with great care, then sat and waited.

For some minutes I felt nothing. However just as I was about to voice my disappointment, something lurched deep within me, and the terrible power of the creature I had consumed exploded in my body. I bellowed in an inhuman voice, then lifted a massive oak chair with my weak arm and flung it against the wall. The wood splintered. The pieces scattered. My sight became keener, my hearing painfully acute. A rage such as I had never felt before took hold of me. I, and the monster within me, were ready for the kill.

The potency of the dark spirit made me uneasy. "If anyone in Espar detects sorcery, I will be an outcast in my own land," I reminded Raven, astonished at the force and strange hollowness of my voice.

"When the creature is released, it will be visible to you only. Even Lord Romul will not see it, though he will certainly feel its effects. He is an old man. If he dies during the duel, no one will think it odd. And you will have the satisfaction of knowing that you have indeed killed your greatest enemy."

With difficulty, I softened my tone to a hoarse whisper. "And if my greatest enemy is someone else?" I asked.

"Do you suspect anyone else?" he asked with some concern.

I shook my head.

"Then look at me."

I did as he asked. In a moment he began the final chant, ending with, "I charge the spirit that dwells within this man—when this human shell is cut and your host's blood is spilled, you will be released. Seek out Lord Sharven's worst enemy. Enter that body and drain its life, but do not destroy the spirit. Instead let the ghost of Lord Sharven's foe walk these halls forever, an impotent observer of all that happens here. When your task is finished, depart this place and return to your own nightmarish abode."

I listened to the words with great satisfaction, for they gave voice to the essence of my revenge. For the rest of our days, Lord Romul's ghost would watch Atera and me together. I could think of no more fitting end for his treachery.

Once Raven had finished his spell, I practiced walking with my new strength. When I thought it safe, I took the potion to Atera.

I had never seen her look so magnificent. Her long thick hair was braided with multicolor scarves. The black bodice of her gown gave way to skirts of the same rainbow hues as in her hair. Her eyes sparkled with anticipation of the gathering.

The creature inside me raged, trying to escape my body —prompted not by anger, but by lust. Such was the beauty of my wife at that moment.

"Would you share some wine with me?" I asked her, my voice trembling as I fought to keep it soft.

"Sharven, you sound so strange. Are you all right? If you're ill we can—"

"No, not ill, just excited. After all, this is my first feast as head of the estate." I kept my back to her as I slipped the potion into her goblet, then poured our wine. I watched her carefully to be certain she drank it all.

By then, the first of our guests had arrived. I went down to join them, Atera walking joyfully at my side.

As we greeted our guests, the potion began to do its work. Atera's face flushed, and her voice grew high and sharp. "She's a bit anxious, but I think the wine did more than relax her," I confided to one of the guests. I heard him repeat the comment to his wife. Soon the entire room assumed Atera was already tipsy.

Lord Romul and Lady Laudrel were among the last to enter the hall. As Atera went to greet them, I hung back. I could not get too close, not with the beast inside me looking through my eyes at my enemy, demanding to be released.

Some time later, Atera and I took our places at the table's center. Lord Romul sat to Atera's right, then Lady Laudrel. After all her planning of the evening's feast, Atera only picked at the food. Her attention became, as the potion directed, fixed on Lord Romul. Soon she seemed openly infatuated. I pretended not to notice, not even when her hand disappeared from the table, resting no doubt in his lap. A few of the guests near us began to whisper to one another.

The farce could not continue much longer. I gave the signal and the music began. I asked Lady Laudrel to dance.

Lord Romul would give too great an insult if he refused to ask Atera. Red-faced and cautious, he led her onto the floor. As I danced with the stout Laudrel, I watched Atera and Romul carefully. She pressed close to him, whispered in his ear. I saw his confusion. No, he had never expected his conquest to act so boldly.

With a firm grip on Atera's arm, Romul led her back to the table. She pulled him beyond it to the tapestry that hung from the wall. In spite of the shadows, I and a number of others saw her kiss him. I pushed Laudrel aside so roughly that she would have fallen had someone not caught her.

"What is the meaning of this!" I bellowed.

Laudrel followed my gaze. She saw her husband's embarrassment, heard Atera's startled cry. "Your wife is . . . not well," Romul said.

"Well enough to kiss you. Is this the first time or only the most obvious of many?"

My guests began muttering. Most sided with me. Others, seeing Romul's confusion, were not so certain of his guilt. Laudrel began to cry.

"She is gone from the house far too often, and when she rides, she always heads north," I went on.

"To visit me," Laudrel mumbled. Atera, fighting the effects of the potion, nodded. No one paid any attention to either woman. Fine people that they were, my guests were eager for blood to spill.

"I demand satisfaction," I said. "I will defend the honor of my wife!"

I saw his resignation, yet still he attempted to placate me. "Your wife is ill, I tell you. And your sword arm is weak. Isn't there some other way to settle this?"

"Honor will make me strong." I heard the murmur of my neighbors. Most were pleased at my response.

Romul sighed. "Very well. But you must loan me a blade. I brought none."

I surveyed the crowd. There must be no hint of treachery in our duel. "Does someone have a blade for Lord Romul?"

Five were offered. As I expected in one his age, he picked a light, thin sword more geared for fencing than battle. One of the other men offered me a similar weapon; I took it. There would be no accusations of poison when this was done.

We squared off in the center of the hall, where only moments ago we had been dancing. As metal met metal, I felt the strength of Raven's minion. I could win the battle at any time. Instead, I fought down the urge to attack and moved stiffly, as if the very act of holding the sword pained me.

In his youth, Lord Romul had acquired a deadly reputation with a blade. He had not lost the skill. Were it not for my terrible inner speed and strength, he would have bested me easily. However, he continued to maintain the ruse of reluctant victim, parrying my more deadly thrusts, letting the others reach him. No doubt he hoped I would shed the first blood and, honor satisfied, call off the duel.

When I nicked his shoulder, I saw real fear in his eyes. His face was florid and sweat formed on his brow. Exertion could kill the old as easily as a knife. I counted on that excuse. I smiled. Yes, you fool. Yes, you perverter of my wife, coveter of my lands. Yes, old man, as soon as my skin is cut, you will die.

I forced him back to the dining table, then in a move no one could have expected, I deliberately fell against him. My arm sliced open on the edge of his blade.

The shell was cracked. The creature inside me departed with the first drop of my blood, taking all its strength with it. "Have you had enough?" I heard Lord Romul whisper as I lay at his feet, too exhausted to move, barely able to breathe.

I looked up. I wanted to whisper that it would never be over, but words failed me as I saw the thing I had unleashed.

Black and formless as the clouds of a deadly storm, its only clear features were its huge red eyes, which smoldered with a predatory light. The creature examined Lord Romul, standing with his sword lowered, looking less like an enemy than a concerned father who had unwittingly wounded his son during training.

It looked at Atera, trembling as she stood at the head of the table, frightened of me, of Romul, of the strange impulses within her brought on by the potion.

It looked at Raven. I think perhaps Raven lied to me. I think he saw the spirit; its summoning was his doing, after all.

And finally it turned to me. Its expression became one of interest, of need. Raven had said it killed with its touch and the power of its gaze. I tried to look away and found I could not. I tried to move but was paralyzed. "I'm not responsible!" I screamed. Though I knew I damned myself, I had to say the words, "You were charged to protect me. Now, kill my enemy."

It obeyed.

The blackness of its form rolled over me. A deadly weight pushed down on me. My heart fluttered, my body became cold.

"Sharven!" Atera shrieked. She tried to rush to my side, but Raven held her back. Her tears were genuine, and the grief tore at my soul. I would have apologized for all my wrongs had I not already been robbed of the power to speak.

And through the unblinking eyes of one already dead, I saw Raven move behind Atera and gently pull her away from my body, holding her as she sobbed uncontrollably. I saw his expression as he looked over her shoulder at me—one of triumph. He had won. And suddenly he appeared much younger than I'd believed him to be.

But then, there are spells for youth as well as strength.

I thought of his remarks to me, and understood their meaning for the first time. Yet, the creature he had conjured for me had done exactly what I had demanded—it had found my worst enemy and it had killed. Now my spirit remains.

*   *   *   *   *

Raven required no spells to make Atera love him, though he did give her one to soften her grief over my demise. I do not hate him for that; there are many more valid reasons for hate.

I stood in the hall with the other guests and watched him wed my wife. I went into the bridal chamber, and after, with fury to give me strength, I went into the little room where I had studied with Raven. Though it took tremendous effort, I have managed to put pen to parchment and finish this account.

Perhaps Atera will one day read it. More likely Raven will find it first and destroy it. If so, I will set the words down again, as often as I must.

Even petty revenge is sweet. Raven will never rest easy in my house.

THE THIRD LEVEL

R. A. Salvatore

The young man's dark eyes shifted from side to side, always moving, always alert. He caught a movement to the left, between two ramshackle wood-and-clay huts.

Just a child at play, wisely taking to the shadows.

Back to the right, he noticed a woman deep in the recesses beyond a window that was just a hole in the wall, for no one in this section of Calimport was wealthy enough to afford glass. The woman stayed back, standing perfectly still, watching him and unaware that he, in turn, watched her.

He felt like a hunting cat crossing the plain, she just another of the many deer, hoping he would take no notice.

Young Artemis Entreri liked that feeling, that power. He had worked this street—if that's what it could be called, for it was little more than a haphazard cluster of unremarkable shacks dropped across a field of cart-torn mud—for more than five years, since he was but a boy of nine.

He stopped and slowly turned toward the window, and the woman shrank away at the merest hint of a threat.

Entreri smiled and resumed his surveying. This was his street, he told himself, a place he had staked out three months after his arrival in Calimport. The place had no formal name, but now, because of him, it had an identity. It was the area where Artemis Entreri was boss.

How far he had come in five years, hitching a ride all the way from the city of Memnon. Artemis chuckled at the term "all the way." In truth, Memnon was the closest city to Calimport, but in the barren desert land of Calimshan, even the closest city was a long and difficult ride.

Difficult to be sure, but Entreri had made it, had survived, despite the brutal duties the merchants of that caravan had given him, despite the determined advances of one lecherous old man, a smelly unshaven lout who seemed to think that a nine-year-old boy—

Artemis shook that memory from his head, refusing to follow its inevitable course. He had survived the caravan trek and had stolen away from the merchants on the second day in Calimport, soon after he had learned that they had taken him along ultimately to sell him into slavery.

There was no need to remember anything before that, the teenager told himself, neither the journey from Memnon, nor the horrors before the journey that had sent him running from home. Still, he could smell the breath of that lecherous old man, like the breath of his own father, and his uncle.

The pain pushed him back to his angry edge, made him steel his dark eyes and tighten the honed muscles along his arms. He had made it. That was all that counted. This was his street, a place of safety, where no one threatened him.

Artemis resumed his surveillance of his domain, his eyes scanning left to right, then back across the way. He saw every movement and every shadow—always the hunting cat, looking more for prey than for danger.

He couldn't help but chuckle self-deprecatingly at the grandeur of his "kingdom." His street? Only because no other thief would bother to claim it. Artemis could work six days rolling every one of the many drunks who fell down in the mud in this impoverished section and barely scrape enough coins together to eat a decent meal on the seventh.

Still, that was enough for the waif who had fled his home; it had sustained him and given him back his pride over the past five years. Now he was a young man, fourteen years old—or almost fourteen. Artemis didn't remember his exact birthdate, just that there had been a brief period right before the even briefer season of rain, when times in his house were not so terrible.

Again, the young man shook the unwanted memories from his head. He was fourteen, he decided; as if in confirmation, he looked down at his finely toned, lithe frame, barely a hundred and thirty pounds, but with tightened muscles covering every inch. He was fourteen, and he was rightly proud, because he had survived and he had thrived. He surveyed his street, his domain, and his smallish chest expanded. Even the old drunks were afraid of him, showed him proper respect when they addressed him.

He had earned it, and everybody in this little shanty town within the city of Calimport—a city that was nothing more than a collection of a thousand or more little shanty towns huddled about the white marble and gold-laced structures of the wealthy merchants—respected him, feared him.

Everybody except one.

The new tough, a young man probably three or four years older than Artemis, had arrived earlier in the tenday. He did not ask permission of Artemis before he began rolling the wretches in the mud, or even walking into homes in broad daylight and terrorizing whoever was inside. The stranger forced Artemis's subjects into making him a meal, or into offering him whatever other niceties could be found.

That was the part that angered Artemis more than anything. Artemis held no love, no respect, for the common folk of his carved-out kingdom, but he had seen the newcomer's type before—in both his horrid past and in his troubled nightmares. In truth, there was room on Artemis's street for two thugs. In the five days that the new tough had been about, he and Artemis hadn't even seen each other. And certainly none of Artemis's wretched informants had asked for protection against this new terror. None of them would dare even to speak with Artemis unless he asked them a direct question.

But there remained the not-inconsiderable matter of pride.

Artemis peered around the shack's corner, down the muddy lane. "Right on schedule," he whispered as the new-comer strolled onto the other end of this relatively straight section of road. "Predictable." Artemis curled his lip up, thinking that predictability was indeed a weakness. He would have to remember that.

The new thug's eyes were dark, his hair, like Entreri's, black as the waters of the Kandad Oasis, so black that every other color seemed to be mixed together in its depths. A native-born Calimshite, Artemis decided, probably a man not unlike himself.

What tortured past had put the invader on his street? he mused. There is no room for that kind of empathy, Artemis scolded himself. Compassion gets you killed.

With a deep, steadying breath, Artemis steeled his gaze once more and watched coldly as the invader threw a stag-gering old man to the ground and tore open the wretch's threadbare purse. Apparently unsatisfied with the meager take, the young man yanked a half-rotted board from the uneven edge of the nearest shack and whacked his pitiful victim across the forehead. The old man whined and pleaded, but the tough struck him again, flattening his nose. He was on his knees, face covered in bright blood, begging and cry-ing, but got hit again and again until his sobs were muffled by the mud that half-buried his broken face.

Artemis found that he cared nothing for the old wretch. He did care, though, that the man had begged this new-comer, had pleaded with a master who had come uninvited to Artemis Entreri's place.

Entreri's hands went down to his pockets, slipped inside, feeling the only weapons he bothered to carry, two small handfuls of sand and a flat, edged rock. He gave a sigh that reflected both resignation and the tingling excitement of impending battle. He started out from the corner, but paused to consider his own feelings. He was the hunting cat, the master here, so he was rightfully defending his carved-out domain. But there remained a sadness Artemis could not deny, a resignation he could not understand.

Somewhere deep inside him, in a pocket sealed away by the horrors he had known, Artemis knew things should not be like this. Yet the realization did not turn him away from the battle-to-come. Instead, it made him even angrier.

A feral growl escaped Artemis's lips as he stepped around the shack, out into the open and right in the path of the approaching thug.

The older boy stopped, likewise regarding his adversary. He knew of Artemis, of course, the same way Artemis knew of him.

"At last you show yourself openly," the newcomer said confidently. He was bigger than slender Artemis, though there was very little extra weight on his warrior's frame. His shoulders had been broadened by maturity, by an extra few years of a hard life. His muscles, though not so thick, twitched like strong cords.

"I have been looking for you," he said, inching closer. His caution tipped observant Artemis that he was more nervous than his bravado revealed.

"I've never lived in the shadows," Artemis replied. "You could have found me any day, any time."

"Why would I bother?"

Artemis considered the ridiculous question, then gave a little shrug, deciding not to justify the boastful retort with an answer.

"You know why I'm here," the man said at length, his tone sharper than before—a further indication that his nerves were on edge.

"Funny, I thought I was the one who'd found *you*," Artemis replied. He hid well his concern that this thug might be here, might be on Artemis's street, with more of a purpose than he'd presumed.

"You had no choice but to find me," the invader asserted firmly.

There it was again, that implication of a deeper purpose. It occurred to Artemis then that this man, for he was indeed

a man and no street waif, should already be above staking
out a claim to such a squalid area as this. Even if he were
new to the trade, this course would not be the course for an
adult ruffian. He should be allied with one of the many
thieves' guilds in this city of thieves. Why, then, had he
come? And why alone?

Had he been kicked out of a guild, perhaps?

For a brief moment, Artemis feared he might be in over
his head. His opponent was an adult, and possibly a veteran
rogue. Entreri shook the notion away, saw that his reasoning was not sound. Young upstarts did not get "kicked out"
of Calimport's thieves' guilds; they merely disappeared—
and no one bothered to question their abrupt absence. But
this opponent was not, obviously, some child who had been
forced out on his own.

"Who are you?" Artemis asked bluntly. He wished he
could take the question back as soon as the words had left
his mouth, fearing he had just tipped the thug off to his own
ignorance. Artemis was ultimately alone in his place. He had
no network surrounding him, no spies of any merit and little
understanding of the true power structures of Calimport.

The thug smiled and spent a long moment studying his
opponent. Artemis was small, and probably as quick and
sure in a fight as the guild's reports had indicated. He stood
easily, his hands still in the pockets of his ragged breeches,
his bare, brown-tanned arms small, but sculpted with finely
honed muscles. The thug knew Artemis had no allies, had
been told that before he had been sent out here. Yet this boy
—and in the older thief's eyes, Artemis was indeed a boy—
stood easily and seemed composed far beyond his years.
One other thing bothered the man.

"You have no weapon?" he asked suspiciously.

Again, Artemis only offered a little shrug in reply.

"Very well, then," the thug said, his tone firm, as if he had
just made a decision. To accentuate that very point, he took
up the board, still dripping with the blood of the old man.
Decisively he brought it up to his shoulder, brought it up,
Artemis realized, to a more accessible position. The thug

was barely twenty feet away when he began his approach.

So much more was going on here, Artemis knew, and he wanted answers.

Ten feet away.

Artemis held his steady and calm pose, but his muscles tightened in preparation.

The man was barely five feet from him. Entreri's right hand whipped out of his pocket, hurling a spray of fine sand.

Up came the club, and the man turned his head away. He was laughing when he looked back. "Trying to blind me with a handful of sand?" he asked incredulously, sarcastically. "How clever of a desert fighter to think of using sand!"

Of course it was the proverbial "oldest trick" in sneaky Calimshan's thick book of underhanded street fighting techniques. And the next oldest trick followed when Artemis thrust his hand back into his pocket, and whipped a second handful of sand.

The thug was laughing even as he closed his eyes, defeating the attack. He blinked quickly, just for an instant, a split second. But that instant was long enough for ambidextrous Artemis to withdraw his left hand from his pocket and fling the edged stone. He had just one window of opportunity, an instant of time, a square inch of target. He had to be perfect —but that was the way it had been for Artemis since he was a child, since he went out into the desert, a land that did not forgive the smallest of mistakes.

The sharp stone whistled past the upraised club and hit the thug in the throat, just to one side of center. It nicked into his windpipe and deflected to the left, cutting the wall of an artery before rebounding free into the air.

"Wh—?" the thug began, and he stopped, apparently surprised by the curious whistle that had suddenly come into his voice. A shower of blood erupted from his neck, spraying up across his cheek. He slapped his free hand to it, fingers grasping, trying to stem the flow. He kept his cool enough to hold his makeshift club at the ready the whole time, keeping Artemis at bay, though the younger man had put his hands back in his pockets and made no move.

He was good, Artemis decided, honestly applauding the man's calm and continued defense. He was good, but Artemis was perfect. You had to be perfect.

The outward flow of blood was nearly stemmed, but the artery was severed and the windpipe open beside it.

The thug growled and advanced. Artemis didn't blink.

The thug stopped suddenly, dark eyes wide. He tried to speak out, but only sputtered forth a bright gout of blood. He tried to draw breath, but gurgled again pitifully, his lungs fast-filling with blood, and sank to his knees.

It took him a long time to die. Calimport was an unforgiving place. You had to be perfect.

"Well done," came a voice from the left.

Artemis turned to see two men casually stroll out of a narrow alley. He knew at once that they were thieves, probably guildsmen, for confident Artemis believed only the most practiced rogues could get so close to him without him knowing it.

Artemis looked back to the corpse at his feet, and a hundred questions danced about his thoughts. He knew then with cold certainty that this had been no random meeting. The thug he had killed had been sent to him.

Artemis chuckled, more a derisive snort than a laugh, and kicked a bit of dirt into the dead man's face.

Less than perfect got you killed. Perfect, as Artemis soon found out, got you invited into the local thieves' guild.

* * * * *

Artemis could hardly fathom the notion that all the food he wanted was available to him with a snap of his fingers. He had been offered a soft bed, too, but feared that such luxury would weaken him. He slept on his floor at night.

Still, the offer was the important thing. Artemis cared little for material wealth or pleasures, but he cared greatly that those pleasures were being offered to him.

That was the benefit of being in the Basadoni Cabal, one of the most powerful thieves' guilds in all the city. In fact there were many benefits. To an independent young man such as Artemis Entreri, there were many drawbacks, as well.

Lieutenant Theebles Royuset, the man that Pasha Basadoni had appointed as Entreri's personal mentor, was one of these. He was the epitome of men that young Artemis Entreri loathed, gluttonous and lazy, with heavy eyelids that perpetually drooped. His smelly brown hair was naturally frizzy, but too greased and dirty to come away from his scalp, and he always wore the remnants of his last four meals on the front of his shirt. Physically, there was nothing quick about Theebles, except the one movement that brought the latest handful of food into his slopping jowls, but intellectually, the man was sharp and dangerous.

And sadistic. Despite the obvious physical limitations, Theebles was in the second rank of command in the guild, along with a half-dozen other lieutenants, behind only Pasha Basadoni himself.

Artemis hated him. Theebles had been a merchant, and like so many of Calimport's purveyors, had gotten himself into severe trouble with the city guard. So Theebles had used his wealth to buy himself an appointment to the guild, that he might go underground and escape Calimport's dreaded prisons. That wealth must have been considerable, Artemis knew, for Pasha Basadoni to even accept this dangerous slug into the guild, let alone appoint him a lieutenant.

Artemis was savvy enough to understand, then, that Basadoni's choice of sadistic Theebles as his personal mentor would be a true test of his loyalty to his new family.

A brutal test, Artemis realized as he leaned against the squared stone wall of a square chamber in the guild hall's basement. He crossed his arms defensively over his chest, fingers of his thick gloves tapping silently, impatiently. He found that he missed his street in the city outside, missed the days when he had answered to no one but himself and his survival instincts. Those days had ended with the well-aimed throw of an edged stone.

"Well?" Theebles, who had come for one of his many unannounced inspections, prompted again. He picked something rather large out of his wide and flat nose. Like everything else that fell into his plump and almost babylike hands, it quickly went into his mouth.

Artemis didn't blink. He looked from Theebles to the ten-gallon glass case across the dimly lit room; the chamber, though fully twenty feet underground, was dry and dusty.

Swaying with every step, the fat lieutenant paced to the case. Artemis obediently followed, but only after a quick nod to the rogue standing guard at the door, the same rogue who had met Artemis on the street after he had killed the thug. That man, Dancer by name, was another of Theebles's servants, and one of the many friends young Artemis had made in his time in the guild. Dancer returned the nod and slipped out into the hall.

He trusts me, Artemis thought. He considered Dancer the fool for it.

Artemis caught up to Theebles right in front of the case. The fat man stared intently at the small orange snakes intertwined within.

"Beautiful," Theebles said. "So sleek and delicate." He turned his heavy-lidded gaze Artemis's way.

Artemis could not deny the words. The snakes were Thesali vipers, the dreaded "Two-Step." If one bit you, you yelled, took two steps, and fell down dead. Efficient. Beautiful.

Milking the venom from the deadly vipers, even with the thick gloves he wore, was not an enviable task. But then, wretched Theebles Royuset made it a point to never give Artemis an enviable task.

Theebles stared at the tantalizing snakes for a long while, then glanced back to the right. He stymied his surprise, realizing that silent Artemis had moved around him, toward the far end of the room. He turned to the young rogue and gave a wry snicker, that superior chuckle that reminded Artemis pointedly of his position as an underling.

It was then that Theebles noticed the quarter table, partially concealed by a screen. Surprise showed on his pudgy, blotchy features for a moment before he caught himself and calmed. "Your doing?" he asked, approaching the screen and indicating the small and round glass-topped table, flanked on either side by a waist-high lever.

Artemis turned slowly to glance over one shoulder as Theebles passed him by, but didn't bother to answer. Artemis was the milker of the snakes. Of course the table was "his doing." Who else, except for his taunting mentor, would even bother coming into this room?

"You have made many allies among the lower members of the guild," Theebles remarked, as close to a word of praise as he had ever given to Artemis. In fact, Theebles was truly impressed; it was quite a feat for one so new to the guild to have the infamous quarter table moved to a quiet and convenient location. But Theebles, when he took the moment to consider it, was not so surprised. This young Artemis Entreri was an imposing character, a charismatic young rogue who had ruffians much older than him showing a great degree of respect.

Yes, Theebles knew that Artemis Entreri was not an average little pickpocket. He could be a great thief, among the very best. That could be a positive thing for the Basadoni Cabal. Or it could be a dangerous thing.

Without turning back, Artemis walked across the room and sat down at one of the two chairs placed on opposite sides of the quarter table.

It was not a wholly unexpected challenge, of course. Theebles had played out similar scenarios several times with the youths under his severe tutelage. Furthermore, young Artemis certainly knew now that it had been Theebles who had sent the rogue out to the shantytown to challenge him. Dancer had told Entreri as much, Theebles guessed; he made a mental note to have a little talk with Dancer when he was done with Entreri. Laughing slightly, the fat man sauntered across the room to stand beside the seated young rogue. He saw that the four glasses set in the evenly spaced depressions about the table's perimeter were half-filled with clear water. In the middle of the table sat an empty milking vial.

"You understand that I am a close personal friend of Pasha Basadoni," Theebles said.

"I understand that if you sit down in that chair, you accept the challenge willingly," Artemis replied. He reached in and removed the milking vial. By the strict rules of the challenge, the table had to be clear of everything except the four glasses.

Theebles shook with laughter, and Artemis had expected no less. Artemis knew that he had no right to make such a challenge. Still, Artemis breathed a little easier when Theebles clapped him on the shoulders and walked about the table. The fat lieutenant stopped and peered intently into each of the glasses, as if he had noticed something.

It was a bluff, Artemis pointedly told himself. The venom of a Thesali viper was perfectly clear, like the water.

"You used enough?" Theebles asked with complete calm.

Artemis didn't respond, didn't blink. He knew, as did the fat lieutenant, that a single drop was all that was needed.

"And you only poisoned one glass?" Theebles asked, another rhetorical question, for the rules of this challenge were explicit.

Theebles sat in the appointed chair, apparently accepting the challenge. Artemis's facade nearly cracked, and he had to stifle a sigh of relief. The lieutenant could have refused, could have had Artemis dragged out and disembowelled for even thinking that he was worthy of making such a challenge against a ranking guild member. Artemis had suspected that cruel Theebles would not take so direct a route, of course. Theebles hated him as much as he hated Theebles, and he had done everything in his power over the last few tendays to feed that hatred.

"Only one?" Theebles asked again.

"Would it matter?" Artemis replied, thinking himself clever. "One, two, or three poisoned drinks, the risks remain equal between us."

The fat lieutenant's expression grew sour. "It is a quarter table," he said condescendingly. "A quarter. One in four.

That is the rule. When the top is spun, each of us has a one-in-four chance of sipping the poisoned drink. And by the rules, no more than one glass can be poisoned, no more than one can die."

"Only one is poisoned," Artemis confirmed.

"The poison is that of the Thesali viper, and only the poison of a Thesali viper?"

Artemis nodded. To a wary challenger like the young rogue, the question screamed the fact that Theebles didn't fear such venom. Of course he didn't.

Theebles returned the nod and took on a serious expression to match his opponent's. "You are certain of your course?" he asked, his voice full of gravity.

Artemis did not miss the experienced killer's sly undertones. Theebles was pretending to offer him the opportunity to change his mind, but it was only a ruse. And Artemis would play along. He glanced about nervously, summoned a bead of sweat to his forehead. "Perhaps . . ." he began tentatively, giving the appearance of hedging.

"Yes?" Theebles prompted after a long pause.

Artemis started to rise, as though he had indeed changed his mind about making such a challenge; Theebles stopped him with a sharp word. The expression of surprise upon Artemis's young and too-delicate face appeared sincere.

"Challenge accepted," the lieutenant growled. "You cannot change your mind."

Artemis fell back into his seat, grabbed the edge of the tabletop, and yanked hard. Like a gambling wheel, the top rotated, spinning smoothly and quietly on its central hub. Artemis grabbed the long lever flanking him, one of the table's brakes, and Theebles, smiling smugly, did likewise.

It quickly became a game of nerves. Artemis and Theebles locked gazes, and for the first time, Theebles saw the depth of his young adversary. At that moment Theebles began to appreciate the pure cunning of merciless Artemis Entreri. Still, he was unafraid and remained composed enough to note the subtle shift of Artemis's eye, the hint that the young man was quietly watching the spinning glasses more intently than he was letting on.

Artemis caught a minute flicker, a subtle flash of reflected light from the table, then a second. Long before Theebles had come to visit, he had chipped the rim of one of the glasses ever so slightly. Artemis had then painstakingly aligned the table and the seat he'd chosen. With every rotation, the tiny chip in the glass would flicker a reflection of the torch burning in the nearest wall sconce—but to his eyes only.

Artemis silently counted the elapsed time between flickers, measuring the table's speed.

"Why would you take such a risk?" wary Theebles asked, verbally prodding the young man's concentration. "Have you come to hate me so much in a few short tendays?"

"Long months," Artemis corrected. "But it has been longer than that. My fight in the street was no coincidence. It was a set-up, a test, between myself and the man I had to kill. And you are the one who arranged it."

The way that Artemis described his adversary, "the man I had to kill," tipped Theebles off to the young rogue's motivation. The stranger in the dusty street had likely been Artemis Entreri's first kill. The lieutenant smiled to himself. Some weaklings found murder a difficult thing to accept; either the first kill, or the inevitable path it had set the young man on, was not to Entreri's liking.

"I had to know if you were worthy," Theebles said, admitting his complicity. But Artemis was no longer listening. The young rogue had gone back to his subtle study of the spinning glasses.

Theebles eased his brake, slowing the rotation considerably. The hub was well-greased—some even claimed there was a bit of magic about it—so the top did not need much momentum to keep spinning at a nearly constant rate.

Artemis showed no sign of distress at the unexpected speed change. He kept completely composed and began silently counting once more. The marked glass flickered exactly an eighth of the circumference from Theebles's chair. Artemis adjusted his cadence to make each complete rotation take a count of eight.

He saw the flicker; he counted and as he hit nine, abruptly pulled the brake.

The tabletop came to a sudden stop, liquid sloshing back and forth inside the glasses, droplets of it splattering to the table and the floor.

Theebles eyed the glass in front of him. He thought to remark that the young rogue didn't understand the proper protocol of the quarter table challenge, for the brakes were supposed to be applied slowly, alternately between the opponents, and the challenged party would make the final stop. The fat lieutenant decided not to make an issue of it. He knew that he had been taken, but didn't really care. He'd been expecting this challenge for almost a tenday and had enough antivenin in his blood to defeat the poison of a hundred Thesali vipers. He lifted his glass. Artemis did likewise, and together they drank deeply.

Five seconds passed. Ten.

"Well," Theebles began. "It would seem that neither of us found the unfortunate quarter this day." He pulled his huge form from the chair. "Of course, your insolence will be reported in full to Pasha Basadoni."

Artemis showed no expression, didn't blink. Theebles suspected that the young rogue was hiding his surprise, or that he was fuming or trying to figure out how he might escape this unexpected disaster. As the seconds passed, the young man's continued calm began to bother the fat lieutenant.

"You have had your one challenge," Theebles snapped suddenly, loudly. "I am alive, thus you have lost. Expect to pay dearly for your impertinence!"

Artemis didn't blink.

Good enough for the young upstart, the fat lieutenant decided with a snap of his fingers. As he departed, he thought of many ways that he might properly punish Artemis.

How delicious that torture would be, for Basadoni could not stop Theebles this time. The guildmaster, who by Theebles's estimation had become much too soft in his old age, had intervened many times on behalf of Entreri, calming Theebles whenever he learned that the fat lieutenant was planning a brutal punishment for the young upstart. Not this time, though. This time, Basadoni could not intervene. This time, Entreri had certainly earned the punishment.

The first place Theebles went when he returned to his lavish private quarters was the well-stocked cupboard. The antivenin to Thesali viper poison was known to cause great hunger after the poison was introduced, and Theebles had never been one to need much prompting toward food. He pulled out a two-layered cake, a gigantic, sugar-speckled arrangement, decorated with the sweetest of fruits.

He took up a knife to cut a slice, then shrugged and decided to eat the whole thing. With both hands, he lifted the cake for his mouth.

"Oh, clever lad!" Theebles congratulated, returning the cake to the table. "Sly upon sly, a feint within a feint! Of course you knew the effects of Thesali antivenin. Of course you knew that I would run back here to my personal cupboard! And you have had the time, haven't you, Artemis Entreri? Clever lad!"

Theebles looked to the window and thought to throw the cake out into the street. Let the homeless waifs find its crumbs and eat them, and all fall down dead! But the cake, the beautiful cake. He couldn't bear to be done with it, and he was so, so famished.

Instead, he moved across the room to his private desk. He carefully unlocked the trapped drawers, checked the wax seal to be certain that no one had been here before him, to be certain that Artemis could not have tampered with this supply. Satisfied that all was as it should be, Theebles opened a secret compartment at the bottom of the drawer and removed a very valuable vial. It contained an amber-colored liquid, a magic potion that would neutralize any poison a man might imbibe. Theebles looked back to the cake. Would Artemis be as clever as he believed? Would the young rogue really understand the concept of sly upon sly?

Theebles sighed and decided Artemis just might be that clever. The vial of universal antidote was very expensive, but the cake looked so very delicious!

"I will make Artemis Entreri pay for another vial," the now-famished lieutenant decided as he swallowed the antidote. Then he romped across the room and took a tiny bit off the edge of the cake, testing its flavor. It was indeed poisoned. Experienced Theebles knew that at once from the barely perceptible sour edge among the sweetness.

The antidote would defeat it, the lieutenant knew, and he would not let the young upstart cheat him out of so fine a meal. He rubbed his plump hands together and took up the cake, gorging himself, swallowing huge chunks at a time, wiping the silver serving platter clean.

Theebles died that night, horribly, waking from a sound sleep into sheer agony. It was as if his insides were on fire. He tried to call out, but his voice was drowned by his own blood.

His attendant found him early the next morning, his mouth full of gore, his pillowcase spotted with brownish red spots, and his abdomen covered with angry blue welts. Many in the guild had heard Dancer speak of the previous day's challenge, and so the connection to young Artemis Entreri was not a hard one to make.

The young assassin was caught on the streets of Calimport a tenday later, after giving Pasha Basadoni's powerful spy network a fine run. He was more resigned than afraid as two burly, older killers led him roughly back to the guild hall.

Artemis believed Basadoni would punish him, perhaps even kill him, for his actions; it was worth it just to know that Theebles Royuset had died horribly.

He had never been in the uppermost chambers of the guild hall before, never imagined what riches lay within. Beautiful women, covered in glittering jewels, roamed through every room. Great cushiony couches and pillows were heaped everywhere, and behind every third archway was a steaming tub of scented water.

This entire floor of the hall was devoted to purely hedonistic pursuits, a place dedicated to every imaginable pleasure. Yet to Artemis, it appeared more dangerous than enticing. His goal was perfection, not pleasure, and this was a place where a man would grow soft.

He was somewhat surprised, then, when he at last came to stand before Pasha Basadoni, the first time Artemis had actually met the man. Basadoni's small office was the only room on this floor of the guild hall not fitted for comfort. Its furnishings were few and simple—a single wooden desk and three unremarkable chairs.

The pasha fit the office. He was a smallish man, old but stately. His gaze, like his posture, was perfectly straight. His gray hair was neatly groomed, his clothes unpretentious.

After only a couple moments of scrutiny, Artemis understood that this was a man to be respected, even feared. Looking at the pasha, Artemis considered again how out of place a slug like Theebles Royuset had been. He guessed at once that Basadoni must have hated Theebles profoundly. That notion alone gave him hope.

"So you admit you cheated at the quarter challenge?" Basadoni asked after a long and deliberate pause, after studying young Artemis at least as intently as Artemis was studying him.

"Isn't that part of the challenge?" Artemis was quick to reply.

Basadoni chuckled and nodded.

"Theebles expected I would cheat," Artemis went on. "A vial of universal antidote was found emptied within his room."

"And you tampered with it?"

"I did not," Artemis answered honestly.

Basadoni's quizzical expression prompted the young rogue to continue.

"The vial worked as expected, and the cake was indeed conventionally poisoned," Artemis admitted.

"But . . ." Basadoni said.

"But no antidote in Calimshan can defeat the effects of crushed glass."

Basadoni shook his head. "Sly upon sly within sly," he said. "A feint within a feint within a feint." He looked curiously at the clever young lad. "Theebles was capable of thinking to the third level of deception," he reasoned.

"But he did not believe that I was," Artemis quickly countered. "He underestimated his opponent."

"And so he deserved to die," Basadoni decided after a short pause.

"The challenge was willingly accepted," Artemis quickly noted, to remind the old pasha that any punishment would surely, by the rules of the guild, be unjustified.

Basadoni leaned back in his chair, tapping the tips of his fingers together. He stared at Artemis long and hard. The young assassin's reasoning was sound, but he almost ordered Artemis killed anyway, seeing clearly the cruelty, the absolute lack of compassion, within this one's black heart. He understood that he could never truly trust Artemis Entreri, but he realized, too, that young Artemis would not likely strike against him, an old man and a potentially valuable mentor, unless he forced the issue. And Basadoni knew, too, how valuable an asset a clever and cold rogue like Artemis Entreri might be—especially with five other ambitious lieutenants scrambling to position themselves in the hope that he would soon die.

Perhaps I will outlive those five, after all, the pasha thought with a slight smile. To Artemis he merely said, "I will exact no punishment."

Artemis showed no emotion.

"Truly you are a cold-hearted wretch," Basadoni went on with a helpless snicker, his voice honestly sympathetic. "Leave me, Lieutenant Entreri." He waved his age-spotted hand as if the whole affair left a sour taste in his mouth.

Artemis turned to go, but stopped and glanced back, realizing only then the significance of how Basadoni had addressed him.

The two burly escorts at the newest lieutenant's side caught it, too. One of them bristled anxiously, glaring at the young man. *Lieutenant* Artemis Entreri? the man's dour expression seemed to say in disbelief. The boy, half his size, had only been in the guild for a few months. He was only fourteen years old!

"Perhaps my first duty will be to see to your continued training," Artemis said, staring coldly into the muscular man's face. "You must learn to mask your feelings better."

The man's moment of anger was replaced by a feeling of sheer dread as he, too, stared into those callous and calculating dark eyes, eyes too filled with evil for one of Artemis Entreri's tender age.

* * * * *

Later that afternoon, Artemis Entreri walked out of the Basadoni guild hall on a short journey that was long overdue. He went back to his street, the territory he had carved out amidst Calimport's squalor.

A dusty orange sunset marked the end of another hot day as Artemis turned a corner and entered that territory—the same corner the thug had turned just before Artemis had killed him.

Artemis shook his head, feeling more than a little overwhelmed by it all. He had survived these streets, the challenge Theebles Royuset had thrown his way, and the counterchallenge he had offered in response. He had survived, and he had thrived, and was now a full lieutenant in the Basadoni Cabal.

Slowly, Artemis walked the length of the muddy lane, his gaze stalking from left to right and back again, just as he had done when he was the master here. When these had been his streets, life had been simple. Now his course was set out before him, among his own treacherous kind. Ever after would he need to walk with his back close to a wall—a solid wall that he had already checked for deadly traps and secret portals.

It had all happened so fast, in the course of just a few months. Street waif to lieutenant in the Basadoni Cabal, one of the most powerful thieves' guilds in Calimport.

Yet as he looked back over the road that had brought him from Memnon to Calimport, from this muddy alley to the polished marble halls of the thieves' guild, Artemis Entreri began to wonder if, perhaps, the change was somewhat less miraculous. Nothing really happened so quickly; he'd been led to this seemingly remarkable state by years spent honing his street skills, years spent challenging and conquering brutal men like Theebles, or the old lecher in the caravan, or his father. . . .

A noise from the side drew Artemis's attention to a wide alley where a group of boys came rambling past. Half the grimy mob tossed a small stone back and forth while the other half tried to get it away.

It came as a shock to Artemis when he realized that they were his own age, perhaps even a bit older. And the shock carried with it more than a little pain.

The boys soon disappeared behind the next shack, laughing and shouting, a cloud of dust in their wake. Artemis summarily dismissed them, thinking again of what he had accomplished and what heights of glory and power might still lay before him. After all, he had purchased the right to dream such dark dreams at the cost of his youth and innocence, coins whose value he did not recognize until they were spent.

BLOOD SPORT

Christie Golden

"I understand you're used to being on the other side of these iron bars," said the woman called the Shark. Her black eyes were hard as she gazed through the barred window into the Mistledale prison cell. "Weren't you once captain of the Riders? They called you Rhynn 'the Fair,' right? Oh, but that was before you turned traitor to the people you were sworn to protect."

Inmate Rhynn, an indigo-haired moon elf, did not reply. Only her clenched hands, their slim wrists encircled by metal shackles, betrayed her tension.

The Shark opened the door with the key given her by the new captain of the Riders. She leaned her tall, well-muscled frame casually against the cold stone of the cell. The elf's glare grew more hostile, though she trembled violently. A malicious smile spread across the Shark's tanned face. Her functional, masculine garb—wool tunic, breeches, and cape — kept her warm, even in the middle of the month of Hammer. Rhynn Oriandis was clad only in a shabby tunic that dozens of prisoners before her had worn. Her skin, pale as that of the quarry the Shark had been summoned to hunt, was covered with gooseflesh.

The Shark knelt and brought her tawny face within an inch

of Rhynn's. "It's all come out, Rhynn. I want the vampire."

"I don't care what lies you've heard. He deserved to go free."

"Ah, you elves do protect your own, don't you?" The Shark's lips curled in a sneer. "I've never heard of an elven vampire before. I'm looking forward to this case."

"Race had nothing to do—"

"It had everything to do with your actions!" the Shark interrupted. "What you forgot is that this creature is *not* an elf any longer and therefore did not deserve your misplaced protection. He's a vampire. They are things of purest evil. They know no race, and the only thing they 'deserve' is a stake through the heart. Give me the information I want, or I'll simply take it from you."

Rhynn's eyes remained steady. "Torture me all you like. I won't break."

"I wouldn't be so sure. They call me the Shark because I'm the predator's predator. I've fought twenty-two vampires and countless humans, and I've always made my kill." Pride colored in her words. "Now—" her hand was a swift blur as she tangled strong fingers in Rhynn's hair "—cooperate, and you come out of this with your sanity and maybe your freedom. Fight me—" she tightened her grip until Rhynn gasped softly "—and you'll have neither."

The Shark chanted an incantation, blunt-nailed fingers digging into Rhynn's skull. Rhynn arched in pain, her shackles rattling furiously, but she could not resist. The Shark's spell tore open the elf's mind.

The woman's emotions had obviously been confused by the vampire's magical charms, for she saw him as a being devoted to good rather than the monster he was. The Shark had probed other minds in this manner before, and always, in the victims' memories the blooder was a veritable saint. The Shark concentrated on the elf's appearance, his name, his destination, even as Rhynn tried frantically to secret the information. In her weakened condition, Rhynn could not bear the mental violation. Her mouth opened in a soundless scream, then unconsciousness claimed her.

She's luckier than she knows, thought the Shark; had she resisted further, the struggle to protect the vampire would have destroyed her sanity.

Triumphant, the Shark released her hold on Rhynn. On a whim, she tossed the keys within the elf's reach. Rhynn might revive and free herself before her captors realized it. Maybe she'd escape. Maybe they'd kill her. It didn't really matter. The Shark slipped the hood of her cloak over her head and vanished, thanks to the cape's enchantment. With hardly a thought, she walked out of the small prison and passed the two guards. Her horse was waiting for her behind the jail, out of sight of the guards. Quietly she mounted. Snow muffled the hoofbeats as the Shark headed toward Mistledale's single main gate. The idiot guards there noticed nothing.

According to Rhynn, the monster wanted to return to Evermeet, the elven homeland. The Shark snorted with contempt. Did the blooder actually think he could cross *water?* No, he'd be stranded along the Sword Coast, probably in Waterdeep. He already had a three month head start. She'd have to ride hard to catch up with him.

The Shark turned her mount westward, toward the place that was becoming known as the "City of Splendors," and kicked the animal savagely.

The hunt was on.

*　*　*　*　*

A bawdy song spilled out of the Orc's Head Inn. The Shark, clad in demure feminine attire and appearing deceptively fragile, entered the noisy tavern. She brushed snow off her cape as she observed the noisy, slightly drunken crowd, then unobtrusively seated herself in a shadowed corner. The blooder wasn't here yet, but her sources had assured her he would make an appearance tonight.

She had only been seated a moment when a pretty young barmaid plunked a foamy tankard of ale in front of the Shark. The girl was small but full-figured, with a tumble of golden curls cascading down her back.

"On the house tonight," the barmaid explained. "Shallen Lathkule—" the girl gestured to an extraordinarily handsome youth surrounded by merry companions "—is to be wed tomorrow afternoon. He's buying drinks for all, in memory of his lost bachelorhood."

"Well, to Shallen and his bride. He seems to be a popular young man," ventured the Shark, hoping to draw the barmaid into conversation. Perhaps this Shallen knew the blooder.

"Oh, he is indeed. Friendly as you'd like. And talented. Crafts the prettiest baubles this side of Evermeet, so they say."

"He's a pretty bauble himself, isn't he?" joked the Shark. Before the girl could answer, the door opened and the barmaid's eyes lit up with pleasure. The Shark followed her gaze—and her own eyes flashed in excitement.

A slim figure entered, carrying a large crate. He leaned on the door to close it behind him. Though he wore a gray cloak over his blue tunic, his shoulder-length hair was uncovered, brilliant wheat-gold dusted with snowflakes. No hood shadowed his fair features and bronze skin. His eyes perused the scene with subtle caution, a furtiveness that the Shark recognized. The silver gaze settled on her for a moment, then moved on.

Her elven vampire had arrived.

She watched him intently as he moved gracefully to a spot near the door and set down his crate. Unobtrusive as he was, Shallen spotted him. "There you are!" the young man cried happily, extricating himself from his less sober companions. "Khyrra told me to talk you into coming to the wedding tomorrow."

"I'm afraid I cannot," replied the elf. The Mistledale folk hadn't exaggerated when they had described the blooder's voice as sweet, like music. "But this might take the sting out of my refusal." With a small dagger, he cut the rope that had secured the crate and pulled out a small statue. Carved of soft pine, the figurine was a mere eight inches high, but the moment the elf brought it into the light, all eyes were upon him and his work.

Balanced in his golden palm was a miniature of Lliira, Our Lady of Joy. Her long hair flowed about her, merging into her swirling dress as she danced in sheer delight. One hand was raised, palm flat, while the other one curved around her body, following the drape of her garb.

"Her hand is empty, but there's a little hollow right here," the elf pointed out. "Fill it with a jewel that has a special meaning for you and Khyrra. Our Lady of Joy will stand in my stead at your wedding tomorrow."

Shallen's blue eyes were wide and sparkling with tears. The Shark's own eyes narrowed. How easily tricked they were, all of them—Rhynn, Shallen, and probably that little barmaid as well, judging by her reaction to the elf's entrance. Like the vampire who had made it, the gift was beautiful, but surely also dangerous.

"Thank you. I—" Shallen's throat closed up and he turned back to the bar, embarrassed by his emotion.

"Too much ale," quipped a friend. The awkward moment dissolved into laughter, and the performers resumed their tune. Though the music was loud enough to drown out most conversation in the tavern, the Shark had come prepared to eavesdrop. She rested her chin on her hand, ostensibly engrossed in the singing. As she did, she held a tiny, perfectly formed horn to her ear, easily concealed by her flowing black locks. She whispered a spell, and the voice of the barmaid came clearly to her ears.

"That must've taken you months! What's Shallen done for you that you give him so pretty a thing?"

The elf glanced back at the jeweler. "He wears his youth and happiness like a beautiful robe, for all to see and share in. That's enough. When it's time for you to get married, Maia, I promise I'll give you and your husband something even prettier."

Maia's response was an uncertain laugh. "Don't know as I'll ever have a husband." Slender, nervous hands gestured at her body, a shade too ripe for modesty, and her beautiful face, a touch too hard for innocence. "Most men like uncharted territory, Master Jander, and I'm more like their own backyard."

The vampire reached to still her suddenly anxious hands. Gently, he said, "You told me something of that sort six months ago, when I found you in the City of the Dead. I told you then that your past need not destroy your future. I was right—Kurnin hired you at once, didn't he?"

A sheepish smile played on her full lips. "Aye," she admitted. "But, Master Jander, none of these people know what I *am!*" Her voice had dropped to a near-whisper.

The elf's teasing expression grew more solemn. "You're wrong, Maia. They know what you are. They don't know what you *were,* and that no longer matters."

"You think so?"

"I know so."

As Shallen had been a moment earlier, Maia seemed close to tears. She blinked them back and allowed herself a true smile, revealing the purity of the beauty that lurked behind the hard facade. "You'd charm the very birds off the trees," she laughed, trying to lighten the mood.

Just as he's obviously charmed you, the Shark thought with a slight sniff of contempt. Charmed you into being his next meal.

Maia left to refill the mugs of the celebrants, and the elf turned his attention to his wares. He carefully emptied the crate of at least a dozen small carvings, turned it over, and spread his cloak over the makeshift table.

The Shark's heart beat faster with anticipation. What she was about to do next was risky, but it was part of the deadly game she loved to play, needed to play. She rose and went to meet her quarry.

The vampire glanced up as her shadow fell across him. The Shark noted, as if she needed further proof, that the undead cast no shadow of his own in the flickering lamplight.

"Your work is impressive." She met the vampire's gray eyes evenly. There hadn't been a blooder yet that could charm her, but she enjoyed the danger of flirting with the possibility. To her disappointment, this golden vampire didn't even try. He merely continued placing his carvings on the crate.

"Thank you."

"Do you have your own shop here in Waterdeep?"

"I find it more congenial to work during the day and visit different taverns at night."

I'll bet you do, the Shark noted silently. She ran a finger along the hull of a tiny, incredibly detailed elven sailing vessel. "People are freer with their money when their throats are wet, I would imagine."

He chuckled politely. "Perhaps they are. Do you like that piece?"

"I do, but I don't have enough with me to buy it tonight," the Shark replied, feigning disappointment. "Could I come to your home tomorrow and purchase it then?"

"I value my privacy when I work," responded the vampire, a touch too swiftly. "I'll be back tomorrow night. Shall I keep it for you?"

"I have an engagement, but I'll send one of my servants for it. Who should she ask for?"

"Jander Sunstar," the elf replied. "And you are?"

"Shakira Khazaar. Thank you for holding the piece for me."

"Standard business practice. I'd hate to lose a sale," Jander answered.

There was a strange expression in those silver eyes, and the Shark felt vaguely uneasy. She had done something wrong. She had gotten careless somehow. The thought was like a slap in the face. She smiled, hoping to allay his suspicion, and was relieved when he returned the gesture with the artless, seemingly genuine smile she had seen him use with the others, his "friends." Still, she felt his eyes boring into her back as she left.

Once outside, the Shark crossed the street and slipped into an alley. After making sure she had not been observed, she drew the hood of the cloak over her head. Woven and ensorceled by her own hands many years ago, the cloak not only made her invisible, but also disguised the aura produced by her body heat—something vampires could see. The snow-speckled wind was strong, but she maneuvered herself so that it blew directly in her face. Though she was now invisible to the eyes of blooder and human alike, she was not about to risk being betrayed by her scent.

Her wait was not long. Just as the inn closed, the vampire emerged. The barmaid Maia was with him. Carefully, silently, the Shark followed, noting that Jander deliberately left bootprints in the snow, perpetuating the illusion that he was nothing more than an ordinary elf. Too many blooders, used to walking without tracks, forgot that little detail.

Maia and the vampire chatted quietly as he escorted the girl to her home, a single room atop a tailor shop. The Shark waited for the inevitable. The stupid girl, hypnotized by the creature, would invite him in. Of course he would accept, then drink his fill. That was the way it worked, and the Shark never interfered. She knew from a particularly harrowing experience in Suzail that it was unwise to startle a feeding vampire.

Her expectations were fulfilled. Casually, Maia invited the vampire inside, as if she had done so often. Courteously, the blooder accepted. The Shark waited with practiced patience, ignoring the cold. Eventually the vampire emerged, descended the stairs, and turned to stride down the street—still taking care to leave footprints. The hunter followed, slightly puzzled. Rather than assume the form of a bat or dissolve into mist, Jander chose to retain his elven shape and simply walk the distance. He seemed tense, though, and repeatedly glanced over his shoulder.

He thinks someone's following him, she realized suddenly. How could he know?

The Shark's mind raced back to the incident at the inn, and she finally recognized what she had done to arouse the blooder's suspicions. She had not asked the price of the carving. Shame and fear rolled over her, bringing hot blood to her invisible face. Idiot! her mind screamed silently. How could she have jeopardized herself so? Her carelessness could have cost her life—and might still. At that instant, Jander paused to look squarely at her, just for a moment. The Shark's heart lurched. . . . But no, he hadn't seen her. The blooder turned and continued on his way.

At last he stopped in front of a small, stone cottage near the city's outskirts. It wasn't until Jander removed a key and unlocked the door that the Shark understood, with some surprise, that this was the vampire's home. The wooden shingles and door were solid and in good shape. Beneath the shuttered windows stood the winter skeletons of rose bushes, carefully pruned and planted in neat rows. With a final, anxious glance around, Jander carefully knocked the snow from his boots and went inside.

The Shark tasted disappointment like ashes in her mouth. What kind of a challenge was a vampire who planted *rose bushes?* How could she prove herself against so feeble a foe? Surely something as exotic as an elven vampire ought to push her to her limits, test every bit of cleverness and skill she possessed! She almost felt that she could walk in right now and dispatch the creature without breaking a sweat, but her earlier carelessness tempered her resentment. She would come back tomorrow and kill him. It would be easy, she knew, yet she still needed to devise a back-up plan just in case something went wrong.

With a final, disgusted look at the cozy cottage that was home to a vampire, she turned and retraced her steps to town. There was one more thing to do tonight.

* * * * *

Protected from all eyes by her magical cloak, the Shark arrived at the blooder's cottage the following afternoon. The vampire's domicile was part of a small row of houses, which all seemed vacant at the moment; Shallen Lathkule's wedding, held at the other end of Waterdeep, had indeed drawn a huge crowd. With speedy efficiency, the Shark picked the lock and slipped inside. Closing the door behind her, she allowed her eyes to grow accustomed to the darkness, then looked around.

On this, the ground floor of the two-story building, she saw nothing sinister, apart from the shutters that were nailed closed and coated with pitch to seal out sunlight. There was a large workbench, with the woodcarver's tools neatly organized. Half-formed carvings sat patiently on shelves. Where they were not covered with shelving, the walls bore lovely paintings and tapestries. In one corner, carefully preserved, was a suit of mail, a sword, and a shield. Relics, no doubt, from the vampire's days as a living being. The stone floor was strewn with fresh rushes. Small squeaking sounds came from behind a curtain toward the back. Senses alert, the Shark moved forward carefully and drew back the curtain.

Dozens of rats milled about in a large pen. She watched them carefully for a few moments, aware that sometimes such simple beasts could be controlled by vampires, but the rats behaved in a perfectly ordinary fashion. Wrinkling her nose at the smell, she let the curtain fall. "Between meal treats," she said softly. Most blooders kept something of the sort on hand.

She checked the wooden floor for any hidden doors, but found none. The Shark frowned, puzzled, and glanced at the ladder that led up to the upper floor. Most undead liked their lairs cool and dark, belowground if possible. The Shark shrugged. Upstairs, downstairs—it made no difference to her. Soundlessly, she climbed up to the small loft. She raised her head cautiously, then drew a swift intake of breath.

This vampire had no coffin. Neither did he lie rigid with his hands neatly folded atop his chest. He slept sprawled on the floor, arms and legs bent at unnatural angles. The beautiful features that had smiled in the lamplight last night were contorted in what looked like fear. For an instant, the Shark hesitated. She'd never seen a blooder sleep in that position. Could she possibly have been wrong?

No, she decided in the next heartbeat. She had never been wrong where blooders were concerned. Quietly she climbed the rest of the way up and walked carefully over to Jander. No chest movement. He was certainly dead—but why this position? Then it came to her. Blooders slept as they had died, and most had been laid out and buried in coffins. Jander Sunstar had obviously met his vampiric fate in a less tranquil fashion and had never seen a proper ritual burial.

She leaned forward for a better look, and the hood dropped into her eyes. Annoyed, she slipped the hood to her shoulders, instantly becoming visible. It didn't matter. Jander, like every blooder she'd ever slain, was vulnerable, unable to move, let alone fight, during daylight hours. He would die, too. The only question in her mind now was how she would kill him. Her strong hands fell to her wide belt, which hosted her tools. Jander's contorted position did not give her a clear shot with her favorite weapon, a small, specially crafted crossbow she could wield with one hand. She had to go with the traditional implements—the stake and hammer.

Straddling the undead body, she placed the tip of the sharpened stake to his breast. She raised the hammer and said the words that she always uttered before a kill: "The Shark sends you to the Nine Hells." Then, in a disgusted tone, she added, "You were too easy."

A gold-skinned hand seized her left wrist. Silver eyes gazed up at her. "Not that easy," replied the vampire.

The Shark recovered almost at once from her shock. A quick flick of her wrist liberated a small glass ball from up her sleeve. Liquid—holy water—sloshed within the delicately blown sphere. She shoved it down toward the vampire's face, but he was unbelievably fast. He loosed his grip on her arm, his hand flying up in a blur to protect his face. The glass ball broke, but instead of searing his eyes, the holy water ignited his fingers.

Before the monster could take mist form and flee, the Shark leapt clear, pulled her crossbow from its harness behind her back, aimed, and fired. The slim wooden bolt sank deep into the vampire's chest. Immediately his body began to desiccate; the flesh shriveled and turned from golden to dull tan. Gasping, he dropped to his knees on the wooden floor. The Shark watched eagerly, hungry for the creature's pain. She hadn't expected the vampire to retain so much of his former race that he could move during the day. But she had gotten him, in spite of—

Flailing golden hands closed on the shaft, and the Shark realized that, although the wooden arrow had hit Jander's chest, perhaps even grazed the heart, it had not pierced that most vital of the vampire's organs. With a mighty tug, Jander pulled the shaft free. His golden coloration returned in a rush, and his features took on their normal shape—save that the gentleness was gone from his face.

The Shark scrambled for the ladder, Jander in furious pursuit. She could not defeat him here, not now, and was intent on leaving with her skin intact. Behind her, she heard a savage growl and knew he had taken wolf form. She let go of the rungs and dropped the rest of the way down to the first floor, but not before sharp teeth clicked shut mere inches from her fingers.

She hit the ground running. Shoving her left hand into one of the pouches on her belt, she felt the gooey combination of bat guano and sulphur. "Twelve feet ahead, three feet high!" she commanded, then pointed her right index finger at the far wall of the cottage.

A small ball of fire appeared at her fingertip, growing in size as it hurtled toward the wall. It exploded on contact, igniting many of Jander's beautiful carvings. Sunlight streamed into the cottage, and the Shark dived headfirst through the opening.

Despite the cushion of snow, she landed hard, and the wind was knocked out of her. For a wild instant, she wondered if this vampire, in addition to being active during the day, was also immune to sunlight. But Jander did not follow her.

The Shark rolled over, gasping for breath. At last she stumbled to her feet and peered in through the hole in the wall. He was nowhere to be seen, of course; he was hiding from the burning light. She was glad now that she had taken the time last night to plan for just such trouble.

"Vampire," she called. Silence. "Vampire! I know you can

hear me!"

"I hear you." The same voice as last night, melodious, but this time laced with pain and anger. The sound gave her pleasure. He had surprised her up in the loft. Now, she had a surprise for him.

"I have Maia."

Silence. Then, "You lie."

"I followed you both from the inn last night, then I went back and got her."

A low groan was her reward, and her pleasure grew.

"Don't hurt her. . . . Please. She's innocent. She doesn't know anything about me. I'm the one you want!" The sounds of movement came from within. "I'll . . . I'll come out."

Alarms sounded in her head. "No!" she cried with more emotion than she had intended. She'd fallen for that trick before, let a vampire volunteer to die in the sunlight, only to discover that the blooder was also a mage who could cast a sphere of darkness about them both. Unconsciously, her hand went to her throat, touched the healed scar there. She'd been bitten, but she'd won—and had learned a lesson about the treacherous nature of vampires.

But if this blooder were acting, he was quite the thespian. The Shark heard real pain in his voice. "Why would you want to do that?" she asked. "What is Maia that you would surrender yourself?" She wanted to hear his answer, but she kept alert for any attack.

From inside, Jander said softly, "She's lovely, and I appreciate beauty."

The Shark snorted. "So you were simply admiring her beauty last night in her room."

A pause, then: "She is untouched. I visit her each night. I'm teaching her how to read."

"Untouched is hardly the term I'd use to describe a two-copper whore, and as for reading—"

"What she did to survive does not concern me." Anger thrummed in the rich voice. "What she is now, and what she might be, is what I care about. She is eager to learn. I want to help."

"You want to help, not kill, is that right?"

"Someone once gave me a chance to atone for my past. How can I not do the same for Maia?"

The Shark couldn't help it. Her amusement grew until she actually laughed aloud. He couldn't possibly expect her to believe such a wildly preposterous story. "You are most entertaining, Master Elf. But I remain unconvinced. If you truly wish to insure Maia a pleasant future, you'll follow through on your offer. My terms are simple: your unlife for her true life. Meet me tonight, at the monument in the City of the Dead. If you don't show up—well, the slut means nothing to me."

Another pause. "Most who hunt the *nosferatu* are holy people. You are not, Shakira Khazaar. Had you been, I would have rejoiced that you had found me, and I would have known why I was hunted. You have asked questions of me, now I ask you: Why would you use an innocent like Maia so? Why do you wish to kill me when I have done no one in this city harm?"

The Shark was taken aback by the unexpected query. No one had ever asked her this before. She killed because that was what she did. She'd done it all her life—first in self-defense, then for money as a hired assassin. When the pleasure of taking human life paled, she'd turned to stalking the undead. Blooders were a challenge, and everyone wanted them destroyed. She was no longer the thief Shakira, afraid and alone. Neither was she a nameless assassin, who hunted and hid in shadows. She had transformed herself into the Shark, who always caught her prey, whose prowess in the fine art of killing was sought after and widely praised. But these reasons did not come to her lips now. Instead she spat venomously, "Because Captain Rhynn Oriandis wants you destroyed, you gods-rotted bloodsucker."

Jander's soft gasp made the Shark's hatred-blackened heart skip a beat. *The fool believes me!* Her face contorted in a grimace that she thought was a smile as she left the vampire alone to agonize until nightfall.

*   *   *   *   *

For a place of death, the City of the Dead was very popular with the living. Many generations and many classes of Waterdhavians crumbled to dust side-by-side in pauper's graves and gorgeously carved mausoleums: warriors, sea captains, merchants, commoners. The struggles they had with one another in life ceased to matter as, united in their mortality, they slept the final sleep. Waving grass, shady trees, and beautiful statues lent the place an aura of tranquility. During the day, this little "city" was a peaceful haven for visitors. Night, however, brought a different class of people to the cemetery—those who conducted business best transacted under the vague light of the moon and stars, business handled by people who did not want witnesses.

The centerpiece of the City was a giant monument erected only a few years past. Designed to pay tribute to the original settlers of Waterdeep, the statue was a gorgeous work of art. Dozens of individual stone carvings, depicting life-sized warriors battling with all manner of nonhuman adversaries, comprised the sixty-foot high monument. Wide at the base, it narrowed with each level until a lone hero stood atop the fray. Frozen forever at the moment of greatest action, orcs speared their adversaries, doughty swordsmen slew bugbears, and heroes and monsters alike died in a variety of dramatic poses.

Here the vampire had met Maia several months ago, plying her unsavory trade. Here he hoped to see her again tonight.

Jander came in elven form, walking, but leaving no footprints. He stopped as he neared the monument. A pale white ring encircled the grand statue, and the pungent scent of garlic filled the cold night air. There came a sound of muffled sobbing, and he glanced upward. With deliberate irony, the Shark had tied the barmaid to a conquering stonework hero, who stood atop the mountain of fighters, arms raised in victory. The girl was lashed securely with rope at hands and feet. A piece of cloth shoved in her mouth stifled words, but not her sounds of fear.

Jander walked slowly around the ring of garlic until he came to a two-foot wide gap in the otherwise unbreachable barrier. He hesitated only an instant before stepping into the circle. It was obviously a trap, but what choice did he have?

At the base of the monument Jander cried out and fell. His foot had been caught in a cleverly concealed, sharp-jawed animal trap made of wood, not steel. And when he hit the ground, a second trap clamped on one of his hands. Holy water soaked the traps' jagged teeth. Steam and blood hissed from the vampire's wounds, glittering black in the moonlight.

With his good hand, Jander splintered the wood that bit into ankle and wrist. On his feet at once, he glanced around, clearly expecting a second attack. None came.

He moved toward the statue more cautiously now, his eyes on the snow in front of him rather than the monument itself. There were several more concealed traps waiting to close upon him. Treading delicately, he avoided them.

"I'm here, Maia," he called. "You're safe now."

The stone figure in front of him was a warrior woman with a single braid of long hair. He reached out to it, prepared to begin the climb up to Maia. But the statue smiled and sprang to life. The illusion shed, the Shark drew a small crossbow and fired a wooden shaft directly at Jander's chest. She was no more than two yards away.

Jander grunted at the impact, but the shaft bounced off his body and fell to the grass.

The Shark gasped. The vampire smiled and tapped his chest with a golden forefinger. It clinked; too late, the Shark recalled the chain mail shirt she had seen in Jander's cottage. She pulled down her hood, safely invisible, and jumped aside. The vampire's hand closed on her cloak, but she yanked it out of his grasp and began to run.

Jander followed without pause.

It took the Shark a moment to realize the blooder didn't need to see her to follow her churning tracks in the snow. At once she leapt straight up, seized the mighty arm of a stone orc, and hauled herself atop it. She scrambled to the left, balanced precariously on a helmeted head and a stone shoulder, then paused, holding her breath.

For a time, the golden vampire stood still as a statue himself, gazing about, as if he could penetrate the magic that concealed her by sheer force of will. His gaze traveled over and past her. Then Jander turned and began to climb.

When he had gotten halfway up the monument, the Shark lowered herself to the ground as quietly as she could. She readjusted the hood of her cape, making sure it would not slip off as she moved. She hoped she could complete her task before the vampire noticed her telltale footprints.

Hastening to the circle of garlic, she closed the opening with the remainder of the bulbs she had with her. He now had no escape—he couldn't even fly over the ring. She returned to the statue and followed the vampire up.

His movements were swift and sure, but not unnaturally so. Jander was taking great care not to reveal his true nature to Maia. Thus far, his deception was to the Shark's advantage. She followed at her own brisk pace, climbing up the battling warriors as easily as if they were limbs of a particularly gnarled tree.

He had reached the top now. There was silence, and the Shark knew that the blooder was staring at the holy symbols she'd draped across Maia's body. Carefully, quietly, the hunter continued to climb, listening all the while.

"Lathander, protect me!" came Maia's fear-shrill voice as Jander pulled the gag from her mouth. "Don't kill me! Please! She—she told me what you are. I'll do whatever you want, but, please, don't kill me!"

Stunned silence. The Shark pulled herself up over a dying archer, awaiting the blooder's response with malicious glee. "No, Maia," came Jander's voice, filled with an ancient weariness. "I won't kill you. I just—here, let me set you free."

The Shark was able to see him now. Safely invisible, she watched, tense, as Jander moved to untie the hands of the still-hysterical young girl. He successfully freed her hands and knelt to work at the knots that bound her ankles. Light exploded from the small pink medallion hidden in the folds of Maia's skirts. The Shark's spell had worked beautifully.

The vampire flung his arms up to shield his eyes, stumbled, and hurtled off the monument. The Shark hastened forward. One hand gripping a dying troll, the hunter watched Jander's fall. His body shimmered, recasting itself into a small brown bat. He began to fly back up to the top.

Behind her, the Shark heard Maia sob as she worked loose the knots. Then, whimpering, the barmaid started the climb down from the monument. The Shark ignored her; Maia had served her purpose.

Instead, the hunter kept her attention focused on the vampire. Leaning out precariously over the raised stone swords and braced javelins that pointed up from below, she clung to the troll statue and withdrew a small pouch from her pocket. Grains of wheat fell in a shower over the bat. This was the Shark's favorite trick to play on a vampire in bat form. The grain would confuse the vermin's senses, making it fly wildly. And that would give the Shark a chance to prepare another, more deadly attack.

But Jander did not veer off. The little bat flitted crazily for a moment, then continued moving directly for the Shark's face. No cloak of invisibility could protect her from the heightened senses provided to the vampire in his bat form. She could see the vermin's tiny, sharp-toothed jaws opening as it approached her eyes.

Startled, the Shark ducked. Her foot slipped from the snow-slicked perch, and she dropped toward the upturned stone javelins below. She did not cry out, merely grunted when her death plummet was abruptly cut short. A spear wielded by a bugbear had snagged her cloak. Her throat was bruised from the sudden tug, but she was alive.

The Shark hung, dangling, swinging slightly back and forth. Her mind raced, and she cursed herself. She'd prepared no spells for this eventuality—no floating, flying, or transformational magic. Grunting with the effort, she reached up, trying to grab the stone spear that held her suspended. She could not reach it. She then stretched to the right as far as she could in hopes of seizing the ugly, porcine face of an orc beating down a hapless stone hero. She grasped only empty air.

More frightened than she had been in decades, the Shark craned her neck to look upward.

The blooder was an elven silhouette against the star-filled sky as he bent to look at her. Then, slowly, he moved. One arm reached down.

Crying incoherently, the Shark twisted away. Her cloak tore a little, and she dropped four inches. At least the vampire was too far above her to reach her—but, ah gods, he could crawl. . . .

"Give me your hand."

For a moment, she couldn't comprehend the words, so unexpected were they. Jander stretched his hand farther. "Give me your hand. I can't quite reach you!"

The cloak ripped again. The Shark stared down at the next tier of battling warriors and their pointed stone weapons. It was at least a twenty-foot drop.

"I'm coming, Shakira. Hold on." And indeed, the golden vampire began to climb, headfirst, down to reach her.

She suddenly knew, knew with a deep, inner certainty, that Jander Sunstar was not coming to kill her. He was coming to save her life, to pull her back to safety. She, the Shark, the woman who had spent her life perfecting the art of murder, had finally failed to kill. And having failed, she would owe her life to the creature she had sought to destroy. If his forgiving hands closed on her, she would never be able to lift a weapon again. She would cease to be the Shark.

She didn't even have to think. Reaching up, she twined both hands in the cloak. "The Shark sends you to the Nine Hells," she said aloud, but this time the words were intended for her own ears.

As the vampire's fingers reached out to her, the Shark smiled like the predator she was, spat at his despairing, beautiful face, and tore the cloak free.

GALLOWS DAY

David Cook

They did not look like the most dangerous of thieves. Desperate perhaps, as they sat at a wobbly table covered with half-filled tankards that clung to the wood in sticky pools of spilled drink. Drunk, too. It was barely midmorning, but already the four thieves had drained two skins of hosteler Gurin's cheapest ale, and they showed no inclination to stop.

Of course, their crimes didn't shine in their drunken faces. Nobody could look at the little one and know he was the man who'd poisoned all the pets in Lord Brion's kennel just to silence the guard dogs. Slouched over her drink, the woman hardly looked the type to spell-torch a jeweler's shop to cover her escape, nor the old man across from her the kind to settle a turf fight with a quick knife thrust on a rooftop. At Gurin's they looked like any other collection of sorry drunks.

They weren't the only ones in the alehouse. It was crowded enough with other drinkers who shared their desperate looks. The four of them huddled at a poor table near the back. In their dark corner, past the stalls and benches that made the small tavern all the more crowded, they drank and talked, their voices low out of habit. No one paid them any mind—Gurin's alehouse was for serious drinking. With its dirt floor and rickety furniture, there was no other reason to be there.

"Pour me more," demanded Sprite-Heels, a halfling and the smallest of the four. Leaning back in the big chair, the impish fellow could only waggle his furry feet impatiently above the floor. His childlike face soured with annoyance that his cup was drained.

"Yer cup's all yer caring for," grumbled the thin old man astraddle the chair beside the halfling. This one was skull-bald and pockmarked, lending the taint of walking death to his already frightening looks. "It's Therin's last day on earth. Can't you care about 'im more than yer drink?" Nonetheless, the ancient hefted a skin and poured the halfling a drink—and one for himself.

"Better him to the leafless tree than me, Corrick," the halfling mocked as he cracked open a walnut and picked out the meat.

"Sprite, you're a horrible creature," sniffed the woman who sat on the halfling's left. She was no more sober than the rest. She might have been striking once. Now she was just hard-used. Her face was mapped by fine red veins from too many late nights and too much drink, her brown hair a disheveled cascade that tumbled down over her ample bosom. "My poor Therin, waiting to be hanged—"

"Yer poor Therin!" snorted Corrick, blowing ale-foam from his lips. "Before 'im it was yer poor Emersar, then it was that barbarian oaf—"

"Xarcas weren't no oaf! He would've been a grand one for the highwayman's law. He could ride and use a sword more than you ever could, you poxy nip," the woman snapped back. Her fingers wove patterns on the table that the other two did not notice. "Xarcas would've been a terror to coach-men on the Berdusk Road."

"If he hadn't boozed himself to death on Gurin's cheap bub," the halfling slipped in with a snigger. "You do pick them, Maeve."

The woman shook with drunken fury. With an over-grand sweep, she raised her arms archly, a pinch of wax and a bit of feather between her fingertips. "Let's see how you two like being—"

"Stow you, Brown Maeve. There'll be no sorcery here." The fourth drinker at the table finally broke his peace, his voice iron calm and cold. Dark eyes watched the woman over the lip of a raised mug. They glittered with confidence, knowing she would not defy him. They were dark eyes that mirrored the gray streaking in his curly, black hair. Though he'd been drinking, the man's gaze was as clear as a card-sharper's during the deal.

At a distance he appeared not tall, not short, neither dark nor fair. He was a plain man, and there was always one like him in every crowd. Only his clothes were distinctive—linen, thick velvet, and rare leathers. In another alehouse, onlookers might believe he was a fop about to be gulled by the other three. Here in Gurin's ale shop, as out of place as he might seem, folks knew better. He was Pinch, wild rogue and upright man. He'd come to Gurin's to drink a wake, for it was his man that was due to be hanged today.

"No spells, no trouble, Maeve." The words carried in them the expectation of obedience.

Maeve pulled short as soon as Pinch spoke. For a moment she drunkenly challenged his gaze—but for only a moment. It might have been the faint frown on his lips that discouraged her, reminding her of the boundless limits of his revenge. Whatever the cause, Maeve reluctantly lowered her arms.

"It ain't right, Pinch," she slurred as she fumbled self-consciously with her mug. "It's gallows day. They got no cause talking like that, not today." The wizardress peered venomously at the pair who had roused her ire.

"Course not, Maeve," Pinch agreed smoothly, playing her like a sharper's mark. "Corrick, Sprite—let her be." Only after he spoke did the thief turn his gaze to the others. Old Corrick twisted uncomfortably under Pinch's hard gaze while Sprite casually took an interest in the nutshells on the table.

"Just a little sport, that's all—to take our minds off the

day's gloom," the halfling offered as his drink-clouded countenance transformed into one of childlike innocence.

Pinch poured himself another mugful of ale and scowled at the halfling. The little fellow's smile might work well on the conies he cheated, but it didn't soften him one bit. "No more of it. Maeve's got the sense of things. It's not right to go mocking Therin's hanging." He drained the draught in a single long pull, all the while keeping his dark eyes on the other two.

"It's not like we haven't seen folks swing, Pinch. Even of our own." Sprite leaned forward to prop his chin on the edge of the table. With a small dagger that seemed to come from nowhere, he began to play an idle pass at mumblety-peg on the tabletop. "Besides a hanging's always good for trade. Draws a nice crowd. We should be striking the gawkers while they still got their purses full."

"We should be leaving town, that's what we should be doing, not sitting 'ere boozing," Corrick growled. "Therin's still got time to turn on us all."

Pinch raised a sharp eyebrow at that. Therin had been his choice as lieutenant. With a snake's speed, the master thief shot out a hand, seized Corrick by a ragged collar, and jerked the old man closer, till their faces were practically cheek to cheek. "Tell me, Gran'," he hissed, "who's the upright man here, you or me?" Even as Pinch asked, one hand slipped to the dagger in his boot.

Ancient Corrick wormed in the grasp, his eyes flickering in panic as he saw the black-haired rogue's hand move south. "You be, Pinch. No one else," he gasped in breathless sincerity.

"That be so?" Pinch mocked as he let Corrick's dirty shirt slip from his fingers. The ancient slid his chair away from the master thief's side of the table. His own hand started to drift toward the sheath knife at his side.

"Here now—Pinch, Corrick—your cups are empty," Sprite-Heels offered eagerly. He hopped up on his chair, dragged their tankards to the center of the table, and sloshed the last ale from the serving skin until both cups were filled to the brim. "To Therin's memory," he toasted, his own mug held aloft.

Neither Pinch nor Corrick moved, eyes locked on each other.

"To poor, dear Therin," Brown Maeve nervously added, clinking her mug to Sprite's.

The master thief's expression shifted into a thin smile as he lifted the mug set out for him. He held the cup there till Corrick followed suit. Still their eyes watched each other, ignoring the other two at the table. "To Therin—would all my children be so true," the master rogue offered. He tapped his mug to Sprite's and Maeve's.

"To Therin—may 'is tongue stay still." With that toast Corrick broke away from his leader's gaze. The mugs clinked once more, and Sprite muttered a benedictus for them all under his breath.

Pinch leaned back and unkinked his stiff leg, the reward of a bad tumble while on a roof-breaking job. "Therin's kept his peace till now. He'll keep his trap shut till the end," was the master thief's confident prediction.

Composure already regained, Corrick shook his bony head, once again sputtering off the golden foam of drink. "Knowing the 'igh lord's permanently canceled yer debts got a way of changing a man," he counterpredicted.

"I trust Therin," Pinch replied breezily, as if his previous displeasure were all forgotten.

"I still wish the Hellriders hadn't taken him," Maeve pined. "He was a good man to me. We was fixing to do up the town that night. Why, I barely shimmied down the back when they broke in the door."

"You should get yourself a crib on the first floor," Sprite jibed as he clambered back into his seat. "Still it was damned quick, the way they found him right after the Firdul job."

"Aye, it was," Pinch agreed. "If they hadn't caught him with the garbage, I could've gotten someone to swear in court that Therin had been out boozing with them when old Firdul was robbed." His words dropped to a weary mutter. "It was too quick, though. Damned queer."

DAVID COOK

The rasp of the tavern door opening interrupted the master thief's ruminations. From the front of the taproom there was a hubbub of voices raised in alarmed surprise.

"Hellriders!"

Pinch, who always sat with his back to the corner, was the first to see the soldiers come through the door, and he quickly gave a nod of caution to the others.

There were six of them, dressed in the unmistakable leather armor of the lord's men. The metal studs that pierced the red leather glittered with brilliant polish. Their scimitars clinked against the steel points as the troop swaggered in. They went from table to booth, brusquely grabbing each customer for a hard scrutiny. Pinch recognized in their midst the stocky build of Troop Commander Wilmarq, an arrogant bastard of an officer. Wilmarq made a business of extorting money from fellows like Pinch, only to arrest them whenever there was a chance for a promotion. His only grace was his greed. Pinch barely held back his wince, knowing the borsholder was probably looking for them.

"Stow all your bilge and drink sad. We're mourning Therin, clear?" Pinch hissed to the others as he snatched up his mug and put it to his lips.

"Here's to poor Therin," Sprite, always quick to follow his master's lead, said loudly.

"May he have a clean drop," Pinch added, seconding another round of toasts. He purposely turned away from the approaching guardsmen.

Before the toast could be downed, a gloved hand clapped hard on the lead rogue's shoulder. "Master Pinch," sliced the nasal voice of Wilmarq. "Not at the hanging? I was certain you'd be there." The officer casually took the wineskin from the table. "You're dry," he said sadly, shaking the empty sack. "More drink, innkeep, and mugs for my men. I'm sure our friend can pay."

As Gurin hurried over, Pinch shrugged the hand off his shoulder and turned his chair to face Wilmarq. "It's a sad day for some of us, Hellrider." His words were a monotone.

"Losing one of your gang is always a cause for sorrow,

eh?" Wilmarq sneered as he held his tankard out for the hostler to fill. "Seems like a good day to me."

"Do you have business with us?" Pinch demanded. "If not, you're making the place smell like an unclean stable."

Wilmarq reddened and his nasal voice reached a higher whine. "I could arrest you for that lifting job on Crossmarket Lane last night! Some pretty parcels went missing."

"And I'd stand before the court with a score of witnesses swearing I was here last night, boozed in my sorrow," Pinch countered. "Go ahead, make yourself the fool, Wilmarq. Maybe they snipped your wits, too, when they made you a horse-loving eunuch."

"Horse-loving eu—? Damn you, you poxy bastard!" the Hellrider blustered. The officer's body trembled so violently that the metal studs of his armor clattered out his rage. Behind him, his men grinned at their commander's humiliation. "I got your Therin, and I'll get the lot of you yet!" Wilmarq finally snarled.

With a polished boot, he kicked the leg of Pinch's chair, snapping the flimsy wood. The thief sprang from his seat just before it clattered to the floor. He landed in a half-crouch, fingers trembling eagerly to hold a blade. At another time Pinch would have gutted the Hellrider without a thought. With the officer backed by his men, now was not that time. The drunken crowd was suddenly alive as bleary eyes watched the confrontation. Hands reached for heavy mugs, blades scraped softly from scabbards, and Gurin suddenly became interested in putting away his battered plate. The troopers backing Wilmarq stiffened.

Pinch calmly straightened as the situation's tenor became clear to all but Wilmarq. "Some counsel, Commander," the thief finally offered. "Never hit a man in his own house." Only then did the Hellrider see what his men had noted—little Sprite-Heels fondling his dagger as he crouched beneath the table, Maeve idly tracing out a mystic rune on the damp wood, even Corrick warming a dirk in the candle-flame.

Wilmarq sneered, wheeled about, and pushed through his men as they backed their way toward the door. " 'Lo, they bravely rode into battle,'" caterwauled a lusty voice in the crowd, singing the opening verse of a popular song. The shoddy tavern shuddered with the howl of laughter that rose from the crowd, a humor that only the Hellriders did not share. Within moments a hodge-podge chorus played the bard to serenade the fleeing patrol.

"Thank your gods for making Wilmarq an ass," Pinch chortled as he pulled up another chair.

Corrick looked up from wiping the soot off his blade and fixed a glaring eye on his boss. "Maybe, but 'e caught Therin on the double-quick."

"And word is Wilmarq'll get promoted for it," Sprite added as he scrambled out from under table. "Maybe Therin was good for something, after all."

"It ain't right," Maeve moaned as she plopped drunkenly into her chair. She made a clumsy kick at Sprite. "He gets a promotion and Therin hangs. It ain't right!"

"Not right indeed—tracking him down to your own house, Maeve," Pinch mused as he leaned back in the chair. His fingers flexed just under his chin. Sprite, Corrick, and Maeve waited and watched, knowing their leader's scheming moods.

Suddenly Pinch's thoughtful visage brightened. "Two with one stone. That's it! Two with one stone." He sat forward and pulled the others in close. "We're going to humiliate Wilmarq by springing Therin from the very branches of the triple tree."

"Off the gallows?" gulped Sprite, sputtering his ale.

"Yer mad!" Corrick bellowed.

Only Maeve kept silent, fuzzily pondering the possibilities.

Pinch ignored the protests. "Sprite, the old catacombs—they run under Shiarra's Market, don't they?" His eyes glittered with devious fire.

"Yes," Sprite answered warily, "but not close to the gallows."

"Yer mad. I'm not risking the rope for that fool Therin—especially on one of yer mad schemes." Corrick heaved back from the huddle, shaking his bare head.

Before the old cutpurse could stand, Pinch laid a hand on his arm and squeezed right down to the bone. "You'll do it because I tell you to, Corrick, or I'll see you're the next one to stand before the hangman's crowd. Maybe it'd get me in good with Wilmarq to give you up to him. Understand?"

Corrick's gaunt face went pale. The old man nodded.

"Good," Pinch purred without loosing his grip. "Corrick, you'll borrow us a wagon with a fast team. Sprite, figure how to get us as close to Therin as you can." The halfling raised a bushy eyebrow in acknowledgement.

"That's set," Pinch concluded, releasing Corrick's arm. "To your duties, lads. I'll be meeting with Therin, just to be sure he knows where his friends stand." The upright man gave Corrick a hearty pat on the shoulder. "We can't have him break before we spring him. Go to your tasks. We'll meet where Dragoneye Lane joins Shiarra's Market an hour before the hanging."

The speed and certainty of Pinch's resolve left the pair dazed. "Get going," he had to repeat before they actually stirred. "And, Sprite, mind your wandering fingers for now. I don't want you caught before the hanging."

The halfling's expression moved from dazed to disappointed. "All those purses, and I can't touch them. It was the only good to come out of this whole hanging," he muttered as he slid from his chair and made for the door. Corrick rose, eyes filled with dark misgivings, and followed the halfling. He rubbed the filthy wool of his jerkin, getting the blood back into the arm Pinch had squeezed.

"What about me, dearie?" Maeve asked. "What you got for me?"

The master thief cast a look toward the door before speaking, making sure his accomplices were on their way. When it was closed fast, Pinch turned back to the woman beside him. "Now, Maeve—good Maeve—you said it was queer how poor Therin was bagged."

"I said it weren't right, Pinch, that's what I said."

Pinch poured her a drink from the skin Wilmarq had ordered. "And it was, Maeve. It was *unnatural* the way they came to your place. You spoke true; it weren't right. The whole thing's no better than a forger's will, I think." He pushed the mug in front of the doxy. "Tell me, Maeve, you know how long it takes a man to hang?"

* * * * *

The towering three-story stone edifice known as the High Prison was one of Elturel's lesser known oddities. No other city of her size could boast such a magnificent structure for the incarceration of the criminal classes. Elturel's Lord Dhelt, in a fit of enlightenment, had the place built "for the reformation of those godless wretches held within." There, prisoners once kept in the dank cellars of the High Hall and the nobles' palaces could be treated as humanely as they deserved. That was the intent anyway.

Pinch didn't care what the high rider's stated purpose was. The High Prison was just another part of his life, like the thin drizzle blowing in from the River Chionthar. The thief pulled up his cloak to keep the mist from forming cold beads on the back of his neck while he waited outside the prison. Finally the latches rattled and the gate yawned open with a creaking moan. The hinges on the old wooden door always needed oiling, perhaps so their harsh rasp would inspire a little more terror in those about to enter. It would be sensible to think that a thief, especially a thief who'd spent time behind the prison's walls, would feel a shiver of dread as he stood on that portal. If Pinch was uncomfortable, he showed not a sign of it.

"Good morn, Dowzabell," the thief greeted the turnkey who opened the door. "How is your trade these days?"

"Not so good as when you paid me for a room in the Master's Side," Dowzabell groused. He was a stooped-shouldered ox of a man and blind in one eye to boot. He'd been jailed himself fifteen years ago for his bad debts. Now he was the turnkey and all but ran the prison, collecting "fees" from the prisoners to keep them from the worst cells the place had to offer. His profits were usually good. "I suppose you're here to see Therin off, Master Pinch?"

"A kind word for his last day," the thief said as he stepped inside, pressing a coin into the turnkey's open hand. "Here's a flag for you. Now lead on."

Dowzabell didn't move until he'd inspected Pinch's silver, holding it up to his one good eye to make sure it wasn't the work of some false coiner. Finally he stuffed it into his breeches and shuffled through the anterooms and down the hall.

The way did not take them to the rooms of the Master's Side, where a prisoner could have a suite that included a bath and servants, or to the Knight's Side, which was barely less well appointed. Therin, who'd never been close with his money, couldn't afford either, though he had at least enough to pay for one of the better cells on the Common Side.

They finally stopped at a row of wooden doors lining a hall strewn with matted straw. In a far alcove stood a small dusty altar. A robed priest sitting at a battered table next to it looked up with interest as they entered, then continued his prayers for the condemned. The words were a soft drone, said without much conviction, and the priest kept peering Pinch's way. After a few tendays of unrelenting boredom, any diversion came as a welcome break.

Pinch waited while the trustee fumbled for the key that unlocked one of the cell doors. "Visitor, Therin. Make sure you're dressed," he shouted through the thick wooden door. Jiggling the passkey in the lock, the trustee kept talking. "Therin's not living as well as you did, sir, when you stayed here. I mean, the Commons is a far cry from the Master's Side. I thought he was your friend." Dowzabell's comment was stated with some puzzlement.

The great tumblers in the lock clanked as the key turned. "No point wasting money on a hanged man," Pinch coolly answered. As he spoke, the trustee drew the bolt back and pushed the door open. The odor was thick with the smell of the cesspits, so much so that Pinch covered his face with a sweet-scented handkerchief.

Therin sat on the hard bed at the back of his cell. The only light in the chamber came from a small, barred window high on the wall. Thick gloom cloaked the prisoner, half-hiding his big, farmhand's body. With his broad shoulders and gangly arms, Therin hardly looked the thief, but Pinch had found his size more than useful for keeping the others of his gang in line.

"Master Pinch!" Therin breathed in surprise as the graying thief entered the small, untidy cell. The prisoner sprang up and brushed the mattress clean. Little black specks hopped out of the ticking at the sweep of his hand. "Please sit, sir!"

Pinch ignored the offer and pressed three gold coins into Dowzabell's hand. "Go join the priest for a round of prayers. I want to be alone with him. Understand?" The trustee looked at the money in his fat hand, then silently closed the door. Pinch could hear the bolts and locks rattling into place.

"Lad," Pinch started, at no loss for words, even to a doomed man, "I'm—"

"Have the magistrates found some cause for my plea? Have they stayed the execution?" Therin blurted, asking with the overeagerness of a man who knows his chances are already lost.

"No. You're to be dropped on the gallows this afternoon, Therin," Pinch stated baldly through the lace he pressed over his nose.

"Did you try challenging the writ?" the other asked helplessly.

"It's all done for. You saw it. The writ was proper." The master thief lowered his napkin to see if he'd acclimated to the stench yet. With the first breath his nostrils curled, and he had to fight back a wave of repugnance; it passed quickly. Stuffing the kerchief away he looked deep into Therin's pleading eyes. Pinch disliked the man's desperation.

"Listen well, Therin. You were nabbed with the garbage in your hands. There wasn't a witness to be had who could stand by you for that. You're going to hang."

Therin sagged onto his cot, head clasped in his hands. He moaned to the floor, "I could still give somebody up. They might pardon me for—"

"Stow that noise if you want to live!" Pinch snapped. He seized the condemned man by the chin and pulled his face up till their eyes met. "You've done us rightly till now and you'll not turn stag. Keep your silence and you might not hang—understand?"

Therin's eyes grew wide with hope and amazement. "You've bought me free of here?" An eager hand clutched at Pinch's velvet sleeve.

"Something like," Pinch lied. "You've stood us true till now, and I've not forgotten it." Pinch knelt beside the other so their voices could be hushed. "I've got a plan."

With those words, Therin shoulders eased with relief. He knew that when his master plotted, nothing was impossible. "What's my part in it?"

"Too little and maybe too much," Pinch said mysteriously. "When they cart you through the streets, give them a couple of good sermons on your sins. I'll need the time."

"Look upon me, citizens, and learn! Dishonestly I have lived my life and this is my reward!" Therin solemnly pronounced as he rose to his feet in a pose of mock piety. "How's that?"

"Good enough," Pinch allowed. "Just remember, no matter what happens after that, or how bad it may seem, don't lose your nerve."

Therin sat back to huddle by his chief. "I won't. I been true up to now, ain't I?"

"Well and true, well and true." With his bad leg protesting at kneeling so long, Pinch had to surrender to the fleas and sit beside his companion. His eyes were distant as he mulled over a puzzle no one else could see. "Tell me, Therin," he finally broached, "tell me again how you got taken."

The prisoner snorted at the curious request. "I don't know why. You've heard it before."

Pinch said nothing, but waited for Therin to get on with it. When the condemned man finally realized Pinch was serious, he struggled to remember. His brow knitting from the effort to recall the facts, he began:

"I'd just done a bit of the lifting over on Stillcreek Lane, the Firdul job we'd plotted. I was the lift. Corrick was the marker. I'd snagged some pretty pieces of plate from the silversmith, so I went over to Maeve's to show her the garbage. Just about as soon as I get there, the constables raise the hue and cry. Before I can make for the broker, the Hellriders come bursting in."

"Where was Corrick?"

"We was to meet at Gurin's to split the purchase and do some boozing."

The farmhand-turned-thief waited for more questions, but his chief suddenly seemed to lose interest in the tale.

"Like Maeve said, it weren't right," Pinch finally murmured as he set the kerchief back to his nose.

"You thinking somebody gave me up? Corrick?"

"Maybe, just maybe."

"What're you going to do to him?" Therin asked eagerly, a dead man looking for revenge.

"Right now, nothing. I've got him stealing a cart and team." Pinch smiled at the irony of it. "That much he'll do."

Their musings were interrupted by the rattling of the lock. "Your time's over, Master Pinch," echoed Dowzabell's voice from the other side of the door. "The patrico's here to take your man's prayers."

"To your plans, Pinch," Therin offered in empty toast.

"Bar your talk, Dowzabell's coming."

The door swung open and the trustee entered. Behind him followed the thin, robed priest, a chapbook of prayers clutched in his pious hands. "He's yours, Patrico, though I wouldn't expect much repentance from him." The priest shot Dowzabell a sour look before the door closed between them.

Dowzabell led Pinch back to the gate in silence, but along the way the trustee seemed unusually watchful for eavesdroppers. The thief knew the old turnkey's ways. The man had eyes and ears everywhere, and a mind for profit. It was clear he had something to sell, if Pinch would meet his price.

When Dowzabell turned back from unbarring the gate, he found a gold noble sitting on the bench by the entrance.

Though his greedy eyes widened a little, the trustee pocketed the coin as if it were a copper penny. He motioned Pinch toward a quiet alcove.

"What I know's worth more," the turnkey promised as they huddled in the shadows. "In advance." Dowzabell held out his hand.

"I'll judge," was Pinch's cool reply as he fingered another coin under the trustee's nose.

Dowzabell scowled. "Your man was turned."

"Not even worth the coin I gave you. I knew."

"But you don't know who. Wilmarq was drunk and bragging about it in a tavern a few nights ago. I heard it from his men."

"So who'd they say it was this time, Sprite or Corrick?" Pinch lied glibly.

Dowzabell's jaw sagged like a limp sail. "Corrick," the trustee mumbled.

With a contemptuous laugh, the thief stuffed the second coin down the man's shirt. "You were always too greedy, Dowzabell. Someday it'll catch up with you."

The trustee closed the gate as Pinch strode into the growing rain, his mind already turning on the interlocking wheels of plots within schemes.

* * * * *

The streets to Shiarra's Market were never hard to follow, but today a blind foreigner could have found the square. A hanging was as good as a holiday in Elturel. The better part of the city turned out for the event, so many folk that the tide of traffic flowed only one way. While passing through the rain-slicked streets, Pinch was offered "The True and Tragic Life of Therin Jack-a-Knaves as Confirmed by this Gentleman," by three different pamphleteers, all for only a few coins. Judging from the covers thrust under his nose, each work was different from the others. They were, if not completely false, highly exaggerated, for in each Therin was the master of a whole gang. Pinch wondered just what lies would be written about him the day he was finally scragged on the leafless tree.

By the time he reached the square, it was already packed with eager onlookers. Most of the town's apprentices had contrived to escape their masters and come for the hanging. Their masters were probably here, too, blissfully believing their apprentices were minding their shops. An enterprising bard had got himself onto a roof that overlooked the square and was serenading his captive audience while a shill worked the crowd for money. Pinch resisted the urge to palm a coin out of the hat when the boy came by, but he took careful note of the musician overhead. The bard would have money later tonight and just might be worth tracking down.

Reluctantly the upright man stowed thoughts of other business and worked his way round to Dragoneye Lane. He was on edge. The plan was at stake. If Corrick or Sprite failed him now, everything would come to naught. Pinch was less worried about Corrick's part in things. He guessed the old cutpurse would play at being loyal just to avoid discovery. Sprite's was another matter, and the rogue could only hope the halfling kept his fingers out of other people's pockets.

The whinnies of a nervous team and the shadow of a wagon told Pinch that at least one of the thieves had come through. He wormed through the crowd and into the alley where Corrick and his wagon waited.

They were all there—Sprite, Corrick, and Brown Maeve. She was soothing the horses, which had been made skittish by the crowd. Pinch slapped her on the rump as he squeezed past. "Keep watch," he ordered before turning to the others. Corrick sat on the seat, reins ready, while Sprite hung over the cart's rail, munching an apple he'd no doubt lifted from a peddler's basket. Sprite never paid for anything that wasn't locked down. "All's done?" Pinch demanded.

Corrick gave a peg-toothed smile and waved to the cart and team. "Best I could get, Pinch," he bragged. The team was actually nothing to brag about—a scrawny pair, spotty with mange, their necks callused with years in the collar. At least the wagon was sound. The back was covered with a patched canvas awning where they could hide. Somewhere, Pinch guessed, there was a rag-and-bone man trying to find his wagon.

"Well, Sprite? The sewers—how close can we get?"

The halfling threw aside his apple core and climbed onto the wagon's seat. He pointed over the heads of the crowd to a shop across the square. "Better'n I thought. See the weaver's? In line with that, maybe a stone toss from the triple tree." At this distance, the weaver's and the gallows were no more than a hand's breadth apart.

"Can you guide us once we're in the tunnels?"

"Marked it out this morning, Pinch."

Pinch suppressed the urge to congratulate himself. The job wasn't done yet. "Well done, boy." The master signaled his accomplices to join him, and join him quick they did. "Maeve, you two, listen wise, 'cause here's the plan.

"We're body collecting. Maeve's already spread it through the crowd that a group of wizards are wanting the body for dissecting." The wizardress mock-curtsied slightly at mention of the part she'd played so far. "That should suit the crowd out there fine. Saves them the fear of anyone resurrecting Therin after he's dead."

Sprite scowled—he'd always been picky about grave-robbing and the like—but Pinch added, "That's just so we can get the wagon close. Then, just before the drop, Maeve'll use her spells to whisk Therin out of the twined hemp. When that happens, Corrick will whip the team into the crowd. We'll all make for Sprite's bolt-hole and be out of here before they know what's happened."

"That's your plan?" Sprite asked incredulously. "I think old Corrick here was right—we should have been huggering this out in another town."

"Well, we're 'ere and there's no point 'uggering now, Sprite," Corrick croaked. "I say we give Pinch 'is due. Don't 'is plans always work?"

"There's no time to waste," Pinch barked. "In the cart, all of you." With easy grace, he swung into the back, then helped the less-agile Maeve alongside. Sprite tumbled in beside them and pulled up a span of canvas to roughly cover them. From the shadowed interior, the three had a narrow view of the still-vacant scaffold.

A roar went up from the crowd as a crier mounted the gallows platform, the writ of execution rolled under his arm. The official swung his bell in a futile attempt to get silence.

"Go, Corrick."

The ancient gave a flick of the reins, and the horses got the cart moving with a rough lurch. The passengers bounced in the back as the wheels rolled down the cobbled street.

A wild cheer, part savage, part joyous, rose from the crowd as the cart entered the square. The roar died down as quick when the mob realized the covered wagon was not the executioner's cart. With a vigorous application of the whip on the horses and the crowd, Corrick was able to force their passage through the pressed throng.

While the bald Corrick was absorbed in driving the team, Pinch leaned forward for a whispered word in the halfling's slightly fuzzy ear. "Sprite, listen close. I need five hundred in nobles. Can you fig it for me quick?"

The small cutpurse's eyes widened at the mere mention of the amount. "Five hundred—now?"

"Or Therin swings. It's the only way."

"Send Therin to the denizens!" Sprite swore under his breath; but Pinch was counting on the halfling's love of the challenge, not his love of Therin. "Five hundred?" Sprite asked again as he scanned the crowd, taking the measure of the gulls. The congregation was teeming with them—fat masters enjoying their mistresses, overworked vendors unmindful of their wallets, drunken craftsmen, even a gentleman with his entourage. "Me and Purse-Nipper can do it," the halfling noted boastfully, palming a small knife from the sheath strapped to his wrist.

"Then go and strike, boy!" Pinch hissed with urgency. At that Sprite sprang lightly from the cart and vanished into the crowd.

A fresh roar went up from the multitude, this time as they correctly sighted the executioner's cart. It was already close to the gallows, having entered the square by a side street so as to avoid the riotous celebrators that awaited it on the main routes. Pinch could see Therin standing tall in the back, cheerfully waving his bound hands to the crowd. The hooded hangman rode next to him, impassive in his duty. His hood was stitched with a crude death's head to remind the condemned man of who shared this ride.

The crowd surged toward the executioner's cart. So eager were they for their entertainment that they almost overturned the vehicle, forcing the hangman to get Therin out of the wagon and onto the platform with unseemly haste.

The rush of the crowd served the thieves too, for it thinned the press ahead of them. Corrick drove the wagon through the gap as fast as the old nags would pull it. As they closed, Maeve passed Pinch an old workshirt she had brought, along with a battered cap and a bloodstained cloak. The clothes quickly covered the thief's fine velvets. After a few adjustments, Pinch, looking like a bloody surgeon's aide, climbed into the seat by Corrick. There was barely time as the wagon lurched to a stop at the base of the gallows.

A squad of Hellriders, their red and silver armor glittering in the sun, formed a wall around the gallows. The twenty or so soldiers held the crowd at bay with a bristling ring of spears. On the inside was a bearded sergeant, exhorting his men to stand ready.

"We be sent to buy the body for our master, Wizard Shildris, so 'e can cut it up," the cloaked Pinch shouted to the sergeant. For that extra touch, he held up a purse, jingling it meaningfully. It was filled with nothing more than coppers, but the sergeant didn't know that. Once again the lies flowed smoothly off Pinch's lips with less hesitation than the truth.

On the platform above, the crier was reading out the death warrant while the hangman fitted the noose. Maeve shifted uneasily, watching Therin's progress, while Corrick kept a grip on the reins.

The sergeant of the command smiled with avarice and nodded to his men to let the wagon pass through their bristling ring. As the cart creaked forward, the small streak of Sprite darted through the throng and hopped onto the wagon's bed. A wink and a nod were all Pinch needed to tell him the halfling had met with success.

At Therin's side, a priest of Tyr was intoning the benedictus for the dead. All that remained was the hood and then the drop when the hangman pulled the trap.

Pinch touched Maeve and cautioned her to be ready. Corrick, Sprite, and Maeve clambered from the cart. Pinch readied to follow them.

"I told you I'd get you sooner or later, *upright man*," shrilled a nasal voice as the master thief swung off the seat. Pinch dropped from the cart and whirled around to come face to face with Commander Wilmarq, sliding out of the crowd. As the soldiers parted to let their commander in, Corrick scurried to the officer's side. "Now, with some small thanks to your friend here, I've got the lot of you," the pudgy Hellrider gloated.

Sprite-Heels and Maeve stood helplessly by, encircled by swords.

"And thus Tyr's justice is done," the priest concluded from the platform.

The crowd drew a collective breath.

"Oh, Pinch, save me!" wailed Therin through the silence.

A tear trickled down Maeve's cheek.

Pinch's hand slid slowly toward his dagger.

There was a rattling bang as the trap fell open, followed in the next instant by a shriek of delight from the crowd. The cheer almost drowned out the twanging snap as the rope reached the end of its drop. Therin's feet, still kicking, almost touched the cart's bed before they recoiled up again. The crowd roared with each sway and bounce.

"Yer a failure, Pinch!" Corrick gloated from where he stood, safe by Wilmarq's side. "Yer'll be gone and I won't, so guess who'll rule this town now! The commander and I 'ave an understanding."

"Do you?" Pinch let his hand fall away from his dagger. Even with Therin still kicking overhead, the mob roaring for blood and swords all around him, the master thief remained remarkably calm. Maeve was already sobbing, perhaps more for herself than her departed Therin. Sprite looked ready to take up religion—any religion.

"Perhaps the commander and I can reach an understanding, too. Sprite, do you have it?" Pinch asked without ever taking his eyes off Wilmarq or Corrick. The old cutpurse's brow furrowed at the turn things were taking.

"Yes—and then some. Struck a gentleman, I did," the halfling replied nervously. He passed the leather purse to Pinch's outstretched hand.

"It might be best, Commander, if we talk in private." Pinch nodded toward the covered wagon. "Therin's not going to distract this crowd forever."

Wilmarq hesitated, looking from Pinch to Corrick and back again, like a dog choosing between two bones. "Bring these two," he ordered the guards nearest him, then pointed at Pinch and Corrick. "And watch those two for tricks." Wilmarq climbed into the shadows of the wagon. The guards shoved Corrick in afterward.

Pinch slowly climbed in. He noted Therin still swinging on the scaffold, his legs slowly jerking. In the darkness of the wagon, the upright man could see Wilmarq, sword poised but uncertain, perplexed by Pinch's game. Taking care not to startle him, Pinch tossed the leather bag to the commander's feet. It hit the wooden boards with a loud, clinking plop. Wilmarq scooted back in surprise.

"There's over five hundred nobles in gold here," Pinch pronounced. "If you take it there could be five hundred more tomorrow, if . . ."

"If?"

"If you give me Therin's body and let us go." The upright man couldn't suppress the smile he felt inside, a cold, evil smile like a cat's grin. He had Wilmarq; he knew it. The offer was more than the bastard could refuse.

The officer glanced at his men outside. "I'll need a body to replace him," he said slowly.

"Yes, you will," was Pinch's confident reply.

"It'll have to look like him."

"It will."

Corrick's old eyes widened as he listened to the exchange, barely audible over the noise of the crowd. "Pinch, you don't mean—"

"His body," the thief said to the soldier.

"Wait," Corrick said, "I—"

With a sudden single thrust of his sword, Commander Wilmarq cut the rest of Corrick's quavering words short. "The thief's dead," he shouted to his men outside. "Cut him down!"

Without waiting, Pinch went into action, poking his head out the front of the wagon. "Maeve, your spells. Sprite, get Therin in here!"

Brown Maeve, suddenly dry-eyed and calm, heaved herself into the cart and knelt by Corrick's body. The wizardress mumbled a few words of a spell as she passed her hands over the corpse. The old thief's wrinkled flesh softened and flowed until it appeared that Therin lay on the boards. Sprite was already heaving the unconscious but very much alive Therin from the scaffold into the back. Pinch dragged the boy in. Side by side, the pair looked like twins in death.

The crowd, still hungry for thrills, rushed the scaffold in a mad attempt to seize the corpse. The Hellriders sprang to their duty to hold the mob in check. They struggled against the bloodthirsty tide, unwilling to use their weapons against honest citizens.

"Get going," Pinch shouted as he half-shoved Wilmarq out of the cart. With a heave the rogue tossed Corrick's ensorcelled body out of the wagon. "Let the crowd have him! No questions that way!" Pinch advised as he clambered into the driver's seat.

Pinch wasted no time in savagely whipping the team forward, plunging it into the crowd. Chaos erupted as those in the wagon's path scrambled to get out of the way while others fought to seize the body left behind. In his last look back, before his cart disappeared down Elturel's backstreets, Pinch guessed the crowd was winning.

* * * * *

A tenday later, in a wineshop in Scornubel, four travelers sat at a table littered with bottles. Two of them, a little halfling and a faded woman with brown hair, had long since passed out. The other two men were still boozing. It was late, but the owner didn't mind; the two were free with their money. Every once in a while the older man, a nondescript fellow who dressed too well, would flex one leg as though it were stiff. The other, a big farmhand, had the equally odd habit of rubbing a scarf around his neck.

"Told you I had a plan," slurred the older as he sloppily poured another round.

"Fine plan—hang him and buy him back. You should try it sometime," groused the farmhand. "By Cyric's ass, these scars itch! How'd you know I weren't going to die up there?"

"Didn't," the older mumbled wearily.

"You mean I could have died?"

"Didn't matter. You were only part of the plan."

"Only *part*—Corrick! You wanted Corrick."

"You're alive. . . ."

"And the one who turned me's dead. You knew he'd done it all along."

"I suspected. The Hellriders' showing up at Maeve's crib —it was too easy. Somebody'd turned on me." The dark-haired one dismissed the question with a wave of his hand.

The first streaks of dawn shone through the cracks in the tavern's shutters, glinting off the bottles. "Then this whole plan, it wasn't about rescuing me at all, was it?"

The older man raised his glass to play the wine in the morning light. "I like to think of it as a lesson in loyalty."

A MATTER OF THORNS

James M. Ward

It was a meaningless little castle, perched on a high hill overlooking an insignificant spur of the Immerflow River, protecting nothing. The military minds of neighboring Cormyr didn't consider the keep—known as Castle Stone— worth the troops it would take to occupy, so they left it alone and labeled it strategically useless. The sixty-odd souls who lived in the village that squatted around the castle walls thought otherwise. They were fiercely proud that Castle Stone had never been defeated in battle. Small wonder: the granite towers and oaken gate had never been attacked.

In truth, Castle Stone's unusual garden was the fortification's only real claim to fame. Two hundred years past, wild rose hips planted in a small bower at the center of the main courtyard had grown into stunningly beautiful roses, red as new-spilled blood and thorned like morning stars. More luck than skill had allowed them to prosper and bloom over the decades, but their remarkably deep color caused the castle lord to claim them as his own. From that day to the present, the lord's banners all bore the blood-red rose as their emblem.

Those same banners had been flying at half-mast for two days now, ever since death had come for the old lord of the keep. The new Lord Stone, filled with the foolishness of youth, thought himself a builder of empires. He reorganized the sixty-man army, set his accounts to right, and replaced all his father's advisors with younger, more farseeing men.

This wasn't to say that the new Lord Stone's thoughts were focused only on matters far afield. Musing, the young nobleman wondered if there shouldn't be a new symbol for his domain, a unicorn or great dragon, something to gain him respect—or even fewer snide remarks—from his enemies. At the very least, it was time to get rid of the gardener. The old sot had been at his post for five decades, at least.

Pleased with his decision, Lord Stone sent his young chamberlain with the appropriate orders. The head of the household hurried to obey his lord's wishes, his scepter of office thudding against the stone floor in staccato rhythm. For his part, Lord Stone turned his mind toward another matter vital to the keep's continued prosperity—the menu for dinner.

He had barely decided upon a choice of soups before the seneschal's scepter came thudding quickly back.

"There is a slight problem, milord," murmured the head of the household. "Goodman Grim . . . refuses to retire."

"What!" Lord Stone bellowed. "When I give an order, I expect it to be carried out!"

"I understand, milord. I agree."

"Well, why wasn't it?"

The seneschal toyed nervously with his heavy chain of office. "I tried to tell Grim your command honored him, that you were rewarding him with retirement. He didn't see it that way." Swallowing hard, he added, "He's still out there, digging at the roses. I could hardly have him hauled away from his post. Grim has—begging your pardon and with all due respect—been in your father's and grandfather's service. He's rather popular with the rest of the staff, and such a scene might cause unrest in the household."

"Unrest indeed!" The young nobleman jumped from his throne and stomped out of the chamber. "We'll see about this!"

*　*　*　*　*

All Grim had ever wanted to do was tend Castle Stone's roses. Forsaking all other possible careers—including a promising apprenticeship with a traveling mage—the frail, bent gardener had grown up, grown wise, and grown very old working with his lord's beloved plants. He fondly remembered his father, who had been the gardener before him, bringing him to the castle to view the prized plants. Their huge buds and gentle fragrance had entranced him even at that tender age; the young Grim had cultivated a garden of his own, nursed with loving care and the little magic he'd picked up almost instinctively, but none of his hundreds of blooms could ever equal one of the castle's roses. He'd sworn then and there that growing the special flowers would be his life's work.

"Now, after all these years, they want me to go. If old Lord Stone were alive, he'd give them what for. There was a man for you. There was a man who appreciated the care it takes to raise roses."

Grim dug his hoe into the earth with more force than usual. Each stroke of the tool punctuated a colorful but silent insult he directed toward the new Lord Stone.

The sound of footsteps in the garden finally drew him from his angry reverie. Turning, he saw his new lord and the new lord chamberlain. He bent his head in respect, but didn't kneel, as he would have to the old castle ruler.

The lord was a well-fed strapping young man, full of the strength of youth. The run from the throne room to the bower hadn't even winded him. That couldn't be said for the chamberlain. Of the same age as his master, he was bent over, gulping in huge breaths. It took both hands gripped tightly on his scepter just to keep him on his feet.

"Grim, what's this I hear you won't retire?" Lord Stone began without prelude. "Listen, everyone needs to retire sometime or other. It's time for new blood here at Castle Stone, men with new ideas—in *every* office. That's what progress is all about." He waited for Grim to nod his agreement. When the old gardener merely stood there, staring blankly, he continued. "Perhaps I'm not making myself clear. Be a good fellow and run along. We're giving your job to someone else. There, that's an end to it."

The lord turned to leave, smiling at a job well done.

"That's far from the end!" Grim wailed. "After all these years of service, I'm not going to be thrown into the dung heap just because your lordship is foolish enough to think he's done with me!" Each word was louder than the last, until the gardener was fairly shrieking. "I've worked for this castle and the lords of this castle since before you were born! You've no right to set me aside this way!"

Old Grim's face grew perilously red, almost the hue of one of his prized buds. He could see the anger growing in the young lord, too, but he didn't care. He raised his hoe to punctuate his words. "I'll not—"

That was the last straw for Lord Stone. No subject of his—especially not this withered old weed puller—was going to raise a weapon against him. He picked up the skinny old man, lifted him effortlessly over his head, and threw him with great force into the cold stone wall of the arbor. Grim's body made a crunching sound as it hit, then slid wetly down the wall. Skin broke, ancient bones broke, and the old man's heart broke.

But as his blood pumped from his torn flesh, into the ground of his beloved rose garden, Grim raised his eyes to his murderer. "Curse you and your li—"

Grim's final words went unheard. The lord was already on his way out of the gardens. He was a busy man, after all, and the matter of the dinner menu was far from resolved.

"Clean that mess up," Lord Stone called over his shoulder to the chamberlain. "And make sure none of Father's roses were damaged."

"Yes, my lord. I'll see to it right away."

The chamberlain dutifully made a circuit of the rose garden, thankful not to find one damaged flower. He made a mental note to find a new gardener to start the next day, then hurried to his other tasks.

It took nearly an hour for the guards to get around to removing Grim's body—Lord Stone had sent most of the troops to the village, scurrying like trained hogs after truffles. By then, everyone in the castle and village knew what had taken place. And those who predicted nothing good would come of Grim's untimely death were absolutely right.

* * * * *

Grim's blood, tainted by his curse, oozed over the freshly turned earth and sloshed against the inner wall of the castle garden. Soaking into the well-tilled dirt, the crimson fluid bathed the roots of the largest rose bush. In brief hours the root system had fed on the wetness and transformed. Root hairs and root tendrils thickened and grew coarse. The earth began to ripple and shift in the rose bed.

No apparent change occurred in the exposed part of the bush until later that night, when the moon's light caressed the plant's leaves. A soft rustle of its pliant vines marked its pleasure. Thickening, the rose's leaves and stems spread at unnatural angles and lengths to claim as much of the moonlight as possible.

Growing, doubling, even tripling in size, the cursed rose bush spread it sickness swiftly. It joined itself to the other roses in the garden, melding the root systems together into a gigantic, pulsing network beneath the soil. Rose thorns became huge hollow daggers along the pliable vines. The outside of every rose petal grew thorny teeth that sucked the life from the flies, moths, and bugs that ventured too close. The root system was busy, too, searching out and spearing every worm, grub, and beetle in the earth.

A smooth, melon-sized gall developed at the monstrous plant's center. The gall's white markings pulsed in the last rays of the setting moon. The thing could sense the many life-forms contained in the castle, life-forms that offered more sustenance than the insects it had consumed until now. Slowly, stealthily, it sent creepers out to investigate.

The rising sun, however, with its harsh and unpleasant light forced the leafy spies to retreat before they could learn anything of value. The monstrous rose shrank back against the walls, shifting its bulk into the shadows. It was considering some other way to investigate the castle when voices just outside the garden gate drew its attention; it didn't really understand what the creatures were saying, but that didn't matter. Its interest in the creatures was more basic than conversation.

"The roses and the garden are behind that gate. It's never guarded, so you'll be able to come and go as you please."

"Yes, Lord Chamberlain."

"Take your duties seriously. You've been given a great honor."

"Yes, Lord Chamberlain."

"Do a good job every day. Lord Stone and everyone else here at the keep takes those roses very seriously."

"Yes, Lord Chamberlain."

"Now get to work." The chamberlain thudded off to attend to several hundred other less-than-thrilling assignments given him by young Lord Stone.

Foley Cornbottom, left standing at the garden gate, was not a happy man. He'd been plucked from his fields and informed that he was the new gardener of Castle Stone. Not that he wouldn't enjoy the position in and of itself, but Lord Stone didn't pay enough for him to abandon his farm completely, and he couldn't imagine how he was going to manage both jobs. And then there was the manner in which his predecessor had been hurried on his way to the Realm of the Dead.

Still, there wasn't a thing to be done about it. When confronted by armed guards who tell you the lord will be *very* upset if you turn away his offer—well, you can only nod a lot and smile. With a sigh of resignation, Foley set about surveying his new domain.

"What do we have here?" At first, Foley's eyes grew huge at the impossibilities around him. His mind filled with wonder at the size and color of the plants. He'd heard about them from old Grim, but no commoner was ever allowed in the lord's gardens to see the legendary roses for himself.

And these were truly marvelous. Each blossom was the size of a man's head, and the flowers all faced the garden path. It was almost as if . . . well, they seemed to be looking at him! A shiver of fear scrabbled down Foley's spine.

"Never mind that, Goodman Cornbottom. You've got a job to do and you'd better get to it." He tapped his chin and looked about. "There's where you should start. That obviously doesn't belong here."

Foley's rough hands reached into the shadows for the melon-sized gall. Lifting it, he noticed an unusually thick tangle of thorny vines connecting it to the earth. One of the thorns scraped along his palm, but it didn't draw blood; he'd been tending plants for over a decade now, and his hands were tougher than thick leather.

"A gall like this should've been cut clean long ago. What could old Grim have been thinking?" He turned the gall roughly. "Maybe he just never noticed you, eh?"

The cursed vegetation tried to shrink back; the gardener only gripped it tighter. The rose monster ached to absorb this creature, but the skin on its hands was like stone. Perhaps there was another way. . . .

Vines with long, hollow thorns reached out behind the gardener. They quickly snaked up Foley's legs, wrenching his hands away from the gall, pinning his arms to his side. The thorns penetrated at the neck and began to draw out the man's life. And with the blood and marrow, the thorns drained something else from the gardener—his will and his intellect.

Shocked at the sudden insight Foley's mind afforded it, the plant paused. It did not kill the gardener as it had the flies and earthworms. It only drained enough of his life-force to sustain itself, enough of the man's mind to leave him a helpless slave. Then the plant fell back, sated.

Weak from the effort and reeling from its new perception of the world, the monstrous rose rested. As it did, Foley cleared some bothersome rocks away and watched for intruders until the sun set and the soothing light of the moon bathed the garden.

Refreshed and certain it could protect itself once more, the plant sent the glassy-eyed Foley away, but ordered him to return with the sun—along with more of his kind.

*   *   *   *   *

Late the following morning, Lord Stone took a stroll past the garden. He'd just finished debating the captain of the guards about the color of his troops' new uniforms. Earlier he'd had a row with the chamberlain over the finer points of menu-planning. He talked to himself as he walked; it was a habit he'd fostered since the day he'd proclaimed himself the only fit conversationalist in the keep.

"Well, that's a good morning's work!" The nobleman laughed to himself. He couldn't see how the domain had survived all those years without his enlightened rule.

"A little sword practice is just the thing right now," he announced. "I mustn't let myself get too out of shape—though it would be easy enough to do, sitting on a throne all day. Off to the practice field with me, then. It'll be good for the troops to see their leader working—"

It was then that the smell hit him.

"What in Tyr's blind eyes is that? It smells like someone built a slaughterhouse in the rose garden. Foley!" Lord Stone bellowed as he flung open the gate and stormed into the arbor. "What do you—"

Foley and the castle cook had just upended a barrel of blood into the garden's earth. They stood there, slack-jawed and glassy-eyed, staring at Lord Stone.

The nobleman shared their dumbfounded expression, though his was born of shock. His father's beloved roses had turned into monster things with thorns as long as daggers. Half-eaten pigs and chickens lay everywhere, entangled in vines. Then he saw three of his castle guards and the blacksmith spitted on thorns, expressions of horror on their ripped faces.

A watermelon-sized gall lifted on a thorny tendril and moved toward Lord Stone. The nobleman raised his sword and swung powerfully at the gall, but hardened rose vines caught the blade midswing. Other vines smashed thorns into Stone's bare arms and neck. Like Foley and the cook before him, Lord Stone gained a new appreciation for roses.

"This plant must prosper and be properly fed, Foley," Lord Stone said dully when the plant had finished with him. "I'll order you more helpers. We'd best double the guard around the castle walls, too. Can't be too careful, eh?"

* * * * *

"Stop right there!" The gate guard called. "Who do you think you are, trying to enter Castle Stone without so much as a by-your-leave?" The gruff soldier, backed by three of his equally gruff fellows, raised his pike to stop the riders from crossing the wide drawbridge.

The smaller of the two travelers was a squire, dressed all in red and feeling rather self-important. He rode a few paces ahead of his lord and stopped. "Since when is it necessary to answer questions before entering Stone Keep—especially for such an important knight as my master? Any king or baron worth the title would gladly welcome him at table!"

The squire glanced back, looking for approval, but found only a frown on his master's face. He probably should have waited for the knight to speak, but the upstart gate guards had irritated him so!

"Back off, spratling!" The commanding gate guard snorted his disregard, then flourished his pike. "Your master will speak to me, or I'll run you both out of here in a heartbeat. Now, who are you and what do you intend with the folk in the castle?"

"Who am I, you ask?" There was a forced sense of wonder in the knight's voice. He spurred his massive war-horse forward. The mount's snort seemed as dismissive as the guard's had been. "Is this Castle Stone?"

"It is." The guard planted the butt of his pike in the ground, aiming the blade at the armored chest of the great beast in front of him. Stop the mount and you stop the rider, his father used to say.

"Is this still Castle Stone, ruled by my *good friend,* the ancient Lord Stone?" Before the guard could answer, the knight turned his handsome features to the sky and added, "And is it not now highsun, the one time of day this castle has always allowed travelers entrance to escape the heat?" Now there was a note of genuine incredulity in the warrior's voice.

"Things have changed here," the guard said coldly. "But I'll not be discussing that with you until you tell me what your business is with the castle." The gate guard signaled a brace of crossbowmen to appear on the upper wall.

The knight tipped his war visor down, preparing to deal out a few bruisings if necessary. The squire mirrored his movements and unsheathed his morning star.

"I'm Sir Ganithar, known as 'the Hammer Knight' to some, or simply 'the Hammer.' I'm a member in good standing of the High Moor Heroes' Guild. I have just returned from three years of highly successful adventuring in the ruins of the Fallen Kingdom, if you must know. I now intend to spend at least a month in the tubs of this castle's only inn. I'm going to eat something other than trail rations and spend my afternoons looking at every pretty woman bold enough to pass my way. Do you have a problem with that?" The last was said hopefully, as if the knight wanted a challenge.

The guard quickly lowered his pike and handed it to one of his fellows, then signaled the archers away. His disdainful expression was one of bemusement, if not outright fear. If what he'd heard about this warrior was true, he didn't want to be the one responsible for bringing about the ruin of the castle's front gate. "The Hammer," he said lamely. "Er, sorry I didn't recognize you."

The guard knew the tales of Sir Ganithar the Hammer as well as his own life story. It was said that the knight's enchanted warhammer was a thing of the gods. Others said Ganithar could walk unseen into any well-guarded place and take whatever he wanted.

The guard bowed and backed away, but at that precise

moment, a group of mounted soldiers appeared in the gate, heading from the courtyard out on patrol. Spotting the leader of the troop, the Hammer waved a friendly greeting. The young Lord Stone led these men on patrol. Now he would get to the bottom of this situation.

"My lord, how goes the realm?"

The young warrior ignored the greeting and made to ride past, ignoring Ganithar and his squire completely. The knight bristled at the insult. The boy owed him civility, at least; he'd rocked the mewling little whelp on his knee all those years ago. This insult just wouldn't do. It wouldn't do at all.

With a flourish, the knight raised his hammer. A flurry of magical lightning bolts lashed out of the clear sky and struck the ground around Sir Ganithar's war-horse. The battle-hardened mount reared majestically, an impressive move that the squire's smaller war-horse mimicked.

The patrol's horses were not so hardy; they screeched in panic at the lightning and retreated. Only Lord Stone's mount stood its ground.

Ganithar raised his visor and shouted, "Now you recognize me, eh? It's good to see you again. I'm looking forward to drinking with your father. You're looking well." This last was a lie—well meant, but still utterly false. The young castle lord looked haggard, years older than his true age.

"Oh . . . Ganithar. Well met," Lord Stone said vaguely. "I didn't see you before. I'm glad you're alive and well. The castle can use all the bold adventurers it can get right now."

"What's wrong? Is there some attack coming? My hammer is always at your service."

"No, no attack. My father died five days ago. It was quite sudden. His heart just stopped." The young lord advanced as if to ride on, but Sir Ganithar was far too perplexed to let that happen. The knight spurred his mount to block the nobleman's path; the squire followed his master's lead and hemmed the lord in.

From his high war saddle, the Hammer looked down on the new ruler of the castle. "Friends usually invite friends to dinner when they haven't seen each other in years. Let's sup together and drink to your father's honor."

The expression on the young noble's face was a pained one. He obviously wasn't thrilled at the thought of dining with Ganithar, but found it difficult to refuse.

"I don't get out much these days. The castle and the things in it demand more and more of my time. I'm sure some of your old village friends will be wanting to hear your latest tall tales."

"I'm sure that's true, but there's no one I'd rather break bread with than you."

Lord Stone winced as if he'd been struck. "So be it. Please come to dinner with the rising of this night's moon. I should be back from patrol by then. We can raise a glass or two and speak of my father."

"It's a pact then!" The Hammer grinned. "Let me introduce you to my squire. Tomkin Woodsmanson, front and center."

The squire, all of fifteen and not very worldly for his travels with Sir Ganithar, was quite pleased to be introduced to this particular nobleman. He'd come from the lands around Castle Stone and seen the young lord during high market days. He bowed as low as the jousting saddle allowed.

"Ganithar, I didn't think you were the type to take on a squire." The castle lord looked the lad over with an appraising eye.

"Oh, I admit he's rough around the edges, but he saved my life."

The look of surprise was plain on Lord Stone's face, so the Hammer elaborated: "It's a rather longish story. Suffice it to say I was in the woods when a wyvern surprised me. It knocked me right off my horse and pinned me to the ground. I would have been a corpse had this foolish boy not put a woodsman's axe clean through the monster in one swing. In return for the deed, he asked me to make him as good a warrior as I am. I couldn't say no—not after he'd saved me." Ganithar smiled warmly. "But we'll talk about it more tonight. I want to get the road dust off my old hide. Tonight, my lord?"

"Tonight—if we must." Lord Stone turned to find his patrol reassembled. He nodded to both knight and squire, then pushed past them and rode away.

"Is he a great lord, like in the old tales?" Tomkin asked eagerly.

"His father was. That lad riding off has been a bit of a bully in the past. Only time will tell what type of ruler he makes." The knight narrowed his eyes as he watched the patrol ride away. "But something is terribly wrong with him. I think you and I will ferret it out during dinner."

"He wouldn't want me dining with the likes of you both."

"It doesn't matter what he likes. You're my squire and go where I go." Ganithar patted the boy on the shoulder. "You must learn to serve me. Loyal service is as important to a squire as the arts of war. Do you understand, boy?"

"Yes, sir, I'll always serve you to the best of my ability. I'll do whatever you tell me to do, Sir Ganithar."

"No, no, lad. That's not what I want. Try to *anticipate* what I need. Anticipation is vital in a warrior, too. Figure out what I need and respond to me before I ask. I'll teach you to do the same to your foes. That's the way of a good warrior. Now, let's prepare ourselves for some fine food. You know they grow some excellent watermelon here. It boasts some of the best in Faerûn—though the roses make a better symbol for the castle, eh, Tomkin?"

The squire nodded, only half-listening to what his master said, his mind caught up in the lesson the knight had imparted.

"Anticipate, that's what I need to do," Tomkin repeated softly as, now unchallenged, they rode into the castle.

*   *   *   *   *

"Two plates. Lord Stone obviously doesn't want me to dine with you." Dressed in full livery, with a two-handed broadsword strapped to his back, Tomkin felt decidedly

overdressed and more than a little foolish as he gazed
through the garden gate at the small table within.

"Nonsense, lad. Lord Stone has taken the time to serve us
dinner in his fine garden. Admittedly, the garden has gotten
rather smelly of late, but we'll both find out why at dinner.
Another plate is easily gotten."

"No!" the squire squeaked for fear that the castle lord
could hear them while they whispered outside the garden
gate. "I couldn't eat in front of him. I'd be afraid of dribbling
soup down my surcoat. Couldn't I just eat my meal with the
horses?"

Ganithar, remembering his days as a squire, took pity on
Tomkin. "All right, lad. You don't have to attend the dinner.
But I want you to stay outside this gate and guard it with
your life. No one is to disturb our dinner without my permission. I want to get to the bottom of the strange goings-on
around here."

Much relieved, Tomkin took his post as the Hammer
strolled into the garden and met Lord Stone.

"Anticipation, anticipation, anticipation," the boy muttered to himself over and over. "Should I draw my sword, I
wonder? Or maybe I should stand inside of the door, not outside. Should I call for help if attacked, or die silently, defending my lord?" Sweat began beading on the squire's forehead
as he looked in all directions, ready to sell his life dearly for
the Hammer.

Standing just outside the garden, the woodsman-made-
squire craned his neck this way and that, trying to see both
the Hammer and the doorway into the keep. So caught up in
his duty was the boy that he could barely hear the words of
the two men in the arbor.

"I no longer rule this castle," Lord Stone said. "I serve
another, and here it is!"

Tomkin caught a glimpse of a large melon resting on several rose stalks. It was unusual all right, but wild roses alongside melons were nothing strange in the forest. Tomkin
didn't like roses very much, but he did like watermelon.

The leaves on the melon vine looked larger than normal,

spear-shaped things as big as plates. Inch thick vines spilled out all over the plant. The bloated, blood-red roses seemed to be fashioned of impossibly thick petals coated with oil.

Tomkin tore his gaze away from the garden. Even the weirdest of plants must not distract him from his duty. If the Hammer wanted to eat dinner surrounded by weird plants, that was his choice. They'd both seen many stranger sights than that on the trail.

After surveying the area around the garden, Tomkin once again glanced into the arbor; he saw his master tugging at a rose vine connected to the melon. There were rose vines wrapped around his back, too.

The squire shook his head. What a silly game this seemed to be. He and friends held such contests of strength in the woods, but they used small trees to bend and snap; this melon-stalk didn't seem like much of a test for what he knew of his master's considerable strength. The scene also confused the squire, for the knight had laid strong prohibitions against playing with food—and that melon looked ripe for the picking.

Again Tomkin shook his head. Strange were the ways of his betters, and he was nowhere near experienced enough a warrior to judge them silly for it. He sighed and turned back to his watch.

"Anticipate, anticipate, antici—"

A shove from behind sent Tomkin reeling. Sir Ganithar and Lord Stone pushed through the garden gate, barely noticing that they'd knocked the boy down. The squire glanced back into the garden and saw the plates still heaped with food. A glance back at his master revealed a terrible look on the Hammer's face. His cheeks were flushed, and his eyes were glassy.

Their contest of strength must have become a squabble, Tomkin decided. Sheathing his sword, the squire followed his master away from the garden.

Sir Ganithar dismissed the boy's concern with a stiff-limbed wave. "No, nothing's wrong. You and I will be sleeping in the hall tonight. Tomorrow we have much work to do—and a trip to take."

That was decidedly odd. Just a few hours ago the squire had heard the Hammer order special baths to be prepared every day for three tendays. Ganithar had also ordered the fixings for a huge party. Tomkin himself had carried the invitations to all of the knights' local friends, and sent off even more to the High Moor Heroes' Guild.

Tomkin hoped that he hadn't done something to cause the argument between Lord Stone and his master. Perhaps, the squire realized grimly, I failed to anticipate something Sir Ganithar needed at the dinner. The knight must surely have been furious, for he left without eating a bite.

Sir Ganithar's chilly silence as Tomkin helped the knight prepare for bed only confirmed the boy's suspicions. Tomkin was miserable as he went about his chores: though he could barely lift the magical hammer, it was his duty to stow it so Ganithar could reach it easily if an attack came upon them at night. The special cloak of silence, boots of leaping, and belt of invisibility were entrusted to the squire every night, as well. The Hammer figured no one would ever suspect the young squire of holding such fabulous items.

Before he dozed off, the Hammer ordered his squire to sleep on a pallet outside the room's only door. Tomkin did as he was told, but only pretended to sleep. A short time later, hearing the snores of Sir Ganithar, he rose from the pallet. He donned the cloak to prevent the guard from hearing his movements. The boots would allow him to spring great distances and move as lightly as a feather over any floor. The belt, activated with a magic word only Ganithar and he knew, made his form vanish from the sight of man, plant, and animal. Thus girded, he could set about "anticipating" his lord's needs.

The dreams of Ganithar the Hammer and all the other minions of the rose were the same. Huge vines of enormous size twisted around their bodies and squeezed the life out of them. The twenty entranced men and women sleeping in the castle all twisted and turned in their beds, caught up in the nightmare images filling their minds. Thorns plunged into their bodies, ripping out their still-beating hearts. They tried to cry out, but vines filled their mouths.

Then, quite abruptly, the dreams ended, and each of the rose minions fell into a deeper, less-troubled sleep.

* * * * *

"Sir Ganithar! Wake up! See what I have anticipated for you."

Ganithar leapt up, his warhammer in hand. At first he saw only the stupid grin of his squire. "You have on my cloak," he rumbled. "And my boots and belt!" Then he noticed the huge covered silver platter in his hands.

"I'm sorry something spoiled your dinner with Lord Stone last night," Tomkin said. "And since you went to bed without eating, I anticipated you'd be hungry this morning. I found this serving thing and got your breakfast ready before you woke up." He lifted the tray's lid to show his master the lovely great melon he'd chopped off the rose vine in the garden.

Seeing the look of shock in his master's face, he reddened. "You're upset about the piece I cut out of it, aren't you?" the squire asked sadly. "I'm sorry, but I only wanted to make sure it was ripe. It tastes rather good, but not like any melon I've ever had before. And it smells a bit like roses. I suppose it's from growing so close to them."

STOLEN SPELLS

Denise Vitola

On the sign hanging outside Bareen Tykar's shop, there was the symbol of a spinning wheel and below it the words "Country Spell Crafts and Implements for Daily Living." I cast my gaze over the door, noting the deep, rich color and the carving of a twisted tree. It was a beautiful piece of art, gloriously old and fashioned from timber found only in Cormyr. The man who owned such a door would have money enough to buy a magical lock that would keep thieves like me standing out on the street.

I had just arrived in Kendil, a quiet hamlet in the foothills of the Sunset Mountains, just east of Asbravn. The village had a mercantile look about it; the majority of the buildings were well-kept, whitewashed affairs edged with flower boxes, each decorated with a quaint, homey motif. An inn fronted the swept cobbled street, and farther down the way, there was a tiny shrine honoring Sune Firehair, Goddess of Beauty and Patron of Love.

I felt inside my jerkin pocket to check the bits of helpful magic I carried. A thief is never far off from his tricks and spells, and knowing that I had come to this place adequately prepared made me feel more confident about meeting the proprietor of this shop.

Entering the establishment, I paused to glance around. The place was empty except for an old, fat clerk wearing a green apron and brushing a beefy hand through his shock of white hair. He stood before a wall of shelves arranged with rows of glass jars, tins, boxes, and intricately plaited baskets. The light from thick, stubby candles set among the goods gave these mundane treasures a bright sparkle, but there was so much dark wood that the large room had an oppressive feel to it.

The man squinted at me as I kicked the door shut and halted to smooth my beard and braid. "Bareen Tykar?" I asked, stepping up to the polished stone counter.

"Aye," he answered, "and who would be asking?"

"My name is Arek Adar. You sent a message along the trade route to Triel about wanting to find a certain elixir from the Sunset Mountain region. An elf named Latine Firewalker spoke with me."

He didn't reply immediately. Instead, he studied me. Finally he smiled. When he did, his lips disappeared into the bag of wrinkles that made up his face. "Firewalker came by earlier and said to expect you." Leaning forward, he continued in a low voice. "He tells me you locate hard-to-find objects, objects of some antiquity."

I nodded. He made it sound as if I were a bona fide dealer of heirlooms, but the truth of it isn't nearly so mundane as that.

I'm a thief of magical objects. I've stolen icons from all the cities clinging to the edges of the River Chionthar. My adventures have even taken me to Cormyr and beyond, and yes, I love antiques. The old spell-stuff had such romance to it, such charm. Nowadays, it's different, what with mages by the hundreds flocking into the Heartlands hawking their crude, magical wares. How dull.

"It's true, then?" the merchant asked.

"Perhaps."

He pursed his lips, and I saw the tip of his tongue dart out to wet them. "Look around you," he said. "In this shop, I sell magical teas and balms. These things are drubbed up by the people of the southern range of the Sunset Mountains, and while in the past these elixirs were held in contempt by the elite living in the big cities, that's no longer true. I employ several agents and they travel into the lesser-known places looking for things for me to sell. One of them returned from a trip to the village of Urlok, and he told me about a brew called Spring Tonic. It's so potent that it revitalizes a man and takes him back to the spring of his youth."

"I've not heard of it, nor have I heard of Urlok."

"I can supply you with a map."

"Traveling the Sunset Mountains in unfamiliar territory can be dangerous. Zhentarim, you know. Red Cloaks. Monsters, too."

Bareen Tykar shook his head. "Yes, yes, I understand. Your commission will reflect the added cost of danger. Are you willing to try?"

"Tell me more about the Spring Tonic first."

"Apparently, this brew is drawn from a hidden pool. The people of the Sunsets have kept the location of this spring a secret, as much a secret as the spell employed to create the tonic. My colleague is sure it's the reason for the health and vitality of the people in Urlok."

"Why doesn't your associate just go into the mountains and buy it for you?"

"We've tried this, but Jig Elbari, the dwarf who blends it, is unwilling to sell it."

"So you want me to steal it?"

"That's right."

I always take a moment to prime the client by pretending to be wary of him and his request. Folks expect thieves to be suspicious. It's part of the little dance we do to get a better price for our services and silence. I've found it is also a good way to drive the bargaining my direction.

He turned to pour a cup of tea from a free-standing samovar, finally filling in the quiet between us. "All right. I'll make it worth your time and risk. If you find the Spring Tonic, I'll triple your fee. That should salt the soup a bit, don't you think?"

* * * * *

Two days later, my black war-horse, Stealth, and I traveled a narrow trail through the southern range of the Sunset Mountains on this mission for Bareen Tykar. The path was barely visible, blanketed with autumn leaves, moist from the silky mist curling low about my horse's feet. It was a heavy, dark wood we passed through, and dusk was coming on. Night bugs started to peep and twill about me, greeting the evening with a heralding symphony.

I had seen many abandoned dwarf-dug mines along the way. Passing through these places where the hemlock hid the sun, my imagination fed my anxiety. At one point, I thought I heard the echoes of ghostly workers breaking rock with pick and mallet. To make it worse, Bareen Tykar's map did little to point me toward Urlok.

I was entertaining thoughts of camping for the night when Stealth turned a bend and stopped with a snort and a head shake. Just beyond the path, guarded by an outcropping of boulders and a low wall of tangled undergrowth, a large glade opened. I squinted through the trees to see the bobbing light of small, hand-held lanterns. Laying an ear that direction, I heard excited voices and the rattle of armor.

Urging Stealth forward, I used the shadows from the rock altar to hide our cautious advance. I halted to blink several times—a thief's trick to adjust to the contrasts of bright and dark.

Goblins. Sure as I had stolen swords from their kind, I knew the commotion in the grove was caused by goblins. Ugly, stinking, cowardly goblins. Where were the Red Cloaks when you needed them?

Goblins are some of the best highwaymen in the Realms, and they don't care whom they attack. I glanced about, looking for those who might still be concealed in the creepers and vines bordering the path. I even looked overhead, thinking they might drop out of the trees on me at any moment. Except for the ruckus in the glade, all was still. I dismounted.

Clinging to the boulders, I came close enough to count six goblins and one female dwarf. She was trying to keep the group at bay with grunting shouts and a wooden staff. The goblins poked back at her with their swords. One swung a club. She ducked this attack, jabbing at another with her staff. He fell, and she assured he stayed down by punctuating her parry with a savage kick.

Being that I'm not given to heroics, I'm the first to admit that I thought of turning back down the trail and running away from the problem. I was here to find Spring Tonic, not to save people from nasty, little ravagers. Besides, where there was a goblin, there was sure to be a bugbear or an ogre or two. A shiver jittered through me when I considered the possibility.

Still, leaving a maiden—any maiden—in distress is not a thing I could forgive myself for easily. And as I considered the situation, I realized, too, that frightening the life out of a few of those monsters was a prospect I would enjoy. A plan suddenly figured in my brain as I remembered the light catcher I carried with me.

I'd picked it up while doing a second-story job on the house of a minor lord in Scornubel. The light catcher was a precision item, styled with a spell that allowed it to capture a flame at a hundred paces, even as it created shadows so black that a panther from Chult would have a hard time seeing. Shaped like a tube, it was fashioned from hammered brass and was as thick as an elf's forearm.

I returned to my horse and quietly unbuckled my saddlebag, doing it by feel as I scanned the darkening forest for lurking ogres. My fingers found the light catcher and I hurried back to the rocks again.

The receded daylight became my ally as I padded closer to the fray. I could see the goblins taunting the dwarf, and their game made them oblivious to my approach.

Stopping beneath the drooping overhang of a willowy tree, I aimed the tube and murmured the simple incantation that freed the magic. Instantly, the lanterns lost their charges and the glade was thrown into utter blackness. The goblins screeched in unison. I moved quickly, my own eyes barely adjusting to the darkness before I contacted the jaw of my first goblin. He screamed out and when he did, I brought the end of the light catcher toward the noise to bang him full in the face. My instincts drew me around into a lunge as I felt the breeze of an arcing sword and saw the hint of movement. I tackled another goblin, slamming him into a tree. The others dashed from the glade, barreling down the slippery path.

I may not be much for heroics, but I do like a good brawl, especially when I know I can come out the winner.

I spoke the light catcher incantation backward and those lanterns left behind flickered to flame, forcing the shadows to recede. I bent to pick up a lamp, glancing at the terrified dwarf still wielding her staff.

"I won't hurt you," I husked. "I'm not a killer."

She stared at me for several heartbeats. I noticed that she had a beard as blond as mine, and I couldn't contain a small smile. I tried to cover it by whistling for Stealth.

"I'm obliged to you, sir," the dwarf said, lowering her weapon. "If you hadn't come along, I'd be dead now."

"You're welcome," I answered.

"What might I do to make us even?"

"You can tell me if there are any inns nearby. I don't want to camp in the woods tonight with goblins about."

She nodded and pointed up the path. "The village of Urlok has an inn. It lies a league or so up the trail, but it's hard to find, being hidden in a deep hollow. I'll show you."

I nodded and, catching Stealth's reins, fell in beside her. We walked a while in silence before I thought to ask her about the dwarf, Jig Elbari.

"I've heard of him," she said. "He's a secretive old man, though. A hermit."

"I understand he has some old spell-stuff."

"Yes, that he does. He brews up tinctures and elixirs for folks. Used to be a doctor for one of the mines hereabouts,so I guess he's knowledgeable in the ancient ways."

"Do you know about his Spring Tonic?"

She laughed. "Everyone in these parts knows of it." She paused to consider me with a long look. "You're not from here, so you must be an agent for one of those lowland merchants. They keep irritating the blazes out of us!"

*　*　*　*　*

It was late the next day when I found the deep ravine that the innkeeper at Urlok said would lead me to Shimmer Hollow, where Jig Elbari lived. I reined in Stealth to consider the fern- and lichen-covered corridor ahead. The trees had closed in around me and the sun was at a long slant. In the distance, I heard thunder.

Such isolated, gray places give me the jumps. As a youngster, I'd heard stories about how these areas should be avoided. In realty, I know it was just a way to keep a mountain boy obedient and safe, but I couldn't shake the uncertainty that these wilderness alleys led to holes entering the Underdark.

A moment's thought of turning back had me brace my legs against Stealth's sides. He snorted and pawed the mossy ground, as if chiding me for my cowardice. Yet, common sense told me that those in Urlok may have lied about the route to Elbari's homestead. They hadn't willingly given up directions to Bareen Tykar's agent—that was why I was here. Though the dwarf I had saved from the goblin pack had made a sound plea to the innkeeper to help me, I couldn't be sure he had.

Pulling a deep breath, I tapped Stealth's reins and we moved forward into the trench.

It was cool inside this furrow, almost cold, but despite the chill, sweat beaded on my forehead, seemingly stealing the moisture from my mouth. The tiny sounds of the forest closed in around me and with each whistle and burble, my stomach clutched tighter. The thunder grew closer.

Stealth's hooves struck through a stream bubbling through the ravine. The water sang softly, filling in the background noise and mellowing my anxiety. I concentrated upon the sound, but still kept an eye out for such horrors as might hide in this place. An hour passed before I could take another good breath.

The innkeeper said there would be a house at the end of this little canyon. When the ravine opened up, I did find the house—a shack really, all broken stones and rotten wood. I believe the most protection the owner had from the elements was given by the surrounding trees. They formed a high, thick canopy overhead. Still, the land was muddy and wet, and Stealth slipped twice as I guided him down the steep trail leading to the homestead.

"Hello?" I called. "Anybody about? Hello?"

The breeze ruffled through the hollow, but no voice overlaid its current. I nudged Stealth forward, deciding to follow the stream onward past the dilapidated barn.

In the years spent roaming the Sunset Mountains, I've come across many such hovels. There was a time in my early youth when I would charge into these places hoping to find treasure, but I mostly found the wrong side of a protection spell. I learned that trying to enter such homes uninvited was just too much trouble.

The ravine resumed and the huge ferns closed down the wan light again. My horse was forced to move slowly, the noise from his steps gentled by the water where he strode. After a while, the stream fed into a quiet pool. There, surrounded by a legion of glass bottles, an old dwarf hunched over the water's edge.

My approach startled him. He reared back, losing the conical-shaped brown hat he wore. It dropped into the pool and floated there like a parchment boat, the sail shot through with holes.

"Who are you?" he demanded.

"My name is Arek Adar. Are you Jig Elbari?"

He nodded.

"I've come seeking your wisdom for my grandmother. Her eyesight is failing."

He stared at me for a long moment. Abruptly he began to laugh, punctuating his guffaws with squeaks and whistles.

"Come seeking my wisdom? A human? I doubt that. Tell me the truth. What do you want from me?"

"I can pay."

"Of course you can, young man." He dipped back down toward the pool to retrieve his hat. Plopping it on his head, he considered me with hard, dark eyes. "You one of those merchant-fellows from the lowland?"

A thief can sniff a mark from ten paces off, and with Jig Elbari, I knew he was a perfect setup right away. Maybe he was bored or lonely. Whatever. It didn't matter. He was already playing the game.

He didn't wait for a reply. "Well, if you have the money, I have the tincture. Coming out this way says a lot about your courage. See any ogres or trolls as you came through the fissure back there?"

"No, sir," I answered, feeling the hair rise on the back of my neck.

"On the return, you probably will." He cackled again.

I watched as he filled each bottle with the pool's clear liquid. "You know about Spring Tonic?" he asked, after a bit.

"I've not heard of it," I said casually.

"It's right expensive, but the price is worth it. One flask can make a man young again. It's the water, you know. There isn't much of a spell spliced to the tonic, but most folks seem to think the words are what gives it the power. It's nonsense." Jig grinned and pulled at his hair. "You've got to bottle the water during the night of a blue moon, and only once a year does Selune go full twice in the same month. We'll see it again during Midwinter, but not until."

"Still for all that, I can't see why the tonic would be expensive. You could have several bottles of it stocked away."

"I do, but it's not that easy," he answered. "The elixir has to age. You take it before it strengthens up all the way, which is about fifty years, and nothing will happen. Besides, not only do you have to mix it on the night of a blue moon, you've got to drink it during one, as well."

"How can you tell if you have an aged bottle?"

He laughed. "You can't. That's the whole trouble, don't

you see? Most people want assurances. They just plain don't trust me when I say it's the good stuff."

"I suppose you have a bottle that's properly aged?" I asked.

He nodded. "Yes, I do. Are you a decent judge of moral character, young man? Do you trust me to be fair and honest? Would you be interested in buying my Spring Tonic?"

"I might."

"Then follow me to the house, and we'll talk about it." He scooped up his jars and clinked on by me, disappearing into the fern hedge.

I rode in behind him, and he invited me into his hovel without another thought to it.

A small bit of light came from a miner's lamp sitting on the board of a dry sink, but it was still a gray, little place inside, decorated with tattered chairs and two crooked wooden tables. Every available square inch and flat plane in the room was covered by a bottle. The containers were everywhere, glinting and sparkling in the lantern's shine. Elbari dumped his new load into the seat of a lumpy recliner.

"Is all this made from the pool?" I asked.

"Yes. Blended with different mountain herbs and the water is good for whatever ails you." He led me to the smallest of the rickety tables and picked through the bottles. Finding what he sought, he handed one to me. "This is some of the elixir. That's the only potent brew I have now."

"How much does it cost?"

"A single bottle is thirty thousand tricrowns."

No wonder Bareen Tykar wanted me to steal it. "Are you mad? That's outrageous!"

"I told you it was expensive. Is your grandmother worth it to you? With Spring Tonic, she'll get back her sight and her youth."

"I can't afford it."

"And you can't be sure it will work," he said.

"If it's the real thing, then why don't you take it yourself?" I asked.

"I'm not interested in being young again. Once around in

this life is enough for me. I'd rather have the money." Rubbing his long, crusty beard, he cast a look across the room. "Well, it was worth a try, anyway. We can at least help your grandmother get back her sight. She'll need some rootwart balm enhanced with a brightening spell."

He stepped toward the dry sink, and I saw my opportunity.

Most thieves carry the mundane things of the trade—lockpicks and glass cutters. Some also use whatever enchanted items they can lay their hands on—things like magical pouches complete with spells to shrink large objects for easy transport. Yet, with all that, the one thing a good thief depends upon is natural-born ability. In the years that skulduggery has earned me a living, I've always found my talent for sleight-of-hand the most useful. With the dwarf looking away from his precious bottle of Spring Tonic, I found my chance to nip the goods.

I made a small movement, turning a bit to the side to hinder the dwarf's full view of the table. Scraping the bottle against the wood, I pretended to return it to its square inch. In the few seconds it took, I gently fingered a neighboring container closer to the relinquished space and slid the Spring Tonic into the inside hem of my cape sleeve.

Elbari moved to search the other table. "Yes, here it is," he said, turning back to face me. "For five pieces of gold, your grandmother will get her eyesight back. She'll need to use the balm three times daily."

"I'll see that she does." I answered with a smile.

* * * * *

After visiting Jig Elbari, I knew one thing for certain: Bareen Tykar was a liar and skinflint. He could have bought the tonic for the right price, but instead thought to steal it. I can't fault a man for resorting to these tactics. If they didn't, I wouldn't be in business. Still, such people give me concern when they're not up front with their motives.

I stood in the center of his shop, and took my weight low

in the legs in case I needed to spring toward the door. Bareen Tykar licked his lips and looked at his two associates. They were moon elves, and in their silver-tinged beauty they appeared like stone statues waiting to be freed by some wizard's spell. Stationed to either side of the old merchant, each elf leaned on a glittering scimitar, the point of which ground into the wooden floor. To crystalize the scene, a hundred candles sparkled on the shelves behind the counter. The effect was beautiful, but my wariness didn't allow me to enjoy it.

"You have the elixir?" Bareen Tykar demanded.

"Do you have my commission?" I asked.

"Of course."

"Show it to me."

"After I see the goods."

"No."

He snapped his fingers and the two elven statues animated. They raised their weapons, approaching. "Search him," their master ordered.

I slowly retreated, meeting their advance by unsheathing my hunting knife. I could feel the taut pull of my riding leathers along the inner sides of my thighs, and I took a heartbeat to wonder what tricks I had buried in my boots. The elves were on me before I could remember.

I sliced at one, but my blade fell wide of its mark, cutting empty air and enraging the fellow. He smacked me in the face with the flat of his hand and pain shot through to my ears. I growled, kicking his partner in the stomach. He buckled for an instant, recovering with a snarl of his own. Backpedaling, I tried for the door, but they wedged me against the wall, instead. I was pinned there while they searched me for their elixir.

"He doesn't have it on him," one elf said.

"Where are you hiding it?" Bareen Tykar asked.

"The bond is broken between us, Merchant," I barked. "You won't get it from me. Send one of your thugs back to the mountains to find it for you."

"You were going to take my money and run."

With that, I received a slap to the head, and the room spun.

"One more chance," Bareen Tykar said. "Where is it?"

Spitting blood, I cursed him. "To Shar with you! May the Lady of Loss dog your every step!"

My answer only made matters worse. "See that he doesn't steal again for a long while," Bareen Tykar ordered.

I squirmed against the strong arms pinning me down. My knife was gone, snatched from my grip, and my legs were wound up with those of my assailants. One elf grabbed my hand. Before I could react, before I could untangle myself, he yanked on my wrist and twisted hard. Stabbing agony ran up my arm, and I screamed out. They tossed me into the empty street, shutting the door on my cries.

I lay in the gutter staring up at the heavens. For how long, I can't say. A street sweeper brushed by, ignoring me, intent on his evening duties. All the while the pain in my broken hand grew, and with it, my rage. Finally I rolled to a stand and returned to the carved door of Bareen Tykar's shop. Glancing in the window, I saw that it was dark and empty inside, the old merchant and his bodyguards gone out some back way.

Reaching my good hand out, I felt in the darkness for the intersection of the twisted wood design of the door. Gouging my fingers into the deep recess, I pulled out the small bottle of Spring Tonic I had hidden there.

*   *   *   *   *

Revenge smudges the sensibilities. Nothing matters except getting even, and as far as I was concerned, I would hurt Bareen Tykar. He would suffer a thousand times for what he did to me.

My hand had been mangled. The cleric with all his healing magic wasn't sure I'd ever get full use of it again. I was lucky to have a storehouse of goods to sell, so while I tried to recover my mobility, I could at least earn a living. After hearing the prognosis, I returned to my lair in the Sunset Mountains.

The moon courted me as I rode toward the wall of shrubs and boulders hiding the entrance to my retreat. A stream-fed waterfall spilled over the granite face of the mountain's upper brow, and I angled toward its gentle sound.

Stealth stepped into the wide groove formed by several huge rocks and stopped when he neared the lair's door. I paused in dismounting to breathe in the cold, fresh air, fill-ing my lungs and reviving my spirit as no spell-slicked Spring Tonic could. My horse nickered, seeming to agree. Grunting when the wrappings on my hand snagged on a saddle buckle, I slipped off, slapping Stealth gently on the rump. He made for the overhang of his stone barn.

My lodge was situated in a deep cave on the ridge over-looking Oak Island, a spit of land breaching into a high, wide lake. Here, in shacks and shanties, were the remains of the village where I grew up. I returned here often, though the mountaintop had long turned toward ghosts and memo-ries. The people were all gone, my family included, trading the freedom of alpine life for a living in the lowlands.

A rock slab set on a swinging pinion served as the door to the lair. Tipping back the recessed handle, I entered, imme-diately comforted by familiar surroundings.

I lit the lantern on the shelf by the door, tapping the stone portal closed with my shoulder. My mood brightened as the flame glow picked up the wondrous things I had stored in my burrow. I moved into the room, and as always, lingered to touch these ancient magical objects. Many had been cre-ated in the Heartlands and many had come to the Sunset Mountains by the old trading routes.

I'd stolen artifacts from peasants and aristocrats, alike. The gentry had rare, fanciful items that I loved and used to adorn my home, collectibles such as the banquet board cut from northern wood and fashioned in the Year of the High-mantle, when Azoun IV took the throne of Cormyr. It was rubbed to an exquisite luster by some craftsman of long ago, and the spell, too, was laid on like silk. Three short, lyrical words pronounced while standing at the long end of the table made the magic come together and the finest, tastiest foods appear.

Such classic antiques were in great demand, but high in price. The merchant class of the Heartlands couldn't yet afford them, so they settled on buying those more home-spun objects I collect from the peasants. Their particular fancies were spell-sewn quilts that kept a person warm on the chilliest days, and cinnabar leaves once grown in the long-dead city of Shoon and used by their magicians to conjure *feng shui*—good luck.

I flamed up another lantern and flooded the cave with soft, orange light. There was one item here for which I had come specifically. Opening the top drawer of my storage chest, I unwrapped the delicate packing paper surrounding my favorite possession. I carefully removed it from its parchment nest, lifting out the ancient, hand-sewn shawl.

Spun through with gold and platinum, and strung with tiny bronze beads, it was shaped like an arrowhead, lacking fringe or ruffle-edging to mar the simplicity of its lines. The weaving's antiquity and worth? Beyond comprehension.

I stole it and the incantation from a mountain wizard who used the shawl to capture his enemies. With a little ingenuity, it was possible to trap a person's life-force in the very fibers of the weaving. When I claimed the shawl as my own, I discovered that it had imprisoned many people already. By reversing the spell, I released them whole and complete. They went away thankful for their freedom and the chance to retaliate against the man who had done them wrong. Emptied, the cloak was packed away, though I knew that one day I would have an opportunity to try its magic on someone like Bareen Tykar.

* * * * *

Thieves can be masters of disguise. It helps to deflect the possibility of being recognized when out and about on business, and I, for one, take such things seriously. I move around too much in the towns and cities of the Heartlands to risk being recognized by my many enemies.

This night I walked through Kendil wearing coarse, brown linen. My long blond hair and tight beard were stained dark. I had added the tracks of a false scar along my cheek and an eye patch to balance the look. Sporting a limp, I hoped to distract attention from the filthy bindings wrapping my bad hand.

I entered Bareen Tykar's shop just before closing time, waiting silently by the door until he'd finished with a customer. The old man stared at me, and it looked as though he was going to summon his thugs.

Lowering my voice and wheezing a little, I spoke before he could call them. "You're the owner of this store?"

"Aye. So?"

"I just came to town and there be people here who tell me you like to buy old things."

"Who said that?"

"Some moon elf over at the inn. He was into his cups, but I thought I'd check it out. The year's been hard and funds are down. I'm selling off my personals, you see."

He stared at me—silent, calculating, distrustful. After a moment, his curiosity won over his caution. "What do you have?"

I shuffled up to the counter and grinned, making sure I breathed on him as I leaned close. The smell of onions and brown bread made him flinch. "What I have is a shawl," I said in a conspiratorial tone. "Struck through with powerful mountain magic."

"Let me see it," he said.

I opened my carry sack and gently pulled out the shawl, spreading it on his stone counter. The weaving glistened in the shop's candlelight. Bareen Tykar's eyes grew wide for a moment, then, as if he remembered his bargaining stance, he pasted on a bland expression.

"What does it do?" he asked.

"It'll mint you coins: gold and silver and platinum and copper."

His mouth came open a bit on those words, but after a sputtering inhale, he shook his head. "I've never heard of such a thing as this shawl. It's a fake."

"No, it's not. See these filaments in the weaving itself? Look how bright they are with the metals. It's through these fibers that the magic works to make the coins. I can't do much with it anymore, though."

"Why?"

"With each speaking of the incantation, the shawl's power wanes. It'll give up only so much gold, silver, and platinum per owner. I've used my turn, you see, and all I get now are copper pieces and not many of them."

He leaned in again and touched the shawl lightly. "You say this shawl is old? How old and from where does it come?"

"It belonged to a dwarf living in the Sunset Mountains and was made before the first Orcgate Wars in Thay."

"That old, then, is it?" Bareen Tykar asked. "Do you have letters of authenticity?"

I laughed. "From a dwarf? Are you mad?" I smoothed my chuckling into a glaring frown.

He snorted and crossed his arms, propping them on his huge stomach. "I'll require a demonstration. If copper is all you can make, then do it so I can see if this shawl really does what you say."

I counted to ten before nodding. Straightening. I took the shawl from the counter and placed it over my shoulders. It was a gossamer delight, so soft and billowy. How it sparkled against my linen shirt. I twisted slightly to pick up the candlelight as I slowly wrapped myself in it. The man's nostrils flared in response.

Being the careful man I am, I'd spent time planning out this encounter. I made a small, leather bag, designing it so it would easily fall open after pulling a slender, almost invisible thread attached to the clasp. This delicate task took me days with my bad hand, but in the end it worked well. I could place several coins inside it and by regulating the tension on the string, I could dump a few at a time. Before coming to Bareen Tykar's shop, I had slung the pouch over my shoulder and packed it beneath my coat.

Standing in the middle of the room, I muttered a useless incantation and released the copper pieces. Three fell clear and rolled across the floor.

The old merchant frowned. "Do it again," he said.

I repeated the motions and the nonsense words, dropping the rest of the contents from my bag. It looked good, like the shawl actually worked.

"I'll try it now," he said. "Give it to me."

I did as he commanded, watching him as he fitted the cloak around his body.

"What are the words I need to speak to make gold?" he demanded.

Digging into my britches pocket, I pulled out a small tear of parchment. I had written down the incantation that triggered the shawl's real power. "Can you read?"

His response was to grab the paper and whisper the ancient words to the spell.

The shawl began to shimmer. From where I stood, I could feel the warmth coming off it as the magic surrounded him. In the candle glow, I saw a distinct, woven texture forming on the skin of this encasing bubble. It sparkled and glittered. At one point I had to glance away from the brightness. A minute passed and it was, then, too late for the merchant to escape without my help.

He realized he was trapped. His growing panic fed the constricting power of the cloak and he began to beg for mercy, but the shell around him muffled his voice. I watched as the tears of anguish rolled down his fat cheeks, then finally, he squeezed his hands against his temples and opened his mouth to scream. Before he could, the shawl captured him.

He disappeared in sparks and glitter, the cloak falling to the floor with a soft flutter. I picked it up and felt the heaviness as the man's very being settled into the threads. Throwing it about my shoulders, I sagged beneath this weight, but after another moment slid by, the weaving grew delicate and silky again. Turning a slow circle, I smiled, then laughed. Such sweet revenge!

Bareen Tykar will remain in this filament prison for years, aware, yet helpless. It's only after I've grown old and think I've seen my last blue moon that I'll finally release him. When I do, I'll make him watch as I drink his precious Spring Tonic.

THE GREATEST HERO WHO EVER DIED

J. Robert King

The stormy winds that swept up from the Great Ice Sea often brought unwanted things to lofty Capel Curig. Tonight, in addition to pelting snow and driving gales, the wind brought a hideously evil man.

None knew him as such when he tossed open the battered door of the Howling Reed. They saw only a huge, dark-hooded stranger haloed in swirling snow. Those nearest the door drew back from the wind and the vast form precipitating out of it, drew back as the door slammed behind the dripping figure, slammed and shuddered in its frame. Without discharging the ice from his boots, the stranger limped across the foot-polished planks of the Reed to a trembling hearth fire. There he bent low, flung a few more logs on the flames, and stood, eclipsing the warmth and casting a giant shadow over the room.

The rumble of conversation in the Reed diminished as all eyes in the tiny pub turned furtively toward the ruined figure.

Silhouetted on the hearth, the stranger looked like some huge and ill-formed marionette. He lacked an arm, for his right sleeve was pinned to the shoulder and his left hand did all the adjusting of his fetid form. Deliberately, that widowed

hand now drew back some of his robes, but the sodden figure beneath looked no less shapeless. For all his shifting, he
did not remove the hood from his head, a head that appeared
two sizes too small for his body. Beneath the hood, the
man's face was old and lightless, with cold-stiffened lips, a
narrow black beard, and a hooked nose. In all, his form
looked as though a large man hid within those robes, holding some poorly proportioned puppet head to serve as his
face.

He spoke then, and his hollow voice and rasping tongue
made the patrons jump a bit. "Can any of you spare a silver
for a bowl of blood soup and a quaff of ale?"

None responded except by blank, refusing stares. Not
even Horace behind the bar would offer this stranger a
glass of water. Apparently, all would rather dare his wrath
than know their charities had provided sustenance to him.

The man was apparently all too acquainted with this
response, for he shook his head slowly and laughed a dry,
dead-leaf laugh. A few staggering steps brought him to a
chair, vacated upon his arrival and still warm from its former
occupant. There he collapsed with a wheeze like a punctured bellows.

"In the lands of Sossal, whence I hail, a man can earn his
blood and barley by telling a good tale. And I happen to have
such a tale, for my land gave birth to the greatest hero who
ever lived. Perhaps his story will earn me something
warm."

Those who had hoped to dismiss him with bald glares
and cruel silence now tried turning away and speaking
among themselves. Horace, for his part, retreated through a
swinging door to the kitchen, to the gray dishwater and the
piles of pots.

Unaffected, the shabby wanderer began the telling of his
tale with a snap of his rigid blue fingers. Green sparks
ignited in air, swirled about him, and spread outward like a
lambent palm in the heavy darkness. The sparking tracers
lighted on all those seated in the taproom, and each tiny star
extinguished itself in the oily folds of flesh between a

patron's knotted brows.

The faint crackling of magic gave way to a single, hushed sigh. In moments, the place fell silent again, and the tale began. "The lands of Sossal were once guarded by a noble knight, Sir Paramore, the greatest hero who ever lived. . . ."

* * * * *

Golden haired, with eyes like platinum, Sir Paramore strode in full armor through the throne room of King Caen. Any other knight would have been stripped of arms and armaments upon crossing the threshold, but not noble Paramore. He marched forward, brandishing his spell-slaying long sword Kneuma and dragging a bag behind him as he approached the royal dais. There the king and princess and a nervous retinue of nobles ceased their conference and looked to him. Only when within a sword swipe of His Majesty did Paramore finally halt, drop to one armored knee, and bow his fealty.

The king, his face ringed with early white locks, spoke. "And have you apprehended the kidnappers?"

"Better, milord," replied Paramore, rising with a haste that in anyone else would have been arrogance. He reached into the bag and drew out in one great and hideous clump the five heads of the kidnappers he had slain.

The king's daughter recoiled in shock. Only now did King Caen himself see the wide, slick line of red that Sir Paramore's bag had dragged across the cold flagstones behind him.

"You gaze, my liege, on the faces of the hoodlums you sought," the knight explained.

In the throat-clenched silence that followed, the wizard Dorsoom moved from behind the great throne, where his black-bearded lips had grown accustomed to plying the king's ears. "You were to bring them here for questioning, Paramore, not lop off their heads."

"Peace, Dorsoom," chided the king with an off-putting gesture. "Let our knight tell his tale."

"The tale is simple, milord," replied Paramore. "I questioned the abductors myself and, when I found them wanting of answers, removed their empty heads."

"This is nonsense," Dorsoom said. "You might have simply cut the heads off the first five peasants you saw, then brought them here and claimed them the culprits. There should have been a trial. And even if these five were guilty—which we can never know now—we do not know who assigned these ruffians their heinous task."

"They were kidnappers who had stolen away the children of these noble folk gathered around us," Paramore replied with even steel in his voice. "If anything, I was too lenient."

"You prevented their trial—"

"Still the wagging tongue of this worm," Paramore demanded of the king, leveling his mighty sword against the meddling mage. "Or perhaps these warriors of mine shall do the task first!"

The great doors of the throne room suddenly swung wide, and a clamor of stomping feet answered . . . small feet, the feet of children, running happily up the aisle behind their rescuer. Their shrill voices were raised in an unseemly psalm of praise to Sir Paramore as they ran.

Seeing their children, the nobles emptied from the dais and rushed to embrace their sons and daughters, held captive these long tendays. The ebullient weeping and cooing that followed drowned the protests of Dorsoom, who retreated to his spot of quiet counsel behind the throne. It was as though the sounds of joy themselves had driven him back into the darkness.

Over the pleasant noise, the grinning Paramore called out to the king. "I believe, my liege, you are in my debt. As was promised me upon the rescue of these dear little ones, I claim the fairest hand in all of Sossal. It is the hand of your beautiful daughter, Princess Daedra, that I seek."

Paramore's claim was answered by a chorus of shouts from the joyous children, who now abandoned their parents to crowd the heels of their rescuer. From their spot beside him, the children ardently pleaded the knight's case.

Daedra's bone-white skin flushed, and her lips formed a wound-red line across her face. The king's visage paled in doubt. Before either could speak, though, the children's entreaties were silenced by an angry cry.

"Hush now, younglings!" commanded a thin nobleman, his ebony eyes sparkling angrily beneath equally black brows and hair. "Your childish desires have no say here. The hand of the princess has been pledged to me these long years since *my* childhood, since before *she* was born. This usurping *knight*—" he said the word as though it bore a taint "—cannot steal her from me, nor can your piteous cater-wauling."

"'Tis too true," the king said sadly, shaking his head. He paused a moment, as though listening to some silent voice whisper behind his throne. "I am pressed by convention, Paramore, to grant her hand to Lord Ferris."

Sir Paramore sheathed his sword and crossed angry arms over his chest. "Come out, wicked mage, from your place of hiding in the shadow of this great man. Your whisperings cannot dissuade my lord and monarch from granting what his and mine and the princess's hearts desire."

With that, Paramore touched the handle of his mighty sword, Kneuma, to dispel whatever enchantment Dorsoom might have cast on the king. Then he snapped his fingers, and the tiny percussion of his nails struck sparks in the air. The king's retinue and the king himself, as though awakening from a dream, turned toward the shadow-garbed mage. Dorsoom sullenly answered the summons and moved into the light.

"Milord, do not be tricked by the puny magicks of this—"

"Hush, *mage*," replied King Caén evenly, regarding Dorsoom through changed eyes. He turned, then, to address the thin nobleman. "Lord Ferris, I know the hand of my daughter has been pledged to you since before you could understand what that pledge meant. But time has passed, as it does, and has borne out a nobler man than thee to take the princess's hand. Indeed, he has taken her heart as well, and mine too, with many great deeds that not a one of them is equalled by the full measure of your life's labors."

"But—"

The king held up a staying hand, and his expression was stern. "I am now convicted in this matter. You cannot sway me, only spur me to anger, so keep silence." His iron-hard visage softened as he looked upon Sir Paramore. "By royal decree, let the word be spread that on the morrow, you shall wed my darling child."

A cheer went up from all of those gathered there save, of course, Lord Ferris and the mage, Dorsoom. The joyous voices rung the very foundations of the palace and filled the stony vault above.

It was only the plaintive and piercing cry of one woman that brought the hall back to silence. "My Jeremy!" cried the noblewoman, wringing a light blue scarf in tender, small hands as she came through the doors. "Oh, Sir Paramore! I've looked and looked through all this crowd and even checked with the doorguards, and he is not here. Where is my Jeremy?"

Sir Paramore stepped down from his rightful place before the king and, tears now running down his face, said, "Even I could not save your son, with what these butchers had already done to him. . . ."

* * * * *

"And her cries were piteous to hear," the cloaked man muttered low, and the crowd in the pub soaked in the sibilant sound of his voice, "so that even evil Dorsoom shut his ears—"

"That's it, then. No more ale for any of you. I don't care how strong the gale's ablowin' out there; there's a stronger one in here, and it's ablowin' out this stranger's arse!"

It was Horace, fat Horace who'd tended this bar in this tiny crevice of the Snowdonia Mountains and fed eggs and haggis to the grandfathers and fathers and sons of those gathered here. In all that time, the good folk of Capel Curig had learned to trust Horace's instincts about weather and planting and politics and people. Even so, on this singular night, regarding this singular man, Horace didn't strike the others as their familiar and friendly confidant.

"Shut up, Horace," cried Annatha, a fishwife. "You've not even been listening, back there banging your pots so loud we've got to strain our ears to hear."

"Yeah," agreed others in chorus.

"I hear well enough from the kitchen, well enough to know this monstrous man's passin' garbage off as truth! He makes out King Caen to be a dotterin' and distracted coot when we all know he is strong and just and in full possession of himself. And what of Dorsoom, cast as some malicious mage when in truth he's wise and good? And Lord Ferris, too?"

Fineas, itinerant priest of Torm, said, "I'm all for truth—as you all know—but bards have their way with truth, and barkeeps their way with brandy. So let him keep the story coming, Horace, and you keep the brandy coming, and between the two, we'll all stay warm on this fierce night."

Now the stranger himself extended that trembling left hand that did the work for two and said with a rasping tongue, "It is your establishment, friend. Will you listen to your patrons' desires, or turn me out?"

Horace grimaced. "I'd not throw a rabid dog out on a night like this. But I'd just as soon you shut up, friend. Aside from lyin', you're puttin' a dreamy, unnatural look in these folk's eyes, and I don't like payin' customers to go to sleep on me."

This comment met with more protests, which Horace tried unsuccessfully to wave down.

"All right. I'll let him speak. But, mark me: he's got your souls now. He's worked some kind of mesmerizin' magic on you with the words he weaves. I, for one, ain't listenin'."

Nodding his shadowed and dripping head, the stranger watched Horace disappear into the kitchen, then seemed to study him hawkishly through the very wall as he continued his tale. "Though Lord Ferris's forked tongue had been stilled that morning before the king and nobles and children,

his hands would not be stilled that night when he stalked
through the dim castle toward Sir Paramore's room.

"But one other child of the night—the ghost of poor dead
Jeremy—was not allied to the sinister plans of Ferris.
Indeed, the ghost of Jeremy had sensed evil afoot and so
hovered in spectral watch on the stair to Paramore's room.
When he spotted Lord Ferris, advancing dark at the foot of
the stair, Jeremy flew with warning to the bed foot of his former bosom friend, Petra. . . ."

*　*　*　*　*

Petra was a brown-haired girl-child and the leader of the
pack of noble children. Jeremy found her abed in a castle
suite, for the children and the parents had all been wel-
comed by King Caen to spend the night. Poor Jeremy now
gazed with sad ghostly eyes on the resting form of Petra,
sad ghostly eyes that had once gazed down on his own still
body, lifeless and headless.

"Wake up, Petra. Wake up. I have terrible news regarding
our savior, Sir Paramore," the child-ghost rasped. His phantom voice sounded high and strained, like the voice of a
large man pretending to be a child.

And Petra did wake. When she glimpsed her departed
friend, her brave girl-heart gave a start: unlike greater
ghosts decked in diaphanous gossamers, poor Jeremy had
no body upon which to hang such raiments. He was but a
disembodied head that floated beyond the foot of her bed,
and even now his neck slowly dripped the red life that had
once gushed in buckets. So grotesque and horrible was this
effect that Petra, who truly was a brave child, could not
muster a word of greeting for her dead companion.

"It's Lord Ferris," the ghost-child said urgently. "He plots
to slay our Sir Paramore where he sleeps tonight."

Petra managed then a stammer and a wide stare.

"You must stop him," came the ghost's voice.

She was getting up from the feather mattress now, array-
ing the bedclothes around her knees. With the sad eyes of

small boys—who see small girls as mothers and sisters and lovers and enemies all at once—poor Jeremy watched Petra's delicate hands as she gathered herself.

At last she whispered, "I'll tell Mother—"

"No!" Jeremy's voice was urgent, strident. "Grown-ups won't believe. Besides, Sir Paramore saved your life this morning. You can save his life now, this evening!"

"I cannot stop Ferris alone."

"Then get the others," Jeremy rasped. "Awaken Bannin and Liesle and Ranwen and Parri and Mab and Karn and the others, too. Tell them to bring their fathers' knives. Together you can save our savior as he saved us."

Already, Petra was tying the sash of her bedclothes in a cross over her heart and breathlessly slipping sandals on her feet.

"Hurry," commanded Jeremy. "Even now, Lord Ferris is climbing the stair toward Sir Paramore's room!"

Upon this urgent revelation, Petra gasped, and Jeremy was gone.

Alerted and assembled in the next moments, the children followed Petra to the stair. It was a long and curving stairway that led to the high tower where Sir Paramore had chosen to bed. The steps were dark, lit mainly by a faint glow of starlight through occasional arrow loops in the wall. But when Petra and her child warriors began to climb, they saw ahead of them the vague, flickering illumination of a candle.

"Quiet now," whispered she.

Bannin, a brown-haired boy half her age, nodded seriously and slipped his small hand into hers. The twins Liesle and Ranwen smiled at each other with nervous excitement. Meanwhile, Parri and Mab and Karn and the others clustered at the rear of the pack and set hands on their knives.

"That's got to be the candle of Lord Ferris," Petra mouthed, indicating the light. "We've got to be quiet, or he'll know we're coming."

The children nodded, for they adored Petra as much as Jeremy had when he lived. And they followed her, doing their very best to be silent and stealthy, though children

have a different sense of that than do adults. They pro-
ceeded on tiptoes, fingertips dragging dully across the
curved inner wall, childish lips whispering loud specula-
tions. As they climbed, the light grew brighter, and their
fear welled higher, and their voices became froggy from the
tension of it all.

With all this muttering, it was no wonder that they came
round one of the cold stone curves of the stair to find the
narrow, black, long-legged Lord Ferris poised above them,
his wiry body stretched weblike across the tight passage.

"What are you children doing here?" he asked in an ebon
voice that sent a cold draft down the stairs and past the children.

The brave-hearted crew started at this rude welcome, but
did not dart. Petra, who alone hadn't flinched, said stonily,
"What are *you* doing?"

The man's eyes flashed at that, and his gloved hand fell to
the pitch-handled dagger at his side. "Go."

The group wavered, some in the rear involuntarily drawing back a step. But Petra did something incredible. With
the catlike speed and litheness of young girls, she slipped
past the black-cloaked man and his knife. She stood now,
barring the stairs above him.

"We stay. You go," she stated simply.

Lord Ferris's lip curled in a snarl. His hand gripped her
shoulder and brusquely propelled her back down the stairs.
Her footing failed on the damp stone, one leg twisting unnaturally beneath her. Then came a crack like the splintering of
green wood, and a small cry. She crumpled to the stone-
edged steps and tumbled limply down to the children, fetch-
ing up at their feet and hardly breathing.

They paused in shock. Young Bannin bent, already weeping, beside her. The others took one look at her misshapen
leg and rushed in a fierce pack toward the lord. Their young
voices produced a pure shriek that adults cannot create, and
they swarmed the black-cloaked nobleman, who fumbled
now to escape them.

They drove their fathers' knives into the man's thighs. He

toppled forward onto them and made but a weak attack in return, punching red-headed Mab between her pigtails and, with a flailing knee, striking the neck of Karn, too. The first two casualties of battle fell lifeless beneath the crush, and the steps under them all were suddenly slick with blood.

As though their previous earnestness had been feigned, the children now fought with berserker rage. They furiously pummeled and stabbed the man who lay atop them, the once-bold Ferris now bellowing and pleading piteously. At one point in the brawl, Parri dropped down to take the crimson dagger from Mab's cold hand, then sunk it repeatedly into the back of the nobleman.

Yet Lord Ferris clung tenaciously to life. His elbow swept back and cracked Liesel's head against the stone wall, and she fell in a heap. Next to go was her twin, Ranwen, who seemed to feel Liesel's death in kindred flesh and stood stock-still as the man's fallen candle set her ablaze. Ranwen, too, was unmade by a clumsy kick.

Aside from the bodies that now clogged the path and made it treacherous with blood, Lord Ferris had only poor Parri and two others to battle now. His weight alone proved his greatest weapon, for these next children went down beneath him, not to rise again. That left only bawling Bannin and broken Petra below, neither able to fight.

The man in black found footing amidst the twisted limbs of the fallen, then descended slowly toward Bannin and Petra. "Put the knives away," said he, sputters coming from his punctured lungs.

The boy-child—young, eyes clouded with blood, ears ringing with screams—drew fearfully back a few paces. Petra could not retreat.

"I told you to go, you little fiends!" growled Lord Ferris. Red tears streaked his battered face. "Look what you've done!"

Bannin withdrew farther, his whimpering giving way to full-scale sobs. But Petra, with a monumental effort, rose then. The desperate cracking of her leg did not deter her lunge. Through bloodied teeth, she hissed, "Death to evil," and drove Parri's blade into the nobleman's gut.

Only now did Sir Paramore come rushing down the stairs, just in time to see wicked Lord Ferris tumble stiff past a triumphant Petra. She smiled at him from within a sea of scarlet child's-blood, then collapsed dead to the floor.

* * * * *

The death of the child in the story coincided oddly with the death of the fire on the hearth; the stormy night had reached its darkest corner. But the rapt crowd of listeners, who sat mesmerized in the storyteller's deepening shadow, did not even notice the cold and dim around them. Horace, in the now-frigid kitchen, did.

It was Horace, then, who had to trudge out in the snow for more wood. He wondered briefly why none of the patrons had complained of the chill and dim in the taproom, as they had tirelessly done in days and years past. As soon as the question formed in his mind, the answer struck him: The stranger's story had kindled a hotter, brighter fire this evening, and by it the people were warming themselves.

Aside from lying slurs on King Caen, Dorsoom, and Lord Ferris—*dead now?* Horace wondered, fearing that much of the story might be true—no crime had yet been committed by the stranger, not even a stolen bit of bread or blood soup. And his story kept the patrons there when Horace would have thought folks would flee to their lofted beds. But something was not right about the stranger. The hairs on the back of Horace's neck, perhaps imbued by the natural magic of apron yokes and years of honest sweat and aches, had stood on end the moment the man had entered with his swirling halo of snow. Now, as the darkness deepened, as Horace heard snatches of the wicked tale that held the others in thrall, his uneasy feeling had grown to wary conviction. This man was not merely a slick deceiver. He was evil.

Despite this certainty, despite the outcry of every sinew of his being, Horace knew he didn't dare throw the man out now or he would have a wall-busting brawl on his hands.

Even so, as he bundled wood into the chafed and accustomed flesh of his inner arm, he lifted the icy axe that leaned against the woodpile and bore it indoors with him.

In the taproom beyond, the stranger was bringing his tale to its inevitable end. . . .

* * * * *

There was much that followed the cruel slaying of the innocent children: Sir Paramore's shock at the assassination attempt, the shrieks of parents whose children were gone for good, the trembling praise of the king for the deeds of the fallen, the empty pallets hauled precariously up the curving stair, the filled pallets borne down on parents' backs, the brigade of buckets cleansing the tower, the stationing of guards to protect the princess's betrothed. . . .

And after it all, Sir Paramore prayed long to the mischievous and chaotic heavens, to Beshaba and Cyric and Loviatar, seeking some plan behind the horrific affair. When his shaken mind grew too weary to sustain its devotion and his knees trembled too greatly beneath him to remain upright, Sir Paramore hung the spell-slaying Kneuma on his bedpost and crawled into his sheets to vainly seek sleep.

Without alarm or movement, and as soon as the knight was disarmed and disarmored, the mage Dorsoom suddenly stood inside the closed and bolted door. Sir Paramore started, and an approbation rose to his lips as he sat up in bed.

But the mage spoke first, in a sly hiss: "I know what you have done, monstrous man."

Sir Paramore stood up now, gawking for a moment in rage and amazement before reaching for his spell-slaying sword. His hand never touched the hilt, though, for in that instant the mage cast an enchantment on him that froze his body like ice.

Seeing Paramore rendered defenseless, Dorsoom spoke with a cat's purr. "Most folk in this land think you a valiant knight, but I know you are not. You are a vicious and cruel and machinating monster."

Though he could not move feet or legs or arms, Sir Paramore found his tongue. "Out of here! Just as my young knights slew your assassin, I will slay you!"

"Do not toy with me," said the black-bearded mage. "Your sword dispels magic only when in your grip; without it, you can do nothing against me. Besides, neither Ferris nor I am the true assassin. You are."

"Guards! Save me!" cried Paramore toward the yet-bolted door.

"I know how you arranged the kidnappings. I know how you hired those five men to abduct the noblemen's children," said the mage.

"What?" roared the knight, struggling to possess his own body but bringing only impotent tremors to his legs.

The guards outside were pounding now and calling for assurances.

"I know how you met with your five kidnappers to pay them for their duties," continued the mage. "But they received only your axe as their payment."

"Guards! Break down the door!"

"I know how you took the clothes of one of the kidnappers you had slain, dressed in them, masqueraded in front of the children as him, and in cold blood slew Jeremy for all their eyes to see. I know how later, in guise of the noble knight you never were, you rushed in to feign saving the rest of the children," said the mage, heat entering his tone for the first time.

The guards battered the bolted door, which had begun to splinter.

Paramore shouted in anguish, "In the name of all that is holy—!"

"You did it all for the hand of the princess; you have killed even children to have her hand. You orchestrated the kidnapping, played both villain and hero, that you might extort a pledge of marriage in exchange for rescuing them."

The tremors in Sir Paramore legs had grown violent; by the mere contact of his toe against the bedpost, his whole pallet shook, as did the scabbarded sword slung on the bed knob.

"I know how you sent this note," the mage produced a crumpled slip of paper from his pocket and held it up before him, "to Lord Ferris, asking him to come up tonight to see you, and knowing that your '*knights*' would waylay him."

"It's not even my handwriting," shouted Paramore. He shook violently, and the rattling blade tilted down toward his stony leg.

Louder came the boot thuds on the door. The crackle of splintering wood grew. With a gesture, though, Dorsoom cast a blue glow about the door, magic that made it solid as steel.

"And in that bag," cawed the mage, knowing he now had all the time in heaven, "in the bag that late held the five heads of the five abductors lies the head of Jeremy—the head you carved out to form a puppet to appear at the foot of Petra's bed!"

The mage swooped down to the sack of heads, but his hand never clasped it. In that precise moment, the mighty sword Kneuma jiggled free and struck Paramore's stony flesh, dispelling the enchantment on him. A mouse's breath later, that same blade whistled from its scabbard to descend on the bended neck of the sorcerer.

As the razor steel of Paramore sliced the head from the court magician, so too, it sundered the spell from the door. The guards who burst then into the room saw naught but a shower of blood, then the disjoined head propelled by its spray onto the bed and Dorsoom's body falling in a heap across the red-stained sack, soaked anew.

Seeing it all awrong, the guards rushed in to restrain Paramore. Whether from the late hour or the outrageous claims of the wizard or the threat of two warriors on one, Sir Paramore's attempt to parry the blades of the guards resulted in the goring of one of them through the eye. The wounded man's cowardly partner fell back and shouted an alarm at the head of the stair. Meantime Paramore, pitying the man whose bloodied socket his sword-tip was lodged in, drove the blade the rest of the way into the brain to grant the man his peace.

An alarm went up throughout the castle: "Paramore the murderer! Stop him! Slay him!"

Sir Paramore watched the other guard flee, then knelt beside the fallen body at his feet. A tear streaked down his noble cheek, and he stared with unseeing eyes upon the sanguine ruin of his life. Determined to remember the man who destroyed it all, he palmed the head of Dorsoom and thrust it angrily into his sack, where it made a clottering sound. Then he stood solemnly, breathed the blood- and sweat-salted air, and strode from the room, knowing that even if he escaped with his life, he would be unrighteously banished.

And he was.

* * * * *

"And that, dear friends," rasped the robed stranger, his left hand stroking his black beard, "is the tragic tale of the greatest hero who ever lived."

The room, aside from the crackle of the hearth fire and the howl of the defiant wind, was dead silent. The people who had once scorned this broken hovel of a man now stared toward him with reverence and awe. It wasn't his words. It wasn't his story, but something more fundamental about him, more mystic and essential to his being. Magic. Those who once would have denied him a thimble of water would now happily feast him to the best of their farms, would gladly give their husbands and sons to him to be soldiers, their wives and daughters to him to be playthings. And this ensorcelled reverence was only heightened by his next words.

"And that, dear friends, is the tragic tale of how *I* came to be among you." Even the wind and the fire stilled to hear what had to follow. "For, you see, *I* am Sir Paramore."

With that, he threw back the yet-sodden rags that had draped him, and from the huge bundle that had been the body of the stranger emerged a young and elegant and powerful and platinum-eyed warrior. His face was very different from the wizened and sepulchral one that had spoken to them. The latter—the dismembered head of Dorsoom—was jammed down puppetlike past the wrist on the warrior's right hand. The dead mouth of the dead wizard moved even now by the device of the warrior's fingers, positioned on the bony palate and in the dry, rasping tongue. Throughout the night, throughout the long telling, the gathered villagers had all listened to the puppet head of a dead man.

The old man's voice now came from the young man's mouth as his fingers moved the jaw and tongue. "Believe him, ye people! Here is the greatest hero who ever lived." A brown-black ooze clung in dribbles to Paramore's forearm.

Only Horace, stumbling now into the taproom, was horrified by this; the depravity did not strike the others in the slightest. The simple folk of Capel Curig left their chairs and moved wonderingly up toward the towering knight and his grisly puppet. They crowded him just as the children had done in the story. Cries of "Teach us, O knight! Lead us, Paramore! Guard us and save us from our enemies!" mingled with groans and tongues too ecstatic for human words.

In their center, the beaming sun of their adoration stretched out his bloodied hand and enwrapped them. "Of course I will save you. Only follow me and be my warriors, my knights!"

"We would die for you!"

"Let us die for you!"

"Paramore! Paramore!"

The praises rose up above the rumble of the wind and the growl of the fire, and the uplifted hands of the people could have thrust the roof entire from the inn had Paramore only commanded it.

The adulation was so intense that none—not even the god-man Paramore himself—saw Horace's flashing axe blade until it emerged red from the knight's gurgling throat.

TWILIGHT

Troy Denning

The world was young.

And on the shores of Cold Ocean sat the woman, and she had the size of a mountain and the shape as well. She had great hips as large as hillocks and she had a bosom of craggy buttresses. The woman had also a sharp chin and a crooked nose, and cheeks as flat as cliffs. She had eyes round and black, as are caves, and white billowing hair, like snow blowing off the lofty peaks.

Ulutiu, the Ocean King, knew not the woman's name, nor did he care, as long as she came often to dangle her feet in his sea. Then he liked to climb to her shoulders and come sliding back down, to twirl his sinuous body around her peaks, to slip down her stomach and glide along the cleft where her thighs pressed together, then to leap off her knees at journey's end and splash back into the freezing waters. So much did the Ocean King like this game that he would climb onto the icy shore and do it again and again, doing it for days with no thought of hunger or fatigue or anything but joy, temporal and fleshly.

And the woman, who was called Othea, also loved the game well. The feel of Ulutiu's slick hide slithering over her skin she craved as her lungs craved air. She liked to brace her hands against the frozen ground, lean back, close her eyes, and think only of the icy pleasures ravaging her body. Deep into torpor would she fall. She would sink into a stupor as blissful as it was cold, and at last she would collapse in utter ecstasy. Then would her body quake, rocking lands far away, ripping green meadows asunder and shaking the snow from the mountains to crash down into the valleys with a fury as great as her rapture.

All this Annam the All Father saw. Mighty was his wrath, and mightier still because it was his curse to hear their thoughts and feel their lust. He raised himself from the canyon where he had lain, and even the crashing flood waters when the river flowed again were not as fierce as his temper. The All Father spat out his disgust, and a storm of sleet raged across the gray waters of Cold Ocean.

Annam strode forward. So heavy were his steps that the creatures of the air forsook their nests and flew, geese and harpies together, eagles beside dragons; so many were there that they darkened the sky with their wings. The beasts of the land also fled, hooves and claws tearing the plants from the meadows, and also the monsters of the sea, their fins and flukes churning the ocean into a cold froth.

Then did Ulutiu know he had transgressed against a high god. He peered over Othea's knee, and his whiskers twitched and his ears lay against his head.

"Othea!" Annam's voice howled across the shore like the blustering wind, and truly there had never been a tempest so terrible. "Have I not spoken against your dalliances?"

Ulutiu's dark eyes grew wide with terror, and he disappeared behind Othea's bulk. Annam heard a splash in Cold Ocean and was not pleased. He rushed to the sea in two quick bounds and there he knelt, and when he spied a dark figure slipping from shore he stretched out his long arm and scooped the Ocean King from the icy waters.

"Annam, harm him not!" Othea's voice rolled across the icy shore as the rumble of a fuming mountain, and it was plain that she spoke in command, not supplication. "Ulutiu bears no blame in this. He was playing, nothing more."

"I know well enough what his games beget!" The All Father rose to his exalted height and faced Othea, and the cold water that dripped from his hand fell over the land like rain. "Firbolgs, verbeegs, fomorians, ettins!"

"Nay, not the ettin," Othea corrected, and when she spoke she showed Annam no fear. "That one *you* sired."

"Perhaps, but that is not the matter here."

Surely, it would have pleased Annam to deny the ettin's paternity, but the All Father knew he had sired the monster, and Othea would not say it had been someone else. That she denied him even this boon made his anger greater, and he thought that her punishment would be very hard indeed.

Othea paid no heed to Annam's ire, for she was not happy to have her game interrupted. "What *is* the matter, Husband?"

"I took you as Mother Queen of the *giants*," Annam answered. "You are to people Toril with my progeny—true giants—not with Ulutiu's bastard races!"

"Toril is as empty as it is young," Othea responded. "There is room enough for giant-kin."

"Did you not claim the same defense after your dance with rat-faced Vaprak?" Annam demanded. "And now ogres overrun Ostoria. Everywhere, they plague the empire of my children, gnawing at its seams like vermin."

"Perhaps your children are weak and Vaprak's are strong."

"I should have drowned the ogre when first you bore it!" Annam stormed, and a blizzard swept across the shore on roaring winds. "I should have crushed Vaprak's skull for daring to cuckold me. I shall not make the mistake twice."

The All Father made tight his grip. Though the shriek that rose from the Ocean King's throat was long and loud, it was a mere gust against the tempest of Annam's anger. Ulutiu saw he would soon die, so he pulled with hands that were like flippers and he kicked with feet that were like flukes. But Annam was the strongest of the strong, and nothing could escape his grip.

"Do not!" Othea's tone remained sharp.

Annam was not pleased. "This shall be a lesson to you."

The All Father bore down, and bones snapped and organs burst. Ulutiu wailed, and a tremendous swell rose far out in Cold Ocean. It came rolling to shore with a terrible speed and crashed against Annam's looming figure, breaking over his head and tearing at the Ocean King's body.

Even the sea could not defy Annam. He stood against the torrent as steady as the pillars of his palace, and when the receding waters no longer swirled about his waist, the All Father held Ulutiu. The Ocean King was limp and silent, but still his heart beat. Weak and erratic it beat, and Annam thought his punishment had been just.

"As with Ulutiu, so it shall be with all your lovers," Annam proclaimed. The All Father turned and whipped his arm toward the center of Cold Ocean, and Ulutiu's body raced through the sky as a shooting star. "I will have no more bastard races loose in the empire of my children!"

Othea watched a long time, until Ulutiu faded to a fleck of darkness in the sky. She watched until that speck arced downward, and still she watched as it splashed among the icebergs at Cold Ocean's distant heart. Then she looked at Annam, and the tears in her eyes were as large as ponds.

"There shall be no more giant-kin," Othea promised.

"That is good." Annam smiled, to make plain she had pleased him. "For I will not tolerate them."

Othea smiled not. Verily, she twisted her mouth into a sneer, and the sneer was more angry than a fiend's snarl. "Neither shall there be more true giants."

"What?" Annam demanded, and he was not happy.

"I will bear no more races for you," Othea said again. In her eyes shone a black gleam of anger, and it was a fury so cold that her tears turned to ice and tumbled down her face like an avalanche. "I love Ulutiu's children more than I love yours, and so I have done with you."

"I am the All Father!" Annam's voice tore at Othea's face as a fierce wind tears at a mountainside. "You cannot refuse me!"

"Why can I not?" Othea demanded. "Will you punish me as you punished Ulutiu? I welcome it!"

So mighty was Annam's fury that he could but roar, and the winds howled as they had never howled before, on their breath bearing shards of ice that scoured the plants from the soil and the soil from the stone. From his belt the All Father took the great axe Sky Cleaver and raised it to strike.

His rage did not frighten Othea, for she had spoken in truth and would gladly follow Ulutiu. When Annam saw this, the fury in his heart changed to shock. Sky Cleaver slipped from his hand, and the axe sailed far over the plains, until at last it came down on a mountain and split it asunder, and so Split Mountain was created.

Annam did not see this, for his thoughts were as mad dragons, whirling about his head in a tumult more befitting a mortal than a deity. He was the All Father. It was his right to have Othea, and he could have her by force, if he wished. Yet Annam was no evil god, and it would not please him to loose the spawn of a wicked union on this young world. The ettin had been horrible enough. Anything worse would destroy the empire of his children and not strengthen it.

But Annam could not yield to Othea. He had seen that Toril would be a world of many races, not just ogres and giant-kin, but of humans and dwarves and dark-loving beings even more horrible. The All Father saw that if his children were to fare well, they would need a wise and powerful king to lead their empire.

So he spoke to Othea, saying, "You shall bear me one more giant, and he shall be the greatest of all, wise and strong and just, for he shall be king of giants."

"I have already borne you a titan," Othea replied. "Let him be king of the giants."

"Nay!" Annam decreed, and his mighty voice rocked Othea on her heels. "The titan is keen and strong and forthright, but he is also proud and vain. The empire of my children must have a better king than that."

Annam took breath, drawing it not into his chest, but deeper into him, down into his loins, and there he held it.

"Storm all you wish," Othea said. "I will not yield."

The All Father exhaled. The wind that came from his

mouth was not a tempest, but a divine zephyr, warm with the breath of spring and the promise of life, and Annam blew this breeze upon Othea, so that it passed over her body as chiffon passes over a bride's head, and the Mother Queen trembled.

No obsidian was ever as black as Othea's face grew then. "What have you done, Annam?"

The All Father smiled, for his trick had pleased him well. "Can you not feel the answer in your womb?" he asked, and in his eye he had the look of a wyvern. "I have got a king on you."

"A king that shall never be born!" A bottomless rift shot across the plain, for such was Othea's anger. "I will hold him until the end of time!"

"Ha! That you cannot do," Annam said. "If you try, he shall grow within you until he splits your bulk asunder."

The Mother Queen gave thought to her husband's words, and after a time she said, "Then will I spill him out early and summon Vaprak's brood. They always have need of tender fodder!"

Annam's mouth fell open and out rushed the thunder and lightning. "He is your child too!" the All Father roared. "You would not feed him to ogres!"

"Not if you have gone," Othea said, and now a crooked smile was upon her craggy lips.

"You offer a bargain?"

"Leave Toril, and I will hold the infant until he can fight his own way from my womb," Othea said. "But if you return before he is born, then will I force him out, and then will Vaprak's brood feast on your spawn."

So cold was her voice that the clouds froze in the sky, and they fell to ground to become the glaciers of the mountains.

The All Father grinned. "Well do I like this game, for my seed is strong and will not long be denied," he proclaimed. "I shall return when my king-child calls my name, and then shall I watch the empire of my children spread over Toril as wind speeds across the plains."

Annam waved an arm toward the heavens. From his hand

spilled a rainbow of five colors; onto this rainbow he stepped, and climbed into the sky with strides as long as rivers.

Othea watched him go, and when the blue firmament had swallowed him up, she looked toward the heart of Cold Ocean. Though the distance was immeasurably vast, she saw the terrible vengeance of her husband. There Ulutiu lay upon an iceberg all streaked with crimson, his body twisted as bodies cannot twist. From his ears trickled dark blood and from his mouth bubbled red froth, and together they spilled into the gray waters of his sea.

"I swear the voice of Annam's child shall never sound outside my womb." Though Othea but whispered, the waves caught her voice and carried it across the waters to the ears of the Ocean King. "I wish I could avenge you better, but the All Father is powerful and this little is all I can do."

Ulutiu raised his head and to his lips came a smile. Across the ice he dragged himself, to where Cold Ocean lapped at the brink of his death-raft, and into the crimson waters he plunged his arm. For a long time he remained there, motionless, until it seemed the life had passed from his body, and the Mother Queen wailed forth her grief. From her mouth spilled the Hundred-Day Night, and that is why winter and darkness are as brother and sister in the northlands.

But Ulutiu had not yet passed from this world. The Ocean King rolled onto his back and pulled his hand from the cold waters, and on his fingertips hung five crystals of ice. They had the color of gems; they were emerald and sapphire, ruby, amber, and one as white as a diamond. The Ocean King plucked the crystals off his fingers and pressed them all to his collar, and there they hung as on a chain.

Ulutiu closed his eyes and from his throat came a long sigh; then did his spirit leave the world, as fog rises from the cold waters, and a shimmering fan of color soared from each crystal to dance like ghosts high in the sky. Thus were the Boreal Lights born. Then Cold Ocean encircled his death-raft with a towering waterspout and sprayed a shroud of ice over his body. The spout spun faster, and the shroud became a veil; faster it spun, and the veil thickened into a mantle, then into a coffin, and soon the ice had grown thick as a tomb.

The waterspout whirled faster, spraying the tomb with layer after layer of sleet, until the mound became a drift, the drift a hill, the hill a mountain, and still it grew. The winds raged harder. The sea waters froze into an endless white plain, and the heavens grew as gray as steel. Cascades of snow tumbled from the sky. The tempest whipped the flakes to every corner of the Cold Ocean, to the east and west, and to the north and south, and to all places between, and the vastness of the frozen sea vanished into the white haze of blizzard.

The storm continued without end, month after month, and the seasons grew into years and the years into centuries. All this time did Othea watch, and though her hunger howled as the blizzard, she took no food. Inside her stomach, Annam's child gnawed at her womb, craving the sustenance to grow, but always the Mother Queen denied him, and kept herself alive only by drinking from the Well of Health. Never did the unborn giant-king grow strong enough to free himself, and the Mother Queen returned often to Cold Ocean to watch the snow pile layer upon layer. The sea became a looming wall of ice, as broad as the horizon and so high it scraped the belly of the sky, until it had grown so vast that the ocean bed could not hold it, and it slipped the ancient shore and began to creep southward, slow and inexorable.

Then did Othea's laughter burst across the land like the crack of a distant volcano, for in the glacier's path lay the pride of jealous Annam: Ostoria, Empire of Giants.

* * * * *

Upon the floor sat an orb of blue ice, its perfect surface polished as smooth as glass and its pith as transparent as air. The sphere's creator, the titan Lanaxis, stood beside it. Gathered around him were Nicias, dynast of cloud giants, and Masud, khan of fire giants. There were also Vilmos, paramount of storm giants, Ottar, jarl of frost giants, and all the other Sons of Annam, the eternal monarchs born of Othea and destined to rule the races of giant-kind as long as Ostoria endured.

It had been thousands of years since Othea had sent their father away, but even lacking Annam's guidance, Ostoria had grown large and powerful. It stretched so far that in two ten-days Lanaxis could not walk from one end to the other. The empire extended almost as far southward, to where kingdoms of dwarves and humans were rising. Each race of giants held dominion over one area of this vast realm, and so the Sons of Annam were scattered far and wide.

Rarely did the Sons convene, but when they did, it was here at Bleak Palace, Lanaxis's home. This day, the titan had summoned his fellows onto his wind-blasted veranda. Here, no wall or pillar blocked the northward view, where the vastness of the Great Glacier loomed beyond the frozen plain, creeping relentlessly southward to swallow their empire.

Lanaxis said, "I have called us together for good reason." As he spoke, wisps of inky blackness gathered in the depths of his ice orb. The giants showed no surprise, for magic came to titans as naturally as smashing to hill giants.

Lanaxis continued, "I have found Ulutiu's grave. Now can we destroy his crystal necklace, and with it the Great Glacier."

A murmur of support rustled among the Sons of Annam, for they hated the Great Glacier as they hated nothing else. But one giant, Dunmore, thane of wood giants, did not add his voice to the approving chorus.

"You have called us here for nothing." The thane's voice was as stiff as the bole of an ironwood tree. "Has Othea not forbidden us to set foot upon the Great Glacier?"

"We will not tell her we are going."

Lanaxis eyed the thane as he spoke. Dunmore was a runt for a giant, thinly built and standing barely as tall as the titan's thigh. With a hairless body, oversized head, and oak-colored skin, he looked more like kin than true giant, and Lanaxis often wondered if Othea had not lied about the wood giant's sire.

"You can't deceive Othea!" Dunmore gasped. "Her punish—"

"I love our empire too much to let ice wipe it away," Lanaxis interrupted. "I will save Ostoria—and after that is done, I'll gladly bear any punishment Othea lays on me."

Lanaxis shifted his attention to the other giants. "Let me show you where Ulutiu lies, and then it is my hope you will vow to help me."

The titan stepped away from the ice sphere and spoke a mystical command word. The inky wisps inside coalesced into the image of a winter night, with the Boreal Lights stretched across the darkness like a curtain of gossamer color. The lights danced for a moment, then a white cloud churned up from the orb's depths to engulf them in a raging blizzard. An instant later, the jagged tip of a mountain appeared in the storm.

The peak grew larger until its massive bulk completely filled the interior of the orb—then the sphere seemed to pass inside the mountain. The crag was made not of stone, but of blue clear ice, and it was streaked with the gemlike colors of the Boreal Lights. The globe drifted downward, following the dancing aura deeper into the mountain, until it reached a pool of crimson blood frozen in the ancient ice at the heart of the mountain.

In the center of the red stain, suspended in the ice, hung a slick-furred corpse that seemed part otter and part human. The figure had a slender body, broad flat arms ending in flipperlike hands with long fingers, and feet turned outward to resemble a whale's fluke. On his chest lay a necklace of five crystals, and from each crystal shot one of the Boreal Lights.

"The ice mountain stands near the center of the Great Glacier," said Lanaxis. A chill as cold as his magical orb ran down his spine, for the titan hated the glacier as he hated nothing else on Toril. "To save Ostoria, we must go there and exhume Ulutiu, so that we may crush his necklace."

"That will be easier said than done," hissed Ottar. As the frost giant spoke, a cloud of vaporous breath spewed from his blue lips, then rose to obscure his white face and icy blue eyes. "The Great Glacier is vast, and the Eternal Blizzard will not make it easy for us to find our way."

"Leave the storm to me!" blustered Vilmos, paramount of storm giants. He was almost as large as a titan, with violet skin and a flowing beard of silver. "But what about the glacier itself? After we reach the mountain, we'll never chop through all that ice. It could be ten thousand feet thick!"

It was Nicias, the cloud giant, who answered. "The ice does not concern me, my brother." His voice was as wispy as his white hair. "Together, we Sons of Annam can accomplish much."

Lanaxis smiled broadly, pleased to have the support of so many brothers. "Nicias, you speak truly and wisely, as always."

Nicias nodded politely, then went on. "But I wonder if we should be asking *how* to reach Ulutiu's grave, rather than *whether* to reach it. Deceiving Othea is not something to undertake lightly. Good sons venerate their mother."

"If our mother loved us, she would have stopped the glacier before it took half our lands!" ranted the fire giant Masud. "I'm for Lanaxis's plan, and into the forge with Othea!" The khan's skin was as black as coal and his beard as orange as flame. When he spoke, he filled the air with sulfurous fumes, but the choking cloud did not stop the other giants from croaking out a chorus of support.

Nicias raised his white brow and glanced around the veranda, then spread his hands in abdication. "It appears the question has been considered and decided." The cloud giant cast a disparaging glance in Masud's direction. "But I do trust that your comment about throwing the Mother Queen into the forge was mere exaggeration."

"Why should it be?" demanded Dunmore, his disgust plainly etched on his wooden features. "If you would disobey Othea, you would do anything."

"We have no wish to harm her." Ottar's cold eyes showed no emotion as he answered the wood giant. "Nor do we wish her to harm our empire."

"Othea gave life to our races! What is an empire compared

to that?" Dunmore retorted. "If the Mother Queen asked, I would tear my palace apart with my own hands."

"And I would burn it for you!" scoffed Masud. "But does that mean I'm fool enough to do the same? I think not!"

The fire giant's retort drew a few amused chuckles.

Dunmore shook his head sadly, then glared up into the faces of his brothers. "I will have no part of this." The thane stepped away from his brothers, then announced, "Now I will drink from the Well and take my leave."

"You may drink from the Well of Health," said Lanaxis. The Sons of Annam customarily drank from the Well of Health before departing Bleak Palace, since the magical waters kept the mind clear and the body free of illness. "But you cannot depart. I fear you intend to tell Othea of our plans, so I insist that you remain here until we return. My servants will see to your comfort."

"Lanaxis, you are too kind." The wood giant's voice was as bitter as sapwood.

The titan smiled, then looked toward the three cavernous archways leading into the interior of his palace. "Julien, Arno!" he yelled. "Come here, I have a task for you!"

As Lanaxis called for his servant, Dunmore spun and hurled himself at the magical ice orb, smashing into it with a tremendous crash. The sphere shattered into a hundred pieces, releasing a howling tempest of wind and snow. Blinded by the raging blizzard, the Sons of Annam bellowed in surprise and began to stumble about, filling the air with crashes and grunts as they collided with each other.

Lanaxis dropped to all fours and crawled toward the center of the room, sweeping his hands back and forth through the accumulating snow. A heavy foot came down on his wrist, and when he jerked his hand free, a giant crashed to the floor beside him. The titan ignored the fellow and continued to sweep his hand across the floor until he found a shard of the ice orb. Taking the fragment in hand, he spoke the sphere's command word, this time backward. The raging wind died away, and the snow began to settle on the floor in a thick blanket. As the confusion faded, a pair of legs kicked through the snow and stopped beside Lanaxis.

"You called?" asked Julien's smooth voice.

"We come, fast!" added Arno. His voice was a stark contrast to Julien's, gravelly and harsh. "What need?"

The titan raised his eyes and found himself looking at the contrasting faces of his two-headed servant, the ettin. Julien's features were swarthy and handsome, with curly dark hair and a cleft chin. Arno was a pale-skinned brute, with a pug nose and double chin encrusted with reminders of his last several meals. Their necks descended to a single point, joining atop a broad-shouldered body that, at Julien's insistence, they kept reasonably clean.

Lanaxis rose, looking around the veranda for the thane. The only sign he found of the wood giant was a set of half-buried footprints leading to one entrance of Bleak Palace.

"It seems Dunmore has left," observed Nicias. "No doubt to do as you feared and tell Othea of our intent."

The giants were silent, for they all knew how great the Mother Queen's anger would be when she heard of their plan.

"I'll go," said Masud. The khan started for the archway. "It won't take me long to stop that runt."

Nicias caught the smaller giant's shoulder. "The Sons of Annam do not fight each other."

"Nor do they betray the confidences of their brothers!" Masud raised his fiery eyes to seek support from Lanaxis. "For that, I say we throw him in the smelter!"

"There's no need to incinerate him," replied the titan. "Just bring him back, and the ettin will hold him here."

"No! There will be a struggle when Masud captures him." Nicias continued to clutch the shoulder of the fire giant. "Dunmore will be injured—perhaps killed."

"Better that than let him go!" boomed Lanaxis. "If Dunmore tells Othea of our plans, none of us will ever set foot on the Great Glacier, and Ostoria will be lost!"

"If we attack our own brother, or even hold him prisoner, we have lost it already," said Nicias. "I will not stand for that."

"And I will not let the glacier scour our empire from the

world!" Lanaxis fixed an angry glare on Nicias.

The cloud giant returned the stare. In Nicias's eyes there was no anger or fear, only determination, and Lanaxis knew his foe would never concede the argument. The titan's anger grew hotter than Masud's forges, and his fists burned with the urge to strike, but he locked his arms at his sides and kept them there. Many other giants held Nicias in high esteem, and to strike the dynast would be to cast Ostoria into a carnage that would destroy it as surely as the Great Glacier.

Vilmos laid his hand on Lanaxis's shoulder. "I am sorry, my brother," rumbled the storm giant. "Perhaps Nicias is right. To move against Dunmore is to destroy Ostoria's spirit—and I'm sure none of us wants any part of that."

With that, Vilmos turned to leave the veranda, as did Nicias. The other giants moved to follow, for they all knew that, without the help of the cloud giant and storm giant, even Lanaxis was not powerful enough to reach Ulutiu's body. Nor did anyone suggest open defiance of Othea. So great was the Mother Queen's power that only a fool would dare such a thing.

Still, Lanaxis could not bear to watch them go, for with them went the future of his beloved empire. "Wait!"

The giants stopped and looked toward the titan. "Accept our fate," advised Nicias. "Let Ostoria die in peace."

"I'm not asking you to move against Dunmore," said Lanaxis. "Only to give me time. Stay until morning. Perhaps I can think of a way to convince Othea to let us save Ostoria."

Nicias and Vilmos exchanged glances, then Nicias asked, "You will raise no hand against our brother Dunmore?"

"I will leave the thane alone," the titan promised. "All I want is time. If Ostoria has hope, I will find it tonight."

The cloud giant nodded. "Then we will all try to think of something." He looked to the other giants. "We meet beside the Well of Health tomorrow at dawn."

With that, Nicias and the other guests entered Bleak Palace. Once they were gone, Lanaxis turned to glare at the mountainous glacier that loomed over his empire.

"Traitors!" Though Lanaxis had only whispered the word, it echoed across the plain as though he had screamed it from the highest mountain. "What do they care for Ostoria?"

"Them cowards!" offered Arno. "They 'fraid to—"

"Quiet!" hissed Julien. "Can't you see Lanaxis is thinking?"

"No—Arno's right," said Lanaxis. "They *are* cowards—as am I, quivering in Othea's shadow!"

The titan smashed his fist down, so consumed by his growing rage he did not notice when the blow broke an entire section from the veranda railing.

Julien raised a brow. "It's merely prudent to be cautious. After all, Othea *is* a goddess."

"A demigoddess," Lanaxis corrected. "And I am done venerating her. She is my enemy. I will treat her as such!"

"What?" gasped Arno. "Attack Othea? She butcher us!"

Lanaxis heard the objection only as a distant echo, for the heinous task ahead had already caught his thoughts in its dark web. The titan stood staring at the distant glacier for many minutes, then suddenly spun around and stepped toward one of the archways leading into Bleak Palace.

"Fetch me an empty vial and bring it to my chambers— and be quick. We have much to do before dawn," he said. "Say nothing to my brothers. Let tomorrow's events surprise them."

* * * * *

At dawn, the morning sun hovered just above the snowy horizon, a crimson disk that filled the open end of the colonnade. The orb's rosy rays coursed down the length of the arcade, running almost parallel to the floor, so they just skimmed the Well of Health's bubbling waters and set the pool aglow with scarlet light. Despite the fiery colors, to Lanaxis the colonnade felt as cold as the Great Glacier.

The titan's brothers had already gathered, and none of them raised their eyes to meet his as he stepped out of Bleak Palace. Without asking, the titan knew the giants had thought of no way to save Ostoria. They had left that task to

him, and now they would have no excuse for shirking the
price.

Lanaxis stepped over to the Well. The ettin followed close
behind, bearing a tray of silver chalices, each sized for a particular giant.

"My brothers, I bid you drink."

Nicias and the others finally met the eyes of their host.
"Then you have reached the same conclusion we have," said
the cloud giant. "Ostoria cannot be saved."

Lanaxis did not answer. Instead, he took the two largest
chalices from the tray and offered them to Nicias and Vilmos. "Have your fill from the Well of Health." The titan
smiled, taking care that his guests saw that it was bravely
forced. "By now, Dunmore has found our mother. She will
come quickly."

Nicias did not accept his chalice. "We were all willing to
deceive our mother. We should bear the consequences."

Lanaxis's smile remained frozen on his face. He had not
expected to endure such pretensions of nobility. Exhausted
as he was from his long night of labors, it took him a moment
to think of a suitable response.

At last he said, "It would be foolish for all of us to suffer."
Inside his mind, an angry voice was screaming for his
cowardly brothers to drink and leave. He had to prepare the
Well before Othea arrived. "Besides, the blame lies with me."

Lanaxis was about to continue when the floor trembled
beneath his feet. A series of distant rumbles sounded from
the other side of Bleak Palace, each one growing progres-
sively louder. Othea was coming.

"My brothers, I'm sorry," said the weary titan. "But it
appears there is no time for you to drink from the Well of
Health today. Julien and Arno will show you out."

The ettin set the tray of chalices on a bench, then started
down the arcade. Masud and most of the other giants followed at once, but Nicias and Vilmos lingered behind.

"We will not let you bear Othea's wrath alone." The cloud
giant's voice was as soft as breath. "We shall stay."

"I have asked you to leave Bleak Palace," Lanaxis said,

struggling to remain patient. "Will you not honor my wishes?"

"If you ask that way, we have no choice," Nicias said. "But we are not happy—"

"I don't care!" Lanaxis pointed down the arcade. "Go!"

Nicias's mouth dropped open, and he was too astonished to move. Lanaxis grabbed Vilmos's hand and guided it to the cloud giant's arm. The titan shoved them both after the other giants, who had already reached the end of the arcade.

"Take him away!" Lanaxis yelled. The Mother Queen was so close that he could feel the floor buck with each of her steps.

Vilmos nodded, his admiring eyes fixed on Lanaxis's face. "As you wish." The storm giant turned away, dragging the astounded cloud giant along. "But we will not forget what you have done today, my brother."

"I know you won't." The titan slipped his hand into his robe pocket. He grasped the vial he had spent all night preparing, then whispered, "No one will."

Lanaxis waited only until Nicias and Vilmos had turned away before taking the tiny bottle from his pocket. The colonnade's columns now shook constantly from the power of Othea's footfalls. If not for the massive bulk of Bleak Palace interposed between them, the titan suspected she would already be looking down on him.

Lanaxis pulled the cork from the vial and dumped a stream of tiny blue crystals into the bubbling waters. A few wisps of turquoise vapor rose from the pool, then the steam returned to its normal color and the titan knew his poison had dissolved.

The colonnade began to shake so hard that the water sloshed from the well. Lanaxis saw a great bulk step from behind the corner of Bleak Palace and move swiftly toward the end of the arcade.

"Stop, cowards!" boomed Othea's voice. "Come back and stand with your brother!"

Nicias and Vilmos, who had just reached the last column of the arcade, stopped and knelt near the ettin. Farther out on the frozen plain, Lanaxis saw his other brothers turn and reluctantly begin retracing their steps.

A purple, dusklike shadow crept down the arcade as Othea's mountainous shape trundled into full view, eclipsing the red disk of the sun. Though the Mother Queen remained as large as ever, her long abstinence from food had rendered her features jagged and sheer, and even the draughts she drank from the Well of Health had not stopped her skin from turning as gray as slate.

Lanaxis called to the ettin, "Fetch Othea's cup. She must be thirsty after her journey."

The ettin bowed to the Mother Queen, then scrambled down the length of the arcade to do as Lanaxis commanded.

Othea studied Lanaxis with her black eyes. She said nothing, waiting for the titan's brothers to return and kneel at her side. Even the runt, Dunmore, appeared—though he took care to stay well away from his brothers.

Masud was the last to return. "My brothers and I are not cowards," the fire giant sputtered. He cast an accusatory eye at the titan. "Lanaxis sent us away because we don't deserve your wrath. We have done nothing wrong, save hear him out."

"That is not what Dunmore told me," the Mother Queen replied. Her rumbling voice seemed to reverberate from the colonnade's stone pillars and granite floor. "He said you all intended journey onto the Great Glacier. He said you all hoped to uncover Ulutiu's burial place."

"Dunmore left early," said Ottar. The frost giant avoided looking toward Lanaxis. "He was not there to hear us later."

Othea turned her black eyes upon Lanaxis. "Is this true?"

"It's true enough." As the titan spoke, Julien and Arno returned with Othea's enormous chalice and knelt at the edge of the well to fill it. Lanaxis continued, "It was my idea to deceive you. All the others did was listen."

The titan locked gazes with the Mother Queen and remained silent. An icy tranquility had settled over him. He felt nothing, no fear, no anger, not even impatience. It did not matter what punishment Othea chose for him. Soon, she would drink, and then Ostoria would be saved.

The corners of Othea's craggy mouth twitched, as though she were about to smile. Then, as the ettin rose and carried her chalice down the arcade, she looked down at the titan's brothers. "Lanaxis shall bear the punishment for you all."

Many of the giants sighed in relief, and Masud asked, "Are we free to leave, then?"

"You are," Othea replied. She reached down and took her goblet from the ettin's hands. "But it may be some time before Lanaxis can invite you to drink from the Well of Health again. Perhaps my son Julien and Arno should fill your chalices before you leave."

As the ettin turned to fetch their cups, Lanaxis's mind filled with a white haze, his thoughts sailing through his head like wind-driven snow. He could not let his brothers drink and yet could not stop them without revealing his plan. The titan looked at Othea's goblet: she had not raised it. Did she know it was poisoned? Was she waiting to see if he let his brothers drink?

Lanaxis fought to regain control of his mind, to clear the blizzard of doubts clouding his thoughts. To save Ostoria, he had to play the game to the end, regardless of the consequences. He could not be like his brothers, afraid of sacrifices or risk. If Othea emptied her cup before the Sons of Annam, the titan would stop them. If not, he would rule Ostoria alone, without foolish and cowardly monarchs between him and his subjects.

Julien caught Lanaxis's eye and, as he and Arno carried the tray of chalices to the well, raised an inquiring eyebrow.

Lanaxis took the largest cup off the tray. "I'll fill the chalices for my brothers," he said, dipping the mug in the bubbling waters.

As the titan filled each goblet, icy beads of sweat ran down his face and his flanks beneath his robe. He ignored this discomfort and kept a polite smile frozen on his lips, nodding to each giant as he filled the appropriate chalice.

Once the titan finished, he looked back to the ettin. "You may serve the Sons of Annam."

Arno's face went pale, but Julien managed to retain his composure and carry the tray to the other end of the arcade. The ettin walked among the giants, allowing them to take their cups off the tray. The Sons of Annam quaffed the poison down, each anxious to leave Bleak Palace as quickly as possible. They did not gag or make sour faces or show any sign of tasting the venom.

The titan was the only one who exhibited illness. Othea still had not raised her chalice, and the fear that he was killing his brothers for naught had crept into his mind. His legs trembled, an icy nausea filled his stomach, and his face felt as cool as snow. As each giant emptied his chalice, the titan grew weaker. By the time Dunmore finally lifted the last chalice off the tray, Lanaxis was swaying.

Dunmore poured the contents of his chalice upon the ground. Lanaxis's knees nearly buckled with shock. He stumbled to a pillar to brace himself. "Dunmore, why do you waste the water of the Well?" The titan feared he already knew the answer: Othea had told the thane not to drink, just as she had not drunk herself. "You insult your host."

The wood giant shook his head. "My intent is quite the opposite. I am the one who brought Othea's punishment upon you. It is not fitting that I drink from your well."

"You were honest in your opposition; for that I thank you," Lanaxis said. "Julien, Arno, fetch him another chalice."

Dunmore shook his head. "No. All the Sons of Annam must suffer with you," he said. "For my part, I will not drink of the Well of Health until you are free to invite me."

The titan's feet and hands grew clammy, and a cold ache seeped into his limbs. He did not believe Dunmore for an instant. The thane would not drink because the Mother Queen had told him about the poison.

Othea shifted her gaze from Lanaxis to his brothers. "Now you may leave, my children," she said. "It seems Lanaxis is growing ill in anticipation of his punishment. If we make him wait any longer, I fear he'll collapse."

The giants filed out of the colonnade, disappearing one after the other behind the Mother Queen's bulk. Othea paid them no attention, and raised her goblet to her cavernous mouth. She poured the contents down in one gulp. A craggy smile of contentment crossed her lips, and she belched, as she always did when she drank from the Well of Health.

To his surprise, Lanaxis experienced no joy. It seemed to him there was a lump of ice where his heart should have been, and it was not pumping blood through his veins, but half-frozen slush. He began to shiver uncontrollably, his skin growing icy and numb, and the tears rolling down his cheeks stung like windblown sleet. He had saved Ostoria.

Othea stooped over to return her goblet to the ettin. The morning sun shone over her back, casting a rosy wash over Lanaxis's pale skin. The rays felt surprisingly warm and comforting, and the titan began to hope the horrible decision he had made that morning would not bring the death of all that was warm and good in him.

"You don't have to share Lanaxis's punishment," Othea said to the ettin. "You can stay with Vilmos or Nicias."

"Make own kingdom," Arno answered. "Tired of being servant."

"That cannot be," Othea said. "You're too hideous. Even on Toril, there is no place for an entire race of your kind."

"Then we will stay," said Julien. The head cast a wistful glance after Dunmore, the last of the departing giants, before he and Arno started back toward the titan. "Lanaxis has always been good to us."

"As you wish," Othea said. The Mother Queen drew herself up to her full height. Once again her immensity eclipsed the sun's rays, plunging the Well of Health into cold dusk. "Now will I tell Lanaxis his punishment."

The titan stood, strengthened by his brief exposure to the sun, and by knowing he had saved Ostoria.

"I am ready," he said. "But first, may I speak?"

Lanaxis knew he could not influence the Mother Queen's decision. He was stalling to let his poison take effect before Othea punished him. By now, his brothers were dying, and it would not be long before the Mother Queen followed.

"You may speak," Othea said. "But it will do no good.

Already have I laid my curse upon you."

"What do you mean?"

"Can you not feel my shadow?" asked Othea. "When I leave here, it shall remain behind. As long as you stay within it, you will be as you are now, cold and sick with regret for speaking against me. You are free to leave at any time—but when you do, you will no longer be eternal monarch of titans. You will become mortal, growing old and infirm, and dying. The choice is yours: to wait in the cold twilight, hoping I will take mercy and release you one day, or to leave and—"

Othea ended her sentence with a gasp. The Mother Queen clutched at the buttress that was her breast and dropped to the ground. The impact shook the entire colonnade. Half the water in the Well of Health sloshed out of the pool and spread, still bubbling, over the arcade floor.

"What have you done?" Othea gasped. She slumped forward, her head hanging over the colonnade like some immense boulder that had been ready to fall for centuries.

"He's murdered you," said Dunmore. The wood giant stepped into the small gap between her hip and the first pillar of the colonnade. "And all of his brothers, as well."

Othea's face paled to the color of milky quartz, and ashen clouds began to gather about her head. "Dead?"

"Save for me, yes," Dunmore replied, glaring into the colonnade. "The Sons of Annam lie scattered on the snowy plain, as still and lifeless as Ulutiu upon his death raft."

The Mother Queen moaned in agony—whether from Dunmore's news or the pain of dying, Lanaxis did not know. Then she looked down with hazy eyes as gray as the snow clouds whirling around her head. To the titan's surprise, she looked more sad than angry. "Why?"

"To save Ostoria," Lanaxis answered.

With the little strength remaining to her, Othea shook her head. "Foolish child. Ostoria could never be what you—or Annam—wished." She spoke with the voice of sloughing snow, gentle and rumbling, so soft that Lanaxis heard her words more with his chest than with his ears. "An empire of giants would dominate the world, and that is not Toril's destiny."

Othea's eyes went as white as snow, then she sat bolt upright and threw her head back. A deep, booming cry broke from her lips and roared into the sky with such fury that it tore the clouds asunder and silenced the wind. The Mother Queen pitched over backward, crashing so hard that the foundations buckled beneath Bleak Palace. Fissures shot through the colonnade, swallowing the spilled waters of the Well of Health, and the pillars began to topple.

"Come, All Father!" Arno pleaded, yelling at the sky.

"Othea is dead!" added Julien. "Help us! Save Ostoria!"

"Fools! The All Father will not come for you!" It was Dunmore's voice, ringing down from far above. "Without the Sons of Annam, Ostoria is already lost—and so are the races of giant-kind. Without their immortal kings, they will fall into eternal chaos and savagery, as surely as you will sink into the everlasting darkness of your own cold hearts."

The floor crumbled beneath Lanaxis's feet, and dark walls of sheer stone rose around him. He felt himself sinking and realized he was descending into the frozen plain, pulling Bleak Palace and all of Ostoria down after him. Soon, nothing would remain of the empire of the giants except the toppled columns and scattered buttresses of their ancient palaces, and for causing that, it seemed to Lanaxis that even the eternal cold of Othea's shadow would never be punishment enough.

Snow began to fall. The flakes were large and heavy, almost like sleet. In the sky, Lanaxis saw, as Dunmore had promised, nothing but cold twilight.

THE WALLS OF MIDNIGHT

Mark Anthony

*And with a single spell, Ckai-el-Ckaan forged a tower of shadow
from the cold bones of the mountain. He named it Gurthang,
which in the old tongue is "midnight," and within its onyx walls
he hid away his greatest relic of power, the Finger of Ckai-el-
Ckaan. It is written in prophecy that he who tries to climb the
walls of Gurthang and fails will lose his life, but that he who
tries and succeeds will lose his soul. . . .*

From *Talfirian Eddas,* circa 342 DR

The warrior stood before a dark fortress, her indigo gaze
calculating, her fine hands resting with easy strength
against her hips. Sunlight glanced off her short, pale hair
and soaked into the close-fitting black leather she wore.

After a time she swore, her breath conjuring ghosts on the
autumn high-country air. The dark fortress soared above the
granite walls of the remote mountain basin, a jagged onyx
knife biting into a cold, windswept sky. Its outer wall looked
as slick as glass. This was not going to be as simple as she
had believed. Yet she had her mission, and she intended to
complete it. The warrior's name was Ravendas, and long ago
she had vowed to do whatever it took to be strong.

A tenday ago, she had pounded a fist against the gates of

Darkhold, the western keep of the Zhentarim, seeking to become an agent of the Black Network. The dark confederation of power-hungry wizards, cruel warriors, and priests dedicated to wicked gods was constantly scheming to extend its dominion over the Heartlands. Thus the Zhentarim were always seeking likely new recruits eager to advance their lots in life. Deadly-looking guards had taken her inside, and she had been granted an audience with Sememmon, the lord of Darkhold.

"To be accepted into the Zhentarim, you must first prove your worth," Sememmon had spoken from the gloom of his subterranean council chamber. He had given her a task: journey deep into the Sunset Mountains, to a tower called Gurthang, and return with a magical object imprisoned there, the Finger of Ckai-el-Ckaan.

Now Ravendas reached out to touch the cold, black stone of the fortress. It felt strangely smooth against her fingers, almost oily, though it left no residue on her skin. The wall's surface was flawless, without cracks or wind-worn pock marks. Gurthang itself was starkly simple in design. A circular curtain wall a hundred feet high surrounded the central tower—a sharp, jagged splinter of obsidian that seemed to pierce the sky.

Ravendas bit her lip in a frown. The absence of any handholds was going to make this difficult. However, she had come prepared. Shrugging her pack from her broad shoulders, she pulled out rope, pitons, and gloves. She held one of the steel spikes against the wall, then hefted a small sledge, striking the spike hard to drive it into the stone.

"Malar's balls!" she swore loudly, dropping the hammer and piton to clutch her stinging hand. By all the bloodiest gods, that had *hurt*. She examined the wall. Her blow had not left so much as a scratch.

Laughter rang out like a bell tolling on the cold mountain air.

With feral grace Ravendas drew her sword. The sun had slipped behind the western rimrock of the basin, and she gazed into the gathering gloom. How had someone come upon her unaware?

"You'll have no need of that sword," a voice called out, echoing off the boulders all around.

Ravendas did not lower the blade. The deep blue shadows swirled beside a granite outcrop. A man walked toward her, clad in a purple cloak, holding a gnarled walking staff. By the pouches, feathers, and animal claws dangling from his belt, she could see he styled himself some sort of mage. However, given his obvious youth, she doubted he was a wizard of much worth.

"You might not want to make a habit of spying on people," she snapped. "Unless you're curious to learn what a sword sliding through your guts feels like."

He bowed gracefully in apology. "And you might not want to make a habit of battling stone walls," he replied. His voice reminded her of a lute. "Unless, of course, you believe your head to be harder than the rock."

Ravendas scowled. Suspicion left a metallic taste on her tongue. "So, apprentice, have you stolen your master's spell-book and slipped away from his tower before your seven years were up?"

The mage's clear green eyes danced with mirth. "On the contrary, my seven years are long past and well served." The two stared at each other. Wind whistled forlornly over jagged stone. "So," he said finally, "they sent you here, too?"

Her eyes narrowed. "What do you mean?"

He shook his head in lieu of an answer. "I have a camp nearby. There's a fire waiting to be lit."

Ravendas gazed at him critically, then shrugged. Night was falling. Already she could see a few pinpricks of starlight in the slate-blue sky. A fire would be welcome. Besides, she knew she could simply kill him if he tried anything she did not like. She sheathed her sword and slung her pack over her shoulder.

"Lead on, mage."

It was full dark by the time they reached a small hollow protected by a granite overhang. The mage spoke a word of magic, and a neatly laid fire burst into crimson flame. At least he could do that much, Ravendas thought grudgingly. In the golden light, she could see that he was handsomer than she had thought, his nose long and straight, his jaw prominent beneath a few days' growth of coppery beard. As she watched, he began fashioning a stew of jerked venison, raisins, and sun-dried tomatoes. Neither spoke as they ate, huddled close to the fire. A thin, sharp crescent of moon rose above the far peaks. When they finished, the mage took her bowl and put away the remaining food. He sat down across the fire from her.

"They sent you here, didn't they?" he asked. "They gave you a mission to prove your worth, just like they did me." Gold flecks danced in his green eyes. "The Zhentarim."

She wondered right then if she should kill him. Perhaps the Zhentarim had sent them both here to see who was the stronger. If so, she intended to win. Her hand strayed toward the eating knife at her belt.

A half-smile touched his lips. "Feel free to kill me, warrior. Of course, know that if you do, you will never discover the way to climb the walls of Gurthang yourself."

Ravendas could only laugh. The mage was young, yes, but he was clever. "And I suppose you would tell me if you knew?"

"Only fate can say," he said mysteriously, drawing a deck of cards from a leather pouch at his belt. He shuffled them deftly with uncallused hands.

"Draw three." He fanned the cards out before her. "Set them face down before you."

"I'm a little old for card games," she noted acidly, but did as he asked.

"This is your past," he said, turning the first card. *The Empress of Swords*. A spark of magical blue light shimmered about the outline of a stern woman standing before a dark, broken landscape, a red-tinged sword in her grip. "A woman of ambition wields death to gain what she desires."

Ravendas nodded. The card suited her well enough. When she was seventeen, she had left her home and journeyed to Baldur's Gate, where she joined the city's elite guard, the Flaming Fist. Within five years, she had risen high in the Fist. But Baldur's Gate was just one city. The Black Network wove its dark webs across all the Heartlands. That was why Ravendas sought to join the Zhentarim. One day she intended to stand mighty among them.

The mage continued. "This is the path you now tread." He turned the second card. *The Scepter.* Again, blue light flickered over the drawing. The mage's eyes met hers. "You seek great power for yourself, at any cost."

She simply shrugged. She did not need a wizard's trick to tell her something she already knew.

"And this is your fate," the mage said, turning the third card. She reached out and snatched it from him before he could look at it. She'd had enough of this game.

"I make my own fate," she said flatly, shoving the card into a pocket of her leather jerkin. He nodded, but she could see a strange curiosity in his expression.

"All right, apprentice, you've had your fun," she growled. "Now, tell me what you know about Gurthang."

He stood to retrieve a book from his pack. It was bound in timeworn leather, its pages yellowed and cracked with age. "This tome contains fragments of a lost cycle of epic poems, the *Talfirian Eddas,*" he explained. "The eddas tell many legends of these mountains, and of the now-vanished people who once dwelt here, the Talfirc. Unfortunately, Talfir, the language this was penned in long ago, is a forgotten tongue. I've been translating it as I journeyed, but it has been tedious work. Only today did I reach a passage that concerned the sorcerer Ckai-el-Ckaan."

Ravendas leaned forward eagerly. "What does it say?"

The mage opened the ancient tome to a place marked with a black ribbon. "It tells many things. But perhaps most importantly, it tells that we are not the first to attempt to gain entrance to Gurthang."

"What do you mean?"

The mage's expression was grim. "The last fragment I translated tells how, in the centuries after the fortress was raised, many tried to climb Gurthang's walls." He bent his head to read the strange, spidery script on the page before him. "'To the sorcerer's keep they journeyed, the walls of midnight to climb: Kaidel the Ancient, Sindara of the Golden Eyes, and Loredoc who slew the great wyrm of Orsil. One by one they came, and one by one they perished. For thus speaks the prophecy of Ckai-el-Ckaan, that no one hero will ever be great enough to scale the walls of Gurthang.'"

Slowly the mage shut the book. "No one has ever climbed Gurthang. Not in a thousand years."

Ravendas could not suppress a shiver. "Then it's impossible," she whispered.

The mage nodded. "Apparently."

She swore vehemently and stood, pacing about the fire. "Then why would the Zhentarim send two prospective agents here, to prove their worth by attempting a task that mythical wizards couldn't accomplish? It makes no sense!"

"No, it doesn't," the mage said quietly. "Unless they considered these prospective agents a mere nuisance, of no great ability or use. Unless they never had any real intention of allowing them to join the Zhentarim."

Instantly Ravendas knew it was true. The Zhentarim had simply wished to be rid of her. Just like the mage. *A nuisance of no great ability.*

"We are fools," she spat.

The mage shrugged at this. "Perhaps. But then, the game has not been played to its end." He rose and banked the fire. "It's late. We should sleep."

Ravendas let out a deep breath. She locked away her fury, saving it for the morning light, when it might serve some purpose. She pulled her blanket from her pack and spread it on top of the mage's bedroll. He regarded her in surprise. Yes, she thought, he was indeed handsome.

"It's going to be cold tonight," she explained with a crooked grin. She burrowed beneath the woolen blankets. The mage laughed—the bells again, low and soft—and moved to join her.

* * * * *

The warrior and the mage rose early the next morning to begin the impossible—the scaling of Gurthang. His name was Marnok, and he came from the city of Illefarn far to the north. That much he told her as they broke camp in the steely predawn light.

"I am curious, warrior," he said as they gathered their things. "What makes you think we can accomplish something no other has in a thousand years?"

"Sometimes a rat can find a way into a castle barred against wolves," she replied mysteriously, shrugging her pack onto strong shoulders. "Besides, I'm not willing to let the Zhentarim defeat me. At least not yet. This isn't the first time I've done something others had said was impossible." She fixed him with her night-blue gaze. "Why? What makes *you* think we can do it?"

"You shall see," was his only answer.

She frowned at this, then set off across the barren, rocky basin, heading toward the beckoning finger of the fortress. The mage followed behind.

"So, am I to know your name or not?" he asked as they scrambled over a jumble of boulders.

"Ravendas."

He paused to look up at her, the cold wind tangling his long, copper-colored hair. "That's not your real name."

She froze without looking at him, then continued on. "It *is* my real name. Now. But when I was a child, I was called Kela."

"Why did you take another name?" he asked as they reached the top of the boulder heap.

They sat for a moment, catching their breath. The tops of the peaks surrounding the basin looked molten with the first touch of sunfire. "I'll tell you a story, Marnok. My father was a mercenary, one of the proudest warriors between the Sword Coast and the Caravan Cities. Then a woman caught his eye. He married her, and to please her he put down his sword to take up farming. They had two daughters, and I suppose they were happy." She ran a hand through her short, white-gold hair. "Until one day when three brigands rode onto the farm. My father wanted to kill them, but my mother begged him not to resort to violence. So he strode outside to tell the highwaymen to leave. They just laughed, and while my sister Kera and I watched, they gutted him where he stood."

Marnok regarded her sadly. "I'm sorry."

She laughed, a harsh sound. "Don't be. It taught me something I will never forget. Love shackled my father, made him forget his strength, and he paid for it with his life. That day I vowed I would never be weak like him. So when I was finally free of that house, I took a new name, a strong one. Kela was a child's name. It is not *my* name." With that she started down the slope, leaving the mage to scramble after her.

The sun had just crested the eastern escarpment of the basin when they reached the fortress. Despite the new morning light, Gurthang was utterly black, an ancient sentinel keeping watch over the valley.

"All right, Marnok, how do we accomplish the impossible?" she asked.

From one of the myriad pouches at his belt he drew out a small clay jar marked by strange runes. "With this." He broke the jar's lead seal. She could see some sort of emerald green salve inside. "Give me your hands." She held them out, and he carefully spread a thin layer of salve over them. "Now, try to grip the wall."

She glared at him. Did he take her for an idiot?

"Grip the wall, Ravendas," he urged again.

She supposed she might as well discover what game he was playing. Walking to the wall, she reached out and attempted to grasp the smooth black surface. Her fingers sank into the stone. She recoiled in shock, staring at her hands. Gradually realization dawned over her.

"Where did you get this, Marnok?"

His expression was unreadable. "I have my sources."

She turned back toward the wall and dug her fingers once more into the rock. It was a strange sensation, like plunging her hands into thick, cold mud. She began pulling herself upward. Why should she wait for the mage, now that she had the means to reach the top herself?

"I wouldn't recommend climbing any higher."

Something in the mage's voice made her halt. She glared down at him. "Why?"

"Come down and I'll show you."

She paused, thinking. True, there must be some reason Marnok had not simply used the salve himself to climb the wall. She let go and dropped lithely to the ground. The mage was peering into crevices and under rocks, searching for something.

"This will do," he said after a minute.

She approached and squatted down to see what he had found. It was a small, unidentifiable animal, long dead. Its flesh was gone, but dried sinews bound its bones together. She could see by the worn, flat stubs of teeth in its skull that it had died an old animal. A few ragged tufts of fur still clung to the small carcass.

"If you're hungry, you might want to find something a little fresher," she noted caustically.

Ignoring her, he carried the little skeleton to the ground before the dark wall. After dabbing a small amount of the emerald salve on the dead creature's paws, he chanted a dissonant incantation in a low voice. The skeleton began to move. Ravendas raised a curious eyebrow. Perhaps the mage was more powerful than she had guessed.

"Climb," he whispered.

The animal skeleton lurched toward the wall, then began to scrabble upward, the magical salve allowing it to sink its claws into the smooth, dark stone. The skeleton was perhaps twenty feet above Ravendas when she noticed something strange. The stone some distance to the creature's right was undulating, almost as if it had turned to liquid. Suddenly she swore. As if emerging from dark water, a shape rose from the smooth surface of the wall, long and sinuous, with horns like curved scimitars and teeth like daggers. It was the head of a dragon, as perfectly black as the stone from which it sprang. Two glowing crimson slits appeared above its snout. It was opening its eyes.

"Look there," Marnok said softly, pointing to a section of wall off to the undead animal's left. Ravendas followed his gaze to see another dragon emerge from the stone. Each of the dark, serpentine heads turned toward the skeletal creature that climbed between them. Without warning, a beam of hot crimson light shot from the fiery eyes of the first dragon. The beam arced around the curved wall of the fortress. It struck the animal skeleton, but the reanimated creature kept climbing.

"The dragon's gaze didn't harm it," Ravendas uttered in amazement.

"Keep watching," the mage instructed.

Moments later the eyes of the other dragon flared. A second beam shot from its eyes, arcing around the wall from the opposite direction to strike the undead animal. As the two beams connected, their color changed from violent red to searing white. In a brilliant flash of light, the skeleton of the undead animal exploded. Smoking splinters of bone rained down on Ravendas and Marnok. The two dragon heads shut their glowing eyes and sank silently back into the smooth surface of the wall.

"Now you see why I was not so eager to begin climbing," Marnok said softly.

"How does it work?" Ravendas asked in dread fascination.

"I'm not entirely certain," the mage said, "but I have conducted a few other experiments like the one you just witnessed."

She listened then as he explained his discoveries. It seemed that within the circular wall of the fortress there resided four columns of magical energy, one situated at each point of the compass. When something—or someone—climbed the wall, a dragon's head would rise from each of the two columns that bordered the quadrant where the intruder climbed. The eyebeams of one of the dragons didn't appear to cause harm, but when the eyebeams of both dragons met, the arc of magical energy was completed, and the climber was—as they had so graphically witnessed—

destroyed.

"Why don't you simply wave your staff, mage, and make wings sprout from our backs?" Ravendas said caustically. "Then we could just fly over the wall."

"And we would die just as quickly," Marnok replied evenly. "I have watched birds that flew too close to the keep. The dragons found them with their gazes easily enough."

Ravendas swore in frustration. "So why don't we smear that salve of yours over our entire bodies? Then we could just walk right through the wall."

"Yes," the mage said calmly. "And then we could just as promptly suffocate with our lungs full of rock. The salve does not make our flesh incorporeal, Ravendas. It only causes stone to flow around it."

She threw her hands up in disgust. "I suppose you have some other solution in mind that will absolutely dazzle me with its cleverness?"

A smile danced in his eyes. "No. Not yet, anyway. However, at least I have learned how the tower's defenses work. That is some help."

"Perhaps," Ravendas replied skeptically. "But then, I've found that sometimes knowledge only gets in the way. Sometimes knowing the truth can make one give up in despair." She clenched a fist. "And I am not about to give up yet."

The mage answered only with silence.

As the morning wore on, Ravendas prowled around Gurthang, searching for something that could help them. On the west side of the fortress she discovered a tarn, a mirror to the cold blue sky. The pool lapped up against the outer wall of the fortress, and she half-wondered if there might be some secret portal beneath its surface. But instinct told her that the way into the tower was upward, over the wall. She returned to find the mage sitting on a sun-warmed stone, poring over the old book he had shown her the night before.

"I've just translated the final passage about Ckai-el-Ckaan," he said. The wind tugged at his purple cloak.

"And?"

Marnok ran a finger over the ancient parchment. " 'Know that should the Finger of Ckai-el-Ckaan ever be lifted from its resting place, Gurthang shall fall, destroying all within. There is but a single path for one who would live: he must face the sunset, and give himself to darkness.' " Slowly he shut the book. "I'm afraid that's it."

Ravendas was unimpressed. "Forgive me for saying so, but that was hardly helpful." The mage only shrugged in silence. "So what do you think it is?" she asked thoughtfully then, gazing at the dark spire of the tower. "The relic, I mean."

"A magical wand, maybe. Or a staff of great power. But if we're ever going to find out, we'll have to do something different than all those heroes who died here one by one."

Suddenly it was so clear. Ravendas took a step toward the fortress. "But that's it, Marnok. Don't you see?" By his perplexed expression, he apparently did not. " 'One by one they came, and one by one they perished.' You read it yourself in that damned book of yours. In the past, the arrogant bastards who tried to climb Gurthang did it alone." She fixed him with her indigo gaze. "But there are *two* of us."

"What are we to do?" Marnok asked in astonishment.

She began rummaging through her pack. "Rope," was all she said. "We need rope." Shaking his head in confusion, Marnok moved to help her.

By afternoon, they were ready.

The two stood before the northeast quadrant of Gurthang, Ravendas close to the north column of invisible defensive magic, Marnok close to the east. A coil of rope hung from Ravendas's belt, its end staked to the ground. The rope was knotted at intervals a fathom in length, approximated by the span of her arms. Marnok had a similar coil. The mage had already coated their hands with the magical salve.

"Remember, Marnok—do it just like we practiced on that outcrop earlier. We have to be certain we're always at the same height." Ravendas could not see the mage to her left— the curve of the fortress blocked her line of sight. "If one of us makes a mistake, we're both finished."

"I understand," she heard him call out.

"Then let's do it."

Ravendas sank her fingers deep into the age-old stone. She began hauling herself up. The rope at her belt uncoiled itself beneath her as she ascended.

"Two fathoms!" she called out.

"Two!" Marnok's voice echoed back. Good. He was keeping pace. But the real test of her plan was yet to come.

"I'm at four fathoms!" she heard Marnok shout.

Quickly she checked her rope. The fourth knot had just uncoiled. Perfect. "Four fathoms!" she shouted back. Then it began.

"The stone to my left is moving!" Marnok cried. There was an edge of panic in his voice.

"Hold steady!" she called back. She watched as the wall just to her right began roiling like an angry sea. Sleek and glistening, an obsidian-scaled dragon head rose from the wall and turned toward her, its ruby eyes opening.

"Don't move, Marnok!" She dug her fingers as deeply into the wall as she could stretch them. The dragon fixed its gaze upon her, and a crimson shaft struck her in the chest. A feeling washed through her like warm pinpricks. She waited, holding her breath. But a second beam did not come from her left, from Marnok's direction, to complete the deadly arc of magic.

"It's working!" she heard Marnok's jubilant shout. "I'm blocking the dragon's gaze!"

Moments later, the dragon shut its eyes and sank back into the stone. Ravendas let out a cry of victory. Her hunch had proved right. As awesome as Gurthang's defenses were, they were designed to destroy an intruder who climbed the tower alone, as a bold adventurer might. But the tower's magic was not crafted to stop two who climbed stealthily in the same quadrant of the wall, always remaining at the exact same height. Though it meant they could not see each other, by keeping close to the columns of magic each could block the gaze of one of the dragons. The arc of crimson magic was never completed, and never erupted into terrible fire.

It was going to work. "Five fathoms!" she called out as she climbed on. "Six!" The mage's voice echoed her.

Three times more as they climbed, the stone to Ravendas's right undulated, and a dark, sinuous dragon head rose out to lock its eyes upon her. But each time, the mage blocked the gaze from the dragon of the eastern column of magic. The deadly arc of magic was never completed. The two climbers continued on. A dozen fathoms up, and the top of the wall was in sight.

Then Ravendas heard the mage scream in terror.

"Marnok!" she shouted desperately.

There was an agonizing silence. Finally she heard the mage's voice, faint and quavering. "I . . . I slipped. But I managed to catch myself."

Ravendas swore. Damn him. He had gotten careless. Suddenly a coldness gripped her gut. The stone to her right was moving, molding itself into a saurian shape. The dragon's head. And this time the mage was not there to break the arc.

"What level are you at, Marnok?" she shouted.

"I'm not sure. My . . . my rope is tangled."

"Then untangle it! Now!"

The dragon turned toward her. Its eyelids lifted, revealing two thin, blood-red slits.

"I'm at ten fathoms—no, nine!"

There was no time to make certain he was right. Swiftly, holding on to the wall with one hand, Ravendas hauled her rope up to the ninth knot and lashed it around her waist. Grabbing the end, she plunged her hand deep into the wall. She let go of the rope and withdrew her hand. The rope remained embedded in the stone. She could only hope it would hold.

The dragon's eyes opened, and she felt a prickling against her chest. There was no more time. She let go of the wall. A second crimson beam raced around the wall from the east to complete the arc of magic, inches above her head. A sunburst of blazing fire singed her hair as she fell. Then the rope pulled taut, jerking her viciously.

"Ravendas!" she heard Marnok's panicked cry. "There's a dragon to my left—it's turning toward me."

"It's all right—" she started to shout, but then she realized that was not so. The rope had slipped around her waist in the fall. She was too low. She could see another dragon head rising from the wall a dozen feet above her, turning to send its fiery gaze in Marnok's direction.

Ravendas threw her body up the wall, her salve-covered fingers digging furrows into the ancient stone. She couldn't let the foolish mage die. She needed him to reach the top. Just as the dragon opened its eyes, she gripped the wall with one hand and thrust the other upward to block the monster's gaze. She clenched her teeth in effort. Then, after what seemed a lifetime, the dragon shut its eyes and melted back into the stone. With a gasp, Ravendas dug a second hand into the wall, clinging tightly.

"Marnok?" she called out.

The wind whistled as it whipped past the fortress. Finally she heard his voice. "I'm . . . I'm all right."

Ravendas squeezed her eyes shut. "You'd better be, you bastard," she whispered. "After that, you'd better be."

* * * * *

The sun was just setting as warrior and mage trod where no other had in a thousand years. Like the spokes of a great wheel, eight bridges led from the top of the wall to Gurthang's central tower, arching over the murky abyss below. Despite their grueling climb, Ravendas and Marnok moved swiftly across the northeast span. They reached a portal hewn of dark, gold-flecked marble. Quickly they discovered it was locked. However, there was a small scraping of magical salve left at the bottom of Marnok's jar. He spread the last of it on his hand. Then, with a grunt, he plunged his entire fist into the door. His brow furrowed in concentration as he moved his fingers inside the thick stone.

Ravendas heard a faint *click*.

Marnok grinned at her, pulling out his hand. "I think that should do it."

She leaned hard against the marble slab. There was a hiss of cold, dry air, and the door swung inward. The two stepped inside. An acrid tinge stung her nose, the smell of old magic. Marnok conjured a purple sphere of magelight in his hand. After a few dozen paces, Ravendas realized the passage was tracing a spiral, leading them gradually toward the center of the tower.

"The spiral is a symbol of power," Marnok said softly as they went.

"How so?" Ravendas whispered back.

"The labyrinthine shape of the spiral attracts magic, even as it entraps it," the mage explained.

"Entraps it?" She did not like the sound of that.

Marnok nodded. "Yes. And the stronger the magic, the stronger the spiral's bonds become." His eyes glowed strangely in the eerie light. "Power can be a prison, Ravendas."

"You're wrong, mage," she countered harshly. "Power is what sets one free."

Marnok gave her a curious, almost sorrowful look, but said nothing.

Abruptly the corridor ended. The two found themselves standing on the edge of a circular shaft. A staircase hovered in the middle of the shaft without any apparent means of support, spiraling up into the shadows above. The intruders paused, sitting for a moment to gather their strength before the final ascent.

"So, mage, why the Zhentarim?" Ravendas asked then.

He looked at her in surprise. "What do you mean?"

"Isn't it obvious? We're both going to a great deal of trouble to join the Zhentarim. You know my reasons. But it occurred to me that I don't know yours. And I think you owe me that by now."

He licked his lips slowly. "Power," he said quickly. Almost too quickly. "What other reason is there?"

Ravendas frowned. "Somehow that isn't the answer I would have expected from you, mage. I would have thought that you—" Abruptly she halted. She could see it clearly in his green eyes. He was lying. "Bloody abyss," she swore softly. "You don't want to join the Zhentarim. That's not it. That's not it at all!"

He hung his head, his shoulders slumping.

"Tell me!" she whispered harshly.

Slowly, he drew something from one of his pouches. The deck of cards. "Yours isn't the first destiny I've read," he said quietly. "You see, for the last year, I've been following the cards, trying to find my own destiny. First the cards led me to the ruins of a wizard's tower, where I discovered the jar of salve, and then to the library where I found the history of these mountains. After that, the cards led me to Dark-hold. Always they led me on, as if I were caught in some great spiral myself. And now . . ." He pulled a single card from the deck.

"What is it?" Ravendas asked intently.

"You didn't want to see your fate." He handed her the card. "Well, this is mine."

She turned it over. Blue magic sparked along the outlines of a dark, knife-edged spire. *The Tower.*

"I came here hoping to find my fate, Ravendas." He reached out and gently touched her hand. "And perhaps I have."

Before she could say anything, he stood and moved toward the spiral staircase. Shivering, she followed. For a heartbeat, the card glimmered on the floor where she had left it. Then it lay dark.

"Let's finish this," Marnok said. He leapt off the edge of the shaft, his cloak billowing behind him, and landed on the staircase. Lithely, Ravendas did the same. She drew her sword as they ascended, but nothing assailed them from the surrounding darkness. The stairway ended, and the two stepped into a circular chamber. Silver moonlight spilled from crystalline windows high in the domed ceiling above. A basalt pedestal stood in the center of the chamber. On it lay a small, pale object. Eagerly, Ravendas moved forward, but the mage grabbed her arm.

"Careful," he hissed. "There is magic here."

She nodded, halting a half-dozen paces from the pedestal. Leaning forward, she peered more closely at the object that rested upon it.

"That's it?" she said in disgust, her voice reverberating off cold stone. "That's the wondrous Finger of Ckai-el-Ckaan?"

"It can't be!" Marnok shook his head in disbelief.

Rage blossomed hotly in Ravendas's chest. Was this to be the final joke, then? "By all the blackest gods," she spat furiously, "it's nothing but an old knuckle bone!"

No, it is much more than that, a voice spoke in their minds.

Ravendas and Marnok looked up in shock. A man stood— no, he *hovered*—behind the pedestal. His long crimson robes drifted slowly on the air, as if feeling the touch of a distant wind. A gold skull-cap covered his head, and his yellow eyes glowed eerily in the angular landscape of his face.

"Ckai-el-Ckaan!" Ravendas whispered in dread.

No, I am but an image he conjured in his likeness long ago, when he raised this fortress to protect his most precious relic.

"Precious?" Ravendas snarled, braver now that she knew she was not facing the ancient sorcerer himself. "What's so precious about an old bone?"

Ah, but it is not any bone, the image said. *You see, as great as Ckai-el-Ckaan's magic was, all his sorcery could not reveal to him the time or place he would meet his demise. So he forged this tower, and here within he cut off his littlest finger, and laid it on the pedestal.*

"But why?" Ravendas demanded in confusion.

"I think I understand," Marnok whispered. He was trembling. "The book told how Ckai-el-Ckaan was obsessed with living forever. So he must have left a finger here, knowing that, one day, the bone could be used in a spell that would forge a new body for him, and bring his spirit back from the Realm of the Dead."

Ravendas stared at Marnok in amazement.

The image of the sorcerer nodded serenely. *That is so. He created this fortress so that only one who was strong, and powerful, and clever enough to see him returned from the dead could gain the relic. Climbing the walls was the first test, the test of strength. Now begins the second.* The ghostly wizard gestured toward the relic. *Take it. But know that only one who has magic to match that of Ckai-el-Ckaan's may attempt to leave once he has done so.*

"What . . . what if he does not?" Marnok asked tentatively.

Then he will be imprisoned forever. The image of the ancient sorcerer bowed. *Fate be with you.* Like mist before a wind, the image was gone.

Marnok drew a handful of glistening powder from a pouch and threw it toward the relic. A crimson sphere appeared, surrounding the pedestal. His magic had revealed the ancient trap. They could go no farther.

"So close." Ravendas clenched her hands into fists. "We can almost reach it. Almost." She knew now that the relic was indeed priceless. Certainly the Zhentarim would have the power to resurrect Ckai-el-Ckaan—and to bind the legendary sorcerer as their slave in the process. For that opportunity, the Zhentarim would pay dearly. If only . . .

"Let's go, Ravendas," Marnok said gently, reaching for her hand. "It's no use."

But that wasn't true. Suddenly she knew it. There was a way, after all.

Time turned to ice. For a crystalline moment, Ravendas could see a future. Not *the* future, but one future, one of many. She and Marnok stood in the doorway of a country house, his arms encircling her. Golden sunlight spilled through the windows, and small children laughed as they ran on the green grass outside. Marnok whispered something gently in her ear—she could almost hear his words. But then the thread of that future unraveled, and another, darker tapestry was woven to take its place. She had made her choice. Time melted to flow once more.

She drew Marnok close to her. He did not resist. She brushed her lips softly against his.

"I . . . I'm sorry," she whispered.

His clear green eyes widened in surprise, but before he could react, she shoved him with all her strength. He careened backward, falling hard against the pedestal. Ruby magic flared brilliantly as the basalt cylinder crashed to the floor. A small white object rolled away. Quickly Ravendas moved to snatch it up. The Finger of Ckai-el-Ckaan.

She stood in victory, but when she turned around, her heart caught in her throat. Marnok floated above the fallen pedestal, imprisoned in a sphere of crimson fire. His limbs were contorted in frozen agony, as if he were dead. But his eyes were alive. They watched her with a strange look that was part anguish, part understanding. She could not look away.

Without warning the floor lurched violently beneath her feet, and thunder cleaved the air. The crystal windows high above shattered, shards falling like glittering rain. The floor shook again, sending her to her knees. Just as the mage's book had foretold, the tower was collapsing.

"You must . . . go," a voice croaked. It was Marnok. His face was twisted with the terrible effort of speaking. "Remember the book . . ." Blood flecked the corners of his lips. "The third . . . test. Face the sunset . . . give yourself to . . . darkness."

The tower shook again in its death throes, but Ravendas could not seem to move.

"Go—" Marnok gasped in agony. "Go . . . Kela."

It was like being freed from a spell. Ravendas turned away and dashed toward the stairway. She did not look back. Chunks of stone streaked wildly past her as she leapt off the stairway and sprinted down the spiral corridor. She bounded across the bridge to the top of the wall. A heartbeat later the fortress shook again, and the bridge collapsed into the abyss.

Ravendas did not stop to watch. Marnok's words echoed in her mind. *Face the sunset.* She picked her way precariously along the jagged top of the wall, clutching the stone each time Gurthang convulsed, until she reached the western edge. She peered down but could see nothing in the gloom. The moon had set behind the mountains. There was no hope in light.

Give yourself to darkness. Yes, she thought. Wasn't that the choice she had made? Sounding a thunderous death knell, Gurthang's central tower began its slow, ponderous collapse behind her. Ravendas did not turn toward the grim spectacle. Closing her eyes, she drew in a deep breath. And stepped off the wall.

For a moment, it seemed she was flying. Darkness encloaked her, cradling her gently within its soft, velvet folds. She laughed aloud. It was glorious! Then she plunged into deep, icy water, and the moment was shattered.

* * * * *

Ravendas huddled by a small fire in the scant protection of a wind-twisted cedar, wrapped in the woolen blanket she had retrieved from her pack. The Finger of Ckai-el-Ckaan lay on a stone beside her. She grinned, the glow of victory far warmer than the fire. She had done the impossible. The Zhentarim could not refuse her now. Her path to power was clear before her.

She spread her clothes by the fire, drying them of the tarn's cold water. As she did, she noticed something in the pocket of her leather jerkin. She pulled it out. A card. Though wet and torn, azure magic still shimmered on its surface, tracing an intricate outline, the outline of a spiral. Below it was written, *The Cage*. Words echoed eerily in her mind. *Power can be a prison.*

"No," Ravendas whispered fiercely. "I make my own fate." Shivering, she tossed the card onto the fire.

AND WRINGING OF HANDS

Jane Cooper Hong

I hate my hands. The fingers are long—too long. And sickly thin. They look as if they'd splinter if someone applied the least bit of pressure between the knuckles. And the knuckles bulge like the knobby growths you sometimes see on trees. I've often thought I'd like to chop off my hands and grow new ones, replace the mealy things with the ruddy, powerful hands of a smith or a sword master. I've looked into the possibility, actually. A wizard in Thay, one of the Reds, said it could be done. But he wouldn't guarantee the results. Oh, I'd have working hands. But when I asked if I'd be able to perform the intricate work I do now, he hesitated before nodding and saying, "Sure, I think so." That wasn't good enough, so here they are.

I feel as if I'm someone else, watching from a few feet away as I use my hands to fletch the veins in the correct pattern on the arrow shaft. You see, the master counts on me to get these right. It makes a difference, you know, where I put the feathers, how far apart they are, how tightly they are bound, whether or not they are exactly the right size and shape.

The arrows and darts the master uses must fly true every time, without reliance on magic. The poisons he uses must be mixed to exact proportions in order to inflict death slowly, or quickly, as the circumstances warrant. If they didn't, what reputation would he have? As it is, people come from the farthest reaches to find Renek here in this gods-forsaken fleck on the Sembian plains. You'd think he might move to Waterdeep or Suzail, or at least Tantras. Imagine how much business he might do then. People would call day and night seeking his services. Already, they pay the highest prices.

His last job fetched three perfect one-carat rubies and a gold medallion nearly as big as the palm of my hand. His mark, Han, was a top-ranking member of the thieves' guild —highly visible—and that, of course, drove up the cost. Still, the pay seemed outrageous to me. After all, using one of my darts, the master could hit a victim from a long way off with a movement almost as subtle as stifling a cough. In Han's case, the means of death was even less obvious.

I question whether, considering all the help I provided, Han's murder or any of my master's assassinations have been worth the price people paid. For that matter, when you think about it, should anyone be paid for another man's misfortune, another human being's demise?

When I think of Renek and his profession, I wonder how he became—how anyone becomes an expert . . . a noted expert . . . at killing? Is it something you decide to do? I mean, did Renek wake up one morning and say to himself, "From this day forward, I'm going to devote my energies to murder. I will become a first-rate assassin."? I can understand wanting thugs and murderers—Renek's typical victims—dead. But I find the idea of *wanting* to kill someone difficult to comprehend. I suppose some people might question my own involvement in Renek's deeds. But my work has never required *me* to kill anyone. Really, I'm a craftsman—a researcher and a craftsman.

At least that is how I had always thought of myself.

The first time I saw Ashana, I was working in my apothecary. That's what I call it. It's really just a glorified shed in which I keep the various components I use for my work. I hang branches and leaves to dry in the room, and I have grinding stones and shelving there. I bottle various components and catalog them carefully—everything from octopus ink to zinc powder and a few gemstones.

I was dicing the tender branches of a sweet brandyroot plant into fine slivers for drying when I saw her through the open door. Her hair was dark auburn, and it glistened in the spring sun. She was tall like me, but with none of my ungainliness. Neither did she crouch as some tall women do. She walked quickly and surely toward me.

"Tine?" she inquired.

I nodded. I should have been more polite, said something more, invited her in, but I stood mute, staring, admiring. She stepped toward me. I backed up against a long work table, taking in the elegance of her movement as she stepped past and then turned to speak to me.

"Bokun, a cleric in the village, suggested I come," she said.

I nodded again. I remember thinking I should smile or say something, but I'm not sure if I did.

"My father is ill. It's a growth the healers can't stop. I've talked with several of them. And I've read everything I can find in the library—" Her words spilled out with a sense of urgency. "I've tried everything . . . He has this, this mucous—" She put her fingers to her neck and moved them lightly up and down. "It builds up in his throat, so thick he has trouble swallowing." She gulped hard, moving her chin down and up again with the effort, imitating his struggle.

I was immediately taken with her intensity. She gazed at me, unblinking, and then spoke again. "Bokun said you have many herbs, rare ones. He thought you might have this. . . ." She paused to unfold a paper that had been clutched in her left hand. She moved very close to me and smoothed the note flat on the table alongside us.

As I turned to look at the paper, I found myself so near to her that I was overwhelmed by her fragrance—a whispering cleanness that made me want to close my eyes and inhale deeply. I forced myself to look at the note. The cleric's prescription was penned in large, fluid letters: *Hsin-feng ku gen*.

"I have it," I said. "A small piece."

She stood still, watching as I scanned through my catalog and then the shelves of my apothecary, searching for the datelike root. She talked to me all the while—in the gentle, friendly tones of a neighbor or a close companion. That's when she told me her name and where she lived.

I marveled at how easy it was for her to keep up a conversation. I groped for words to say in response. "This is the herb. It's used by the Wa people. My notes say the name means "bitter root of the fresh wind."

Ashana was impressed and said so. I could see from her eyes that her interest was genuine. I am no healer, but many of the tools of my work can be used to positive effect if applied differently, and I am not ignorant of their other functions. I scraped shavings from the wrinkled root and then mixed the herb in a paste with an inert powder and water. I explained to Ashana as I gave her a vial of the sticky mixture that her father must coat the back of his tongue and throat with the paste and leave it there for several minutes before washing it down with water. "It's exceedingly bitter. He'll think he's being poisoned," I explained, "but mixed at this proportion, it should be harmful only to what ails him."

Ashana gripped my hands in hers as she thanked me. My first reaction was to pull away, but I felt a warmth unlike anything in my experience. I have always felt dreadfully awkward around women, and few have shown any interest in me. I didn't take her touch as a sign of interest, but from that day on, I took every opportunity to ride to the neighboring town she lived in. I watched for her and tried to think of things I could offer to help her father . . . to make her notice me. And she did notice me.

I know I said I think of myself as a researcher, as well as a craftsman. Part of my "research" is observing my master carefully—in order to serve him better. I've always made a point of watching Renek closely—knowing his physical strengths and weaknesses—the fluidity and power of his movements, the slight trembling of hand that overtakes him occasionally during "the hunt." He calls it that. I suppose it makes it seem less like murder to think of a victim as prey, but it's also part of his belief that he is somehow superior, specially talented, somehow uniquely deserving of the rewards of his trade.

He never seemed to realize the disadvantage, the complete unlikelihood of success, he would face without me. The thief he most recently killed was a snake. That was Han. And because of Han's own vile nature, he knew about the wiles of others. If Renek had tried to use ordinary means to kill Han, he probably would have wound up with his own entrails publicly displayed from the tower of the nearest thieves' guild hall.

But I had watched Han for Renek. I knew that he had few regular habits and fewer weaknesses. After several tendays of watching, I alerted my master to his opening. The thief, for all his stature in the thieves' guild, paid tithes to the order of Tymora. I saw no logic in a thief worshiping at the shrine of the goddess of good fortune. Maybe he'd made a habit of gambling. Or more likely he was trying to appease the goddess on behalf of someone for whom he grieved. I could only guess his motive, but my master's good fortune rested in the fact that on the sixth day of nearly every tenday, Han could be found casting the crescent moons of fate and drawing lots before paying his tithe to the cleric at the shrine.

I pondered long over the method of death, and I chided myself for not seeing the possibility sooner. Like so many others seeking luck or blessing, Han would rub the wooden moons in his hands, then blow on them and kiss them before casting them to see which way they would land.

Dressed as a traveling cleric in the faith, my master had easy access to the crescents. A part of Renek's smoothness, his talent, resulted from his ability to blend unnoticed into even small groups of people. He is of ordinary human height and weight. His hair is a medium brown of medium length. His eyes are dark but not unusually so. Even his nose, a telling feature for many, is unobtrusive and indistinctive. Truly, he hasn't a single physical characteristic that would draw attention or set him apart from anyone in a crowd.

I wish I could say the same for myself. I'm tall, awkwardly so, and gaunt. My skin is pale enough that in my youth it was the subject of jokes and cruel comparisons to fish bellies and other pallid things. No amount of exposure to the sun has ever improved my pallor. In fact, when I was young and more concerned about such things, I would stay out on bright days, scalding myself to the color and crepe-like texture of red poppies. But within days my parched skin would peel off in gummy layers to reveal more of the same milky hue I started with.

I also used to gorge myself repeatedly over many days in hopes of filling out my tall frame. Always, I would grow a rounded, ball-shaped paunch but experience no satisfying increase in overall bulk or brawn, and so I would return to my former eating habits.

Renek would not understand such measures. He's not handsome or even striking, but he'd never be the subject of stares or surreptitious snickers. That's why he could move unnoticed through the temple, as he did through every other assassination site.

But anonymity alone would not have put Renek in a position to kill Han. He had another important advantage going into this job: I had given him the perfect poison. Han felt, I'm sure, a faint tingling in his hands within seconds of rubbing the two crescent moons between his palms. And no doubt his lips had begun to tingle a moment after he'd kissed their smooth wooden surface. As Renek told it to me later, Han had, as a matter of curiosity, sniffed his hands and the crescents themselves, inhaling the odorless poison. He shrugged and cast the crescents. My master told me they landed with their points at odds. "A bad omen," Renek had noted, chuckling. As Han walked to draw a lot from the bin indicated by the opposing crescents, he no doubt felt the tingling intensify to a mild burning, extending from his hands to his wrists, from his lips to his tongue and throat, and from his throat into his lungs.

By then, of course, Renek had exchanged the tainted

moons for two harmless objects of worship. He told me how he feigned concern as Han staggered to the priest to have his lot read. And when Han began ranting in poison-induced lunacy, Renek asked a brother of the order if he could help. But two other clerics waved him off as they carried Han to a trough and began splashing him with water—a kind but pointless act. Not long after, as Renek disappeared into the shadows, they would have noticed grotesque and darkening blisters forming on Han's lips and hands. He probably started to heave then—blackened spittle and blood. Renek told me he heard the screams of "Plague!" as he left the site.

I accompanied Renek when he collected his fee. I remember that I was staring at my hands on the saddle horn as he spoke giddily of how smoothly the task had gone. I was thinking about what the Red Wizard had said when I became conscious of Renek's words.

"You should have seen him, Tine," he said to me. "He came in meek as a bug, the way he always does—" I'd told him that. Yet Renek acted as though it was firsthand knowledge "—and walked to the offering table. I've never seen him look so humble—pious almost. Can you imagine?"

He went on like that, providing each detail as if he had observed it first, and describing the action of the poison as if he understood it. At one point I asked him, "Do you suppose you should have used an even slower-acting solution?"

"No. No," he answered. "I had just the right combination. And plenty of time to make the exchange, get out of there, and know I'd accomplished what I set out to."

His words and his pompous, thankless attitude jarred me more than the rough gait of the horse I rode. *He* had just the right combination—not "you provided" or "because of you." He actually credited himself with the success.

When he took his pay for the task, I felt sure he would offer me a share. In my two years of service for Renek, he'd never been overwhelmingly generous, but he had occasionally rewarded me when, as in this case, the craftsmanship was of exceptional caliber. When my master mounted his horse and reined it around to where I sat, waiting astride the old bay, he handed me my wage and a paltry amount extra—hardly more than a barmaid might expect to earn in tips for half a night's work.

I tried to take some consolation simply in the fact that Han was dead. Unlike most thieves, who take great pride in doing their work with stealth and cunning, Han based his pride on and earned his status from the sheer volume of his plunder. I'm sure he had far more murders to his credit than my master, but he had none of Renek's reputation for finesse. He'd left a trail of gore and mutilation that buzzards and monsters of the twilight appreciated. Strangely, though, proof of his crimes was elusive. Gnomes in the Arch Wood had tried him for killing one of their princesses in conjunction with the amazing robbery of an entire royal treasury. Even in places where lynching is the common form of justice, Han had escaped punishment.

Most recently, Han had publicly threatened the entire town council of Gendelarm. Rumor had it that he had dragged a councilwoman's son behind a wagon till he was maimed beyond recovery. The woman said that, with his last breath, her son repeated a death threat from Han.

Ironically, Han's assassination was not commissioned by the councilwoman, her family, or anyone on the council. Instead, a fellow thief seeking to elevate his own position in the guild had contracted for Renek's services. I suppose I shouldn't concern myself with the reasoning behind my master's work—Renek doesn't—but it always feels better when justification can be found in higher principles.

Such was not the case with Renek's next kill. His prey was not a criminal like Han or an undesirable like others he had killed. Always before, I had understood my own role and seen some good in assisting Renek.

Until recently, I also thought I understood how others viewed my role. But I learned otherwise from Ashana. After the assassination of Han, I continued to pass near her home in hopes of seeing her. As her father's illness progressed, she spent more and more time at his bedside, but occasionally when she did come out, she would visit with me.

I could see how the burden of caring for her father weighed on her. Weariness had taken its toll on her posture. Likewise her hair. The first few times I had seen her, it was carefully brushed and restrained with combs, but as she spent more time caring for her father, she spent less time attending to her looks. Wild cascades of loose curls covered her shoulders and back and occasionally fell into her eyes. When we visited—always standing in the street—I would find myself wanting desperately to reach out and touch her hair, gently brush it out of her eyes. But always I hesitated. What if she were to shrink from the touch of my hands?

I couldn't risk it. I enjoyed our conversations far too much. Ashana spoke easily to me of many things—the weather, her father, her childhood, her love of stargazing. Her voice was warm, with a clear, rich timbre. I loved to listen to her talk. More than that, though, I found her outlook on life fascinating. She was more than optimistic; she truly saw some good in everything around her. As much pain as she felt watching her father suffer, for instance, she pointed out how much worse his condition would be if she hadn't gotten the Wa herb from me. Perhaps this was just a polite observance on her part, but I certainly enjoyed hearing it.

She told me her father was a merchant, a successful man who, in better times, had traveled far and returned home with outrageous tales of hunts for griffon scales and dragon eggs. Apparently, though, the family was now of more modest means. Ashana's brother, Menge, had squandered much of the family's wealth. I should point out that this is my interpretation, not Ashana's. In my curiosity about her, I had tried to learn more about her and her family. I found that Menge was best known at local taverns and brothels. By all accounts, he was his sister's opposite—a despicable parasite, incapable of work or accomplishment of any sort.

Yet in the confidences Ashana shared with me, she never spoke bitterly of him. Sometimes I thought I saw a flash of sadness or a hint of resentment cross her face, but she never said anything negative. In fact, she didn't call Menge any of the things others did. Privately, I wondered if she and her brother had been born of the same mother. I'd learned that her father was a widower, but I didn't know how many times, and I certainly would never ask.

* * * * *

I was starting an assignment for Renek—preparing to research his next kill—when Ashana came to my apothecary a second time. It had been at least a tenday since I'd seen her last. She was visibly weary, her eyes sunken from time without sleep. I waited for her to speak.

She locked eyes with me for several long, silent seconds. Finally, she licked her lips and began: "Sometimes he . . . sometimes Daddy hallucinates," she said. "And he's in pain. The cleric has given me a prayer balm, and a healer gave me something to help him with the pain, but if it gets much worse, he'll need something . . . something stronger."

I was startled by her words. At every other encounter she had seemed so positive—as if she would never give up hope.

And then I wondered if I had understood her intent. How could she know of my poisons? It's not something I talk about, and I always assumed Bokun thought of me merely as an amateur herbalist. Certainly, even if anyone knew Renek's occupation, they would not think me his accomplice, but rather his personal valet.

I hesitated, hoping she would clarify her meaning.

She pressed again. "Daddy and I . . . we still have some good moments, but I'm not sure how much longer that will last. I want to be sure that when the time comes, when there are no spaces between the pain, that I can help him cope . . . one last time." She grabbed my hands again. "Please."

She meant it. I couldn't envision what pain her father must be in that she would come to me with such a request.

"Can he still swallow?" I asked.

She nodded.

I found it difficult to imagine Ashana killing her father, even as a matter of mercy. I actually felt queasy thinking about it, but I tried to offer a solution. "There is a poison you can mix with tea," I suggested. "He'll feel nothing—"

"He might not be able to swallow for much longer. Do you have . . . something else?"

Of course I knew of dozens of poisons and even more methods of administering death, but I couldn't help wondering what she must think of me to ask such a thing. I tried to come up with something simple and humane. Finally, I prepared a poisoned lancet she could administer herself. "This will be fast," I assured her. "But be careful. It could k—it could harm you or someone else as easily as it will *help* your father."

She took my hands in hers, then pulled me toward her and kissed my cheek. Like the touch of her hands, her kiss felt amazingly warm. I suppose it was a simple gesture of gratitude, but I wanted very much for it to be more. While I stood reveling in the sensation, she grabbed the packet I'd prepared and dashed off.

I worked numbly after she left, packing, trying to get my mind back on Renek's next victim. Renek had explained that Sil was a mage's apprentice whose death was sought by a senior apprentice. Sil had been watching when the older apprentice's spell went awry, and he threatened to tell the sorcerers' council. For that, the senior apprentice had hired an assassin to kill Sil.

As usual, I was to watch the victim, learn his habits and look for an opening for Renek.

I went to Scardale alone. I found it a seedy, chaotic place, cluttered with brothels and second-rate taverns. Even the most typical-looking pubs catered to black marketers, Zhentish soldiers, thugs and smugglers. My master had said he would arrive in a fortnight, ostensibly after he pursued the terms of another hunt. I've often wondered what Renek does when I am researching the kill. Occasionally, he claims to complete an assassination himself, but I have my doubts. He never provides details.

At any rate, in this case I was able to make my way close to the intended victim quite easily by hawking some of the herbs and special materials I use for my work in the town's makeshift wizards' market. When the apprentice, Sil, chanced near, I tipped a cerulean crystal so that it glistened in the sunlight. The brilliant blue flash caught the attention of several people nearby, including the apprentice. He came my way, and I struck up a conversation.

Sil was young, even for an apprentice—fifteen maybe. His voice still cracked at times, and I'm sure shaving once a ten-day was more than adequate to keep his face free of stubble. He was quick to chatter and show off. Like most young mages, he was constantly trying his magic, casting spells to fetch things when carrying them would be easier. Yet he had a certain aura about him. He could be powerful some day. Already, he appeared to have an unusual capacity to command animals.

A full-grown opossum clung with the stubbornness of a burr to the shoulder of his loosely fit tunic, its queer pink eyes seeming to review anyone passing near the boy. Sil spoke to it, not as one speaks to a pet, but as to an equal. And, clearly, it responded. I could see the animation of its features. The ratlike animal gestured with a free paw and seemed to scratch a rear foot occasionally for emphasis. It certainly looked as if the creature was born of stronger magic than the callow boy could possibly possess. It was because of the opossum that I felt sure Renek would want to be extra cautious with this one.

I found myself liking the boy, yet it was easy to see why others might not. He was not shy about his intelligence, and he exuded the kind of grating self-righteousness that only the truly naive can muster. No doubt the tale he wished to share with the sorcerers' council would be told in a tone of awe, as if he could not imagine how his fellow apprentice could possibly have strayed so far from the teachings of his master.

"A young man like yourself could use a stone like this," I said, flashing the gemstone again in the bright sunshine of early summer.

Sil was tall, nearly my equal in height, and he met my eyes. He tipped his head, waiting for me to say more, but before I could, a gnome, gnarled by decades or likely even centuries of harsh living, pushed his way in front of Sil. "You flashing that thing to get attention, or you planning to sell it?"

"Both," I said, trying to keep a casual eye on Sil as I spoke with the old one.

The gnome extended a deformed hand with two hook-like, reptilian fingers. "May I see it?" he asked.

I must have hesitated. He thrust his stumpy hand up toward me. "I know how to handle it!" he insisted.

I leaned down and held the stone out on the flat of my palm. I tried not to shudder when he touched me.

"Ahhh," he sighed, clearly relishing the cool feel of the cerulean in his fingers. "This will work well, yes?"

I nodded.

Sil moved even closer, looking down at the gnome's contorted fingers and at the smooth, perfect stone. The opossum looked on with the same intensity.

"What do you use it for?" Sil asked.

"Ice magic," the gnome and I responded in unison.

Clearly the boy wanted to ask something more, but the gnome plunked the gemstone back on my small stand and spit a question of his own: "How much?"

I ignored him and attempted to finish my response to Sil. "Surely, a young man like yourself has considered making snow fall out of season?"

"I've tried, but I haven't mastered the spell," said the boy.

"How much?" the gnome asked again, pulling his shoulders back and speaking loudly to make himself more visible between the two of us.

"Your choker should settle it," I said, pointing to the wide gold band around the gnome's thick neck.

I expected him to scoff, but he reached his stunted hands under his wild gray beard to unclip the choker.

"Wait. Will you take this?" The apprentice pulled a large midnight blue cloth from his belt. He fluttered it gently over the crystal, and where the lump should have been, the surface was smooth.

"A parlor trick—or thievery!" The gnome yanked the cloth off the table, but the crystal was where he had set it.

"Rest your hand on the table," said Sil. He motioned to the gnome, who eyed him skeptically but thrust an arm forward. The boy laid the cloth lightly over the gnome's reptilian hand, and again the plush blue material lay smooth on the small table. The gnome's arm appeared to end at the table's edge. "Only works on a flat surface," Sil said, almost apologetically. "But it's handy. And quite valuable."

The gnome jerked his arm out from under the cloth.

Sil looked at me expectantly. "How about it?"

"A parlor trick," the gnome repeated. "*This* is valuable," he said, flopping his gold choker down on the cloth.

"But it's a parlor trick I haven't seen," I countered quickly. I had the choice of angering the gnome or doing what I had intended, which was to use the crystal to learn more about the boy. "And I've seen a good deal of magic in my time."

"Humans!" the gnome harrumphed in disgust. "Your time's so short you don't know the difference between a child's toy and real magic. What'll a boy like him be doing with a stone like that?"

I shrugged. "Making snowstorms?"

"A waste! A bloody waste!" The gnome flailed a twisted arm toward the apprentice.

The opossum hissed, and its fur bristled. I've no idea what sort of sound an opossum generally makes, if any, but this sound was almost human, and filled with malice.

The gnome recoiled and seemed instantly shorter. "Keep it away!"

The boy put a calming hand on the animal, and it immediately quieted. "She'll do you no harm if you do me none," he said matter-of-factly.

"She'll do me no harm on any count!" The gnome gave the animal a hateful gaze.

"Touch her and you'll die," the apprentice hissed back with an edge I found startling. I didn't think he had that kind of venom in him.

The gnome remained withdrawn, seeming especially

small, but rage stirred in his gray eyes. He turned, as if he would leave. And then he lunged my way. I reached, but he seized the crystal and thrust it toward the opossum. He sputtered hasty words, arcane and guttural. Instantly, white light shot from the crystal and connected with the animal.

The opossum leapt, jolted. It landed clutching the gnome's face, clawing and scrabbling for purchase. The gnome flailed at his own head, trying to dislodge the opossum, but his arms were too short.

People pressed in, drawn to the spectacle. But those closest pressed back, perhaps sensing the fury in the young apprentice's eyes. Brilliant light refracted from the crystal still in the gnome's crude hand. The gnome screamed. The opossum screamed. The stone fell from the gnome's hand. And the gnome stood, stiff as a statue, dusted with hoarfrost.

The apprentice gathered up the opossum. In fact, I was quite sure he whispered "Thank you" to it. I expect my mouth was still gaping when the boy picked up the crystal and turned back toward me. "Will you take the cloth for it?"

"How did you do that?" I asked.

"Parlor trick," he said. A hint of a bashful smile flickered across his face, but then he was serious again.

He set the stone on the cloth. "Well?"

"But . . . you're so young. I thought . . . I assumed you were an apprentice," I ventured.

"I am. But Pocket here's had a lot of practice." He patted the ratlike animal affectionately.

"That . . . ?"

"'Possum," he filled in for me. "My father gave her to me before he died. He was a pretty impressive wizard, I guess. I never saw much of him. When he died, I got all his trappings but not much of his talent."

"Really? Isn't he—?" I nodded toward the frost-covered gnome.

"Dead? Most likely. You heard me warn him not to touch her, so I'm not at all concerned about what the local garrison might say. . . ." His actions belied his bold words: He prattled on about the frozen gnome in the market, trying to make it sound like an ordinary event in his young life.

And that's when he volunteered more information. . . . "*I* didn't kill the gnome. It was Pocket. Casting a spell on her is like shining light on a mirror; it reflects back on the caster."

I'd heard tales of such magic, but this seemed unusual in its force. Sil apparently thought so, too.

"But I've never seen it come out so powerful," he said. "I mean, it's a reflection, not the real thing. Do you think maybe it's because of the crystal or something?" He didn't wait for an answer. "Gosh, that old one would have killed me with the same spell for sure," he continued.

I wondered myself at the force of the reflected magic. More than that, I worried about what other unexpected powers the opossum might possess. I mentioned the way it gestured when Sil spoke to it. I was relieved when he blub-bered on as I've seen other pet owners do about the special qualities of the animal. None were out of the ordinary. The opossum was smart the way a monkey is smart, or a rat.

Despite his earlier suggestion to the contrary, Sil's "crime"—or his pet's crime—bothered him so that he enlisted my help to carry the gnome's body to the nearest garrison post for identification and burial, an uncommon and strikingly civilized gesture in these parts. As we strug-gled together through the market with the gnome's then-thawing body, Sil talked with innocent awe and appreciation about his studies. He spoke of a dream his father had passed on of providing limited magical arts to husbandmen to help them grow bigger, healthier plants. I thought at first he was joking; I had never encountered a wizard from whom I would expect philanthropy. But Sil was quite seri-ous, and he planned to carry the torch of his father's dream. He was pursuing special studies of his own, experimenting with weather-control spells to encourage plant growth. He told me that was why he wanted the crystal—to study its weather conductivity qualities.

The more I learned about Sil, the more disturbed I was by my assignment. Always before, Renek had been hired to kill people like Han—thugs of high level who add little or no value to the world around them. I had taken pride, in fact, in using my talents to aid my master in taking the lives of scum and vermin whose wealth and success were built on the daily squalor of underground slave trading and other seamy businesses.

But Sil was party to no such evils. I couldn't help thinking the apprentice who hired Renek was out of line seeking the death of this student. I wanted to call Renek before me and insist that he drop the assignment. But of course, it was not my position to do so. And so instead, when Renek at last arrived, I suggested a plan of assassination that would be clean, quick, and dignified. I certainly didn't want the boy to suffer as Han had.

I offered to teach Sil all I could about the cerulean crystal so I would have further opportunities to spend time with him. We met in the market. The opossum it seemed was permanently attached to Sil's shoulder. I decided I must do my best to always appear friendly to it, despite the revulsion I actually felt for the creature. I assumed that like most animals, it would sense my discomfort, so I expressed to Sil the fact that I was very curious about the opossum but somewhat timid about animals in general. He said he would use Pocket to help me learn to be more comfortable around all beasts. He spoke as though that were some kind of exchange payment for the training I was imparting to him about the cerulean. Such gross naivete.

At any rate, I endured the "lessons," smiling even when he would deign to let me hold his pet. Unfortunately, I always felt tempted to run to a well and wash after handling the animal. Unlike the fur of cats and rabbits, which is soft and pleasant to touch, the opossum's fur was coarse and oily. Worse, I could sometimes see fleas where its wrinkled flesh showed between the hairs on its sparsely furred ears and tail. I also did not care for the way the animal stared at me with its eerie, bulging eyes.

After the fourth such exchange, Sil invited me to his home. He lived alone in his parents' estate, a large, auspicious dwelling of a dozen rooms at least, though I never saw them all. I knew the location of the house, of course, and had passed by it shortly after I arrived in Scardale, as part of my research. I realized almost too late that I needed to remember to let Sil lead me there.

He showed me his father's work area, now his. The library alone was bigger than my quarters at Renek's, and the adjacent storage area for spell components was equally large. Both opened to a huge, vaulted room filled with plants, which Sil said he used for practicing his magic. I had never seen a room like that. The glass that went into the ceiling must have taken the most skilled craftsmen years to complete.

I was still marveling at the sight when Sil handed me the opossum and said he would advise his cook to prepare lunch. I grinned, this time in earnest, as he exited the room and left me holding the animal. I patted the opossum and spoke to it much the way he did, and then, when I heard Sil returning, I pricked a needle into the callused pad of one of its small, ugly feet.

The slow-acting poison took effect much later, after we sat down to our meal. To my disgust, Sil had a perch for the opossum on the table. It was a carefully hewn, treelike structure; the animal climbed it, wound its tail around one of the branches, and hung upside down. The opossum itself was vile enough to look at, dangling there like a gaudy centerpiece, but immediately underneath it, cupped in the lowest branch of the perch, was a silver dish—filled with a mixture of bug larvae and spoiled fruit. My stomach heaved.

Fortunately, the opossum lost its grip and tumbled down headfirst from the perch. And then the spasms began.

Sil was horrified. He grabbed the animal and began screaming its name. He looked at me, accusingly for a moment, I thought, but then distraught.

"I know a healer," I said, "an animal healer." And I led him to Renek, who was waiting, according to our plan, in a dingy flat nearby.

On the way, the animal jerked so violently in the boy's arms, I was afraid it might die too soon, but when we reached

Renek's office, the opossum's paws were still twitching.

I could see the slight hesitation in the boy's eyes as we entered, and I was glad I had suggested to Renek that he outfit the room with several animals in cages and at least a few of the trappings of animal medicine so Sil would not be suspicious. It worked. He rushed to Renek with the opossum, blurting the sudden onslaught of symptoms.

As sorry as I was that Sil was to be Renek's victim, I felt a certain pride in how smoothly everything was going. The boy had arrived as planned. Renek was to ask for his assistance in holding the animal while he performed the examination. A simple slip of the hand, and the poisoned lancet, attached to a tool for blood-letting, would pierce the boy's hand. In moments, it would be over.

But my master did not follow the plan. Sil had barely started talking when Renek lunged toward the boy. Sil jumped back and sheltered his pet from the apparent madman. But Renek charged Sil, flailing at him with the lance. Sil pressed back. Too late, he turned to run. Renek jammed the lancet into Sil's shoulder. The boy shuddered and dropped to his knees in front of me. His body shook in one huge convulsion. Another spasm and he squeezed the opossum so hard that its eyes bulged even more than normal. And then Sil looked at me, and I saw in his eyes the recognition of betrayal.

I had given Renek a perfect means of execution. The *professional* assassin had botched it. And I would live with the memory.

* * * * *

"That was a good one, wasn't it, Tine?" Renek asked. "The poison you whipped up was fast, for sure, but I really moved in on him in a hurry."

When Renek gloated over his role in Han's death, I was annoyed. When he gloated over his role in murdering Sil, I wanted to take the contents of Pocket's food dish and force them down his throat. I wanted to scream at him to shut the gaping hole in his face. But I rode along beside him, silent for almost the entire journey back to our home on the plains. In my mind, though, I raged at him; I called him names and epithets I had never said aloud in my life. The voices of several gods chimed in, yelling alternately at him and then at me for our actions.

It was then, amidst the ranting voices in my head, that my master began describing our next assignment. "Ashana," I heard him say. "The woman's name is Ashana." I willed the voices to stop, and I listened.

"Her father is dying. The brother can't stand the idea of his sister receiving their full inheritance, and he says that's what will happen if she lives. I guess the father's made special arrangements of some kind."

No wonder that. But now I knew for certain he was talking about *my* Ashana.

"He's investigated local laws and says that if his sister is dead, he'll be rightful heir to his family's property."

Rightful heir. The words stung with their inappropriateness. How could he refer to Menge as the rightful heir to anything? The slug was lucky the family hadn't turned him out long ago. Every neighbor knew well enough that he dragged disease-ridden women in with him every night after he'd had his fill of ale and spirits. I'd heard that when his father had been well, he'd beseeched the clod to show more respect for their home. But apparently Ashana's father was too good a man to throw his own son out.

The irony was that Ashana undoubtedly would continue to support her brother regardless of the terms of an inheritance. How could Menge not recognize his own sister's radiant spirit?

How could Renek be talking seriously about killing Ashana—this splendid young woman who had shown an interest in *me?* She was no thug, no murderer. She wasn't even a self-righteous apprentice.

I didn't know what to think or do or say. As Renek continued his description of the assignment, I was suddenly aware that the only emotion in his voice was that sick bit of excitement he always displays before a hunt.

I felt I had to do something, but I was at a loss. Renek was, after all, my master. I was indentured to him for a lengthy term of service, and it was not my place to challenge his business doings.

But I remembered the way that Sil had looked at me, and I finally blurted the only business question I could think of: "The brother—" I didn't say his name "—has a terrible reputation. How can you be sure you'll be paid?"

Renek reined his horse to slow it and glanced at me. "He paid in advance."

I was trying to imagine how he could have, but Renek completed the thought.

"Apparently, a long time before the father got sick, he had set aside his wife's jewelry—she's dead, I guess. Anyhow, he'd put the jewelry away for his daughter's dowry. Menge —that's the client—told me he staged a robbery to take the stuff. Steals his sister's dowry and then has her killed. A really nice fellow, don't you think?" Renek laughed at his little joke. My stomach twisted.

Then Renek started explaining how he would handle the case. I wanted somehow to find just the right words to make him stop, to get rid of this whole ridiculous notion and go on with his business—elsewhere. I could think of nothing appropriate, given my status, but I spoke again anyhow. I actually interrupted him. "Aren't you kind of worried about assassinating someone so close to home?" I asked.

"Tine, I didn't think you concerned yourself with such matters." His tone said he didn't think I *should* concern myself with such matters.

"I—I—"

He waved me to silence. "Really, Tine. You don't need to worry for me. This isn't the usual high-visibility political killing, with some notorious person wanting to take credit for the assassination. No one will even know I'm involved."

He stopped his horse and turned to face me. "If you'd seen the dowry, you'd know why I'm doing this. It's no ordinary sampling of jewelry. I don't think many men make that kind of a haul when they get married anymore."

Greed. Simple greed. That's why so close to home. That's why Ashana. . . . My stomach twisted again. I don't know if he could sense any of my dismay, but he spurred the horse and started on again.

I couldn't do this—couldn't be involved, couldn't let it happen. But what could I do?

Voices started in my mind again. I kept seeing the look Sil gave me before he died. "Liar! Murderer! You betrayed me!" I could hear his voice, cracking, frantic. How could I keep those words from being Ashana's?

"—strangle her." Renek's words jarred the questions from my head.

"What?" I asked too loudly.

"It will look as if a common thug broke into the home. I'll strangle her, take a few things, and leave."

He planned to kill her with his bare hands.

"You're not even going to need to get involved in this one," he said. His voice rose with excitement as he continued. "Menge doesn't have the stomach to do it himself or he would. He'll make sure the door is unlocked. . . ."

Renek was an assassin, a professional. He used arrows, darts, tools for his work. I couldn't fathom how he could think of killing someone with his bare hands. To grasp someone around the throat and hold the neck, squeezing while the person flailed, watching while the eyes bulged. . . .

The voices started again. I knew I needed a clear head. I needed to think, figure out what to do. "Their father," I stalled. "Will he live much longer? Is Menge anxious for his death, too?"

"Menge suggested that if I strangled Ashana in front of their dad, the old man might keel early from the shock. I don't know, though. That's kind of creepy. I wouldn't want his ghost rising up and coming after me."

Now, *there* was a sense of perspective. He found that idea creepy. The voices in my head cheered his sensibilities.

I forced myself to ask routine questions—when, where, what would he have to bring.

I wanted to warn Ashana, but I knew she'd never leave her father's side—not now. I was sure she hadn't left the house since she took the poison from me.

And then it came to me: I could go with Renek. I'd go "just in case." Somehow, I'd figure out a way to stop him.

"What if the father wakes?" I asked. "You might need me there."

"He's bedridden!" he chided.

"Well, what if he shouts a warning? Or what if the woman puts up more of a fight than you're anticipating?"

I could tell he thought it strange, my insisting on participating, but I got the impression that perhaps he believed I had a morbid fascination with the idea of seeing him strangle someone. I didn't care what he thought. I had to be there to find a way to stop him.

When we reached home, Renek showed me the dowry. It was an awe-inspiring collection for sure. There was gold aplenty, and more. An entire necklace of dragon scales shimmered in blue and purple hues. There was an arm bracelet, hewn in detail so fine it could only be from a master dwarven crafter. Emeralds glittered from the intricate bevels on its surface. I wondered at the cache. I had heard Ashana's stories of her father's business, but his wife must have come from royalty to stock a dowry chest like that. And the son truly was a drunken fool to part with those riches to gain claim to a business and house that were probably worth less.

* * * * *

Lights were on only in the front of the large manor. We entered in the back where it was dark. The door was unlocked as Menge had said it would be. Renek said Menge had promised to go out for the night and get too drunk to remember anything. I was sure we could trust him at that.

As soon as we got inside I scanned the darkness for a tray of glasses, a suit of armor—anything that would clatter when it fell. I thought perhaps I could startle Ashana so she would cry out and alert neighbors or passersby before we could get near.

The house was silent. I was thinking Ashana might hear us even before we got much closer. Then she started to sing.

It was an ancient hymn of Myrkul, God of Death. My grandmother had sung it when my grandfather died. Ashana's voice lilted through the vast house, clear, and so mournful it felt as if someone were physically pressing on my heart. Renek started to tiptoe forward, but I put a hand on his shoulder to stop him. I froze, mortified. I had put a hand on my master. I don't know what I thought he would do about such insolence, but to my surprise he just motioned impatiently for me to follow him toward the lighted room. For a moment, I did so, dumbly.

Then it hit me. The woman's father had just died. She was doing her duty and sending his spirit to rest. And none of this fazed Renek. He was still going to kill her.

I stepped forward—three long, quick steps, and I grabbed him.

I caught his head fast in the crook of my elbow. If he tried to yell, it was muffled by my arm. I pulled him back and down, hard. I tripped him to the floor. I straddled him, pushed his shoulders hard to the ground, and then I put both my hands around his throat.

In the dim light, his eyes reminded me of the opossum's as I pressed against his throat. I watched my hands as they squeezed more tightly. The knuckles bulged. So did Renek's Adam's apple. There was a slight gurgling sound as he died.

I thought for a moment of Renek, lunging prematurely at Sil. Perhaps, even for a professional there is something impetuous about murder.

Ashana was still singing in the other room. "Carry, carry. O Dark Soldier. Carry, carry, o'er and away."

I stood and walked quietly to the doorway. Tall candles formed a circle around the bed in the center of the room. Ashana was draping a cloth over her father's body. I felt more an intruder now than I had a moment ago, sneaking in with Renek. Ashana must have sensed I was there, though. She turned and motioned for me to enter the room.

"Menge wanted this?"

She knew. I nodded.

I could see tears forming in her eyes. She looked beyond me at first and then straight at me. "I saw him with Renek one day—after Menge took my dowry. I know what Renek does, what you do."

I recognized the look in her eyes. I'd seen it before. "You knew," she said. "You were here, with Renek, to kill me."

"No." I shook my head. Cold terror pierced through me. She couldn't think—"Ashana! No! I—"

And then I saw a glimmer of her usual warmth. "I understand," she said. She stepped close. "You stopped him." Her voice trailed off. She brought her hands up to her head and ran her fingers back through her hair, pushing it off her face, but loose curls dropped back down over her eyes.

This time, I reached out to brush her hair back. She flinched at my touch and I quickly pulled back my hands.

* * * * *

I hate my hands. I've always hated my hands. But now I'm not sure if its the hands themselves or what I've done with them. I keep staring at them. I've even tried covering them up with that cloth I got from Sil. They appear to end where the cloth begins, just as the gnome's hand did. I try to imagine what new hands might look like—if they might make a difference with Ashana. I wonder if the gnome ever wished for new hands.

I think it's time to go talk to that wizard in Thay.

THIEVES' HONOR

Mary H. Herbert

Teza inched forward another finger's width on the branch and strained her eyes to see through the leaves. There he was, coming slowly, almost wearily, along the forest path below. Teza let her breath out in a soft, appreciative whistle.

By the cloak of Mask, what a stallion! Broad shoulders, muscular legs, powerful neck, large intelligent eyes, and a tail that swept the ground like a black mantle. His hooves gleamed when he moved, and his coat was polished ebony. He was by far the most magnificent horse Teza had ever seen, and she had seen many. She had a passion for other people's horses and had made it her life's profession to trade and sell them whenever she could get her hands on one.

But *this* one! Such an animal would be worth his weight in gold pieces in any horse market in Faerûn. All she had to do was catch him, and he would be hers.

At the moment that task was looking easier and easier. Teza had spotted the horse just after sunrise in the northern edge of the Ashanwoods near Rashemen's great city of Immilmar. He had been alone and nervous, with a broken halter dangling from his ears. Teza had not been able to believe her luck. The stallion was too tall to be one of the mountain ponies favored by the Fangs of Rashemen and too slight to be a draft horse, which meant he had probably escaped from some merchant caravan or a nobleman's stable.

She had followed him through the morning, waiting for her chance while he wandered aimlessly along the rim of the woods. Then he had happened onto a trail familiar to Teza and began to head toward an old oak well known by local road agents for its low-hanging branches and dense foliage. Teza had decided to make use of that opportune tree.

Silently she turned to look straight down between her bent knees. Her muscles bunched; her fingers tightened around the coil of rope in her hand. Already the stallion was only a few steps away from her perch, unaware of her presence.

The morning breeze had died to a mere flutter, and the summer heat brought glistening sweat to Teza's forehead. She ignored the heat and the growing discomfort in her legs, instead straining to see the open patch of ground below.

Her heart suddenly jolted. There he was! His head . . . his neck . . . his broad black back. Like a panther, Teza dropped onto the stallion's back. With a skillful flip, she tossed a loop of rope over the horse's muzzle and pulled it tight. She had him!

The horse stopped in his tracks; his head came up, and for one brief moment, Teza thought he was going to accept her and stand quietly. The hope died aborning when the stallion's ears whipped flat on his head. Instead of a snort of surprise or a whinny of fear, his voice rang out in a stallion's scream of triumph. Before Teza could move, he bolted forward into a dead run.

Teza's head snapped back. Frantically she wrapped her hands in his mane and pulled herself low and forward over his neck. The pounding of his hooves echoed the frightened pounding of her heart as she stared wide-eyed at the woods flashing by her. The stallion was running berserk over an uneven wooded track. Not even her big, rawboned weight hauling on the rope around his nose was slowing him down.

She tried to sooth him with her voice, signal him with her

legs, even grab for his broken halter. The horse only ran faster, his teeth bared and his head low like a striking snake.

Teza prided herself on being able to ride anything on four legs, but this mad, frenzied gallop terrified her. There seemed to be no way to control or calm this horse, and he was showing no signs of tiring. When he burst out of the woods and sped even faster over the open ground, Teza groaned. She wondered for once in her life if it would be wiser to abandon a prize than find herself broken on the rocks or crushed under a fallen horse.

It was only when she tried to move her legs that she realized she had no choice. Her thighs, her seat, and her knees were strangely stuck to the stallion's heaving sides. Panic rose to choke her. She yanked wildly at one leg and then the other, and all that happened was the stallion tossed his head and snorted in contempt.

In that instant, Teza knew she was in desperate trouble. Instead of a velvety brown, the stallion's eyes blazed with a cruel greenish fire and his cold breath, carried on the wind, smelled of dank water and rotting vegetation.

"Gods above!" she railed to the sky. "An aughisky!"

The horse neighed again in agreement, his voice so close to wild laughter it made her blood run cold.

Teza hunched over the aughisky's neck. Struggling was getting her nowhere. She had to think of something else and fast. She could see they were running east toward the Ashane, the long, deep Lake of Tears where the aughisky lived in its silty depths.

Also known as a water horse, the aughisky was rare and wily, seldom seen by humans, but its reputation was well known by anyone who lived within the environs of Lake Ashane. The creatures were predators and fed on unwary or greedy humans who tried to mount them. Held fast by the aughisky's power, the helpless victims were carried underwater, drowned, and completely devoured. Only the liver was left to wash up on the shores.

Teza shuddered at the memory of the tales. She beat the horse's head with her fists. "Stop, you ugly, fish-eaten carp

bait!" The aughisky snorted and stretched his head even farther out of her grasp.

Teza caught a silvery glimpse of water framed between
towering hills. The Lake of Tears. They were nearing the
eastern shore, where high bluffs plunged down into the dark
water. And Teza was no closer to escape than when she
dropped on the aughisky's back.

She sat in shuddering dismay and stared at the water stallion's surging head. There was one more thing she could try.
Her hands cold, she drew her dagger from its sheath. She'd
been forced to use the blade many times in her life, mostly as
a warning against overreaching men, but she had never
turned it against a horse. She had to remind herself that this
shining, magnificent creature was a beast of water and blood
and ravening appetite.

Gritting her teeth, Teza clutched the dagger in her right
hand, leaned forward over the horse's neck, and plunged the
blade with all her strength into the aughisky's neck, just
below his throatlatch.

Nothing happened. The water horse did not even slow.

The woman yanked out her dagger and stabbed him again
and again, but still he raced toward the water. Teza saw no
sign of blood or any liquid leaking from his wounds.

The aughisky neighed a cruel cry of glee. He galloped
past a copse of trees, through an opening between two high
rock walls, and burst out onto a cliff overlooking Lake
Ashane. He stopped so abruptly, Teza was flung against his
neck. Her dagger fell out of her fingers.

She felt his hold on her legs give way. Before she could
regain her balance, the horse lifted his heels and threw her
over his head. Her hands scrabbled for a hold, but he snaked
his black head out of her grasp and all she caught was his
broken halter dangling by his ears. The old leather straps
stopped her fall just long enough for her to look downward.

Her eyes opened wide in terror. There was nothing but air
between her and the rock-studded edge of the lake far below.
In a crazy, slow motion horror, she watched her dagger spin
down, bounce off a half-submerged rock, and sink out of

sight in the lake. Then the halter snapped off the aughisky's head, and she began to drop.

Teza screamed.

Suddenly something snatched the back of Teza's wide leather belt. It yanked her painfully to a stop and held her dangling over the precipice. She felt the aughisky's cold breath chill her back.

"Oh . . . please, you gorgeous creature, don't drop me!" Teza pleaded in a very soft, deliberate tone. Her eyes pinned on the black rocks below her hanging feet, she hung as still as she could.

The aughisky, knowing her fear, snorted gleefully and gave her a little shake.

"No!" Teza almost shrieked. "No." She choked on her words and quickly forced down the hysterical note in her voice. "No! Please, put me down on the ledge. I can't swim, and I hate water. But I love horses, especially magnificent animals like you." Teza realized she was beginning to babble, but she didn't care. "That's why I wanted you. You're the most beautiful stallion I've ever seen. Please, just put me down on that solid rock, and I will do anything for you! Do you hear me?" she shouted into the empty air. "Anything!"

"Do I have your word that you will do anything to regain your freedom?" a voice said behind Teza.

Teza flinched in surprise. Aughisky couldn't speak, even when their mouths weren't full of belt, so who else could be on this cliff ledge? She could not see behind her from her precarious position, and the voice, cool and modulated, gave nothing away about its owner. Teza's suspicion belatedly raised its prickly head. "Who are you?"

"You are not in a position to ask questions," the voice replied reasonably. "All I want is your word."

Teza swallowed hard. "Yes," she said as clearly as she could manage. "My honor."

The aughisky snorted in obvious disappointment. He took one step back and turned, keeping Teza hanging by her belt.

The ledge the aughisky had brought her to was a wide shelf jutting out from the middle of a towering cliff wall. Teza had to crane her neck to see the rock face that soared above their heads to the top of the bluffs. As far as she could see, the ledge and the cliff wall were empty. Grass, weeds, and a few hardy shrubs grew among the rocks, and shadows streaked the walls, but there were no other living creatures and no real hiding places.

Then something moved against the stone face of the cliff, a shifting among the long, dark shadows. A black figure stepped away from the stone wall, and its masked form became clear to Teza.

She sucked in her breath and tried to quell her panic as the figure strode toward her, black robes swaying around her graceful feminine body. The being carried no weapons, and Teza knew she needed none. The impassive gray masks worn by the witches of Rashemen were warning enough of the vast and deadly powers wielded by the mysterious women.

"Put her down," the witch ordered.

The aughisky obeyed by simply opening his mouth. Teza fell heavily at his hooves. Immediately she scrambled out from under him and away from his teeth.

The water horse made a move to stop her, but the witch lifted a hand. "No. She will not leave us. Teza's word has honor even among thieves."

The woman from Immilmar rose slowly to her full height, threw back her shoulders, and stared at the expressionless mask with her own habitual arrogant facade—a facade that hid her nervousness and fear.

Teza, through her profession, had learned to be very observant. She drew on that skill now, hoping to divert her apprehension with some bit of knowledge that could be to her advantage. She quickly noticed several things that interested her. The witch's hands were smooth and supple, like those of a young woman, and her voice, while strong with authority, was still rich with youth. This was a younger witch, not one of the old crones who had tested Teza those years ago. And somehow, she had learned to control an aughisky. That fact fascinated Teza almost more than anything else.

"You brought me here deliberately," Teza said evenly. It was not an accusation, just an observation.

"I have need of your particular talents," replied the witch.

Teza made a sound of disbelief and hid the shaking of her hands by brushing off her pants. "Why not just ask? I can hardly refuse one of your number."

"It was faster this way. You left Immilmar so quickly I had to send the aughisky to find you."

"Yes, well . . . I was tired of the city."

"Particularly after the huhrong found one of his prize white stallions dyed brown and for sale in the horse market."

The witch's voice was so full of humor, Teza easily imagined a smile behind that enigmatic mask. She responded with a smile of her own. "He always did have a good eye for horseflesh." Her voice dropped, and she crossed her arms. "So what do you want?"

"I want you to do what you do best. I want you to steal something for me."

Teza did not allow herself to react. "A horse?"

"A man."

Teza was so startled her mouth fell open. "A man! I'm a horse thief, not a kidnapper!" she cried, throwing up her hands. "What do you want with a man?"

"I need him," the witch replied simply.

"Why don't you get him yourself?"

"Let's just say it will be easier for you to fetch him and bring him here." The witch fell silent, her gray mask nearly lost in the hood's shadow. Without offering another word of explanation, she moved closer to the aughisky and waited.

Teza sighed a breath of exasperation. She had given her word to do anything—and even without that, to disobey a witch's command was suicide. Yet somehow, there had to be something in this for herself. "What do I do?" she asked.

The witch lifted a slender hand. There was a rush of noise and a pillar of red light formed directly beside Teza. The thief leapt sideways just as a richly dressed man rode out of the red light and brought his horse to a stop. He nodded pleasantly to the witch.

Teza's eyebrows rose. She recognized the man immediately, for she had seen his long, dark features several times in the past tendays. "Prince Laric," she said, bowing to the mounted man. "What are you doing here?"

The man's pleasant smile suddenly twisted into a sneer.

The witch's laugh held a subtle hum of triumph. "He does look exactly like the real grand prince of Telflamm, but this is a duplicate who has graciously consented to stand in for Prince Laric while the prince comes to visit me." The witch's voice lowered to a throaty purr. "Laric, you see, is my lover."

* * * * *

Dusk was falling when Teza rode the aughisky on the road back to Immilmar, this time at a more relaxed pace and with the grand prince, or whatever he was, riding by her side.

For the hundredth time she glanced at the man. He was certainly handsome in a noble, polished sort of way, and he did look exactly like the prince: tall, slender build, long face. But who was he really?

The witch wanted Teza to switch him for the real prince for a few days so Laric could meet her for a tryst. Teza knew the witches sometimes sought men outside the realm for matters of procreation, and discretion was certainly necessary when dealing with married noblemen from an allied city, but why set up such an elaborate switch and why trick a common horse thief into performing this task?

Teza couldn't help thinking that the members of the powerful sisterhood of witches rarely did anything for simple, purely selfish reasons. They were the real power behind Rashemen's continued existence, and any plot or spell they devised usually had several layers of motives behind it.

Teza shook her head. She had a thousand questions, no answers, and a totally silent companion. The aughisky was no help either. She was sure the witch had sent him along to keep an eye on her. Yet, she didn't mind his company. When the aughisky was not trying to drown her, he was a joy to ride. His stride flowed like silk and his coat was velvet beneath her hands. The urge to possess him swelled within her until even the plans to switch the prince dimmed in her mind. She had to have this fabulous horse, cold breath and all. There had to be some way to control the beast without ending up as a liver floating on the shores of Lake Ashane.

She mulled over that possibility all the way back to the edge of the Ashanwoods. There she stopped and sought out the hollow log where she had stashed her gear earlier that morning. While the false prince and the aughisky waited, Teza sorted through her packs and picked out exactly what she would need.

At the same time, she tried to remember everything she knew about the grand prince's camp. The real Prince Laric and his entourage had been ensconced on the outskirts of Immilmar for two tendays while the grand prince attended meetings with the huhrong and his advisors. No one in the city knew what the talks were about, but knowing Prince Laric's limited influence and power even within his own city of Telflamm, Teza doubted the talks amounted to much.

Not that she really cared. She had been too interested in visiting the Telflamm delegation. Laric's huge camp had proven to be a delightful change from her normal haunts in Immilmar, teeming with bulging purses and more horses than the grooms could keep watch on. She had learned the layout of the camp and even had a few guards she could count on for a favor or two. Getting near Prince Laric's commodious lodgings was not going to be difficult. The challenge would be avoiding the Fang honor guard stationed around the borders of the camp. They knew her too well.

Fortunately she had a few disguises they hadn't seen yet. Stepping behind the aughisky, she stripped off the tunic she had worn out of the city and untied the special undervest she often wore when she dressed as a man. A long, flowing red skirt was pulled over her pants, and a white, low-cut blouse was added that barely hid the ample evidence of Teza's true sex. She took out a few pins, and her thick brown hair came tumbling down her shoulders.

When she came around the water horse, the impostor

lifted an elegant eyebrow. "My dear, you hid a butterfly beneath those rags," he observed.

Teza grinned wickedly. "So! The false prince can speak."

"When there is reason," he said. He waved a long, manicured hand to the setting sun. "Will you be ready soon?"

In reply Teza fastened her small carry bag to her belt, packed another bag with her discarded clothes, and slipped a new dagger into a decorative sheath at her waist. Soon they were riding again toward Immilmar in the deepening twilight.

"It's generous of you to give up a few days of your time to play this charade for your friend," Teza commented idly.

A faint smile twisted the lips of the man beside her. "Yes," he agreed, his voice low. "A friend."

"But tell me in truth," she went on in the same half bored, half wheedling tone. "Who are you really?"

The smile deepened to a self-satisfied sneer that made the imposter's handsome face look cruel. "It matters not."

Teza nodded. "I suppose it doesn't. But my curiosity is piqued. Since I must deliver you no matter what, what harm will it do to tell me your true nature?"

"Perhaps you're right," the man chuckled. Something in his voice brought her head around, and she saw the prince's form begin to blur. His tall frame dwindled to half the proper size; his limbs turned to gnarled, misshapen sticks. The chiseled features of the nobleman became lumps set on a bald, distorted head.

Teza took one horrified look at the grotesque creature with skin like a knobby old fungus and even her experienced stomach lurched. "A boggan," she whispered. They were one of the particularly loathsome forms of goblins that inhabited the underworld beneath Faerûn. They were vicious, cunning shapeshifters who could change their appearance at will. Teza had no notion the witches ever dealt with them. Of course after meeting the aughisky, she shouldn't have been surprised. This particular witch seemed to have a liking for nasty creatures.

With another chuckle the boggan resumed his princely

guise. "You asked," he smirked.

Teza bit her lip, her curiosity more than satisfied. All she wanted to do now was get this boggan to the prince's camp and make the switch. Then the prince's retainers could deal with it!

Teza and her charge rode silently after that. They soon completed the short ride to Immilmar and arrived at a ridge that commanded a full view of the grand prince's camp. Tents, supply wagons, and strings of picketed horses crowded to the foot of the high ridge and spread out like a makeshift village. To the north, the city of Immilmar and the huhrong's hulking palace sat like a black bulwark against the night sky. To the west lay the vast, whispering depths of Lake Ashane.

"Don't wander off," Teza told the aughisky as she slid off his back.

The black water horse turned his head toward the lake and stamped his hoof irritably.

The boggan sneered, "He won't go far. Not as long as she holds the hippomane."

It took every ounce of self-control for Teza not to react to that statement or to show any sign of the excitement that burst in her. A hippomane? Is that what it took to master an aughisky? Her hand surreptitiously slid to her carry bag and the little cache of treasures she always carried with her. In there was a crystal vial containing a dark brown lump of dried flesh snatched from the forehead of a newborn foal. She had stolen the hippomane and carried it for years in the hope that an opportunity to use its powerful attraction charm would come her way. Maybe this was her chance. Perhaps the aughisky could be lured away with her own little bit of magic.

Teza shot a quick look at the boggan who was studying the camp below. As silently as she could, she drew the vial out of her bag and pulled the cap off. The small dried lump fell into her hand.

The hippomane had a dull but distinctively spicy smell. The aughisky's nostrils flared; his eyes glowed green in the darkness. Teza rubbed the hippomane across her palm, then offered her hand to the water horse to smell. He took a step toward her.

"That's right," she whispered. "Remember that smell, my friend. If the opportunity comes, will you follow me?" The aughisky bobbed his head.

Teza couldn't be sure the water horse understood her words or would obey the power of her hippomane, but the charm seemed to have some effect on the beast. To make the spell permanent she had to swallow the hippomane in the aughisky's presence, and even then she didn't know if the magic would be enough to break the witch's own charm. If the opportunity came to test her hippomane, Teza could only hope it would work. Sighing, she slipped the hippomane back into the vial and tucked it into her bag. When she looked up, she saw the boggan grinning at her.

"You covet the beast, don't you?" he said.

Teza shrugged. How could she explain her desire to own this horse? He was deadly, but he was rare and fantastically beautiful.

"He could kill you if you are careless," the boggan observed.

"I know. So could the witch if she caught me stealing her aughisky."

The false prince smirked. "That is true. But I like you. You are cunning, greedy, and as interesting as that beast. I will give you something to think about. The witch has other useful pets. One more or less may not disturb her."

Teza looked from the man to the horse and back again. It was stupid to risk her life on the mere supposition of a boggan. And yet, if he was right, she had a chance to gain an aughisky—the prize of a lifetime.

Teza tucked his words away with her hopes and set her mind on the task at hand. The moon was rising above the eastern hills and the witch was waiting for her lover.

With the boggan close on her heels, Teza worked her way down the slope of the ridge to the southern edge of the Telflamm camp. Large piles of boxes, bags, and supplies, lines of wagons, and the tents of the servants and camp followers marked the beginning of the impromptu community that had sprung up during the grand prince's visit to Immilmar. Every evening men-at-arms, mercenaries, merchants, thieves, prostitutes, and townsfolk gathered in this part of the camp for pleasure and business. Teza knew from experience that it would be easy to mingle in.

First, however, she had to get past the two Fang guardsmen who stood, hands on sword hilts, beside the path into the camp. If they recognized her, they would certainly try to detain her over that little matter of the iron lord's stolen horse.

It would be best if they didn't see the false prince either. She turned to the boggan and came face to face with a strange man. Her hand flew to her dagger, but before she drew it, the man leered at her. The boggan had already anticipated their problem and altered his features.

"Chase me," she snapped to the boggan. She pulled her bodice down her shoulders until her cleavage gleamed in the moonlight. Then she sprang out onto the trail and ran laughing toward the guardsmen. She did not slow down or hesitate, but darted past the startled warriors, giggling and waving her bag to the man running behind her.

The Rashemen guards saw only the flash of her white blouse and the Telflamm emblem on the nobleman's velvet robes before Teza and her charge were past and moving into the crowded camp. The guardsmen merely shrugged and resumed their watchful stance.

Once among the tents, Teza quickly obtained a flagon of *jhuild*, Immilmar firewine, and thrust it into the boggan's hands. "You are drunk and having a wonderful time," she whispered to him, and he was quick to follow her suggestion.

Soon they were wending a haphazard way among bright paths and merry people, heading toward the center of the camp and the grand prince's tent. Along the way Teza acquired another flagon of firewine, a big wedge of her favorite Sjorl cheese, and the purse of an Immilmar merchant, which she tucked out of sight in her wide, woven belt.

As soon as they reached the grand prince's inner circle, the boggan stepped into a deep shadow and changed his features back to match Laric's. Teza took his arm and they walked toward the ring of Telflamm honor guards who stood watch on the prince's lodging. One guard saw them and snapped to attention. "Your Highness," he gasped. "I didn't know you were out."

"I had a hunger," the boggan said cheerfully before Teza could speak. He slipped an arm around her waist and gave the soldier a broad wink.

The guard grinned at Teza and bowed, and the false prince hurried them past.

"Over there, the big gold tent with the banners," Teza hissed. Her heart was drumming as it always did when a big job was nearing its completion. She felt excitement and nervousness thrill through her in an exhilarating rush.

The tent was dark and still as they approached. They were almost to the entrance when Teza spotted a royal guardsman just outside the doorway. His dark gray surcoat and mail blended into the night shadows. She doubted he could see them very well either, and her suspicion was confirmed when his harsh voice snapped, "Halt! The prince may not be disturbed."

"Oh, let's disturb him anyway," the boggan snarled. His hand whipped around the guard's throat. Without missing a step, the boggan strode into the spacious gold tent, carrying the soldier by the neck.

Teza saw the Telflamm's eyes bulge and heard the cracking of bones, then the man went limp. The boggan threw the corpse carelessly into a dark corner. Exasperated, Teza said, "Now how are you going to explain that?"

The boggan's lips pulled back in a vile expression of pleasure and anticipation. "I won't have to. I'll eat him."

Teza rolled her eyes in disgust. Just then, a man in long robes walked in from the sleeping quarters in the rear of the tent. "What is this? Who are you?" he demanded.

Teza turned and faced the real grand prince of Telflamm. Before he could call for his guards, Teza handed him a small scroll. "Everything is in there, Your Highness."

When he unrolled the scroll a silver rune at the top of the parchment began to glow with a soft starry light. "Ah!" he sighed, and a gleam of anticipation lit his face. He read the scroll, then tucked it into the pocket of his robe. "I shall be ready in a moment," he said eagerly to Teza and rushed into his quarters.

The woman cocked an eyebrow. No hesitation? No questions? No doubts about leaving his retinue and business in the hands of an identical stranger? What kind of besotted idiot was this prince? He certainly put a great deal of trust in a witch whom Teza wouldn't trust as far as she could throw the huhrong's palace. The woman shook her head. No matter. She would deliver the prince, fulfill her duty, and get out with whatever she could take. The prince could handle his own problems.

While the boggan finished his firewine, Teza stepped behind a screen to change her disguise again. The guards had seen the prince go into his tent with a woman. They had to believe both of them were still in there so the prince would be left alone until daylight. That should give her enough time to slip the real prince out of camp and be well on her way to the witch.

Hurriedly she peeled off her skirt, put her undervest and tunic back on, and refastened her hair on top of her head. The dead guard had an embroidered surcoat, a fine pair of boots that just fit, a felt tricornered hat, and several jeweled rings to add to her costume. Last of all, she buckled his short sword to her waist.

"I'm ready, let's—" The prince broke off speaking as he walked in. "Where is the woman?"

Teza made a flourishing bow. "Here, Your Highness."

The prince started, then lifted his lip in distaste. "Of course. A big woman—blue eyes, dark hair, dresses like a man. You must be that Teza woman. I have heard much about you. There is a reward posted for you, my dear."

A reward? That was a nasty surprise. But Teza's grin only grew wider. "So what do you want to do? Collect the reward or visit your lady love?"

He gestured to his clothes: dark pants, shirt, and a hooded cloak fit for traveling. "I will follow you, horse thief, at my lady's bidding. But don't ever let me catch you in my camp again."

"Oh, you won't," the boggan hissed softly.

Teza did not bother to respond to either of them. Turning her back on the boggan, she led the prince to the rear of the tent and slipped out of a smaller back entrance. From there it was easy to amble through the camp, pretending to be deep in conversation with her companion. The Fang guards gave them only a glance when they sauntered by.

As soon as Teza and her companion were out of sight of the guards, she turned south and took the prince by a round-about path back to the high ridge overlooking the camp. The aughisky was there waiting beside the brown gelding, but Teza noticed immediately he had been up to something. His coat was drenched, and his muzzle dripped with blood.

She stifled a shudder, knowing that her blood might have stained his dark nose. To hide her discomfort, she wiped his nostrils clean with the guard's surcoat and tossed it in the bushes. "You could have cleaned off when you were finished," she said, patting his satin cheek. She felt for her bag and was reassured by the hard lump of the vial and its contents. With a quick grin she hopped on the horse's back.

Teza and the prince rode rapidly through the night back to the high bluffs between the Lake of Tears and the Ashanwoods. Shortly after sunrise they came to the faint trail leading up to the ledge overlooking the lake.

Teza slipped off the aughisky and tied the two horses in the shade of the copse of trees while the prince hurried lustily up the trail to find his love. She hesitated to follow. This was an excellent time to disappear before the witch thought of something else for her to do. Then her curiosity got the better of her. Teza could not resist the temptation to witness the witch's meeting with the prince. Maybe she could find out if there was more to this tryst than love.

She walked quietly up the rocky trail, between the stone

walls, and out onto the ledge overlooking the lake. The witch, her back to Teza, was standing perilously close to the edge of the dropoff, Prince Laric held tightly in her arms. The prince had his hands on both sides of her face and was kissing her passionately. The gray mask dangled in the witch's left hand.

Teza caught a brief glimpse of an exquisitely beautiful face when all at once the witch broke the embrace. She stepped away from Laric, raised her right hand, and pointed a finger directly at his chest.

Laric's expression of desire faltered. He moved toward the witch, but she laughed a hard, cold sound of ridicule that chilled Teza and stopped the prince in dismay.

An emerald green ball of energy burst from the witch's finger. The power slammed into Laric's stomach and sent him reeling backward.

"No!" Teza shouted before she could stop herself.

The prince teetered on the edge and cried in terror, but it was too late. His feet slipped, and he fell over the cliff. His agonized wail echoed off the stone walls before the cry was suddenly cut off. Teza stared openmouthed at the black-robed figure standing so calmly on the brink of the rock.

The morning was very still—no wind or cry of birds to hear. The heat was already wilting the last cool shadows of dawn, and the sun poured its light onto the cold, dark waters of the lake. The quiet around the cliff ledge intensified until it became almost palpable. A thousand questions tumbled in Teza's mind until she could no longer bear to be still. "Did you love him at all?" she demanded angrily.

The witch had already readjusted her mask; when she turned, the beautiful face was hidden behind the featureless gray cloth. "Yes," she replied, "and I will bear his child."

Teza was stunned. "Then why?" she yelled. "Why send me on this ridiculous fool's hunt? Why put a boggan in Laric's place?"

The witch regarded her, still as cold and motionless as the rock around her. Then she threw back her head and laughed a warm, rich sound of delight. "Poor Teza. I have played a terrible trick on you. First dragging you here on an augh-isky's back, then involving you in kidnapping and murder. I suppose I could give you an explanation."

Teza might have laughed, too, if she hadn't been chilled by the words, *kidnapping* and *murder*. Thievery was one thing, but those crimes were punishable in Rashemen by several revolting kinds of death. Even if anyone believed her tale about a boggan playing a prince and a witch who threw royalty over cliffs, no one would consider her side of the story—she was only a common thief. Teza swallowed hard and tried to listen.

"Prince Laric was an idiot. A handsome, virile male who ruled a port city that controlled the Golden Way, one of the richest trade routes in Faerûn—but an idiot nonetheless." She gestured to the lake waters where Laric's body now floated. "He and his father before him let Telflamm's power and authority slip away into the hands of the merchant council and guilds, who spend *their* time dipping into each other's profits and squabbling with the cities of Thesk. As a result of their incompetence and the past invasion of the Tuigan Horde, the whole eastern coast of the Inner Sea is a shambles. The area needed someone to take a firm hand and bring city-states like Telflamm back under control."

"Someone who could also be trusted to further the interests of Rashemen and the witches," Teza observed caustically. Her eyes narrowed. This plan did not sound like the usual methods of the masked sisterhood. The witches had some morals and a sense of honor. This young witch behaved more like an unprincipled rogue.

"Naturally," the witch replied, "the boggan is cunning, merciless, and under my complete control. Before long he will bring Telflamm's merchants to heel and Rashemen will expand its influence along the Golden Way and the Inner Sea."

"And I suppose you even had the iron lord invite Laric to Immilmar just so you had an excuse to get close to him."

The witch nodded once. "The huhrong had no more respect for Prince Laric than I did."

"Nice." Teza paused. "Where does that leave me?"

"Free to go. Your help has been greatly appreciated."

"I'll bet," Teza muttered to herself. She knew an obvious dismissal when she heard one, and she also knew there was little she could do about it. She had been used, abused, and tossed aside, and for her own safety, she could never tell anyone. If this witch was a renegade, she would not hesitate to hunt Teza down and destroy her.

Her hand on her small bag and the vial within, Teza stalked away down the trail toward the copse of trees. The witch's laughter followed her out of sight.

The witch took one last long look at the lake far below, at the body still bobbing in the water. She would have to have the aughisky dispose of that. No use leaving obvious clues to murder. She whistled for the water horse.

There was no response.

She whistled again, louder and sharper, with irritation. The path remained empty; there was no sign of the beast.

The witch finally picked up the hem of her robes and strode angrily down the trail to the copse of trees. Only one horse stood tied to a branch: the brown gelding the boggan had ridden to Laric's camp.

Something small glittered in the thin grass near the witch's foot. She bent over, picked it up, and stared in surprise at the empty crystal vial in her hand. A faint yet distinctive odor rose to her nostrils. Hippomane.

Her eyes widened behind her mask, then her voice broke into an amused chuckle.

Teza had stolen her aughisky.

"Let her go," the witch said to herself, and she flung the vial away. The thief of Immilmar had earned her reward.

LAUGHTER IN THE FLAMES

James Lowder

Ask any member of the Society of Stalwart Adventurers about his home—not the place where he hangs his helmet between expeditions, but the address at which he feels most relaxed—and his answer will always be the same: the library at the society's headquarters in Suzail.

In that cavernous room, one thousand years of Stalwart history stood on display, reminding the trailblazers who belonged to the club of their heady contributions to civilization. Bookshelves towered high overhead. Their dark wood cradled journals bound in every type of leather imaginable, tomes scribed in every language spoken across the wide world—and more than a few lost to men and elves and dwarves. Winged monkeys retrieved these books for readers not inclined to scale the tall, narrow ladders. As they went about their aerial portage, these rare apes set the library's massive chandelier to swaying with the soft flutter of their wings. At their passing, the chandelier's magical, ever-burning Halruaan candles winked like so many mirth-brightened eyes.

Trophies filled the remaining wall space. Riven shields and bloodstained swords recovered from distant battlefields hung beside the regimental colors of a dozen victorious armies. Medals and plaques shone gold or silver from glass-fronted teak cases; the awards bore the mark of each monarch to hold Cormyr's throne and more than two dozen foreign potentates. In a corner not too distant from the largest hoard of medals, a stuffed yeti snarled menacingly. Around the shaggy white beast hung the horns of perytons and minotaurs, gorgons and quasits. The Stalwarts' most spectacular trophy—the head of an ancient red dragon—stared from its place of honor over the library's entrance. Even death could not dim the malevolence in the wyrm's eyes.

What the dragon glared down upon was an ever-changing collection of men and women ardently pursuing relaxation. Barons and generals, explorers and high-born patrons of adventure made up the club's majority, but a few erudite souls could also be found in the library's confines. These avid scholars huddled over ancient histories in hopes of gleaning some bit of trivia that would lead them to whatever long-lost relic or magical blade served as their grail. Their solemn study habits sometimes darkened the club's air of cultured quiescence. "Bookwarts" was the name Sir Hamnet Hawklin gave to such fellows, though he himself had authored many of the journals over which the eager young savants pored.

"They should be out creating their own maps," that same revered adventurer now muttered, lifting his port glass with one age-spotted but steady hand. As a cartographer and explorer, he had captured huge parts of the world on paper. The books he'd penned and maps he'd created filled two entire shelves in the library. "That's the trouble with the snot-nosed blighters," Sir Hamnet continued. "Too much time spent looking through books for short cuts when they should be plunging into the thick of it and finding their own way."

The distinguished young soldier occupying the adjoining, overstuffed armchair sounded his agreement. "Just so," said Captain Gareth Truesilver, the words balanced expertly between enthusiasm and cultured restraint. "They're no more likely to discover something new than they are to catch a weasel asleep."

"Yes," Sir Hamnet muttered. "Wretched little beggars."

The epithet was meant to rain shame upon both Bookwarts and weasels alike. Sir Hamnet had despised the latter ever since his expedition to the Hill of Lost Souls. The weasel that had brought about this undying hatred was a particularly huge and mean-spirited example of its kind. According to Sir Hamnet's twenty-third journal, the beast devoured the camp's rations and the exquisitely detailed maps the nobleman had made of the hill and its environs. And in trying to skewer the monster, Hawklin's companions created enough of a racket to alert the local goblin tribe to their presence. Only Sir Hamnet survived the battle that followed. It was neither the first, nor the last time he would report how his expert swordsmanship had preserved his life.

Captain Truesilver knew this tale, being quite familiar with all his mentor's writings. His mention of the most-hated of animals had been intentional, a kind-hearted ploy to fire the nobleman's spirits. A funk had settled over Sir Hamnet in the past tenday. More and more frequently, the accounts written by younger adventurers eclipsed his works. Sometimes, as with Artus Cimber's recent collected writings on Chult, the upstart tomes even usurped his books as primary reference.

"Even if the whole pack of them ran out of the library this instant, their explorations would still depend upon *your* maps, Sir Hamnet," Captain Truesilver offered generously. He struck a noble pose—an easy thing with his athletic good looks—and gazed with open admiration upon the aged nobleman.

Hawklin gulped the remainder of his wine. "The real romance lies in mapping lands untrodden by civilized men," he said, cheeks flushed from both the topic and the port. "Only rabble follow maps."

"Or tourists," the soldier added. The word was a curse on his lips.

"Exploration brings glory, not cataloguing street names in Calimshan or counting the number of words the Bedine have to describe *sand*." The nobleman paused and held his empty glass out at his side. "Uther!"

The butler appeared at Sir Hamnet's side before his name was free of the explorer's tongue. Befitting his service in this unusual adventurers' club, Uther himself was arrestingly exotic. A misfired spell during the Time of Troubles had cursed him with a remarkable resemblance to a denizen of Hades—tall and brutishly muscled, with skin a sooty, corrupt shade of crimson seen only in a burning church. The magnificent set of twisted horns atop his head rivaled any trophy hung upon the library's walls.

"Yes, Sir Hamnet?" Uther said smoothly. He raised the cut crystal decanter with gnarled, black-clawed fingers. "Would you care for another glass of port?"

"No, I'm holding my glass this way to catch the drool when a doddering peer shuffles by," Sir Hamnet said coldly.

Uther bowed his horned head. "My question was needless," he noted, his fiendish face impassive. "I had forgotten how Your Lordship prefers not to waste words upon the staff." Deferentially he filled the nobleman's glass.

"Where was I?" Sir Hamnet drummed his fingers on the chair's padded arm. "Ah, yes. The Bedine. The sun makes them wild, unreliable. Not surprising, the way they wander for days on end across the Anauroch."

Sir Hamnet paused to sip his port, as if uttering the name of the great desert had parched his throat. But a pained look twisted his features before he'd even lowered the glass. With a groan of disgust, Hawklin spat out the wine. "Uther, you subhuman! What is this swill?"

All heads turned at Sir Hamnet's outburst, and a susurrus of murmured speculation slithered through the room. Uther bristled at the undesired attention, but kept his thoughts hidden behind a mask of unearthly calm. "I refilled your glass with the same Tethyrian vintage you've been drinking all afternoon, milord," the butler replied truthfully. "If you wish something else—"

"Dolt," snarled the nobleman. "I know good Tethyrian port from chamber pot lees like this." He spat a blob of crimson spittle onto the Shou carpet at his feet. "You've switched the good port with the servants' dregs, haven't you?"

Uther scowled, the tip of one fang protruding over his lower lip. "That is a grave accusation, milord. I assure you I would never do such a thing. I value my position here too highly to even consider it."

Sir Hamnet leapt from his chair and came face-to-chest with the monstrous butler. "If I say you did it, you did! How dare you challenge my word!" He grabbed for the rapier that hung at his hip during expeditions, but his fingers closed on empty air. "You're fortunate I've left my blade at my quarters, you impertinent behemoth, or I'd have flayed a layer or two of leather from you—just as a reminder."

"I'll need no reminder, Sir Hamnet," Uther said, voice as dead as the stuffed yeti in the corner. "You've impressed your point quite forcefully on me. In fact, if you look around, I think you'll find that you've made it clear to everyone that I've overstepped my position."

Sir Hamnet Hawklin surveyed the now-silent library. He was not surprised to find more than one head nodding in support of him.

With a swiftness not unlike that of the treacherous animals he so despised, the nobleman turned and triumphantly shattered his port glass in the fireplace. For an instant the fragments flashed, starlike, against the sooty backdrop of the chimney. Then the wine-wet shards rained down on the blazing logs. The fire hissed angrily with a sound like a sword tip sliding across stone.

"I'll see to it you're out of this club and begging along the Promenade by morning," Sir Hamnet announced. He met the butler's unblinking gaze and paused, silently daring Uther to reply.

A tense, unpleasant hush settled over the library, broken only by the hissing fire. It was Gareth Truesilver who finally ended the confrontation. Some little part of him pitied

Uther, but mostly he feared that prolonging the menial's degradation might cast Sir Hamnet as cruel.

The captain took the nobleman by the arm and guided him back to his chair. "You've made your case against Uther so well that even the gods agree," Truesilver noted loudly. "When a fire hisses like that, it's supposed to be an echo of Lliira's laughter. Our Lady of Joy finds great mirth in a fool being exposed—and you've certainly revealed Uther as a fool. You'll find no debate about that here."

The clubmen took their cue from the captain and voiced soft support for Sir Hamnet before going back to their drinks or their books or their chessboards. But the nobleman would not be placated so easily. He pulled away from Truesilver and said contentiously, "That story's wrong. It's faint-hearted nonsense meant to help peasants sleep easier at night. The world's a much nastier place than that.

"Each time a fire cracks," Hamnet began as he settled into the comfortable confines of his armchair, "it's the sound of a man's spirit breaking. The hiss is Cyric's amused and satisfied sigh as he drags a condemned soul down to Bone Castle in Hades."

"That's not in your journals," Captain Truesilver noted as he perched casually on the arm of his chair. "You should set it down on paper—perhaps as an addendum to your essay on known magical gates to the Realm of the Dead."

"I never pen what I cannot prove," Sir Hamnet said grandly. "Though I have every reason to believe the tale's veracity, I would have to speak with Cyric himself to confirm it." Eyeing Truesilver frostily, the nobleman added, "That would be a suitable quest for you to undertake, Gareth. The Battle of the Golden Way was a long time ago. You can't live on past triumphs forever."

From where he knelt, working the port stains out of the Shou carpet, Uther cleared his throat. "If I might have your permission to speak, milord?"

Sir Hamnet looked down upon the butler, on hands and knees before him. The utter lack of defiance in his inhuman eyes gladdened the Stalwart's heart. "Yes, go on."

"Should you decide to undertake that journey to Cyric's realm, I . . . I might be able to provide details of a safe route, one unrecorded in the society's journals."

Astonishment blew across Truesilver's handsome features like a cloud scudding across the sun. "If this is a jest, Uther, it's a rather sorry one. After the little exchange earlier, I would think—"

"Oh, I'm not having you on, milords." The butler glanced from left to right, making certain no one else was listening. "You see, from time to time denizens from Hades travel in the mortal realms disguised as men. A few have mistaken me for one of their own, a fellow minion of Cyric trapped here by some wizard's power."

He indicated his nightmarish visage. "The mistake is a natural one, and it prompts the denizens to offer me friendship and solace. Even now I shudder at the things they've revealed in their awful sociability. . . ."

Sir Hamnet shifted uncomfortably in his chair, but Uther's words brought Captain Truesilver to his feet. "And you can help us reach Hades safely?" the soldier gasped.

"I offer this knowledge hesitantly, milords. The way leads directly to Cyric himself."

"Someone's gulled you, Uther," Sir Hamnet interrupted. "I've catalogued all the known paths by which mortals may travel to the City of Strife. They are too well-guarded by denizens for any but the most foolhardy to travel."

"The denizens told me this path is traveled not by heroes, but by common folk," Uther replied. "So it is no surprise its presence remains unknown to great men like yourself."

Sir Hamnet dismissed the notion with a wave of one hand. "Were the story true, I would walk this hidden road to Hades myself. But it has no ring of truth about it. When he ascended to godhood, Cyric promised that any living soul who braved the trek to Hades would be granted an audience and safe passage back to the daylight world when that audience was done.

"It's been a deadly temptation, that promise, drawing many a foolish adventure-seeker to his doom." The nobleman snorted derisively. "Cyric posted denizens a dozen thick along the known roads to his kingdom, and no one has been able to bypass them. It hardly seems likely he would leave a way unguarded, especially one open to 'common folk.'"

"But what if Uther is correct?" Truesilver said breathlessly. "We wouldn't have to face the denizens and the traps and the endless slog across the Fugue Plain. And by his own pact, Cyric would have to grant us an audience! No Bookwart's scribbling would ever challenge the account you'd write of that meeting."

"It's a waste of time," Sir Hamnet snapped.

"If you think my story false, then I apologize for wasting your valuable time." Uther hurriedly gathered up his rags and cleaning brushes. "I mentioned this path only as an apology for my earlier impertinence. I merely hoped the information would help you secure the respect you deserve from your peers and soften your desire to have me fired."

The monstrous butler rose, towering over both the nobleman and the soldier. "However, if you hesitate solely because you think me insincere, I will make this offer: if you search out this path and find it a false trail, then you may have me beaten in just measure to the effort you expend searching. If the road proves true, but guarded by any of Cyric's unearthly minions, you may have me beaten in just measure to your peril."

"An easy promise if we never return," Sir Hamnet noted.

"If either of you fail to return, I will confess to premeditated murder and accept the king's punishment—beheading, if I am not mistaken—without challenge," Uther said. "We can set that to paper before you leave."

"There," Captain Truesilver said, grinning. "Surely Uther wouldn't offer up his life if he thought there'd be the least bit of danger. And if this road to Hades does prove a hoax, you can have him beaten, then fired. The club will be rid of him for good."

Sir Hamnet hunched in his chair, struggling to form some suitable reply, scrabbling to discover some way out of this unwelcome challenge.

After a moment, Truesilver leaned close. The handsome young soldier spoke softly, choosing each word with care. From the strain in his voice, it was clear that what he said pained him greatly.

"I—I would understand if you didn't feel yourself, er, *healthy* enough to come along. You aren't as young—I mean, perhaps the club physician could—"

The disappointment in Truesilver's eyes was a dagger, and the barely concealed accusations of cowardice in his stuttering speech a poison to coat the blade. Together they bit into Sir Hamnet's pride and sent an anguished jolt to the core of his being. The explorer felt his cheeks flush with anger.

"A statue of Sir Hamnet Hawklin has been long overdue in the Hall of Worthies," the nobleman said, eyes flashing defiance. "I'll send a man for my blade and traveling cloak. We leave for Hades tonight."

* * * * *

Captain Truesilver hadn't expected a trip to the City of Strife to begin this way—crammed in Sir Hamnet's plush carriage with the nobleman and Uther, rattling through the fog-shrouded back streets of Suzail at midnight. When he pondered the incongruity of their destination and their mundane mode of travel, he could only shake his head. He'd witnessed some amazing things on the battlefields during the Tuigan campaign, and many of them had sprung unexpectedly from just such unlikely beginnings.

"The tavern's name is the Shattered Mirror," Uther said from where he sat on the floor. Sir Hamnet had insisted the butler take that uncomfortable position to prevent his horns from shredding the carriage's padded ceiling. "The sign in front of it—"

"Depicts a shattered mirror. You've gone over this twice, Uther." Sir Hamnet stifled a theatrical yawn. "It's not that complicated. We go into the tavern and ask to 'see the other side of the mirror.' "

A scowl twisted the butler's leathery lips. "There may not be denizens guarding this place, but there are other perils. I just wish to ensure your safety—"

"Your own safety," the nobleman corrected.

"I couldn't care less if he thinks blathering on will save his own head," Captain Truesilver noted as he turned his scabbarded blade over in his hands. "It's his motherly warnings about footpads and drunken brawls that I find annoying. I've chased off a thief or two in my day. You don't travel with an army on campaign without seeing the world's darker side. And Suzail's twice as civilized as the holes where we billeted during the Tuigan campaign."

"What you'll find in the Shattered Mirror has nothing to do with civilization," Uther said ominously as the carriage rumbled to a halt. Taking a deep, steadying breath, the butler opened the door and slipped outside.

The carriage stood at the crossing of a street and an unpaved alley. The only light came from lanterns hung in the windows of the squalid shanties nearby. Silk scarves had been draped over them to color their light red. The crimson glow lent the swirling fog—thicker so close to the docks—a ghastly hue. It swirled in dense sheets, bodiless souls bleeding in the lanternlight. From time to time a gull shrieking overhead gave those phantom forms a voice.

Sir Hamnet stepped from the carriage as one of those mournful cries echoed through the night. "Disease is the real danger here," he noted effetely, sniffing the fetid air. "Suzail has a sewer system. Don't these ruffians know how to use it?"

Captain Truesilver chuckled. "The regiment's horses keep their stalls sweeter smelling. Perhaps they could lecture the locals on hygiene. You know, public service work."

Uther laid one gnarled hand on the soldier's shoulder. "Please," he said softly. "When you first joined the society you could see clearly enough to treat me as more than a menial, as a friend even. Keep your eyes open tonight and you'll see—"

"My eyes are open enough to see you're overstepping

your place again," Truesilver growled. He hated to be reminded of the generosity he'd shown the servants during his first months as a Stalwart. He'd buried that part of his past, severed that part of himself, when he became Sir Hamnet's protege.

Truesilver brushed the butler's hand away, then straightened his cloak. "This alley leads to the Mirror," he stated icily. "Correct?"

"Yes," Uther replied. He nodded to the driver and stepped back into the carriage. "I'm certain you'll have no trouble finding it."

The Stalwarts listened more than watched as the carriage vanished into the fog. The staccato clomp of the horse's hooves and the creak of tackle faded, then silenced altogether. The gulls had quieted, too, leaving the men to stand in the cemetery stillness that had settled over the crossroads.

"Stay near the center of the alley as we walk," Truesilver cautioned quietly as they started down the narrow, stinking lane. "You watch the doorways. I'll watch the upper floors."

The buildings seemed empty, but both men knew better. The darkened entryways led to rooms where anything might be bought or sold, places dedicated to every corrupt desire known to mortalkind. The hovels lacked doors, and the thick mud coating the alley spread right inside, a universal carpet of filth. Rats moved boldly from building to building, slogging through the mud or swimming through the wide potholes filled with black, oily water.

"Watch your footing here," Sir Hamnet said as he leapt over a particularly large and noxious mire. "There are things floating in this soup you'd never get off your boots."

Captain Truesilver nodded and drew his scrutinizing gaze away from the second-floor windows and rickety balconies long enough to guide himself past the pothole. As he stepped lightly over the mire with his right foot, he glanced down. Ripples spread across the water, then something floated to the surface. Truesilver gasped. It was a disembodied face, small and pale and grinning like a fiend.

A thin arm burst from the muck, a stiletto gripped in its scabrous fingers. "Ambush!" the captain shouted as the blade pierced the sole of his boot. He toppled forward into the mud. As he did, he freed his sword from its peacestrings and its scabbard. But before he could bring the blade to bear, his foe sat up, scrabbled from the muddy pool, and dashed away. A child, no more than five. The filth smearing its face and the sodden rags clinging to its cadaverous body suggested that the little cutpurse had been lying on its back, enveloped in the mire, for quite some time.

"Clever little monster. After your silver, no doubt," Sir Hamnet muttered as he reached a helping hand down to the young soldier. "Good thing you were quick with your steel or—"

The rest of the sentence died in Sir Hamnet's throat; the captain did not reach up for the proffered hand, did not move at all. His handsome countenance was frozen in an expression of angry shock. He held his sword threateningly toward the now-empty pothole. With his other hand he clutched at his injured foot.

"Be a bright swell and step away from 'im now," someone said in a rattling whisper. The voice was unmistakably feminine.

Sir Hamnet spun around to see a tall, gaunt shadow detach itself from a doorway and move into the alley. "You'll hang for this," the nobleman blustered, reaching for his sword.

"I wouldn't draw your steel if I were you, milord," the fog-cloaked silhouette hissed. The warning was followed by a groan of rotting wood from a second-story perch. There, another shadowy figure crouched. It flicked one wrist, and the unmistakable twang of a plucked bowstring hummed over the lane. Sir Hamnet stiffened, braced for the impact of the arrow.

"Just a warning," noted the whispering woman. "Before your blade cleared the leather you'd be sprouting feathers, if you know what I mean. Shouting will get you the same fate." She whistled twice, short and sharp, and a hulking figure wrapped from head-to-toe in black cloth lumbered out of a doorway. "Your mate's not dead—I don't do the out and out no more—but 'e will be if you don't let us lag 'im to a wizard friend of ours. I'm afraid my boy gave 'im a dose of trouble with that cheive of 'is."

"You mean your brat's poisoned him?" A scowl darkened Sir Hamnet's features. "I see your game now. You want us to pay this mage to provide the antidote."

"'Scuse me," the brute said politely. When Sir Hamnet remained stupidly still, the man straight-armed him. The brute didn't exert himself, but the shove sent the old man staggering back a half-dozen steps. "Sorry, gent. I gotta move him now, and we can't have ya grabbin' at the body. Ya might scratch some particular part the wizard wants real bad."

Some *part?* The true horror of their situation finally burned itself into Sir Hamnet's consciousness. "Body snatchers!" he gasped.

"The polite term is 'resurrection men'," the whisperer corrected. "And it's fortunate for you we're that and not more desperate sorts. See, we only need your mate. Nothing personal, but your withered old parts aren't worth a copper thumb to the wizard we work for."

"I dunno," the brute drawled to himself. "I kinda like *body snatchers*." He twisted the sword from Captain Truesilver's fingers and heaved it onto a rooftop. Without even a grunt of effort, he lifted the soldier from the mud.

"Money," Sir Hamnet said. He fumbled with his purse. "I have twenty-five gold lions and . . . a few silver falcons. You can have it all if you leave us alone."

The body snatchers laughed as one, a chorus of wheezing, guttural mirth. "We'll get more then that for one of 'is legs," the whispering shadow said. "But if you drop the purse at your feet, it'll buy you a dozen steps down the alley."

"A d-dozen steps?" Sir Hamnet repeated numbly.

"You get a dozen steps before our friend with the bow tries to bury a cloth-yard shaft or two in your back," came the softly spoken reply. "Your wrinkled arse might not be worth selling, but it'll make for suitable target practice."

"Wait 'til I'm outta the way," the brute said.

But the warning proved unnecessary. Before the black-clad thug had jogged three steps toward safety, Sir Hamnet dropped his coin purse and ran.

Mocking laughter, not arrows, followed the nobleman down the narrow lane. But his panic-ridden mind found horrors to keep his legs pumping anyway. The fog clutched at his arms with phantasmal fingers, and the thick mud closed on his boots with wet, greedy maws. And when Hawklin's imagination cooled for even an instant, a memory of Captain Truesilver's face flared to life in his thoughts. Cradled in the brute's arms, the handsome young soldier had stared help-lessly, pleadingly at Sir Hamnet; the terror in Truesilver's eyes had made it clear that he was well aware of his fate as the thug carried him off.

Sir Hamnet fell more than once, smearing himself with filth. It didn't matter. He pushed himself to his feet and dashed onward, frantically searching the darkened hovels for a likely safe haven.

A triumphant cheer drew him around the next corner to the doorstep of a tavern. The building was no less a ruin than its neighbors, but its facade was brightly lit. Torches burned on either side of the wide doorway, chasing away the fog, casting broad shadows into the street. Spritely music spilled from the interior along with the sour scent of spilled ale and overcooked meat.

Sir Hamnet staggered over the stoop just as another cheer went up. He blinked, thinking his vision blurred by the frantic run, but realized the room was hazed with acrid smoke. Clusters of languid, slack-limbed men and women lounged around a dozen or so hookahs. A few turned to regard him with vague, disinterested eyes; most seemed completely unaware of his presence, so caught up were they in their ardent pursuit of oblivion.

The real center of attention—and the source of the cheer-ing—was a large square cut into the taproom's floor. A mob of rowdy toughs lined the miniature arena, noisily wagering on a bloody fight between a terrier and a small, slim creature, all slick-furred and sinuous. The nobleman stared for an instant, uncomprehending, as the thing locked its jaws on the terrier's throat and tore away a gory, fatal chunk of flesh. Then the victorious gladiator reared up on its hind legs, and Sir Hamnet finally recognized the beast.

A weasel. A large, gray-furred weasel. And its beady eyes were fixed firmly on Hawklin's face.

"Welcome," a smooth, not-quite-melodious voice said in the noble's ear.

A shabbily dressed man stepped before Sir Hamnet. His face was narrow, with a hawkish nose and high cheekbones beneath the grime and the scars. He was thin to emaciation, clad in tattered clothes and suffused with the stink of cheap gin. Like everyone else in the place, he wore his weapon without peacestrings. From its obvious value, the short sword hanging at his hip had certainly been stolen.

"You look a little ragged, old gent." The stranger's broad smile seemed to radiate welcome despite the rotting gums and missing teeth. "Best get you a seat, eh?"

Sir Hamnet was too stunned to object as the hawk-nosed man slipped a hand under his elbow and guided him to a chair at the back of the room. He was sitting before he finally gathered wits enough to speak. "I need to find a watchman," he said. "There's been a—"

"Shhh!" the stranger interrupted, holding up his left hand to silence the nobleman; his fourth and fifth fingers were little more than discolored stubs of scarred flesh. "The locals don't like the king's men much. You'd best keep your voice down. Look, I'll be right back. There's somebody here wants to talk to you. Maybe he can help."

Sir Hamnet watched the hawk-nosed man weave his way to the bar. It was only then that the nobleman took in the details of his surroundings. The place was a cesspit in every sense of the word.

Fist-sized roaches picked through the spilled ale, chunks of age-petrified bread, and unconscious revelers strewn on the floor, while centipedes as long as a man's forearm pulsed up the walls. They ducked under and around the trophies tacked there. Crude sketches of women in various stages of undress surrounded the crumbling hearth. Nearby hung a gallery of finger bones, the penalty exacted from careless pickpockets by the local watch. Parchment arrest warrants and wanted posters signed by King Azoun and a half-dozen other sires of House Obarskyr were displayed beside nooses cut from gallows all across Cormyr. Many of the ropes still bore the fleshy marks left by the infamous footpads and highwaymen who'd dangled in their choking embrace.

The most prized trophy hung over the door—a helmet once worn by a captain of the city watch. As Sir Hamnet stared at the helm, the wavering torchlight illuminated the eye slits. The captain's head was still housed within the rusted steel, its empty eye sockets staring down in defeat at the toughs crowding the taproom.

The hawk-nosed man suddenly eclipsed the vile trophy. "I told you they don't like the city watch," he said as he placed a brimming mug before Sir Hamnet. With his right hand he presented the weasel from the arena. Blood darkened its muzzle, and bits of terrier fur still clung to its claws. "He's got a message for you."

Sir Hamnet recoiled from the weasel and from the mad-man holding it. But his discomfort at the beast's proximity was nothing compared to the horror that gripped him when the animal opened its mouth and spoke.

"You were the lone weasel at the Hill of Lost Souls," it rasped softly, so that only Sir Hamnet could hear.

Heart thundering, blood roaring in his ears, Sir Hamnet exploded from his chair. The hawk-nosed man stepped aside as the aged explorer bolted past. "He usually prefers to chat with his own kind, so the message must've been important," he called to the retreating nobleman. "Say, old gent, does this mean you don't want to see the other side of the mirror?"

Sir Hamnet had just crossed the threshold into the alley, but the shouted question stopped him cold, just as surely, as completely, as the poisoned dagger had paralyzed Captain

Truesilver. He forced himself to look up. As if following some unheard cue, the fog and the shadows parted, allowing the torchlight to shine fully on the sign hanging overhead. The weather-beaten circle of wood was colored by wedges of silver paint, a crude attempt at depicting a broken window—or a shattered mirror.

"Yes, Sir Hamnet," the hawk-nosed man said. "The Shattered Mirror. You came here for an audience. Now you have it."

The nobleman turned slowly, knowing it would be futile to flee. He found the taproom and its patrons transformed. Bones and grinning skulls had replaced the wooden walls and offal-smeared floor. Instead of gin-soaked toughs, denizens and fiends filled the hall. They stood in silent array, the court of Hades in all its terrible splendor. Some gripped razor-edged halberds. Others had only their horns and fangs and claws for weapons, though they were surely enough to rend any man's soul from his flesh.

And in the center of this ghastly host sat the hawk-nosed man. His myriad names flashed through Sir Hamnet's mind—the Lord of the Dead, the Dark Sun, Master of Strife, the Prince of Lies.

Cyric.

He was robed in darkness, the kind that shrouds the hearts of liars and infidels. The weasel curled affectionately around his neck, a living collar to that shirt of shadow. Pages of other gods' holy books soled his boots, and the remains of false martyrs formed his throne. Free of grime, free of scars, Cyric's countenance glowed with hideous glee. Even as Sir Hamnet watched, fingers sprouted to replace the missing digits on his left hand. He flexed the restored hand and caressed the pommel of the rose-red short sword lying across his lap.

"Well, old gent?" Cyric prompted. "Do you have something to ask?"

Sir Hamnet cast his gaze down. "As a son of House Hawklin and a member in good standing of the Society of Stalwart Adventurers, I claim the rights of safe conduct and—"

"Has anyone here raised a talon against you? No. So you've obviously been granted safety." The death god sighed with impatience. "Aren't you going to return my courtesy?"

"C-Courtesy?"

"I've dropped my facade. Are you going to do the same?" Cyric watched Sir Hamnet's face for some sign of recognition, but none came. There was only the typical pall of fear and awe. "Shall I let the weasel explain it to you again? I thought he'd summed it up nicely before, but maybe he should have another go."

At Hawklin's stammering reply, Cyric pounded the arm of his throne. "The facade of the great hero, the great explorer!" he shrieked in a voice like an orchestra of untuned violins. "You didn't lift a blade in defense of your companions at the Hill of Lost Souls. You ran as the first goblins entered the camp—just as you've run from every danger you've ever faced! As my sinuous friend said earlier, you were the only weasel on the hill that day."

The Lord of the Dead closed his eyes and collected himself. "Now," he continued more calmly, "I don't brand you a coward. I'd label your actions—" He paused and looked up, as if the proper word floated just over his head.

"Self-preservation," the weasel on his shoulder rasped.

"Exactly," Cyric chimed. He stroked the beast's bloody muzzle affectionately before turning back to Sir Hamnet. "I applaud someone smart enough to preserve his own life, but I take exception to your imperfect guise of resolute honesty and stout-hearted courage. You haven't convinced yourself that you're a hero, not deep down. So don't insult me by hiding behind a flawed mask and expecting me not to notice it's cracked."

"It's not a mask," Hawklin murmured dazedly. "My books. My maps. The Stalwarts respect all that I've done." He voice grew stronger, his words more certain. "They know the truth. . . ."

Cyric clapped slowly, facetiously. "Not embarrassingly bad, but I've seen you do better cheating your way out of a bar bill at the club."

"Seen me do better? You've been watching me?"

"No more than any other liar."

Hawklin's bushy white brows knit over his dark eyes. "This was a trap! You charged that monster Uther with luring me here, tempting me to search this place out!"

An amused murmur rippled through the assembled court of Hades.

"I hardly need to employ imitation fiends like Uther when I have the endless hosts of the underworld at my beck and call," the Lord of Strife replied blandly. "And I leave this pathway to Hades open, and let my minions circulate stories of its existence, to see who wanders in. It breaks up the monotony of listening to the dead drone on about their tedious past lives, to the damned scream in agony. I just happened to recognize you when you crossed the threshold."

Cyric studied the nobleman for a moment, then shook his head. "I hope I haven't overestimated you, old gent. You forge lies well enough, but you've hidden your heart from them, shielded it with a wall of delusory respect built up by those boors at your club."

The weasel perked up and added, "But the problem with walls is, you never know which way they're going to fall when they finally crumble. Maybe out, maybe in."

Casually Cyric gestured to two of the largest, most hideous fiends in his entourage. "Throw him out—but be careful you don't hurt him. He's under my protection until he reaches the mortal realms."

A scream wrenched itself from Sir Hamnet's throat as the fiends closed on him. They gripped him with fingers liquid and putrefying, but strong as vices, and lifted him from the ground. Cold seeped into his flesh at their touch. It spread up his arms and across his chest, chilling his heart, making it thud against his ribs like a frantic caged animal.

Sir Hamnet was still screaming when the city watch found him at sunrise the next morning, kneeling in the mud before the burned-out shell of an abandoned building. They recognized him, of course, his fame having spread beyond the walls of the Stalwart Club long ago. That was fortunate, since the watchmen would have been less patient, less gentle with a commoner so obviously insane with drink.

"We'll take you to the temple of Mystra, Sir Hamnet," the captain offered. "They'll look you over there. Then we'll take your report."

"No. Take me home."

"Fine. We'll have you to your estate before the servants are done preparing breakfast," the captain replied.

"I said home," Sir Hamnet croaked. "*Home,* damn you. The Stalwart Club."

* * * * *

For three days, Sir Hamnet Hawklin immersed himself in the healing familiarity of the society's library. He slept in his chair, his rapier never far from his hand. He spoke little, and when he did it was only in carefully worded snatches that obscured more than they illuminated. Still, he revealed enough for his fellow Stalwarts to construct their own, utterly distorted account of Gareth Truesilver's demise and Hawklin's own confrontation with Cyric. Their version cast Sir Hamnet as a valiant defender, overcome by a combined cadre of body snatchers and fiends that grew in number with each telling.

The nobleman did not object, and some time during the second day he almost came to believe that he had crossed steel with a dozen assassins and denizens in his friend's defense. Soon after, plans were begun for Sir Hamnet's long-overdue statue. Hawklin had warmed by then to the familiar role of daring trailblazer and all-around stout fellow. In his own mind, he even managed to dismiss the most troubling events at the Shattered Mirror as toxin-induced hallucinations, brought on by a nick from a body snatcher's poisoned blade.

Only one topic rivaled Sir Hamnet's bravery in those three days—the whereabouts of Uther. The butler had been missing since the night of the disastrous expedition, a sure sign of his involvement with Captain Truesilver's waylaying.

Those clubmen who'd befriended the monstrous servant chose to believe he'd fled in fear upon hearing of the soldier's death; kindhearted though they were, these misguided folk found themselves shouted down more and more as the hours passed. No, the butler had clearly orchestrated the captain's murder, and it was only a matter of time before he was brought to justice.

The last place any of the Stalwarts expected the frightful servant to appear was in the library itself. Yet Uther strode into that cavernous, trophy-lined room just as twilight settled upon Suzail that third night.

He ignored the gasps of surprise and the angry, shouted accusations. Anyone who got too close was warned away with a shake of his magnificently horned head, or shoved away by a black-clawed hand. And the mages scattered about the room knew better than to attempt to restrain him through spellcraft; the same misfired magic that had warped the butler's form had made him immune to all further enchantment.

Uther stalked to one particular bookshelf, a place of honor near the hearth, and paused there. With his usual efficiency, he began to withdraw the tomes and scrolls and maps housed there. Most of the Stalwarts knew whose books they were; those few who didn't could guess.

"Outrage upon outrage!" Sir Hamnet cried, finally jolted out of his shocked silence by Uther's astounding impertinence. "Leave those volumes alone, you murderous brute!"

"These books have been shelved incorrectly," Uther noted without looking up from his task. "The cases nearest the hearth are reserved for histories, Sir Hamnet. Your works are fiction."

As he closed on the butler, the aged nobleman reached for his rapier and drew it with a flourish. "I'll run you through unless you put them back."

"Coward."

The voice was labored, the word thick and ill-formed, but it was clear enough to draw everyone's attention to the figure framed by the library's massive doorway. Captain

Truesilver glared balefully with the one eye left him and started into the room.

The crutch braced under his right arm thudded like a coffin-maker's hammer with every other step. Without it Gareth Truesilver couldn't have walked at all; his right leg was missing from the knee down. Nor was that the worst of his injuries. Angry red blotches patterned his arms where the skin had been flayed away. Incisions held closed with thick black stitches snaked across the back of his left hand. There, the body snatchers' patron had pilfered the muscles and sinews, leaving the hand nearly useless. Similar scars creased the captain's once-handsome face; they traversed the angry purple bruises over his cheekbones, disappearing into both the gap that had once been his nose and the dark circle that had held his left eye.

The butler turned, muscled arms cradling two shelves of displaced books. "You should rest, Captain. The city guard will be here soon to take your statement." Uther shifted his gaze for an instant to Sir Hamnet. "I have spent the past three days aiding the watch in their search for the captain. If you'd told the truth the morning the guards found you screaming like a madman, we might have rescued him days ago, before the butchers had time to cut him up."

"Gareth," Sir Hamnet stammered, as if he hadn't heard the accusation. "We thought you lost. Helm's Fist, but I'm glad you're alive!"

"Liar," Truesilver managed in a slow, pained voice. From the way he mangled the word, it seemed likely a part of his tongue had gone to power some wizard's spell, too.

Awkwardly the captain hobbled to a stop in front of Uther. With his right hand, he lifted the largest book from atop the pile and pitched it into the fireplace. The flames danced along the spine. With a sharp pop, the tome flipped open, revealing a hand-colored map of the Hordelands. Fire hungrily devoured the page and set to work on the rest of the book.

Truesilver tossed another volume into the fire, and another. Sir Hamnet raised a hand to stop him, but a low and rumbling growl from Uther warned him away.

Helpless, he turned to the others in the library, his friends, his fellow explorers. But Sir Hamnet Hawklin found loathing in the faces of the Stalwarts, and disgust, and anger. They stared at him with open contempt, silently cheering the destruction of his life's work.

He tried to shrug off the contempt and shore up the barricades he'd built around his craven heart. But the walls were crumbling now. The society's shared glories fled him like deadfall leaves abandoning a winter oak. The myriad ceremonial blades and trophy shields hanging on the walls had been his to wield. The slaughtered monsters and conquered dragon had been his trophies, too, proof of valorous deeds beyond imagining. No longer. The Stalwarts knew the truth, and each accusing eye reflected that truth back at the nobleman like a perfect mirror.

Sir Hamnet Hawklin was a coward.

The room began to spin, and the nobleman covered his face with trembling hands. He could block out the sights, but he couldn't deafen himself to the crackle and hiss of the fire as it destroyed his journals and turned his maps to ash.

And in that instant, just before his heart was crushed by those toppled walls of borrowed honor, Sir Hamnet heard it—the low, sibilant laughter in the flames. He'd been right all along. It was the vicious chuckle of Cyric, the satisfied sigh of the Lord of Strife as a man's spirit shattered and his damned soul went shrieking down to Hades.

VISION

Roger E. Moore

The summons brought me out of a meeting in an over-crowded den where the candles had eaten up the air. My clan head grumbled, but he released me and returned to bullying compensation from an opponent over an imagined slight of honor. Such wars of words, often punctuated by drawn knives and brief duels that left the cavern floors slick with blood, were far too frequent these days among my people. I was glad to go.

I would have been happier for the freedom, but the warrior who called me out told me I was summoned by Skra-lang, shaman of all our kind. My stomach grew tight at the thought of meeting the old goblin. I was no coward, but I was no fool. The warrior hurried off as I bound up my fears and set off myself through the long, narrow tunnels of the Nightbelow, our home under the Dustwalls.

At twenty winters I was a guard captain and assistant to my clan head, a young fist among the many hands of the goblins of the mountains. I had fought on the surface against human intruders on our lands since I was twelve, and had been captured once and held prisoner for a year until I had escaped. My captivity taught me to never let it happen again. I knew humans well and feared none of them, but Skralang was not a human, and some said he was not a goblin, either.

The old shaman's door opened automatically when I reached it at the end of a black, web-filled tunnel. Skralang greeted me with a nod from his bed. He carelessly waved me to a chair at a table on which a lone candle flickered. I steeled myself and entered his den.

I picked my way across the tiny, litter-strewn room. My iron-shod boots crushed bits of bone, bread crusts, and other debris beneath them. Skralang did not seem to care about the filth. The world meant less to him every day, it was said. How he could stand to live in such vile conditions was beyond me, but it was not my place and not to my advantage to say so. Who insults a mouthpiece of the gods?

I sat and waited as the shaman took a small bottle and earthen cup from a box by his bed of rags. He carefully swung his feet off the ruined bed and got up, shuffling over to pull up a stool and take a seat by me. I stiffened and almost stood to salute, but he seemed not to care. His familiarity was astonishing; it was if I were an old and trusted friend.

Even more astonishing was Skralang's appearance at close range in the candlelight. His robes stank of corruption, as if death were held back from him by the width of an eyelash. The skin was pulled tight over the bones of his face and hands; open sores disfigured his arms and neck. Yet even with this, his pale yellow eyes were clear and steady. He gently poured another drink for himself, but did not take it right away. Instead he sat back and regarded me with those cold, clear eyes.

"You are bored, Captain Kergis," he said. His voice was no more than a whisper. In the silence, it was like a shout. "Life here has no appeal for you. You long to be elsewhere."

I almost denied it, but his eyes warned me off from lies. I nodded hesitantly. "You see all, Your Darkness," I said. I knew that with his magic, the old goblin probably did see all within the Nightbelow—even the hidden places of the heart and soul.

The old one toyed with his cup. His spidery fingers trembled. "Has the security of our home begun to wear on you? Do the petty ravings of the clan heads lull your blood to sleep, rather than stir it with fire? Or do you have plans of your own for advancing your rank and position, and your boredom is merely feigned to cover your intentions?"

To be accused of treachery was not uncommon, but hearing it fall from the thin lips of our shaman was like hearing my death sentence pronounced. "I am loyal!" I pleaded, much louder than I wanted. "You wrong me, Your Darkness!"

I bit off my words. Skralang wronged no one. He was the law, and there was no other. I sat frozen, half expecting that his response would be my execution. A swift death was better by far than a slow one, and I prayed for the former.

Instead, Skralang drank from his cup and sighed. "You are loyal, yes," he said, staring at the cup in his fingers. "You are neither coward nor traitor. You merely seem . . . disenchanted, not impure in spirit. You do not carry yourself like a true goblin lately." He was silent for a moment, then looked up at me. "But then it sometimes seems to me that none of us do."

I could not have been more amazed than if he had informed me that he was actually a halfling. I was at a loss for words for several moments. "I do not understand," I finally said. "We are all true goblins. We are not tainted like—"

Treacherous tongue! The words had no sooner left my mouth than I would have cut out my tongue to have them back! Skralang flinched when he heard it, and his aged face became like steel.

"We are not *tainted* like a certain one among us, you say?" The shaman's eyes were icy yellow orbs shining from the depths of his face. His fingers gripped his cup like a web grips prey. For one awful moment, his cup became me.

Then—without warning—the old shaman's face softened and melted. He looked away as he set his cup on the table. "Tainted. You are right. No one has spoken that word to me since the birth of my grandson, but there is no hiding it.

When I call him my kin, it is like swallowing daggers. He is tainted, tainted with the blood of a human."

The ancient visage looked my way again, but in sadness, not anger. "Everyone must talk about it. It is a disgrace, and there is no atonement for it. None but death." He sighed deeply and looked off into the darkness of the room.

I knew better than to say anything more. Everyone knew of his half-human grandson, the child of his mutilated daughter and her human attacker. Both child and daughter had been hidden from all other eyes for over a decade, but we knew from rumor that they yet lived. And that we could not understand. Had the daughter belonged to any of the rest of us, we would have slain both her and her infant before birth, and thus removed the shame from our line. What had happened to prevent this?

The shaman looked back at me as if he could read my every thought. " 'As the gods will, we do without question,' " he said, quoting the maxim in a tired voice. "They spoke to me as I held a knife over my daughter's belly, eager to cleanse our honor, and their words turned my knife aside. It was their will that Zeth be raised among us, in my daughter's den, though they would not say why. I had the girl and her bastard walled up, as the gods did not forbid that. I feed them once a day, give them a candle or two for light, but keep the taint away from the rest of our people. It was the gods' will, and I obeyed them, as would any of us." He rubbed his face with a skeletal hand.

I did my best to hide my surprise at this revelation. The gods' will? He said so but still lived, so it must be true. The sharp, clear eyes turned away again, and the old one refilled his cup and stared into it for a long moment, chewing his lower lip in perplexity.

The old shaman drank again and set the cup down. The ghost of a smile came to his withered lips, but there was no humor behind it.

"I am older than old for our people," he said softly. "If I see another midwinter's day, I will be forty-six. I ache ceaselessly. I pray for death before I sleep, yet the gods want me to live a little longer." His cold eyes looked across the table at me. "Can you guess why, Captain?"

"Why what, Your Darkness?" I asked after hesitating. I had lost the way of the conversation entirely, and I now considered every word I spoke so I might live the longer.

"Why the gods have kept me alive when I have strived so hard to die," he said patiently. "I rot from within, yet awaken every evening and draw breath into my bleeding lungs. Can you guess why the gods still want me to live a little longer?"

"No, Your Darkness." A lesser person would have offered an opinion—a worthless way to risk one's soul.

The shaman's lips pulled back as if he would laugh. "This last day, the gods spoke to me again," he said, as if the other topic were now forgotten. "They came to me in a dream. It was time, they said, to free my grandson and send him out from the caverns with a force of true goblins at his command." The old shaman drew in a deep breath through his nose, staring at me. "I've seen fit to end your disenchantment, Captain Kergis. I've already given orders for three sergeants to assemble their squads for a foray this evening. You will go with them, led by my grandson. Draw rations and equipment for a mission far from our Nightbelow, among the lands of humans."

I believed for a moment that I had gone deaf, so incredible was the news. Goblin warriors led by a half-human bastard?

"What is our mission, Your Darkness?" I managed.

"Zeth will let you know," said Skralang. "Obey his every word as you would mine. It is as the gods command."

The wrinkled face suddenly leaned close to me, and I caught a whiff of the drink he had prepared for himself. It was ale mixed with a pain-deadener made from the blossoms of the corpse lily. I knew its scent from the battlefields, where warriors chewed such blossoms to subdue their pain. Sometimes, if badly wounded, the warriors chewed too much and fell into a sleep from which they never awoke. We left them for the dogs to eat.

"The gods have ordained that Zeth must go out," said the

shaman steadily. I shuddered at the smell of his breath.
"They ordered nothing more. For my part, when he is gone,
I am finally free to clear the taint from my family. I will
cleanse my line with my daughter's blood, but there is the
fear in me that even this will not bring me a long-deserved
death. The gods want one thing more of me, and I cannot
see into their plans."

Skralang sat back. "My other dreams have all been troubling of late. The gods are unhappy, I fear, with the way the
lives of our people have fallen into quarrels and tedium. You
are bored, Captain Kergis, because you sense it, too. We
have not gone out as we did in the old days to remind the
surface world that we exist. We've gotten old in our heads,
old and petty, and we hide in our caverns and complain
about the dark. We are not the children of our fathers, not fit
to be their lowest slaves."

The old shaman's gaze fell, and his face grew slack. "I
believe the gods are especially unhappy with me, their servant, for allowing such deterioration to come about. I have
favored rest and ease over struggle, against their teachings,
and the rot of my words has spread and ruined us." He
looked back at me, and his eyes gleamed. "Did you ever
wonder in your private moments, Captain Kergis, if the taint
among us reflects a greater taint? If Zeth's coming, and the
manner of it, was *purposeful?*"

The old goblin had long ago strayed into territory that
not even the greatest fool among us would have tread. I
wished now I were back in that stale cavern room, listening
to my clan head shriek about his worthless honor.

"Never," I said truthfully.

The shaman's smile deepened. "You will." He dismissed
me with a wave and drank again of his cup of poison, swallowing it without so much as a tremor at its bitterness.

* * * * *

There was much that Skralang had not told me. He hadn't
said that Zeth's skin was the color of a dead toad's belly,

white and dry like the face of the moon. Or that Zeth wore no armor and carried no weapon, and knew nothing of how to use either.

Or that Zeth was blind.

I shivered when I saw the shaman's grandson led out of the mouth of our Nightbelow into the evening air. He was big and long-limbed, no doubt from the human blood in him, but his muscles were slack. I could have thrown him down with only mild effort, had I dared.

And he had no eyes. His eye sockets were dark holes in his face, half-covered by sagging skin that made him appear sad faced. He wore only a short, pale robe, belted with a thin rope. It was the sort of thing only a prisoner or slave would wear, and entirely the wrong color for a warrior at night.

Skralang brought Zeth to me as my warriors looked on with surprise and curiosity. In the failing sunlight, the withered shaman seemed to have deteriorated even more since I had seen him, only hours before. Splotches of blackness dotted his face and arms, marks of a curse on him. I was terrified he would touch me.

"Zeth," said the old shaman with a prompt at his grandson's elbow. "Here are your warriors. Go forth, as the gods have commanded, and carry out their will."

The big half-human stared over me, his unseeing gaze level with the top of my head, then nodded dumbly. I saw that Zeth had no weaponry, and I started to pull an extra dagger from my waist scabbard. Skralang stopped me with an upraised hand. "Not necessary," the old shaman said. "Zeth has no need of blades or armor. He has all he will need."

With a last look at me, the shaman summoned his retinue of guards and servants, then retired inside the cavern. The great doors were pulled shut behind him and barred. Not even the usual guards were posted tonight.

I swallowed as I stared up at the eyeless sockets of the white half-human. He merely looked off to the west, where the sun had vanished a while ago.

ROGER E. MOORE

"What is your wish?" I finally asked. If I were lucky, Zeth
would prove to be mad as well as blind. I wondered if the
prohibition against arms and armor was meant to speed his
death in battle. It made sense to me. His quick death would
release us from this mission, perhaps allowing brief forag-
ing in the countryside to gain a few pigs or cattle before
returning to the Nightbelow.

The big half-human slowly turned his head to the south,
as if he'd heard something in the gentle wind. Southward
lay the kingdom of Durpar, which we had once raided regu-
larly. He nodded slightly, then set off toward that distant
land. After two steps, he almost fell over a log that had been
pulled up to the cave entrance as a bench. He stumbled,
caught himself, and walked on. No one laughed or moved to
help him. We merely watched.

I nodded to myself. With luck, the mission would be a
short one.

"Single file, scout fore and back, standard march," I called.
The warriors glanced at me, then fell into place. We set off
into the coming night.

We marched south for about ten hours by the stars. That
Zeth had some ability to sense his path became more evi-
dent as the night deepened. He would pause at times, then
slowly make his way across a creek or through a rock field.
At other times, he acted as blind as he appeared, running
into low tree branches or dancing out of thistle. Perhaps his
hearing gave him a little help, but I began to think perhaps
his eyes were present but merely small and deeply set.

Dawn was coming on when I finally moved up alongside
the stumbling half-human. I hesitated over proper forms of
address, then ignored them all. I couldn't see that it mattered. "Dawn is near," I said under my breath. "We must
pitch camp soon."

Zeth marched on in silence, his blind gaze fixed somewhere over the horizon. Abruptly he slowed and stopped.
For a moment he stood, his chest heaving from exertion,
then nodded quickly. "We will stop here," he gasped. It was
more an animal moan than speech, the words wheezed out

and half-mumbled. Was Zeth feebleminded as well? What was Skralang up to?

I gave the proper orders anyway and had everyone in hiding among the rocks and brush of a nearby hillside before sun-up. Zeth wandered away in the meantime, but returned to camp as the meal was served. I thought it politic to sit near him for the first meal and see if I could learn a little more about his plans—if he had any—for this expedition. My concerns grew rapidly that he would lead us straight into a human city or worse.

A plate of beans and dried meat was prepared for Zeth, and another for myself. I glanced at him as we ate, and saw that indeed he had no eyes at all. The blind half-human and I sat for a while on the hilltop in silence.

"If you wish any advice," I began, "I am at your service."

Zeth chewed a bit of meat for several moments, rocking slowly forward and back. Abruptly he spoke.

"When I was no more than a babe," he said in a quiet, dry voice, "my grandfather dug out my eyes with a spoon." Empty sockets looked at me from an empty white face. "He loved me very much to do that. Did anyone ever love you like that?"

I stared back, a fork full of beans halfway to my mouth. A cold finger ran down my spine. He was as mad as mad could get. I took a bite of the beans and looked around. None of the goblins was close enough to have heard anything.

"It was the only way he had to open my eyes," continued the half-human, looking toward the predawn sky. "Had he not done so, I'd never have seen at all. I hardly remember it now. I was told that I fought him and the others like an ogre, that my screams caused the dead to cry out. I don't recall it." The blind half-human raised a thin hand and stroked his chin. "It had to be done. I didn't understand why then, but I learned."

It was apparent that more than just Zeth's eyes had been dug out by Skralang's spoon. His words, however, showed him to be smarter than he had first seemed. I could think of nothing to say, so I finished my cold meal.

"It will be light soon," said Zeth. "We will rest, then evening will come and we will march. We will find a village." He paused, lifting his head slightly as if listening to something far away. "They will be halflings, farmers. There we will start."

I swallowed the last bite slowly and chased errant bits of food across my teeth with my tongue. "Start what?" I asked, masking my concerns. I knew from past experience that Durpar's warriors were not to be taken lightly. If any gods were leading Zeth, they could not have been our gods.

Zeth looked up. "There we will start our teaching," he said quietly.

"Teaching," I repeated.

"Teaching, yes," said Zeth, with an unmistakable note of enthusiasm. To my great concern, he then looked directly at me. "We will teach them."

"What? Teach them what?"

"Ah," said Zeth. His smile grew broader. "We will teach them what we have forgotten."

Crickets chirped. A sparrow called down in the fields.

What would the gods do to me if I were to kill you? I thought as I looked at the pale, smiling face. What is Skralang expecting of me? Will I fail his unspoken desires by letting this abomination live? No, Skralang had been clear: I was to obey his grandson. But he was mad, and he was leading us into destruction.

"I should post guards," I said and got to my feet. I needed to think. Perhaps it was unwise to risk the anger of the gods by acting directly. Nature could take its course, with a minimum of help. The half-human would be easy to dispose of just by letting him lead until he walked into a ravine or a Durpar border camp. His grandfather would undoubtedly welcome the news.

I turned to go but got only three steps when Zeth called my name. I looked back.

The blind half-human had a dagger in his right hand, holding it out to me by the blade. I felt at my belt and discovered a dagger missing. It must have slipped out when I sat down.

"You must be more careful," he said. "We have much to do tonight."

He handed the weapon to me, the handle aimed exactly at my stomach. I took back my dagger and left, looking back several times as I did.

* * * * *

We were on our feet and moving before the sun had vanished behind the low western hills. The half-moon lighted our way. Zeth strode easily through the tall grass that paralleled a cart track a half-mile east of us, to our left. I posted a forward scout and two scouts to the left and right. Yet another scout trailed Zeth by a dozen paces, and the rest of us followed after.

As before, the big half-human avoided most obstacles in his path, winding his way around them with unusual care. If he stumbled, he caught his balance gracelessly but quickly. I wondered whether the gods had made Zeth insane and his eyes simply invisible, or if it was all an elaborate trick, something Skralang thought up to test me. I thought of Zeth staring at me that morning, and a tightness grew in my stomach.

I was growing used to the mindlessness of the situation— a company of goblins led by a blind madman—but I saw its dangers as well. The warriors grumbled among themselves, and some began to treat the outing as a farce. They walked with weapons sheathed, laughed at private jokes, pushed and shoved one another in line.

I did not let this go on long. I dropped back among the file and located one of the worst offenders, who had fallen earlier and scraped his knees and hands. As he complained about the pain for the third time, I pulled the lash from my belt and struck him.

The lash caught him full across the face, just below the eyes. Before he could cry out, the lash came back and snapped across his back like a brand of fire. His cry was cut off by his intake of breath at the second hit, and he fell to his knees, hands covering his face.

The column behind him stopped, but at a gesture from me, continued on around him. I waited with the warrior as the column filed past. After a few moments, he regained his feet and picked up his weapon. I watched as he stumbled on to catch up with the column.

I followed, ensuring that the message had gotten through. It had. Silence was kept thereafter, and weapons were held at the ready.

We marched on for only three hours when Zeth abruptly slowed his pace, head turned to one side, and stopped. The scout behind him looked back at me questioningly. I came forward.

"There they are," said Zeth, pointing ahead. "We must begin our teaching."

I looked ahead and noticed a faint light. We were about two miles from a small community that sat astride the cart path to our left. I detected no sign of any military activity, but that meant little. Enemy warriors could be concealed anywhere and had time to prepare a bloody welcome.

"We are safe," said Zeth carelessly. He was smiling again and wasn't breathing as heavily as the night before. "They don't know we're here."

"How would you know?" I asked under my breath. I gave a hand signal for the troops to stay low and keep silent. Before I could do more, Zeth turned to me and grabbed my shoulder, pulling me close to him. I was too surprised to resist.

His breath was visible in the cool night air. "Gather the villagers together. They will not resist. I wish to begin teaching before the night has passed. Our people should gather around and learn wisdom, too." He released me and sat on the ground with a thump, not moving from that spot.

I stared at him, then looked across the dark field. Gather the villagers up for Zeth to teach them? His grandfather had ordered me to obey the mad one as if he were one of the gods. Perhaps the gods would spare me for my obedience if any disaster fell, but I no longer believed it. I obeyed but felt I was as mad as Zeth to do it.

I left the scout with Zeth while I went back and collected the rest of the troops. Moments later, we moved on to the sleeping village.

The attack was over almost as soon as it had begun. Many of the halflings were in their beds when we set fire to their barns. As they rushed out, half-dressed and clutching blankets and buckets, they were shot by our archers. Many were clubbed down and herded together on the road as others of us torched the houses. Some fought back with farm implements—pitchforks, shovels, hammers. Those we killed. The dogs were more trouble than the villagers.

We forced the survivors—about three dozen males, females, and children—to strip and stand naked in the night wind. Warriors surrounded them and amused themselves by prodding bare skin with their spears, laughing and betting as to which of the little people would jump highest. Around us, orange flames roared through the halflings' homes and farms.

I sent a runner for Zeth, but he was already on his way to the burning village with the scout at his side. As I watched him approach, I wondered what purpose there was in this miserable raid besides this nonsense about "teaching." I had always fought armed humans before—guardsmen on caravans, or armored militia at fortified farmhouses on the borderlands. Assaulting such poorly armed and trained halflings was wasteful of our powers. I bit my lip with frustration and tasted blood.

Zeth put out his hands toward a burning cottage as he passed it, his smile clearly visible. He warmed himself thus, then slowed and picked his way with care toward the warriors surrounding the crouching prisoners. The huddled halflings' eyes were like those of caged rabbits. Zeth looked them over, and I believed then that he had to have sight of some kind. Was it magic, then, that let him see? I would not allow myself to think that the gods had anything to do with it. It must be Skralang's doing, though I could not imagine how or why.

Satisfied, Zeth walked to the top of a low mound, then

turned to face the troops. There was silence across the area, except for the crackling of dying flames.

"In the beginning of all things," said Zeth, his voice growing stronger, "there was war between the gods and the rebellious earth, and the world was struck down and slain. Darkness covered its face; winds and sea lashed its corpse. Nothing grew on its naked rock or stirred beneath the cold moon. As the world lay dead, maggots were born from the blood shed by the gods in the battle, and the maggots burrowed into the flesh of the world and feasted upon it, celebrating the victory of the gods.

"Then came forces of light, and there arose a sun over the land. The light burned the eyes of the maggots and made them cry out. The old gods heard them and were moved to rage. One of the old gods put forth his hand and said, 'A debt is owed our children as well as to us, and now our children shall claim it.' He changed the maggots into goblins, and he gave them a commandment, that the goblins would always remember the days of darkness when the old gods were victors, when nothing grew on the world, when there was night eternal and deep. And the goblins would remember always to claim the debt owed them and their gods by the forces of light."

Zeth swept a hand toward the flaming cottages beyond the gathering. "Here we are tonight, the spawn of the maggots, and we are still asked to remember what our god asked of us, but we have forgotten it all." His hand fell. "At highsun tomorrow, a band of riders will come to this place, and they will see what we have done. They will taste the ash from the houses and feel the heat from the blackened fields. But will the riders fear us? Will the old debt have been repaid?"

The half-human paused expectantly, though none of us spoke. "No. The riders will have seen burned villages before. They will have seen slain farmers. Why should they fear us—we, the firstborn, who are descended from the maggots who fed on the world?"

Several goblins stirred restlessly, their faces crossed with confusion. Even the prisoners had ceased whimpering to listen.

"Would *you* fear us?" asked the half-human, pointing at a goblin in the crowd. "Or you? We have only burned a little town. Who is alive in the world who cannot do that? Little pixies could do that." Zeth's face cracked into a shallow grin. "Even *humans* could do that." There was a pause, then he added, "I should know."

He let the silence grow. I shivered. There was a change in the atmosphere when he said the word *humans,* and we looked at him and remembered what he was.

"Even humans could do that," he repeated. "We've lived so long under the sunlight, away from the night and the truth, that we've forgotten who we really are. We've started to think—" Zeth leered as if he would laugh "—that we're *human.*"

None of the goblins moved. Their tight faces were like stone. His words were a mortal insult, the basest slander. Yet they rolled off Zeth's lips as if they were a shabby truth at which the knowing world snickered. Only the warriors' knowledge that Skralang was his grandfather kept Zeth from a speedy death.

Zeth's thin fingers reached into the air. "Are we *human* now?" he called out. "Can we do only things that humans do? Do we remember anything at all that our gods taught us? Has the sun burned it out of us, the memory of where we came from?" He then shouted, his face twisted with rage. "Do you want those riders who come here tomorrow to laugh at our night's work? Do you want them to ride here and see this and say, 'Looks like humans' work, bandits maybe, just nasty old humans, good thing they weren't *goblins.*'?"

The half-human raised a hand to the black heavens. "My father was a human! He cursed me with his taint! My eyes were not red like yours—they were blue! Blue, like a human's! Blue like the day sky! *Where are my eyes now?*"

He suddenly pointed at one goblin in the crowd, his white finger like a sword. "You! Tell me! *Where are my eyes now?*"

The goblin's lips trembled as he mouthed a word silently.

Zeth's face came alive with fury. *"Tell me, dog, or may the gods burn you where you stand!"*

"Your eyes are gone!" screamed the goblin. He fell to his knees. "They are gone!"

"Yes!" Zeth shouted at once. "They are gone! My eyes were human, and my grandfather gave them back! My grandfather gave back my eyes! These holes in my face are a thousand times better than the taint of my blue eyes! What my father was, his human taint, was cut out of me! I am more goblin now than are you, because my soul is free! My soul is clean, yet yours writhe with the taint of *humanity!* The proof is among you, there—the farmers you have taken prisoner! You've treated them as humans would treat prisoners! They beg you for mercy, mistaking you for *humans!* How far have we fallen for them to think we, the children of maggots in the flesh of the dead earth, are capable of *mercy?"*

The silence was absolute save for the crackling of fire. Zeth trembled all over as if in the last stages of a fever.

His face turned up, looking over the heads of us all. "I feel their eyes upon us. Can you feel it? Can you feel their eyes looking down upon us? In another moment, they will turn away, and we will be lost. Our people will be lost. Our Night-below will be lost. All that we once were will be gone. Will you show them, our very gods, that you remember that you are *not human?"*

He looked down. His hand swept in the direction of the prisoners. "Prove it now!" he said. "Let the gods see what I cannot."

No one moved. Then one of the warriors silently pulled his long knife, turned, and lunged for the prisoners, seizing one by her hair. He dragged her screaming from the group. Warriors clubbed down two halflings who tried to pull the prisoner back.

The goblin with the knife snarled his left hand in the little halfling's hair and yanked her head back. Her hands tried to ward off the blows as his knife came down once, twice, again and again and again and again, until her hands flopped down into the dust of the road.

The other prisoners screamed with each blow. Abruptly flinging his dagger aside, the warrior seized the body, lifted it over his head as its limbs swung limp, and hurled it into the mass of prisoners, splashing them with gore.

The halflings screamed anew, but it was a sound I had never heard before from the throat of any being. It was mindless with terror, a sound like that made by animals in a slaughtering pen. In that moment, something old inside me awoke and hungered for the taste of blood. I became a wolf in a pack that had seen its prey go down, prey that could not get up and escape, hot prey that would be salty and wet in my mouth. I stepped forward as the rest of the warriors surged in on the wailing prisoners.

But the step was all I took. I held back, not knowing why, as the warriors who had been mine gave in to their hunger and tried to sate it.

Blood-mad goblins murdered prisoner after prisoner in hideous fashion. Onlookers shook their spears and stamped their feet, shouting their approval more loudly and wildly with each death. I watched from the side as if I weren't really there. I was no stranger to cruelty, but what I watched were not the actions of warriors I had raised and trained. They were the deeds of fiends out of Hades.

When the cries and struggles of the last prisoner had ceased, the warriors broke into ragged cheers. Flasks of ale and foul wine had appeared, and many of the warriors drank deeply from them. What had happened to them? I could not even find words to order them to stop, to turn themselves back into soldiers.

"Leave the bodies out," called Zeth. "Let the sun look down on them tomorrow and review our night's work. Let the world see what the children of maggots do to have a debt repaid. Our work has only begun." He swayed, then turned and headed off again to the south, away from the smoldering village.

The goblins followed him easily, the warriors who had once been mine. Not one looked back at me as they went.

When they were almost out of sight, I recovered sufficiently to make my own feet work. I followed their quick pace, my mind cold with shock. We half-ran in this manner for several hours, until the air smelled of fresh grass without the touch of smoke and the tang of blood. The warriors chattered as they went, heedless of the need for quiet in enemy territory, and they passed their wineskins back and forth. I, who was once feared and respected by them all, could have been invisible.

Dawn was almost upon us when Zeth slowed to a stop. As the warriors drew up to him, Zeth collapsed on the ground to rest.

I looked down at the puffing half-breed.

"Captain Kergis," gasped Zeth, though I had made no sound as I had come up, "you do not understand, do you?"

"No," I said, not even thinking of lying. "It is your will."

"It is my will, you say, but I am empty," Zeth returned, still out of breath. "I am the cup that holds the drink, but not the drink itself. I am the mouth, but not the word."

"I don't understand this," I said. "I don't understand any of this. We are warriors. We don't—" I broke off, trying to frame my thoughts. "We fight warriors, not worthless farmers. This is cowardice, to kill the dregs and the helpless! We fight those who can fight back! It's the way to win wars."

Zeth finally caught his breath and sighed as he lay back on the grass, resting on his elbows. He let his head fall back, staring up into the endless night.

"Captain," he said softly, "you are more blind than I am."

I knelt down on the grass a dozen paces from him. Strength seemed to flow out of me into the air. The warriors were drinking and laughing aloud in the distance.

"You wish to kill me," said the half-breed. "I can feel it. Sometimes I can see things, when the gods borrow my head and I see through their eyes for a few moments. But other things I can hear and taste and feel for myself. You would be glad to see me dead."

Zeth cocked his head in my direction, without looking directly at me. "It was the insult, you see, that drove me to this."

When I did not respond, he nodded to himself. "You do not see, then, not even the insult. The taint. My birth. You do not even see that."

"I see it," I said under my breath. I was thinking about killing him right then with my sword, the gods be damned. It would be easy.

"You see only this body. You see that I am different. You see that you wish to kill me. I hear it in your voice. But you do not see the insult. You cannot learn what I am teaching."

Zeth turned his head away in the direction of the warriors. In a few moments, he got to his feet and walked away.

After a while, I got up, too. Goblins milled around the field, aimless and tired. I guessed from the sky that dawn was only three hours away. We had to be off to make camp. Someone would find the massacred village, and the word would be out. I looked back and saw in the moonlight that our trail would not be difficult for vengeful parties to follow. We had to move or else die here.

I found Zeth sitting on the ground, talking to himself in a low voice. He paused and turned his head as I came closer, my boots crunching sticks beneath them.

"We must get out of here," I said flatly. "We have no time to delay."

Zeth turned away again. He was still talking to himself. Or to someone I couldn't see. "He does not understand," he whispered. "He cannot see where they are weak. It is the same place we are weak."

He was motionless for a time, then got unsteadily to his feet.

"Lead us on," said the blind half-breed. "South. We must hurry to our next teaching."

* * * * *

The following night, about twelve miles south of the halfling village, we attacked an isolated farm. Two of our number were wounded but stayed on their feet. We left the farm a few hours later, after Zeth spoke again about the maggots we came from and the gods who watched us. The dozen humans of the family that had lived there now hung by their feet from the ceiling rafters in the dining hall, butchered like deer.

Those who had been my warriors took some of the meat with them.

"Do you see more clearly, Captain?"

I did not look away from the dark horizon as I marched. "No."

Zeth hummed tunelessly to himself. "It is just as it was with me," he said at last. "They would ask, 'Do you see more clearly now?' And I would cry and say, 'No! Give them back to me!' But that was not possible. They had thrown them out already. They were given back."

"Your eyes," I said after a pause.

"My mother said she would put them back, but she had no hands. My father had cut her hands off after he had attacked her and planted the seed for me. He had cut off her hands and left her to die. He was a human, but it was not a human thing to do. He was a hunter, she said, a hunter who had chosen her as his prey. She went out for water and he caught her. He tried to be a goblin. Surely, now, you see it."

I licked my lips. I had lost my warriors and did not care what happened to me anymore. "No."

Zeth sighed heavily. "The insult," he said slowly, as to a child.

I didn't bother to answer.

The next day, a scout shot a rider from his horse as the latter passed our camp at full gallop. It was a remarkable shot, given that the sun was full and we could barely see. The rider tried to crawl away but was found. Zeth did not even need to make a speech. The goblins knew what to do.

The rider was a human soldier from Durpar. Our doings had been discovered. Someone had sent for help against us.

"We can't go farther south," I told Zeth. "The danger is great. We've got to head back, or at least go west where they won't look for us right away."

"You do not understand," said Zeth.

* * * * *

We went on south. We caught a farmer on a hay wagon, then two field hands, one human and one halfling. We surrounded a cottage on the edge of a woodlot, but there was only an old woman inside.

"We are cowards," I said, looking at the old woman's body as it swung in the breeze. I did not say it loudly, as goblins were all around. I no longer felt like one of them. They had betrayed me. Death was better than this.

"We are goblins," said Zeth. He stood with his back to the tree from which the old woman hung. He looked high into the branches. "We have been like humans for too long. We did not understand what the gods wanted of us. We forgot their lessons. We forgot the maggots."

"I've been listening to you talk about teachings and lessons and forgotten things, and I am sick of it," I said. "Tell me what the lesson is, or I will kill you."

The talking among the goblins stopped. Those who had been my warriors were now motionless, holding drinking flasks and cups and jugs pilfered from the old woman's cottage. The goblins were all around me, watching me.

"We have been like humans for too long," said Zeth. His voice was calm and peaceful. "We forgot that the gods made us from the lowest of all life, then gave us the burning inside to become the highest. They gave us the will to gain supremacy at all costs. Yet humans challenge us at every turn. Humans think they are better than we in every way. All know this—goblins, orcs, giants, elves, dragons—all know this is true. Humans believe only in humans. None of the rest of the world matters to them. Soon we all come to believe that, and we lose the vision the gods gave us to see our way up. We lose our will, and then we are gone."

Zeth pushed away from the tree and walked slowly over to the hanging corpse. He put out his hand and touched the body, causing it to slowly spin.

"It was only when my grandfather put out my eyes that I began to see for the first time," he said. "The gods gave me the vision. Humans do not understand us and call us evil. They think we do terrible things just because we want to, because we are selfish. They call it evil, what we do, and I will call it evil, too, because the humans hate it so."

Zeth looked directly at me. "We do evil, then, but we do this for the gods. Humans do not see that our evil is like love, in that it is greater than the self. Our evil reaches out to embrace the world and slay it, as the gods did, so that it will be ours. Our evil is as warm and red as love, and it enters the world in the same way love enters the heart— through the least defended places."

The half-breed spread his arms, palms up. "You did not understand what I meant by the 'insult,' " he said. "This body is tainted. I am forbidden by the gods to carry a weapon or wear armor to protect the taint." A cold grin formed at the edges of Zeth's mouth. "My father wanted to prove something when he attacked my mother and cut off her hands. He wanted to prove he was stronger than a goblin. Perhaps he wanted to show that he was more evil than a goblin, too. He certainly knew how we feel about humans and what we call the taint—the touch of humanity, of goodness and weakness. We might wallow in it, but we hate the word. And my father rubbed it in our faces.

"How could a human be stronger than a people descended from the worms that crawled in the wounds of the earth? How could he be more evil? Humans say they are so much better than we, and my father's deed was as if humans had also claimed to be so much worse, as if we were nothing. It was an insult to us all. The gods saw it and were angry, and I was born to repay the insult to our people.

"We are now teaching humans how it feels to be weak. What do the strong fear more than weakness? What is more terrible to a warrior who prides himself on his might than to know it means nothing? We strike at the weak and the helpless, and the mighty humans go mad because they cannot protect the weak and helpless with goodness! The gods and our people are avenged! The old debt is repaid!"

Zeth suddenly whirled on his heel and slapped the

swinging corpse of the old woman. It spun around and around in the moonlight. He looked back at me. His face shone like the moon. "*Now* do you understand, Captain? Do you see now?"

I looked at the corpse as it swung, the old woman's dress ruffled by the gentle night breeze.

And I saw.

Zeth knew it. He felt his way back to the tree. The god who had let him see had now left.

"Let us head south," he said. "Our teaching is not yet done."

* * * * *

Three days later, the humans caught us.

"How many are there now?" Zeth asked. He did not shield his face from the sunlight, as the rest of us were forced to do on the flat hilltop. Whatever god or gods had been using him were now gone.

It didn't matter. The teaching had gone well.

"About a hundred," I replied. There looked to be more, but it was hard to tell in all the light. Many of the humans were mounted, so more troops could have been hidden in the dust behind them. Their battle flags were raised. The colors of Durpar flew.

We dug in as well as we could. We could not outrun them on the open fields where the humans had sighted us. The hilltop was no defense, but it gave us the altitude we needed against the tall folk and their mounted riders.

"A hundred is good," said Zeth. "More would have been better, but a hundred is good."

One of our human prisoners screamed at the soldiers marching toward us. I could not understand what she was saying. A goblin slapped her across the face, then began to beat her.

"Stop it," Zeth said mildly. He didn't turn around. "Let her scream. It is better that way. Let the prisoners scream as much as they want."

"They're splitting up," a warrior said. "Some have bows drawn."

"They won't use them," said Zeth, his face at peace. "They know we have the prisoners."

"They'll charge us," I said, squinting at the distant figures. I made decisions and shouted aloud. "The horsemen will come in first—archers, take out as many as you can. I want everyone with a spear to be ready to meet them. Go for the horses first. Ignore the riders. Once a horse is down, ignore it. Draw your swords and go for the next horses. Cut at their legs and drop them. The riders won't be able to get up right away; we can send a second rank over to finish them. Then get ready to meet the foot soldiers. Use your height and go for the heads and arms as they come up the slope."

"Ever the warrior," said Zeth, quietly so only I heard.

My mouth opened, then closed in silence. Ever the warrior. Perhaps so I was. I had known nothing else. Yet my words were wise, even now. More humans would learn from us as a result. It was better that way.

I watched the humans close in, dust flying against the distant rumble of hooves. Though I could not see their faces, I sensed their hunger for our blood. I could almost smell it. It was natural and right.

"It is a good day," I finally said. It wasn't what I had meant to say, but it was true. I was at ease at last, at peace with all. It would be a good fight on a good day. I looked at the oncoming riders, their pennants flying, and a strange sensation passed through me. It was the purest feeling that had ever touched me. I blinked, forgetting myself, and my breathing stopped.

"You feel it," said Zeth softly. "It is good, yes?"

My lips formed the word yes, but gave no sound. I slowly smiled at the humans coming for us, smiled as a child would do. Welcome, I said without sound, full of that feeling. Welcome to our final teaching.

"They will hear of this in the Dustwalls," Zeth said, as if dreaming. "I can see it happen. My grandfather will hear of this from the gods, then he will teach it to our people, then the gods will release him from his shell of life. We will have found ourselves at last. We will be as we should be."

"It is a good day," I repeated, nodding. I felt light, light and strong, eager and pure. I had struggled so long with such simple things. It was so good to let it go.

The human riders charged at us, heads down, swords and axes at their sides, the hooves of their steeds flying through the tall grass. The world grew brighter, sharper, clearer, but I did not look away.

Zeth turned and made a single motion. Arrows hissed from a dozen bows. Horses and men fell. Behind us, warriors began to kill the prisoners in view of their rescuers. A woman screamed in one long howl that rose over us all like a great arch.

Many, many riders were left. They came on faster, growing in size, faces hard as stone. Zeth spread his pale arms to greet them.

It was a beautiful day. The first riders reached our hill, came up the slope, came through our ranks of spears. I ran to meet them with my people, sword high. The feeling touched me again, and I laughed and could not stop.

It felt just like love.

CONTRIBUTORS' NOTES

If it's heaven for climate, it's hell for company.
Sir James Barrie, *The Little Minister*

No one is more surprised than **Mark Anthony** at his apparent penchant for world-hopping. He's explored Krynn (*Kindred Spirits*), tramped across the Realms (*Crypt of the Shadowking*), and was recently lost in the mists of Ravenloft (*The Tower of Doom*). Luckily, he made it back in time to complete his Masters of Science at Duke University, and now hopes to stay put for a time in Colorado. Needless to say, he isn't counting on it.

Elaine Bergstrom is a Wisconsin writer of horror novels and science fiction short stories. She is the author of the RAVENLOFT® novel *Tapestry of Dark Souls,* as well as an upcoming RAVENLOFT trilogy and a story in the anthology, *Tales of Ravenloft.* Her previous novels include the vampire series *Shattered Glass, Blood Alone, Blood Rites,* and *Daughter of the Night,* all recently reprinted by Ace.

REALMS OF INFAMY

David "Zeb" Cook has written four novels, ranging from spy thrillers to space fantasy. His most recent was the Harpers novel, *Soldiers of Ice;* his next, *King Pinch,* features the characters introduced here in "Gallows Day." David recently made the jump from designing role-playing games for a living to designing CD ROM products, including games. He has a passion for his family, giant monsters, kites, food, and drink.

Jane Cooper Hong lives in Wisconsin with husband Dan and delightful daughters, Aleta and Dena. In previous lifetimes, Jane learned to speak Chinese, edited DRAGONLANCE® books, and co-authored the best-selling FORGOTTEN REALMS® novel *Pool of Radiance.* She now earns her living writing about nonfanciful things such as backhoes and beer.

In "The More Things Change," **Elaine Cunningham** sheds some light on the character (or lack thereof) of Elaith Craulnober, the enigmatic villain from her Realms novels *Elfshadow* and *Elfsong.* She is currently at work on several projects for TSR, including a book in the FIRST QUEST™ book line and a series of novels set in the Realms, which will feature a female drow protagonist.

After two years in the deserts of Athas, where he penned the Prism Pentad, the premiere DARK SUN® book series, **Troy Denning** finds his return to Faerûn a refreshing change. His short story for this volume, "Twilight," is the prelude to his current Realms project, the Twilight Giants Trilogy. His previous Realms books include *Waterdeep, The Parched Sea,* and *Dragonwall.*

Christie Golden is perhaps best known for her RAVENLOFT® novels, *Dance of the Dead, The Enemy Within,* and *Vampire of the Mists* (wherein the character of Jander Sunstar, featured here in "Blood Sport," originated). After that kind of practice, she was more than prepared to write a story from a villain's perspective. She is currently at work on an original fantasy novel.

Ed Greenwood is the creator of the FORGOTTEN REALMS® setting and is "like Elminster—only much nicer." He lives in Ontario, Canada, where he's hard at work on yet more Realms lore. His Realms fiction includes the novels *Spellfire, Crown of Fire, Elminster: Making of a Mage,* and the short story "Elminster At the Magefair" in *Realms of Valor.*

Barb Hendee is a grad student and part-time English instructor at the University of Idaho. It snows six months out of the year in Northern Idaho, so it's good territory for writers. She's sold about thirty horror stories to various magazines and anthologies, and is currently shopping a vampire novel—isn't everyone? She likes gourmet coffee, guinea pigs, and friends with a sick sense of humor. This is her first fun-filled venture into the Realms.

Georgia author **Mary H. Herbert** came out of the Dark Horse Plains long enough to discover a whole new world in the Realms. When she isn't writing stories, she takes care of her husband, two children, and numerous pets. Her previous books include *Dark Horse* and *City of the Sorcerers.*

J. Robert King, author of *Heart of Midnight, Carnival of Fear,* and the upcoming books *Rogues to Riches* and *Summerhill Hounds,* is often asked how he thinks of such sick stuff to write about, to which he responds, "How does one not?" He enjoys Fred Astaire movies, Faulkner novels, bourbon, sailing, cigars, and "Beavis and Butt-Head" . . . heh heh, heh heh heh—*Cool.*

After *Realms of Valor,* **James Lowder** forgot how much work went into editing an anthology—until he was hip-deep in first drafts for this volume. Still, as the quotation at the head of the Contributors' Notes implies, working with these "infamous" authors made this sometimes-hellish process a lot more enjoyable. When not drowning in novel or short story drafts, Jim freelances as a writer, editor, and video and book reviewer. As an author, his previous Realms novels include *Crusade, The Ring of Winter,* and *Prince of Lies.*

Roger E. Moore works with the AD&D® product line in the Games Division of TSR, Inc. Former editor of *Dragon®* magazine and mental-health counselor, he listens to too much news radio and writes short stories—many of which have appeared in the various DRAGONLANCE® anthologies—and articles in his free time. Writing "Vision," he says, was not fun.

Bob Salvatore was born in Massachusetts in 1959. His first published novel was *The Crystal Shard* from TSR in 1988, which also introduced Drizzt Do'Urden to the Realms. Since that time, Bob has published eighteen novels, including the *New York Times* best-sellers *The Halfling's Gem* and *Sojourn* (in paperback) and *Starless Night* (in hardcover). His current projects include series with Ace, Warner, and Del Rey.

In 1992, TSR published **Denise Vitola**'s first novel, *Half-Light*. In that same year, her short story "Walk an Alien Mile" appeared in *Amazing®* Stories Magazine. Recently she signed a three-book deal with Berkeley Books; the first novel in that series will be published in 1995.

James M. Ward was born in 1951, which he claims makes him old beyond his imaginings. He has three sons and a charming wife (who aren't old), and a thing for happy endings. The latter has certainly colored the volumes of game-related stuff he's written, not the least of which is his work as co-author of the Realms trilogy begun with *Pool of Radiance* and concluded with *Pool of Twilight*.